The Onyx Hourglass

By Kristy Nicolle

Queens of Fantasy Saga
The Ashen Touch- Book 5

First published by Kristy Nicolle, United Kingdom, May 2018

QUEENS OF FANTASY EDITION (2nd EDITION)

Published October 2018 by Kristy Nicolle

Copyright © 2018 Kristy Nicolle

Edited By- Jaimie Cordall

Adult Paranormal/Fantasy Romance

Disclaimer:

This e-book is written in U.K English by personal preference of the author. This is a work of fiction. Names, characters, businesses, places, events and incidents are either the products of the author's imagination or used in a fictitious manner. Any resemblance to actual persons, living or dead, or actual events is purely coincidental.

ISBN: 978-1-911395-17-1

www.kristynicolle.com

For Angie Pfeiffer-Senft,

You are a testament to the fact that a warrior is not a person who is never knocked down, but a person who always gets back up.

I cannot think of anyone who deserves this book's dedication and story more than you. I hope it's everything you've been waiting for.

PROLOGUE

<u>XION</u>

THE BLUE SUN FLICKERS, illuminating the world lying silent below the lilac sky. It boasts an infinite galaxy of stars despite the overwhelming cobalt solar presence. The sycamore trees behind me stir, butterflies of mauve and fuchsia flapping their wings. It's a somewhat simple act, a beautiful act, but one I have no doubt is starting a tsunami of pain on the other side of the world somewhere.

The smell of wisteria diffuses through the air as I pass dangling purple fruit, lush with delectable juices, amongst hanging cherry blossoms on vines forming the inner curtain of the grove I'm heading toward. I've never been here before, my feet have never punished the soil with the heaviness of my tread, and yet I am not lost.

Rather, I am being summoned, called even, by a force I can't resist. By her.

Dressed in a white cotton shirt and pale blue jeans, an unusual look for me to say the least, I reach out to part the fragile pink flowers. They are silk upon my fingertips as I step across the floor mapped lush with a tangle of roots and vines.

It's here I find her, still, skin like fine china as it rests perfectly pale and preserved. She's lying, raised high by the earth, central to the space and cocooned by heavy mosses, stems, stalks, and blooming flowers, not an ounce of rot or decay anywhere to be seen.

A single beam of light falls onto her face from where the canopy of trees manipulates, multiple branches twisting to ring a natural skylight. The smell of wisteria continues to irk me, mixing in with the pungent moisture seeping into the air from thousands of pale pink roses which surround her on all sides. Her hair is strewn, a halo of perfect fiery curls, around her. My phoenix, no angel to be sure, looks anything but herself, and yet I could not tear my gaze away if I tried.

1

Taking several steps forward, my heart hammers in my chest, yet my breathing is forced into a calm rhythm as though any disturbance of the peace may shatter everything. The silence is deafening, and it seems that even the natural world is in mourning as it stands still for just us two. Reunited, at last.

Her lips are petal pink, matching the roses that climb, possessive of her limbs, as though they've sprung from the very life sapped from her, stolen, pulled out from beneath us.

"Sephy." Her name is gospel upon my lips, escaping in a broken whisper. The sick plea of a diseased heart, infected with feeling, rotting in the absence of a target for such thick and potent affection.

What have you done to me? I wonder, edging closer to her, inch by inch, step by step. I'm surprisingly agile in this state of fear-imposed delicacy, which I'm sure would amuse a certain someone greatly if not surprise her entirely.

I reach the place where she's elevated by nature, a monument to its exquisite fragile beauty, and find her palms draped across her chest, placed peacefully, protecting her heart from what I could not. I know it's wrong, seeing her like this, but I can't help but wish she could stay this way, consumed by the flowers, the vines, safe. Perhaps the earth can achieve what I could not.

And yet— I know she is not a flailing princess, not a damsel in need of a knight with a steed.

She's a warrior.

Still — can't I wish — can't I desire to preserve her this way? After everything.

Reaching out, I place my hand upon the soft matte of the porcelain her skin has become. She's cold, despite being draped in the shroud of sunlight from overhead. Her eyelashes flutter at my proximity, mimicking the butterflies quivering in the endless fragrant sea of thick forest air.

I know what I must do as I reach down, letting my fingertips trace the length of her neck before drifting to her elegant fingers that lay atop the shimmering alabaster of the corset trapping her breath.

Leaning in, I place my lips to hers, closing my eyes and relinquishing to the gnawing, urgent craving she left behind. I give her the kiss of life, gift it to her because I know, even though she cannot save herself, she would if she could.

Deepening the kiss, I find her lips warmer than I could have ever imagined. The heat and proximity of her, it seems, causes the world around me to glow, tingeing a bright orange in the corner of my eyes.

As I try to ignore it, not ready to let go, my heart protests, hammering against my ribcage, my soul fracturing at the fact this is all a dream.

I resist but cannot overcome the inevitable as the world around me begins to dissolve into a plume of fire, ash, and blood.

MR SANDMAN

<u>XION</u>

THE PAIN OF MY sizzling skin overcomes me as the darkness from my dream takes over my sense of sight. The scent of burning fills my nostrils, sending my other senses reeling.

I hang on to her lips, the sensation of her kiss, for as long as I'm able, trying so hard to stay inside the dream despite the fact I know that it isn't real.

How is it that I would rather be in a dream than the real world? Has she broken me so completely that I'm suicidal?

Bringing myself back to the world with reluctance, I can no longer escape the growing and immense heat on the left side of my face. I realise as sensation returns to me that I'm lying atop a warm body, not hers but that belonging to someone else.

Someone with a Y chromosome.

I stare down into the greys of his irises, heart sputtering with horror like an overused and badly maintained engine shocked into failure.

"*What the fuck*?!" Haedes cries as I leap off his chest, retreating from The Eternal Flame he's been holding up to the side of my face, ready to end me. Our lips part slowly, too slowly, as in slower than a snail with asthma.

Fuckkkkkk.

"*Me*, what the fuck? *You*, what the fuck!!?" I exclaim, voice startling in the confines of the small and now entirely too cosy twin room.

"You were kissing me! That, my over-amorous and creepy friend, is a serious *you* what the fuck moment!" Haedes yells, sitting bolt upright in his bed as I spit ferociously, trying to rid my mouth of the taste of him.

"You were kissing me back! Why the fuck didn't you wake me?!?" I bellow, horrified, heart sputtering with the trauma. I'm clammy with sweat, wanting the ground to open up and swallow me whole as Haedes grows more offended by the second.

"I was trying! I was having this great dream— and then I woke up with you on top of me, not exactly who I thought I was kissing! What the hell are you trying to pull? Is there something you need to tell me?!" Haedes' hair is scarlet, matching his complexion which I've never seen flush so vividly.

Both our chests rise and fall, rapid, in the stifling heat of the room. Wide startled eyes stare, boggled, too self-conscious to surrender eye contact for even a second.

After a few moments, shock loosens its hold.

"What? Like I fancy your oh so gorgeous Highness? Get over your god damn self! Ugh!" I spit again, trying to remain calm. Haedes wipes his mouth, the alabaster definition of his chest illuminated by the moon as it falls like an irritating and exact spotlight through wisps of flimsy gossamer curtain.

I feel a breeze at my back, my brow creasing with sudden paranoia.

I didn't leave the balcony doors open. Did I?

Spinning on the bare balls of my feet, I catch the shadow of an intruder sitting cross-legged atop the dark mahogany of the armoire beside the double glass doors leading out to the balcony. The door's ajar, resulting in a chill running rampant down my spine and spiking the all-too-familiar rush of adrenaline in my veins.

I squint into the shadow and feel Haedes rise off the mattress beside me, palm still full of fire. We stand, both dressed in only boxers due to the heat of the Turkish night, ready to fight.

"Oh, for God's sake," Haedes curses, extinguishing The Eternal Flame that's been drying the surrounding air. I relax, the scent of smoke filling my nostrils and bringing unwelcome relief, reminding me of her.

"Good evening to you as well, Haedes." The voice comes from the figure who remains meditative on top of the chest of drawers, encased in clammy dim light.

Haedes rolls his eyes.

"I suppose we have you to thank for that hideous awakening?" Haedes demands, stepping forward so his shins are almost in contact with the edge of the bed where I've been not so peacefully sleeping.

"Perhaps. I can't deny it was highly enjoyable to watch either way. Very entertaining indeed. Though, I would have thought you'd have both realised you were in lucid dreams long before you figured it out. Disappointment is very much present in my heart." The voice is melodious and annoying as all hell, laced with mischief and verging on bursting into spontaneous song.

"I figured out it was a dream," I interject, grumpy, and Haedes shoots me a glare powered with a ferocity rivalling that of the Mortarian sun.

"What do you mean you *knew* it was a dream?!" He's accusatory as he balls his fist at his sides, his edgy frame rippling as what little muscle he has tightens.

"I mean it was obvious. I wasn't crushing everything I touched, tripping over my own feet or scaring off the ridiculous butterflies with my heavy boots. Besides, my internal monologue was like something out of a goddamn Shakespearean tragedy. Not at all convincing," I shrug, shaking my head.

Haedes looks at me with a deadpan expression, his lips forming a morose line.

"So, you knew you were in a dream — and yet — you still got on top of me and kissed me? That's what you're saying?"

I stutter in an attempt to reply as Haedes continues to glare at me over his shoulder, my entire demeanour becoming defensive and enraged at the implication of compliance in snogging his stupid face.

"Gentlemen, gentlemen, please — no fighting. One cannot be held responsible for what they do under my charms — supposedly. Trust me, I've had more than one young man claim helplessness when under my influence," the intruder chuckles. His voice transforms, as though he's not inside a hotel room but rather an opera house. His words echo over and over inside the walls of my skull, eerie and melodramatic all at once.

Unfolding his legs, he hops down off the furniture, his feet not making so much as a sound as they hit the worn carpet beneath him. If I wasn't so pissed, I'd probably ask him how it is he moves so soundlessly.

"Who are you?" I demand, folding my arms over my pectorals as the tall, lanky figure steps into the light.

"This is Morpheus," Haedes announces, his voice a partial growl. I stare at the man, taking him in, realising almost as quickly as the vivid

6

viridian of his hair and the chameleonic nature of his irises become apparent that he's not a man at all.

"What are you?" I demand, noticing the pallor of his skin glowing unnaturally despite the sheen cast by the moon outside.

"He's a Fae. Kindred of Apollo and Aphrodite. Master of dreams, guardian of The Nether." Haedes removes any opportunity for Morpheus to answer, but he doesn't seem to mind.

"Indeed, so nice that you recall my full title. You know who made me, so of course, you know to whom I answer on a higher level, so to speak." His mouth twists into a wicked grin, his too-white teeth gleaming and causing my eyes, still heavy with sleep, to burn. His eyes are sunken into his skull, casting deep shadows across his high cheekbones. His entire face is acute and angular, harsh yet beautiful. He's one of those men you expect to see in an underwear commercial, the kind who get paid extortionate amounts for simply standing and gracing the world with their presence.

"Wait, I thought Fae were winged?" I say in an accusatory tone, scowling at him.

"I take whichever form I choose whether it be this one — or — this," he waves a hand, and his face flickers between his acute features and Sephy's. His skin morphs pale, eyes burning deep cognac and hair flashing scarlet, like a television on the fritz.

My heart falters, the mere inkling of her causing more pain than I'd thought possible.

"Enough! What the hell does Zeus want?" Haedes snaps. His temper is flaring as is visible by the fact his roots are turning, yet again, from their familiar cobalt into a fierce scarlet hue, reminding me only too quickly of his daughter as well.

"It is not what Zeus wants, but what The Aetherial Court wants," Morpheus replies, striding toward us.

He's nimble, posture perfect and yet unnatural in the way he moves so seamlessly through the space between us. The blue-green of his hair reminds me of peacock feathers and when I look closer find it's speckled through with gold. A large feather, attached to a dream-catcher earring, falls from one of his ears, tickling the shoulder of his crushed velvet poet's shirt. Contrasting with the plum of his shirt, he also sports emerald leggings, which leave far too little to the imagination if you ask me.

"And who do you think truly rules The Aetherial Court— because it isn't Apollo. Freaking uppity asshole that he is." Haedes rolls his eyes, turning with less than subtle intent so Morpheus doesn't leave his line of sight.

"It would serve you well not to speak poorly of he who gave me immortal life, Haedes. After all, you're looking old. Who knows how long it will be until you and he are face to face yet again," Morpheus quips with a dramatic flourish of his long pale fingers, and I can't help but want to smile. He's certainly got Haedes pegged; that's for sure.

"You little—" Haedes moves forward, ready to take a swing at the Fae, who merely giggles like a small child as Haedes falls right through him and into the wall on the other side.

"Silly Haedes. You know I cannot venture here in physical form. Astral bodies are my speciality, thus allowing me to walk in worlds you can only dream of. I would have thought you'd have remembered, given that you still hold such disdain for those whom I serve." He cocks a viridian eyebrow, smirking as Haedes' eyes flash dangerously with no available outlet for his fury.

"Why are you here?" I push the conversation forward, sick of his games, of his overly pompous language and demeanour as the scent of wisteria reaches me. It's overwhelming, and I know it's coming from him as I inhale unwillingly, taken back only too easily to the dream world where Sephy lay sleeping. Morpheus smiles as he continues to observe me, a knowing look taking over his face, which I contemplate slapping him for.

"I'm here to deliver a warning. Or— perhaps you will see it as a decree." His pointed ear twitches as he brushes his long hair behind it, causing the lilac feather hanging from his lobe to flutter, irritating me immensely.

"I'm waiting—" I urge him to continue speaking, wanting nothing more than to go back to sleep. After all, Haedes and I have an extremely busy day ahead.

"You must abandon your search now. The Book of The Dead must remain lost, and as for The Nether, I am more qualified than most to tell you it is not to be meddled with either. You could be putting events into motion that will have far-reaching and devastating consequences. Your daughter," he intimates, turning to Haedes and then back to me, "and your lover, is dead. Let her remain so. If you value the balance of this universe at all, you will let her rest in peace." His expression turns serious, which on him looks like anger though whether it is or not is hard to tell. Either way, I find myself getting short-tempered, especially seeing as he's just referred to Sephy as my lover in front of Haedes. I hold my breath, waiting for The God of The Underworld to respond, but it's as though the slip fell on deaf ears.

"Go back to Nirvana. I don't have time for your warnings. Oh, and while you're up there, send a magical pigeon or whatever the hell you use to Zeus, and tell him that if he had let Sephy rise as a Titan, we wouldn't be in this little predicament," he spits, eyes blazing.

Morpheus rolls his eyes, brushing down the velvet falling across his shoulders with long fingers.

"Yes— I'll, uh, be sure to pass that on. Though you know why he has decreed her not worthy of such status. It would not be fair to have her ascend when Hercules remains a halfling." Morpheus speaks in a certain, unmoved tone, and for a moment, I wish he'd go back to giggles and half-song.

"So, because *he's* a shitty father, *I* get to look like a shitty father? Geez. That's *so* fair," Haedes snarls. Morpheus shakes his head, the gold strands of his hair shimmering, an overt external symbol of his grandiose sense of self.

"For a being as old as you, I'd have thought you'd have learned that fair is merely an illusion as are most coveted things. Monogamy for instance. An utter and total illusion. Security— also an illusion."

"And I care because?" Haedes sighs, hurrying to stand beside me and passing through Morpheus without a moment's pause.

"You don't. I'm just making small talk. I figured I'd better be out of my body for at least twenty minutes, or Hypnos would cotton on to the fact that I didn't actually *want* to orchestrate this little rendezvous." He smirks, eyes sparkling as they transition from teal to sapphire and back again. His pupils are rimmed with gold, and I wonder if they're resonant of his mood.

"So— you're saying don't resurrect Sephy because it's dangerous, but that you also don't care? Excuse me if I'm a little far from taking you seriously right now." I roll my eyes, and Morpheus smiles, wickedly mischievous.

"I'd be disappointed if you did. After all, security is, as I said, an illusion. What will be will be. Good day to you." Giving a tiny bow, yet again reeking of an intense narcissism that makes me feel slightly nauseous, he twists, skipping from the room and out of the balcony doors. My eyes trace his spritely path as he disappears into nothingness, fading from existence as quickly as he came.

"Well, that was fucked up," I comment as soon as I'm sure he's gone.

"Utterly and completely," Haedes agrees, but then he smiles.

"What are you so chipper about?" I enquire, sidestepping him to sit on my half of the twin set. He takes a seat on the mattress opposite me, hair a slick cobalt blue yet again.

"If they're warning us off, it means we're close," he concludes. My eyebrows rise on my forehead as I run my fingers across the coarse stubble of my cheek. He's right. No point warning two people who are chasing their tails.

I lay back on the pillow of my bed, looking up at the ceiling.

Tomorrow, we leave for the ruins of Pergamon, an ancient city and one we believe may very well be hiding The Book of The Dead.

I prepare to close my eyes; aware I need my rest. We have no idea what lies ahead or what kind of obstacles will lie between us and our goal.

"Oh, and Xion—" Haedes calls out, his mattress squeaking as he too leans back onto his pillow, ready to return to sleep.

"Yes?" I call out into the dark, yawning.

"If you tell anyone about what happened here tonight, carbon will look undercooked compared to you."

Silence falls, and sleep shortly follows.

"Haedes! Hurry up! We have to check out in five minutes!" I slam my knuckles into the wood of the bathroom door yet again. Every single time we stay overnight in a hotel the morning after is hell on earth. As if his incessant need to summon Cher's voice on repeat in the car or break every single speed limit while singing along isn't bad enough.

A few moments pass, the only sound his hum that now only fills me with dread. He's anticipating further altercations with Cher already.

Jesus Christ, he's worse than a teenage girl! I cuss, rapping on the door with increased vigour.

As I get ready to make a final knock, the door swings back with a swift jerk, revealing Haedes, groomed to perfection like a prize poodle. He's wearing a white cotton shirt with the top button undone that clings to him tightly before disappearing beneath tight navy-blue trousers.

Giving me a look of utter disdain, he saunters past my stiff and unmoved stance as I continue to hang in the doorway.

"Perfection takes time, Xion. Patience," he scolds me.

I stare, incredulous, into his face.

Now I examine him closely, and in the fresh light of day, I can see what Morpheus meant; he really has aged. The edges of his eyes are beginning to show crow's feet, lines around his mouth are starting to etch permanently into his skin, and his eyes appear weary though whether that's because he's aged or because he's sick of travelling the mortal way I can't be sure.

"Can we just go? We have this argument every single time we're about to get on the road," I complain.

He smirks, not looking apologetic in the slightest.

"You seem to be forgetting that when we were in Cairo, it was you who was occupying the bathroom," he reminds me, and I scowl, brow furrowing as I move over to my bed before slinging my leather jacket over my shoulders.

"One time! In six months! And you pushed me into a goddamn sarcophagus, and I got some kind of mutant flu! That wasn't my fault, and you know it!" I retort, and he laughs.

"Well, I'm just saying that I put up with the sound of you throwing up, which was entirely resonant of a dying hippo gargling lava, so you can put up with my styling habits. Besides, what's the point in pissing off my brother if I can't look good while I'm doing it?" he asks, grabbing the duffel bag with our clothes in from the foot of his bed. I don't respond to this, merely sighing and deciding that it's too early to get into it with him.

We both head for the door, the heavy tread of my boots nothing short of comforting. It's funny because I never noticed it before, but now it never fails to remind me of her and our constant sarcastic banter.

Down in the lobby, I hand over the room key to a man who barely speaks English and boasts one hell of a moustache before we head across the chequered gold and cream marble of the floor. Here, we get, yet again, stuck in a pair of glass revolving doors.

Finally, after a lot of yelling and shoving, we emerge into the morning sun of Bergama.

"Why is it you and your godliness can't handle a simple revolving door? It says in big white letters not to get too close to the goddamn glass! Every single time!" I cuss. Haedes shakes his head.

"Hey, I'm not one for patience when it comes to travelling, even on foot. Convecting for eternity will do that to you," he grumbles, placing a pair of shades over his eyes as we take a left and head briskly toward the car. I don't reply, fatigued already from the delicate balance between us which often verges on explosive rage and the entirely inevitable accompanying violence.

11

The Turkish equivalent of The Mean Machine sits where we had left it parked late yesterday afternoon, waiting.

It's a black Range Rover with Haedes' usual blue flame design adorning the hood and wheel arches.

Dread fills my stomach at the thought of being stuck in close quarters with him after the events of last night, but luckily for me, the drive up to the Acropolis ruins today should only take an hour.

Haedes unlocks the car as we approach, and I move around to the passenger side. He's not allowed me to drive once, not even when he was practically falling asleep at the wheel in Berlin before we broke into the Pergamon museum after hours. I mean, we had *tried* to visit during the day, but *somebody* kept touching the exhibits and got us promptly thrown out for disruptive behaviour.

As Haedes takes a seat beside me, places the keys in the ignition, and we both sink back into the supple leather of our seats, I find myself pondering how this trip had begun.

Rolling the windows down, Haedes flicks the signature pair of blue fluffy dice attached to the rear-view mirror for luck, and I turn from him as he waves a hand.

Cher begins to ring throughout the car.

I have never desired silence more in my entire life, I vow, taking a deep breath and trying so very hard not to lose my temper.

The air conditioning starts up with a whir, giving welcome relief from the too-warm Turkish sun, and I prop my arm on the top of the open window frame, looking out into the buzzing streets of Bergama as we pass.

If you'd told me six months ago that I'd be driving around with Haedes, listening to Cher, seeking out a long-lost ancient artefact to resurrect Sephy Sinclair, I would have laughed in your face. But as it is, here I am. Some people would, and have, said in my few trips back to Mortaria for supplies that I'm running. That I'm in denial. That what we're doing is wrong.

But for some reason, I can't stop myself, can't let go of the sound of her laugh or the wicked glint she got in her eye at our sarcastic exchanges. It can't just be gone.

A flame of that ferocity doesn't just extinguish; it just doesn't.

It can't.

Haedes and I clearly share the same thoughts on this, as we spent over two months in Egypt alone, digging through tombs, searching library stacks, and trying, unsuccessfully, to get the sand out of our shoes. The golden grains remain, though I can't say we had any leads or progress in Egypt at all. The book just wasn't there.

There was a record of it having been there, once upon a time, but this was before Moloch had even used the text. After he had gotten his hands on it, all records of the book had fizzled into mystery and mere speculation about its fate.

Our next lead came from satanic texts, revealing we may be best looking in South America, which had also been a complete bust, though Haedes had certainly enjoyed the alcohol of that little trip. Much to my horror, he still refused to let me drive back to the hotel.

From there, we ventured to Peru, then Thailand, and Vietnam—anywhere with even the slightest reference to the dead, worship of the dead, or resurrection.

However, nothing made sense until we stopped looking for the book and started looking for those who followed Moloch himself. It was those followers who had invaded the ancient Greek city of Pergamon and tried to claim it for their Ancient God instead.

Haedes believed that Moloch's grudge against Gaia and her descendants led to the fall of the Acropolis, so we headed next to Berlin. There, in the museum, we examined the Alter of Zeus, which we thought was somehow linked to the book's location. He guessed that Moloch's mortal servants would have placed it in the location most sacred to the people of Pergamon, to their Gods, and yet the trip was still a complete mess.

That though, at least, has brought us here, speeding down a winding country road that curves up a rising incline. Blocked intermittently by trees on the outer side, the sun flickers upon my face as we climb, speeding toward our destination and, with any luck, the end of this wild goose chase.

I'm brought back to the sound of Cher as Haedes hits a high note in his sing-along, and I let the breeze cool my face, trying to remain calm despite the sounds of '*Believe*' fraying my last working nerve.

"Come on, Xion, it's the chorus! You know the words!" Haedes implores me to join in, but I remain silent, fear clutching at me. Every time we near a location we think might hold the book, I become anxious, a pathetic nervous wreck. Though, whether it's because I'm desperate to get Sephy back or terrified I'll bring her back as a brain-dead zombie is hard to tell.

I feel my phone, the one Jules insisted I carry on me, vibrate against my abdomen from inside the pocket of my leather jacket. Taking off my seat belt, I remove my jacket and dig out the small black telephone which does far more than any telephone I'd ever known as a young man.

Knowing it will be Jules, I take a full ten seconds to decide whether to answer. I go with no, as I have the last forty-odd times he's called, hanging up and stashing it back in my jeans.

"Papa Sinclair bugging you again?" Haedes enquires, twisting the steering wheel. His fingers are covered in thick silver rings, some with skulls and others with crosses that catch the light, as I nod.

"I don't get why he keeps calling me." I shrug as Haedes lets the steering wheel fall through his fingers and we straighten on the road.

"You didn't tell him— did you? What we're doing, I mean?" He looks concerned, which makes me curious.

Since when does he give a damn about Jules?

It's not like the guy could make so much as a dent on Haedes physically.

"No. He would have tried to stop me," I express, guilt twisting into a tight knot in my gut.

I run my hand back through my thick black hair, looking at myself in the side mirror as the Turkish countryside continues to fly by outside. My reflection is haggard, torn apart from the conflict that's raged inside ever since the funeral.

"Do you think he would be justified?" Haedes' next question catches me off guard, and I feel myself becoming angry for no real reason.

"Of course! The fears he'd have are reasonable— I mean. She might come back wrong. Anything could happen! We're raising her from beyond the grave, not taking her for a facial." I scowl at him, and he nods in agreement though his face is determined.

"It won't go wrong." He tightens his grip on the steering wheel, pushing his foot down harder on the accelerator.

"You don't know that," I counter. His head snaps sideways.

"You don't know that it won't work perfectly fine," he retorts, silencing me. That is my problem. I'm too easily swayed, too easily coerced into doing something entirely unnatural because I just can't let go of the hope that I could see her again.

For real.

It goes against everything I know to be right and yet I'm in too deep to say no. I need her. Even if she has never and will never need me. She's the only person who's ever made me feel like I'm worth anything. Like I am not only half demon, but half human.

14

Turning a final corner, Haedes silences Cher as we pull up to the ruins on top of the hill. The view is breathtaking, and neither of us wastes any time in getting out of the car and standing, taking it all in along with some well-needed space from one another.

The earth beneath my feet is dusty, and a dry musk fills my arid mouth as though the crumbling of white stone has aged even the air. A few lone columns remain standing from what had once been, erecting themselves into the clear blue of the sky as though in protest of time. The remains are sparse, but we knew that the place had been emptied of all grandeur, having seen the result on the clinical floors of the Berlin Pergamon Museum.

I had known, and yet seeing the complete barren sprawl of what had once been teeming with life makes me feel empty, small. As though one day, perhaps soon, or perhaps far, I will be nothing more than dust on the wind too.

Is it not the natural order of things?

Entropy?

Yes.

Not for her, though. She was a constant. Fierce enough and strong-willed enough to withstand the Demon Lords and their Kindred.

A world without her in it is a world I cannot justify, it's a world worse off in so many ways, and so I will continue to move forward.

"Come on," I murmur as I catch Haedes, his expression odd, out of the corner of my eye. He's removed his shades and is staring at the ruins with a melancholy grimace. "What is it?" I demand, impatient as my anxiety grows by the second. The urgency, like I'm a boy breaking some redundant school rule, creeps unwanted from my conscience.

"I am old," Haedes replies. I smirk, cocking an eyebrow and rolling my eyes.

"No shit," I retort, and he shakes his head.

"I remember when this was built—" he informs me, and I feel my eyes widen in surprise, taking in the man standing in front of me.

He reaches down, taking a worn piece of marble in his hand, turning it over once, then twice in the stark light of the sun, before tossing it aside with a careless swing of one arm.

It's easy, when he's constantly annoying the shit out of me, to forget who he is. The things he must have seen and the life he must have lived become redundant when equated to the man who's taking an age in front of the bathroom mirror. But he's a god. The God of The

15

Underworld. A figure of myth and legend. A pain in the ass for sure but still undeniably remarkable.

"Let's go take a look," I suggest, but he doesn't reply, simply placing the shades back over his eyes as though he's getting misty recalling the past.

We tread through the sparse grass, where nature has tried to reclaim the site but has not yet been given adequate time. Dust lifts with my tread, billowing out and irritating my eyes and skin as we approach crumbling columns.

"We should start at the altar site," Haedes suggests, panting slightly as we bake in the midday sun that continues to pound down, merciless. I don't reply, merely looking around instead, hoping there will be some kind of neon sign.

Unfortunately, there isn't.

Haedes seems to know where he's going though, and so I follow him as he picks his way across scattered ruins and rocks, over the grass and cracked cobblestones where roads had once run like arteries through the body of the place where now only a skeleton remains.

Finally, Haedes indicates we're close to where the altar had once stood, and as we venture forward, my nerves ratchet up a notch. I swing my arms, and hop a little in my step, trying to disperse some of the tension by directing it to my muscles.

"Here we are!" Haedes calls as we approach a flat outline upon the earth. There are a few pillars that have been knocked down at their bases, scattered around the outside of the space, indicating it was a special site.

As I move closer, I find myself increasingly restless.

Stepping up onto one of the pillar's remains, I jump over it and to the other side letting my inner demon stretch its limbs, landing upon the white surface with a thud and then a crack.

Suddenly, I find my stomach continuing to drop as the rush turns to horror. My legs have braced themselves for the impact but have been mistaken about the stability of the ground underneath.

I fall, dust clouds erupting around me, through the seemingly solid ground and down into the dark. The impact of the surface I land on is harsh, rattling my brain inside my skull as I sprawl out flat on my back, gasping for air as all breath is knocked from me, the crash of falling debris ringing in my ears.

Staring up at the gaping hole above that allows a single beam of light to fall, illuminating the dust and debris, I catch Haedes looking down at me, amused.

As I cough, sitting up and spluttering, I squint at my surroundings, dirt falling like dark snow from my hair.

I hear him beginning to laugh overhead with a building and uncontrollable high pitch that echoes around me.

"Well, shit! This place stays hidden for hundreds of years, and one moment of contact with your fat ass, and the entire place is falling apart. What are the odds?"

2

ROCK THE BOAT

LUCE

THE SCENT OF JASMINE rises from the depths of my fine china teacup, curling and twisting in a tendril of steam, calming me as I look to The Fates. Crossing my legs beneath the duchess satin of my burgundy petticoat, I exhale, feeling the whites of their eyes boring into my face.

"You asked to see me?" I enquire, heart fluttering, and the three women nod in unison, despite the fact Moira is deaf as a post. I lean back into the clutch of the bloody, crushed velvet of my brand-new couch, the black velvet of my overcoat making an irritating sound.

"Indeed," Layla replies, eyes unseeing as always. They're eerie as a triplet, withered and ancient in appearance, but undeniably powerful as their hindrances become complimentary when they're together in more ways than you'd expect.

"And?" I ask, exhausted.

This is the first time I've had a moment to sit in days, and I would rather be alone than having this meeting, so I wish they'd hurry up.

"We wanted to talk to you— about the alchemy," Moira begins, her voice raised a little more than her companion's. Volume control never was her strong suit.

She takes a crooked finger and pushes a wisp of silver hair behind the fragile, pale skin of her left ear, coughing so her ribs rattle against the silver boning of her modest corset like the keys of a xylophone.

"What about it?" I'm quick to reply, snappy almost. I don't have time for this.

As it is, Mortaria is currently without Haedes or Xion to pick up the extra slack, and Anubis and Osiris have been less than helpful in assisting us. Thane and I have been running ourselves ragged these past six months, and I'm completely sick of it.

"Child, it has come to our attention that you may be utilising your affinity for the ancient magics a little more than might be wise. We know you had a large role in saving the life of Persephone Sinclair, but it cannot escape our notice that you have been using magic more frequently." Layla gives me a disapproving stare, impressive for a blind woman. She straightens her fossilised spine, which audibly creaks, and folds her hands politely in her lap upon the baby blue velvet of her thin skirt.

"Excuse me? A *large* role? I did save Sephy Sinclair! If it weren't for me and my abilities, she'd be — well, she would have died in that colosseum," I exclaim, defensive as my fatigue reaches fever pitch.

"Does it not occur to you that perhaps her death was necessary? That it was meant to be? That it was—" Moira begins, but stalls as I cock an artfully shaped eyebrow, interrupting her.

"Fated?" I finish her sentence, biting out the word with disdain.

"Destined," Layla corrects me.

I shrug.

"I'd hope if that was the case, you'd have told me. Or do I have to worry about your allegiance as well?" I demand, short-tempered far more than is usual.

Sensing my unrest, Beelz slinks over from the bedroom opposite, laying at my feet and eyeing the three women before me with a suspicious, clementine stare.

I bend forward, running my fingers through the onyx silk of her fur, and try to calm myself as I inhale deeply the scent of my tea, seeking clarity from the pungent, floral fumes.

"You know better than to assume because we harness the name 'The Fates' that we are omniscient. That part of our power was stripped long ago. You know this. Think of it, as I have always told you, like a shattered mirror. Where once we saw the whole picture, we now see only fragments. When those fragments align between the three of us, it is possible to discern certain future aspects, sensory glimpses. But— as I have said repeatedly, you already know this, don't you, Luce?" Layla berates me.

I roll my eyes.

"It's all well and good, lecturing me about my use of magic, but you have no idea what I'm going through. Haedes left this place unattended, with abnormally little regard for the consequences. I'm

19

exhausted. I'm the one trying to run this place, and I have nowhere near his experience or power. He's the son of Cronus and Rhea, and I'm the daughter of a banished ancient god who should never have existed. I didn't exactly benefit from the kind of schooling he did," I defend myself, defend the fact I've been brewing late into the night, trying to concoct ways to travel faster, do better, and be more for the sinners of Mortaria. They've been nothing if not abandoned by their god, if you can call him that.

"Lucifer, there is darkness in you. It makes you susceptible. We care very deeply; please don't—" Moira begins, but I hold up a hand, silencing her.

I turn to Layla, narrowing my eyes.

"You don't care though, do you? If you did, you'd be looking at the situation I've been forced into and you'd understand that the magic I'm using is necessary to keep this place up and running," I sigh, exasperated.

I tear my eyes from their haunting and collective gaze, focusing on the refracted rainbows cast upon the walls by the dark chandelier hanging overhead.

"You care about the risk I pose to others. That's all," I whisper, coming to the realisation quickly as I drop my pale blue gaze back to their faces with decisive speed.

Layla stutters, bumbling like an old fool, and Anya opens her mouth to speak even though no sound will ever fall from her lips. I've been in their care for so long; perhaps I've forgotten that no entity can be flawlessly correct in everything they assume. Maybe I've become brainwashed into believing they have all the answers and honestly care about my well-being. As it is, they're not caregivers — they're parole officers, making sure I don't become a risk to others. They don't care about me. If they did, they wouldn't feel the need for this little intervention over absolutely nothing.

"I'd appreciate it if you would leave," I request, getting to my feet as a sign that they should depart.

Startled, Layla frowns.

"Lucifer, you're overreacting. We're merely concerned." She tries to save the conversation, to make me see her side, but I don't. I see only mine.

"Get out." I gesture to the door.

After the clatter of nervous cups against saucers placed on the glass coffee table between us and their nonsensical ramblings, I feel nothing but utter and complete relief when I'm finally able to slam the door in their wake.

Slumping against the dark wooden grain and finally alone, I find my gaze pulled to the coffin-shaped alchemy cabinet pressed against the left-hand wall. The vials within it capture my fancy, the sparkling effervesce of the power held within calling to me from across the room.

Beelz shifts, startling me for a reason I can't discern, and I shake my head, striding through the apartment, past four still steaming cups of tea, and out onto the balcony, flinging the double French doors open behind me with careless abandon.

I look to the skies, to the lilac of the glowing orb above, to the heavy clouds that hang like a hideously accurate, pathetic fallacy over everything. I wish Haedes would return.

After all, this is his domain, not mine.

Moments pass, and I feel my mind drawn back to last night, to how I had spent hours bent over my cauldron, surrounded by the scent of frankincense and the sizzling of unicorn blood. A kind of peace settled over me that I cannot help but crave, a kind of stillness that never fails to take me away from my problems and that allows me to exist only in the moment. It's euphoria, that kind of contentedness and excitement rolled into one experience, the type that comes only from knowing you are intrinsically where you belong. I know this because it's the same feeling I get when I'm lying in Thane's arms.

As my thoughts turn to her and my heart grows heavy with how little we've seen each other recently, I feel the snug wrap of her arms snake around my waist. I spin, surprised as my heart leaps in my chest. I didn't think she'd be back for hours.

"Hello, stranger," I purr, looking with a loving sincerity into the storms raging inside her irises. She doesn't speak, only places her long, nimble fingers along the line of my jaw and melds me into the jagged edges of her form, kissing me as though she's been drowning and my lips are her very first breath of fresh air.

When she ends the kiss, she leans back, adoring me with her gaze.

"I missed you," she breathes, and my heart swells, pounding ever frantic beneath the delicate flush of my skin.

"It feels like forever since we slept in the same bed, doesn't it?" I sigh, and she nods, taking a step back and placing her hands into the deep pockets of her skinny black slacks.

21

"If Haedes ever returns, he owes us like— something huge, and awesome, and probably shiny."

"Like a Dragon?" I giggle, and she smirks, pursing her lips in approval.

"Sure, then you could fly with me. I could use a Dragon bodyguard," she suggests, and my eyes sheen with affection that's been simmering beneath the surface with no viable outlet for far too long.

"Trouble in the skies?" I demand, hairs on the back of my neck standing to attention as anxiety returns to the pit of my stomach, cooling my desire like a large bucket of ice water unleashed from a great height without warning.

"Not in the skies, but I wouldn't say no to a wing to shield me from all these spark showers we keep getting. It's making recon work a bitch," she complains, rolling her eyes and exhaling a large breath. I examine her, suddenly realising that she's wearing formal attire.

"You're all dressed up, off for dinner with your other woman?" I tease, taking a moment to etch her appearance into my memory. I love staring at her, remembering every detail as though I'm taking a mental photograph, just in case.

"Other woman? As if you aren't handful enough for any single person to manage. I need both my hands to manage your crazy." Her stormy irises glisten as I stick my tongue out at her and roll my eyes. "I thought we could have dinner together. I know you haven't been getting much downtime lately, and we haven't eaten a meal together in months. I wanted to surprise you." Her words touch me, and it amazes me that after all this time, after all these years, she still makes me feel like a besotted teenager who has finally found a place to call home.

"It would be my pleasure. Can I get changed first?" I enquire, and she nods, eyes tinted through with rosy adoration.

"Of course. I'll meet you in the grand hall, but don't take too long. You look beautiful already." She winks, leaning in and kissing me on the cheek, causing my heart to warm at her proximity as my prior worries seem to evaporate into hot steam, setting my insides burning.

As she leaves me, I walk back into the bedroom, not looking back over Mortaria. I'm glad, more than anything, for a distraction from the chaos left in the wake of one Miss Sephy Sinclair, which it seems may never end.

Dressed in a twenties-style flapper dress, I stand with silver beads hanging delicately across layers upon layers of tassels falling heavy from my shoulders, right down to just above my knees where the dress ends. Slipping on a pair of too-high stiletto ankle boots, I give myself a once over in the mirror. My lips are lacquered bloody, and my pale eyes shine out beneath thick eyeliner and mascara. My hair falls in gentle white waves over one shoulder, fastened to the base of my skull with a clip that looks like a raven. Finally, I top off the look with the choker Thane had given me the day she fell to this place, binding the velvet around my throat and examining the indigo crystal pendant as it catches the light. It's definitely the most valuable object I own, for more reasons than one.

Making my way through the apartment, I grab my purse full of newly required essentials off the counter and turn off the lights as I go. Then I descend the spiral staircase after locking the apartment behind me. Admiring my legs, which I rarely have on display, as I move toward the main hall to meet her, my heart is frantic in my chest, excitement palpable on my hurried and shallow breath as anticipation builds.

I reach the main lobby of the Exilia, emerging from the tower and passing several envy sinners who watch on with jealousy plastered, all too predictably, on their faces. My heels click against the grey quartz of the floor, and I watch the sconces flicker, casting an intermittent orange glow onto the ground, making it appear as though it's alight and billowing smoke. I shake my hips, enjoying the feeling of tassels caressing my skin, and smile to myself, bright eyed and ready for a night of romance for the first time in I don't know how long. I catch my reflection in crystal facets of the wall as I pass, my head looking oddly wrong without its usual adorning horns. For some reason I just haven't been feeling like wearing them lately.

Two sinners open the gargantuan double doors, and I step through into the ballroom where I'm greeted by candles flickering everywhere. I smile, stepping over rose petals scattered across the floor in a dreamily random display of her affection. I can't help but grin as she stands from the table set for two in the centre of the room, flushing yet again.

"This is amazing. You did all this?" I ask her, and she beams.

"Sadly no, but luckily for us, Haedes' maids have found themselves with a large amount of spare time of late." She closes the distance separating us too easily, her eyes caressing me from head to toe as the candlelight bathes us both in a creamy peach glow.

"I'll have to thank them," I comment, and she looks deeply into my eyes as she takes my purse from me and throws it over to the table. It lands with a clatter, and my heart drops slightly, afraid what's inside may shatter.

"You're wearing my choker," she notes, a smile twisting her lips and causing her angular features to cast dark shadows, only highlighting her androgyny further.

"I am. I haven't worn it in a long time," I recall, and she kisses my cheek.

"You've been keeping it safe for me. Just as I knew you would." She moves her lips down past my earlobe, brushing aside the silver chandelier earring that dangles against my neck and running her mouth along the path of my throbbing carotid. "Dance with me," she demands, and I smile, inhaling the ever-heavenly scent of blackberry and pine.

"But there's no music," I note, and she cocks an eyebrow.

"You know there's more than one way to summon a song—" She turns, and from the shadows, a sinner holding a saxophone emerges, taking a large breath before beginning to play a sultry rhythm from the room's darkened edges.

"Let's dance," I coax her. She takes me into her arms and we begin to sway together, my soft curves and her jagged edges moving together flawlessly, just as they always have.

"I can't believe how long it's been since we've been alone like this," Thane growls, moving her head back to stare at me as we turn, feet stepping effortlessly in time.

"I know. Things have been crazy. I mean I'm drowning in new arrivals for no reason I can discern. I've slept at Golgotha every night for the last three weeks. Not to mention the fact that we've had to double security and Anubis has been less than helpful with sending souldiers up to The Exilia. It's like she doesn't even care anymore—" I sigh, and Thane nods.

"I know. I know it's been tough. But you know it's funny you should mention her not sending extra security up here because ever since that night at the Colosseum six months ago, The Ashen Waste has been — well — barren. There are hardly any Demons roaming around there compared to the normal numbers you'd expect," Thane elaborates and I frown, eyebrows pinching together on my forehead.

"You think they all gave up and decided to take up knitting?" I ask, trying to be funny to diffuse the tension, but instead of laughing, she shakes her head, eyes laced with poisonous worry.

"I doubt it. I'm concerned. I mean I haven't checked the far side of the volcano because it's always so desolate— but maybe I should. We're weaker than ever, and while low levels of Demonic activity would seem like a blessing, I doubt that's the case," she explains.

I still, no longer in the mood for dancing.

"Can we sit? I'm tired," I ask, and she examines me closely for a moment before leading me over to the candlelit table for two. I sit, opening my purse and pulling out a vial with bloody orange liquid inside. It shimmers in the peach hue of the room, and my heart slows in its beat, relieved.

"What's that?" Thane asks as she takes a seat opposite me, eyes judgemental.

"It's just something I've been taking for my nerves," I explain, placing my bag back down on the table in front of me. She reaches over and grabs it from in front of me as she hears the remaining vials inside clink together. As I un-stopper the draft in my palm and move to down it in one swift gulp, she raises her gaze to me, eyes wild.

"Luce! How many of these have you been taking?" she demands.

I shrug.

"Just enough to keep me going. I'm barely sleeping, and I'm constantly walking around paranoid or worried. It's been a tough six months," I reply, moving to place the vial to my lips yet again. She scowls, rising from her seat and snatching the brew from my fingers.

"Hey!" I exclaim, and she shakes her head.

"No! The Fates were right!" She's confrontational, standing and looking down over me like she's so high and mighty.

"Oh great, so now my not-so-supportive Grandma posse has been telling tales to my girlfriend? Fabulous!" I roll my eyes, folding my arms over my chest and feeling the silver beads of my dress push, harsh, into my skin.

"Luce, they're worried about you! And judging from this little stash, I'm not surprised. This is completely unnecessary," she berates me, and I feel my temper growing like a weed where love and affection had promised to bloom only moments before.

"Unnecessary? You didn't think it was unnecessary when I brewed this exact same potion to give to Sephy Sinclair to calm her nerves after the banshee attack. Or the potion that saved her life," I defend myself, wondering why in a world where I'm constantly running to save everyone else, to mother every single damn person around me, she can't allow me to just help myself for once.

25

"That's different. Those were necessary to keep someone alive. You don't need to be taking all these. It's ridiculous. If you're having anxiety, then talk to me about it—" she begins, but I scowl at her.

"When? Between the hours of six and one minute past six in the morning? When you're around for a whole two seconds before taking off again?" I condemn her, suddenly angry at the entire situation. I didn't realise I was angry, but perhaps this has been bubbling just beneath the surface for a while.

"Luce, this isn't about me! It's about you! You're using magic, and it's dangerous for you. You know that. You know that half of you originates from a Dark God. An Ancient God. You're more vulnerable to this than anyone, and if you become infected, you're also an immediate threat to everyone around you." She reminds me of a fact I have never forgotten, will never forget, and I cross my legs, fury building as I tense every muscle, defiant.

"You sound just like them," I accuse her, my heart beating too fast in my chest for the complete opposite reason than I had been expecting.

"Like who? Like someone who gives a crap about you?" she demands, folding her arms and cocking her head, lips pursed.

"Our mothers," I retort, and she rolls her eyes.

"Well, maybe they were right," she whispers.

I feel my heart break in two.

"Fuck you," I bite out.

She leans forward over the table.

"You can cuss me out all you like; it doesn't stop what I'm saying from being fucking true," she spits.

I roll my eyes.

"You're so goddamn over dramatic you know that? It's a goddamn pick me up. It's not like I'm trying to brew something fatal," I explain again, sick of her judging me. She doesn't know what it's like to be in my skin, to feel these urges, this pull. She doesn't know what it's like to have to be strong every waking hour of the day.

"Then get yourself a fucking espresso, Luce! Get some sleep! This isn't you *needing* magic, it's using magic to take the easy route."

"And why shouldn't I? For once? Given that a whole mountain of shit has spontaneously descended on both of our shoulders without warning, why shouldn't I try to make things a little easier? Why shouldn't I use the skills at my disposal? I never see you travelling on foot. Why? Because flying is fucking faster, and you *can*," I remind her. She exhales heavily as though I'm utterly exasperating her.

"Luce, that's different. You know it is. You're being utterly unreasonable. I love you. I just don't want you to get into trouble." She's trying to make me see reason where I just don't, trying to guilt me with our connection. I stand up, banging my hands down on the table and causing the silverware to rattle.

"No. You love *part* of me. The safe part. If you loved me, all of me. you wouldn't be overreacting about a simple nerve tonic. You'd trust me and believe that I can take care of myself!" I exclaim, tears filling my eyes as she's overcome with a look of utter fury. Her eyes sparkle, the multihued greys of her irises resonant of swirling clouds right before a hurricane hits. She opens her mouth to shout, to really let me have it, to wound me with only her tongue, but as she prepares to unleash a linguistic bullet, the left side of her face is illuminated a bright and electric blue.

The scent of smoke fills my nostrils as I turn and find him standing there, smirking.

"Hope I'm not interrupting you, ladies." Haedes coughs once, then twice, shifting from foot to foot. He's dressed in navy blue trousers and a white shirt, his hair perfectly coifed. I watch him in slight disbelief as he brushes something off his shoulder. As the particles tinkle to the floor, I realise it's a mixture of dust and sand.

"No. You're not interrupting. What are you doing here?" I speak before Thane gets the chance to, not wanting her to get Haedes on her side.

"Xion and I, we found the book." He holds up a hand, and where pale flesh once was his skin is blistered and bloody, mottled and melted into something unrecognisable.

"What the hell?" I take a few steps away from the table, kicking some rogue rose petals aside and taking Haedes' palm in mine.

He winces, a coarse hiss escaping him.

"The damn thing burns anyone who touches it. We thought— well, we thought because you're more powerfully linked to the dark side of things and the daughter of its previous owner that you might be able to shift it." He gives me an expectant look, and I exhale.

"I suppose that's not an unreasonable assumption. How on earth did you track it down?" I ask him, ignoring Thane as she shifts at my spine, moving around the table toward me.

"A lot of dead ends, a pinch of luck, some of my winning charm and wit." Haedes gives nothing away, and I wonder momentarily if he's just playing a practical joke. I mean, I know he said he was going to find the book, but nobody believed he'd do it.

"Where is it?" I query him further, still not quite believing him.

"Pergamon, in Turkey. It was stored in a secret room underneath the Altar of Zeus." Haedes rolls his eyes, no doubt at the fact he never got such a grandiose gesture from mortals, nor their gratitude. Being God of The Underworld certainly hasn't made him many friends, and even fewer fans.

"How on earth did you know there was a secret room? Doesn't sound so secret to me," Thane interjects, and I turn, flashing her a look of warning with my pale blue irises.

"Xion, being the agile and graceful entity that he is, just so happened to fall through the ceiling. I suppose I'm lucky he's such a brute." Haedes smirks, and I can't help but smile, missing Xion more than I'd thought possible, especially with how little I've seen Thane.

"Sounds legit. I can help— no problem." I shrug and hear Thane cough at my back. I spin to face her.

"Yes?" I demand, temper threatening to erupt into a fully-fledged Demonic presence if she doesn't quit with the judgemental crap.

"Do you think that's such a good idea?" She stares at me, expression stern and unforgiving. Haedes looks between the two of us, frowning.

"Did you two have a falling out?" he enquires.

I shake my head.

"Not really. Thane was just making yet another one of her *unwanted* opinions known. It's fine. Shall we go?" I demand, pushing him to convect as I move to stand at his side.

"Ohhh *snap*. Whatever you did you better make it right. Look at that face!" Haedes pinches my cheek, and I scowl at him as Thane glowers, eyes dark.

"Luce. I can't stop you. But I won't be there to pick up the pieces either when this shit goes wrong. If you think you're fine, think you can handle it, you're on your own. Got it?" she threatens me yet again like her love and support are conditional of me acting on only half of who I am.

I shrug, beyond upset but not wanting her to know.

"Fuck you," I cuss again for lack of a witty response, gripping Haedes' arm and feeling the harsh sting of the resurrection flame rise around us. I inhale the heat, the fire, letting it singe my nostrils, embracing the pain as I watch Thane's heartbroken, furious face fade into memory.

3

THE WINDMILLS OF YOUR MIND

PANDORA

"AFTERNOON," I BREATHE OUT into the dry rust of the air, laden with the scent of old blood that fills even the dankest corners of Gorgon's private quarters. He's sat, feet propped up on a threadbare, cobweb-coated, jade velvet chaise longue, and as he raises his eyes to address my unexpected presence, his pupils dilate, scanning me from toe to head.

I know why he's staring; the same reason all the other Demon Lords have been staring lately. I'm wearing tight, black velvet pants and a violet, silk corset that peeks through the undone zipper of a cropped leather jacket. My knee-high, stiletto boots click against the blood-stained cobbles of the floor as I pass him, revelling in his awestruck expression.

"What on earth are you wearing?" he demands, placing the book he's reading down on the chaise longue and erecting himself. He's unable to tear his eyes away from my body, of course, as it's revealed as curvaceous and full of sexual potential. I glimpse the title on the worn spine: *Lord of The Flies.*

"Have you been into the mortal world lately? I won't exactly blend in wearing a ball gown," I remind him, and he cocks one curved eyebrow, the limes of his irises glowing with approval in the dark.

"I have not. Though, Lilliana did tell me you and she had been venturing there more often. Might I ask why?" he enquires, voice barely a whisper, the sibilance of every syllable like the sizzling fuse on a bomb.

I don't reply, running my long nails down the sides of my body with a dark promiscuous stare. I'm enjoying his attention far too much, and yet I can't seem to help myself when it comes to indulging such base urges, especially as I'd been so repressed during my first dance with mortality.

"Recruitment. Time will tell if it's of any use or not." I don't give everything away, playing coy, but Gorgon doesn't pry as I expect him to. Instead, he simply sits, legs cocked apart, tilting against the back of the seat.

A black vanity opposite him beckons, so I lift myself gracefully to sit upon it. Blocking his view of the shattered mirror reflecting his terrifying gaze back seven-fold, I replace it instead with my breasts as I lean forward, resting my elbows on my knees.

"Can I help you with something?" he enquires, straight to the point as usual. I smile, flashing my teeth as my glossy black lips spread wide and catlike across my face.

"I don't know. Can you? I'm terribly bored," I announce, far more casual than I've ever been where he's concerned, swinging one of my legs over the other and crossing them with obvious and concentrated intent. I remove my jacket next, letting the chill of the place encapsulate my arms in slithering paths of cold as I lean back, my hair tumbling in thick curls, onyx and never-ending, down my spine.

"What did you have in mind?" Gorgon's eyes narrow, and I run a fingernail up the bare skin of my throat, looking directly at him.

"I'm curious about you." I am forceful, dominant even, and his eyes deaden in his skull as if giving out his psychological profile is the very last thing he has any intention of doing.

I look around the place, at the slick and wet brick of the walls, at the enormous bed in the corner, barren of any kind of sheet or pillow. The most interesting thing about this room, it could be said, would be the feeling that we're not alone, which I'm certain, as ever, we are not.

"What do you want to know?" The question comes, surprise laden in his tone as the undying hiss of his tongue flicks between the thin crinkled flesh of his lips. I wonder if he's trying to discern an ulterior motive in me, but regardless, I'm eager to ask about his past. I have been for a while, but it's only now, in the long days and even longer nights of this place that I find myself bored enough to pursue the challenge.

"How did you become what you are?" I ask directly and without hesitation. He narrows his eyes, mimicking me as I study him.

"Why would you want to know that?" he sneers, immediately suspicious, as I would expect.

31

"Well, if there's one thing I've learned about gods and goddesses, it's that they love their secrets and hate sharing knowledge. I've always been curious about so many things you see, and knowledge is power, right?" I cock my head, feeling the ends of my locks brushing the base of my spine with gentle yet deadly prowess, not entirely unlike the creeping and fatal lull of nightshade when slipped into one's tea.

"And you wish to have power over me?" Gorgon assumes, crossing his legs and mirroring my pose, expression unamused. His pointed features pinch further, his heavy brow casting darkness over his eyes and making him nothing if not more intimidating, more desirable as a conquest.

"No. I wish to know everything I can about the people I'm working with. If I don't know your weaknesses, how can I adequately form a plan to take back Mortaria?" I ask, and he laughs, the sound entirely unnatural.

"I'd say given recent history you're not equipped for such a task in any capacity. Let alone being the one forming the plan. Wouldn't you?" he baits me, tempting my fury as I exhale heavily, arching my back and smiling, hiding my rage. I'm used to playing nice, pretending to be placid and genteel when I am silently seething just beneath the surface. After all, I had played the role of Nephilim Queen only too well.

I don't reply to the insult, cocking my head and letting my hair fall around one shoulder, a dark silken curtain of angel curls, the only part of me which remains close to what I'd once been.

"When I was in my early twenties. I met a woman, and I fell in love with her. She showed me things, taught me about power and what it meant to be unafraid of the world around you. Taught me what it meant to be that thing people fear," Gorgon explains, and I wonder what made him change his mind. Perhaps I look too innocent to be of any trouble. Perhaps he sees that I have nowhere else to go and nobody else to ally myself with, or maybe he just wants to get back to reading his book.

"A woman?" I query, and he nods.

"Yes, Medusa." Gorgon relinquishes this information, and I feel my expression turn surprised as I lean forward further, intrigued as I generously reward him with more cleavage.

"*The* Medusa?" I demand, and he nods, smirking at my faux naïve tone. However, whether he can tell I'm putting on this little show to pry into his past, I can't discern.

"Indeed. The original Demon Lord, chosen by Moloch himself." This makes sense now I think about it, waiting with bated breath to hear the next words that fall from him.

"What happened?" I enquire, impatient as the chill of the room ebbs into my palms. The longer I sit here, the more I'm beginning to smell not only blood but bodily fluids, as though birth, or more likely, death, has recently occurred.

"I got curious. The more she taught me about her power, about what she was, the more I craved it for myself. The Demon Lords were originally imbued with the power to create new demons—"

"Wait— how?"

I'm suddenly confused. I know demons can't be killed indefinitely, but I had never actually asked myself where they had come from in the first place.

"When the Gods of Ancient fled to Mortaria after they lost control over the Higher Plains, they tethered their power to weapons made of obsidian." He announces, and I feel the cogs in my mind become slick with the lubricant of this new information. It makes sense to me now, for I've always known that the intense magic in the soul of a god would destroy any flesh conduit it was funnelled into. Now I suppose I know what happens to the excess. "These weapons were left to their Demon Lords once they were banished to The Island of The Blessed. A cut from the blade of one of those weapons that drew blood would infect the subject with darkness. The original Demon Lords chose those creatures, which man most feared, to corrupt - the original Demon Lord Barbas' idea as I'm sure you can imagine. The Wolf. The Snake. The Spider. The Bat— and so on." Gorgon continues to explain, and I find myself made humble yet again. Amazing what history is never mentioned between Kindred and God.

"So— what does that mean for you?" I ask, still wondering how he came to be the man he is today.

"I stole Medusa's weapon, killed her in the night, and imbued myself with the darkness absorbed by the obsidian sword. And here we are," he confesses this so simply, as though it is not cold-blooded murder and of someone he claims to have once loved, no less.

"You killed her? But I thought you loved her?" I demand, exhaling heavily in what can only be described as disappointment. I guess somewhere deep down, I'm still a sucker for happy endings, especially when it comes to the underdog.

"You know, I did too, until one night, while we were making love, she said something to me— it changed everything. She said, 'Love, like life, comes and goes, but power is forever. So, thus, is love of power.'"

"How romantic," I snort, and he shrugs.

"It broke my heart and killed her in the end. So, I suppose you could say she wasn't wrong." The slick tendrils of hair that creep down his forehead sheen as he stirs, posture as ever fluid, inside his suit.

"That's a great story," I comment, not wanting to come across as impressed.

"You think so?" He smirks, laughing against his own volition.

"I do. But I just have one question—"

"What happened to the weapons?" He's already three steps ahead of me, knowing immediately that my mind will have moved directly to how the story and its implications can be used to benefit myself.

"Exactly." I smile too sweetly, swinging my legs as I uncross them and lean forward once more, enjoying the freedom wearing pants allows.

"Destroyed. All of them. When Haedes first took over this place he waged war on the Demon Lords, tried to get rid of us for good. He couldn't of course, because of the balance, which is so important to everyone in The Higher Plains, but he did make sure we couldn't multiply in number. Couldn't grow to be a threat. So, he built Mortaria on the hunting grounds of our Kindred and had the weapons crushed into dust." Gorgon shrugs, and my heart sinks a little.

Silence falls over us as I contemplate the story I've just been told; it's the stuff of legends, the stuff great writers would kill to merely put down on paper. Yet, it is also unsatisfactory as far as my own agenda goes, as it seems are most things these days, and thus utterly useless in every single regard.

"Pandora," Gorgon says my name, and I raise my head from where it's fallen so I'm staring past my feet at the ground. Gorgon's face is amused as my eyes find his, and I wonder momentarily if he's about to tell me that the story I've just been told is entirely fake. Instead, though, he stands, leaving its authenticity untarnished.

"My Kindred have a message for you," he informs me.

I slide from the wooden vanity, curious as my acutely angled brows pinch together in the centre of my forehead.

"Yes?" I demand, and as my voice hits the air, I watch a snake-like demon crawl up Gorgon's body, rippling into visibility and undulating too fast for me to follow. Hisses fill the air, slithering and slicing through it with a sound painful to the ear.

"They found it. Luce just left with Haedes," Gorgon announces, the slits of his pupils widening and then narrowing again as he turns from his Kindred and back to me.

"The Book of The Dead?" I know I sound incredulous, but after how Anubis had insisted it was near impossible to find, I would have thought we'd be waiting a year at least.

I guess she was just being overdramatic, as per usual.

"Well, this is good news," I murmur.

Gorgon dismisses the beast that disappears promptly into the pattern of the cobbles underfoot, slithering back from whence it came. I wonder how many of the demons are in just this room alone.

"I'm sure you have a meeting to attend, so I'll let you go." Gorgon sits back down, propping his feet back on the chaise longue and picking up the book he was reading, caressing my body with his gaze in what he assumes is a subtle manner.

"I do indeed." I smile, grabbing my leather jacket and moving to leave the room. "Thanks for the story," I add, rushed and careless in tone as I storm past his lounging silhouette.

"Anytime—" he hisses after me.

I could swear it's as though he means it too.

My feet touch down on the floor of The Icon's throne room, sprawling from me like a lake of flawless, molten gold. The portal still spilling from within, I slide the box's left-hand panel shut, taking in the emptiness of the space as I stow it in my jacket pocket.

The torches are extinguished. Nobody is here. Though I shouldn't be surprised, it's the middle of the night or so I'd guess. You never can tell in Mortaria with total accuracy.

However, given the fact that the entire city is on high alert after everything that's happened, you'd think Anubis' security would be tighter.

I shrug, taking a rhythmic step forward, feeling good. It's been a long six months, waiting around, biding my time, baring the scrutiny of the Demon Lords and their loss of confidence in my abilities after the escape of Sephy Sinclair who had slipped too quickly from firmly within my grasp.

Making my way to the far end of the room, I stride past the swinging pendulum keeping track of nothing specific, and which has the sole purpose of indicating that time is passing endlessly and to no avail.

Stepping through a gilded archway decorated with fine and swirling filigree forming endless columns of hieroglyphs I don't understand, I wonder how many hours of torturous labour it took to craft this archway alone and snort. For someone who claims she hates feeling inferior to pure gods, Anubis sure seems great at making mortals feel the same way.

I know where I'm going; I've been to Anubis' suite before the few times we've met regarding this same matter. Yet, in the dark, I can't help but feel somewhat mischievous as I ascend the staircase that curls like precious smoke to the height of the building.

As I reach the doors, embedded with thick slab cuts of Lapis Lazuli, I hear her call.

"Come in!"

At her welcome, I enter, pushing the heavy golden door aside and stepping through, heels clicking softly against rich metal as my senses are enveloped in the heady aroma of myrrh.

The scene inside is not what I expect — Anubis sprawled, naked across the white, Egyptian cotton sheets that are crumpled and strewn upon the mattress. She startles at my presence, moving upright behind the thin, flowing, white gossamer of the drapes where she's been splayed, touching herself.

I smirk, realising that I'm interrupting a very personal kind of party. Turning left, I find a group of three sinners strewn across a violet and gold chaise longue, too distracted to notice my arrival. One woman, two men, their limbs entangled like the brittle vines formed over long-lost ruins, the only stitch of clothing adorning them being the sin stone pendants of rose quartz that hang, all but forgotten, around their necks.

I blink once, then twice, before clearing my throat. A sinner with dark hair and thick biceps doesn't stop what he's doing, merely raising his gaze from the breast of a woman with flowing blonde hair, nipple still clutched firmly between his teeth as he looks to Anubis for further instruction.

"You should all take your leave. I have business to attend," Anubis orders them, wrapping the soft sheets around herself and giving me a disgruntled stare. The ménage rises to their feet, wrapping loose strips of white cotton around their bodies for decency and shuffling out of the suite, barefoot and ashamed as their eyes remain fast fixed on the rug-strewn floor.

"How can I help you?" Anubis enquires, tone sharp as she lets the sheets fall to the floor before pulling a partially transparent golden robe over her tall and slender form. Releasing her hair from beneath the golden shimmer of the garment's intermittent and carefully placed panelling, she treads from beside the bed as though she is floating on air and utterly superior to everything in the room, including me. I trace her motion as she reaches a drinks cabinet, carved unsurprisingly from solid gold with splashes of garnet embedded into the edge of the flat top surface as though a past murder victim's blood has crystallised and become nothing more than decoration.

"Drink?" Anubis demands, holding an empty martini glass between her fingers and shaking it so the golden rim catches the light falling from a turquoise chandelier overhead. I shake my head, taking a seat in one of the decadently upholstered armchairs facing the couch, refusing to break eye contact with the Titan before me.

"I'm surprised; I didn't take you for the kind of woman who was lonely enough to take the company of sinners," I smirk, judging her, as she cocks an eyebrow.

"Lonely, no. Satisfied, oh yes. You see, the thing about mortals is it doesn't matter to them where you started or where you've been. You're a goddess, and they worship you as such. Very keen to please indeed." Pouring a clear spirit into a solid gold tumbler and skewering two olives with a metal cocktail stick, Anubis shakes the drink by one ear, her tanned leg sticking out from beneath her robe as she cocks one hip.

"But so many? Why not just take one lover?" I demand, curious more than anything, and she shrugs.

"Why not take three? Pleasure need not be in limited supply to people like you and I, must it? We have suffered at the hands of men, haven't we? Felt their weight upon us and their unwanted thrusts for hours while we prayed for nothing more than death. Times have changed. I'd say I deserve it." She pours herself a generous drink and tilts her sculpted chin back as she delivers the alcohol between plush lips. I ponder this a moment, think back on my life, on how I've been nothing but a counterpart to men for the majority of it. I suppose she's not wrong in wanting to turn the tables and serve her own pleasure instead; I guess I'd just rather have long-awaited revenge than the immediacy and short-lived relief of passion.

"Anyway— about why I am here —" I begin, and she swallows fast, rolling her eyes as a tangle of words fall from her newly whetted gullet.

"Oh, I know. Luce departed to help Haedes and that miserable half-breed extract The Book of The Dead." Anubis takes the wind from my sails.

"How do you know that?" I demand, suspicious immediately.

Anubis rolls her eyes yet again.

"Thanatos dropped by earlier to shout at me while I was eating dinner." Her tone is filled with disdain, irritated, and I frown.

"Why would she shout at you?" I enquire, fearful for a moment that The Nexus has become aware of our little rendezvous.

Anubis takes her good time in replying, walking with torturously slow elegance across the thick faded weave of the rugs underfoot before planting herself leisurely atop a violet couch adorned with plump, golden pillows. She crosses her legs, flashing me more than I wish to see, before taking another sip of her Martini, smiling, and pushing her dark silken hair behind one ear.

"She blames me for Lucifer's use of magic increasing." My ears prick at the mention of the girl's name.

"I see. That's not exactly your problem though, is it?"

"Well, no. But Thanatos is, as ever, looking for someone to blame who isn't blonde and doe-eyed, so I guess I was her first thought. Besides, I'm not going to complain; she's keeping me nicely in the loop," Anubis purrs like a feline, almost giddy in her glee as she sucks down an olive.

"I had thought, given your reservations, that The Book of The Dead was lost for good if I'm honest," I pry, wanting so badly to say, 'I told you so', but also knowing I need her more than I want to admit.

"Finding the book is only the beginning, Pandora. You should know by now that resurrection isn't like drafting a simple potion or reading some old words aloud. I've been here before, with resurrecting *my* god. I'm still hesitant no matter how much you want to act naïve and believe in happily ever after." Her words stir something within me, something bitter and angry, something of the person I had once been before my wings. I merely glare at her, keeping my expression dead to hide what I'm thinking.

"You've done this before?" I demand, changing my approach. Before I had perhaps forgotten my place, been arrogant, but now I know if I am to thwart those who truly are arrogant, I must ask the right questions. I must be humble and continue to seek information. Knowledge is, after all, power.

"Do you know nothing of my history in this place?" she sighs, frowning at me like I'm an ignorant schoolchild. I scowl right back but then calm myself, remembering above all that my end goal is what's important.

"I am nowhere near as old as you. You're what— a first-generation Titan? One of the original three Queens of Ancient? I was the first Kindred Titan, but in terms of The Higher Plains, I'm still two entire generations younger than yourself," I remind her, and she exhales, uncrossing her legs and leaning forward to place her empty glass down on the decadent, gold coffee table between us.

"Look, I've been here before. The thing is I succeeded too," she exhales.

My forehead creases, confused.

"Excuse me? You *succeeded* in resurrecting Ra? Then— where is he?" I demand, wondering if she's temporarily lost her senses.

"I did indeed. After this place fell out of the hands of The Ancient Gods, Cronus realised he was at a loss for what to do with it. He needed someone to rule Mortaria, and he had no interest in this place himself, he thought it— beneath him I suppose you could say," Anubis explains, and I find myself listening once again for the second time in as many hours. Turns out I'm learning a lot more than I'd bargained for.

"So, is that how you ended up with the job?" I ask, merciless in my interrogation, and she shakes her head.

"Oh no, I was banished here long before the fall of The Gods of Ancient because you see, I had become one of Ra's closest and most devoted followers."

At her explanation, I become more and more confused. So much had happened before my time it's entirely impossible to keep up with these seemingly petty dramas between gods and titans, which have ridiculously oversized repercussions for the little people down below.

"Wait— but didn't you help overthrow the Gods of Ancient in the first place— I thought that was how you became a Titan?" I sound incredulous, and Anubis laughs.

"Oh yes, I helped overthrow them; I saved The Higher Plains. But once I was welcomed into Hermopolis, reunited with my ingrate husband Horus, and fell pregnant with his child, which I honestly never wanted, I realised that I had been mistaken in thinking I could ever be equal to *actual* gods." Anubis is bitter now, making me smile. We really *do* have a lot in common.

"So, you were banished here for changing tact and realising that Ra was more suited to your personal agenda?" I guess. She nods, dark hair falling over one shoulder.

"Indeed, I was, and I remained in Mortaria, watched the fall of those same gods, and then was approached by Cronus, the very being who had banished me. He presented me with a proposal. He would aid in the resurrection of Ra into a mortal body, and we would rule Mortaria together, under his guidance." I frown, it seems like the perfect solution, and I can see why she accepted, so I'm left wondering why she's sitting here alone.

"So how did you resurrect him into a mortal body?" I press her further, and she smirks, clearly pleased with herself.

"The exacts of the ritual were never known to me, for that part was taken care of by Cronus. You know he was ultimately one of the most powerful entities in the heavens, hence why it took his own prodigies to befall him. I, however, did provide the body. I killed Horus, my husband." She looks too smug about this, and I wonder what their marriage must have been like. Probably abusive, knowing the way most men throughout history have treated their wives.

"So, if the ritual worked— what happened?" I'm beyond curious now and watch with bated breath as her eyes turn sad.

"When Ra was fully coherent again, and I explained what I had done, he killed himself. He couldn't bear the thought of allying himself with a son of Gaia. Told me that he would rather die than rule by the side of a traitor." Her eyes betray heartbreak, though why I cannot discern. Could it be she truly loved Ra? Or that she had been in love with the idea of ruling by his side and finally being perceived as equal, instead?

"And that's how you ended up ruling over Mortaria? Cronus didn't have anyone else—" I muse. She looks affronted momentarily before nodding slowly.

"I was, as ever, the last choice."

"So, do you think that Ra would do the same if you tried to resurrect him a second time?" I ask her, expression falling serious, and she shrugs.

"I don't think it matters. Nobody has the power required to even perform the ritual. You're talking about pulling a soul from The Nether and putting it into a flesh conduit that's been rotting in the ground for the last six months in terms of Sephy Sinclair, and even longer with Ra. The last two gods I knew of who were able to muster that kind of energy, light or dark, are long gone. Moloch and Cronus are both long banished to The Island of The Blessed, and so I feel is the option of resurrection." Her mind is made up, so I exhale, feeling the full sting of her stubbornness. Though perhaps she feels the same way about my hopefulness, seeing it merely as naïve ignorance.

I look around, at the high domed ceiling that moves to form the point of the pyramid; it's covered in mirrors that are fractured a hundred times over into mosaic murals. The walls sheen luxurious in gold, and I'm left wondering if Anubis isn't a little too comfortable with her luxury apartment and her too-keen mortal lovers.

"I see. Well, I suppose that your mind is made up. I will not call on you again, unless— you have something else in mind which may benefit the both of us?" I query, getting to my feet, and she shrugs.

"Not that I can think of." She flutters her long fingers, as though all thought of an alliance between us has long since floated away on the breeze of her subconscious.

"Well then, I'll leave you to your— pleasure." I cock an eyebrow and purse my lips as she gives me a suggestive stare.

"Pandora, a word of advice—" she calls as I spin on one foot to take my leave. I glare back at her over one shoulder — the woman who has been passed over again and again for rulership, and is hesitant to fight to regain any power at all, is giving *me* advice?

"Yes?" I ask, widening my eyes and feigning innocence.

"Don't get yourself into any trouble. It would be an awful shame if I had to watch Haedes torch you to a cinder." Her eyes flash playfully, and I wonder momentarily who the hell she thinks she is.

Is it the drink, going to her head?

Instead of biting though, instead of allowing my desire to be seen and proven as worthy rule me, I simply smile, playing the long game as ever.

"Of course."

With these final two words, I reach into the pocket of my leather jacket and pull out the box, not daring to look back into the lap of luxury as I open a portal to The Fallen Kingdom and step inside.

4

DANGER ZONE

XION

"OOOH OOH! GET THE red jellybean!" Haedes shouts in my left ear, rattling me so I almost drop my phone into the thick layer of dust and sand coating the floor. His voice bounces in a hideous clang off the long-forgotten stone walls of the hidden chamber inscribed with ancient runes I don't understand.

"Can you just stop yelling in my goddamn ear for like two seconds; this is hard, okay? It requires a great deal of concentration," I explain for the fourteenth time this hour, staring hard at the screen. The brightly coloured grid filled with candy is making me irrationally angry yet again, a constant theme since this trip began.

"The way I see it you just have to blow up all the candy, right? That's easy!" Haedes sounds incredulous, like it's me being stupid and not the creators of this game being masochistic assholes.

"Look, why don't you try it if you think it's so easy?" I yell, shoving the phone at him and leaping off the floor so I'm an inch from his face. His eyes light up with wicked delight, gleaming in the shadows as cobwebs stir around us, a light breeze catching them in its charms.

As he snatches the phone from my hand, with a smug smile on his annoyingly self-satisfied face, Luce coughs.

I turn and find her sprawled on the floor, high-heeled shoes strewn around her, squinting at the walls as she has been for the last hour. More importantly though is the pedestal atop which a dusty old volume sits, bound in black leather now adorned with several pieces of melted flesh, some pink, some black, all I'd really rather were still attached to me. I look down at my hand. It's almost healed now, but I won't forget the pain that blistered my palm raw in a hurry, and neither will my demon self.

"Look, can you two just shut up? It's hard enough trying to decipher ancient runes without you two bickering over freaking red jellybeans in the background!" She scowls, the blues of her eyes violently pale against the shadow encasing the far end of the chamber. In fact, she looks phantasmal.

"Uh, sorry," I apologise, glaring back at Haedes who is propped on top of the rubble that had just an hour ago been part of the ceiling. Now, thanks to me, it's making him an ample, if not slightly crooked, pedestal upon which to sit. Staring with malicious intent down at my phone screen, it illuminates his face in a too-white hue.

I frown, observing his fingers dancing, manic, on the screen and decide to turn away, focusing on the book instead.

"So, any progress?" I ask, bored of waiting.

Luce nods, blonde hair shaking against her skin as it falls over one shoulder.

"Actually yes. I think you two are too pure. The book needs to be picked up by a God of Ancient, or someone possessing similar power—" she relinquishes. I nod, snorting.

"Figures, not pure enough to do any good but not tainted enough to match up the big leagues. Typical," I pretend to be sad about this, but I'm relieved. If I wanted proof that I'm not all bad, here it is.

"I did kind of already guess that, Luce. You didn't need to spend an hour of my precious time checking you know." Haedes' voice comes, distracted, and I turn to look at him with a scowl, mirroring Luce's face. Finding him with his tongue stuck out to one side, he's not even looking at us.

Asshole.

"Well excuse me if I didn't want to get my skin melted off like hot wax!" she cusses, and Haedes' body visibly tenses. I watch the roots of his hair morph scarlet, his eyes blazing as he remains utterly enthralled by the game, as if we're not even here.

Luce and I stand, staring at each other, eyes dead, wondering exactly why it is we put up with his crap. Shrugging and shaking her head, Luce spins on the ball of her foot, swooping down with one arm to pick up her heels in her left hand, before swiping the book off its pedestal with the other.

As she does this, Haedes erupts behind me in an audible, "Yes!" and I spin back, finding him smug.

Getting to his feet, he hands me back my phone, unbearable in his self-satisfaction.

"You did *not* just beat that level—" I glower at him and he cocks an eyebrow, smirking.

"I'm God of The Underworld baby! Ain't no candy beating me!" He erupts into laughter, and I ball my fist at my side.

I've been stuck on that freaking level for *a week and a half.*

"Oh, hey! Luce! You got the book! Awesome! Well done, you!" Haedes continues to smile at her, hair fizzling back to cool blue as his eyes sparkle with victory. I could honestly punch him in his stupid face right now.

"Yes, thank you for noticing. Can we go now?" Luce demands, expression unamused as she stares at us both, gaze blank and impatient.

"Sure. You're cool with a walk though, right? I can't convect everyone— well I could, but it's bad for my complexion," Haedes announces.

I sigh, rolling my eyes.

Luce glowers at him.

"So, you mean to tell me you brought me all the way here with no intention of convecting me back to Mortaria? Don't you realise how busy I am since you left your post unattended, Haedes? You're unbelievable!" she scolds him, spinning on the ball of her foot. Pondering the same question as me, her head tilts back, and she looks up at the hole in the ceiling, unamused.

How are we going to get out of here?

"I'll give you a lift up, of course, but no convecting between dimensions or across continents. It's really taking its toll on my skin." Haedes continues to whine about his wrinkles as he grabs Luce by the arm and convects out of the room, reappearing at the edge of the hole overhead. The sun is high in the sky and, as he looks down, I notice a disturbing but wicked look on his face.

"So, I was thinking—" he begins, but I cut him off.

"Haedes! Get me out of here! Stop being an asshole!" I curse, and he shrugs.

"Well, I was thinking, you should probably admit that I'm the best— seeing as how I've got you at a bit of a disadvantage."

"The best?" I demand, fury scorching through my veins like poison as I fight the urge to go full demon right here, right now.

"Yes, at crushing candy!" he announces.

"You're the biggest asshole I know!" I yell, staring up at the cobalt blue speck of his head, silhouetted above me.

"And?" he goads me, but for lack of a better option, I find myself bending to his stupid wishes.

"And— you're the best at crushing candy—" I mumble, cocking my head and giving him a pissed-off glare as I shield my eyes from the sun with one hand.

"What was that? I didn't quite hear that?" he taunts me further, and I hear Luce complaining, though her voice is muffled by the earth overhead. I can only hope whatever she's saying includes a lot of four-letter words.

"I said, you're the best at crushing candy!" I scream up at him, voice reverberating off the walls.

In a flash, he's beside me, appearing in a spontaneous eruption of blue flames.

He grabs my arm, smiling, and simply saying, "Why, thank you, Xion. No need to shout," with a cheeky grin. We convect together out of the ruins, only to find Luce sitting, fury warping her face, on top of one of the half-crumbling pillars of the once magnificent Pergamon.

"Are you two quite finished?" she demands, voice high-pitched and full of superiority.

"Yes, but you know we've still got a long drive ahead of us," Haedes reminds her. She sighs, looking down at her bare feet and then up at both of us, face alarmingly pale in the bright sunlight.

"Brilliant. Just what I always wanted. Being stuck in the car with the dream team all day," she bites.

Haedes simply shrugs.

"Well, if you don't want to make conversation, you could always look inside that book, seeing as how nobody else can touch it."

Her eyes light up as her gaze falls to the volume cupped in the crook of her elbow. Biting her bottom lip, guilty almost, she cocks her head, shuffling on the spot.

If I was a believer in such things, I'd say it was almost as if the book was speaking to her in whispers only she can hear, like a phantom of her past coming back to haunt her.

I frown, worried more than I'd like about exposing her to such clearly potent magic.

She looks up between the two of us, head jerking like she's trying to physically dissipate the dreamy look that's overtaken her face and morphed her powder blue pupils milky with desire.

"Ugh!" she yells, stomping her foot into the dirt and storming off toward the car.

Haedes simply stares at me; his grey eyes not the least bit sympathetic, before giving me a cheesy smile.

"Women, eh? Can't live with em, can't—" he pauses, clearing his throat of dust as Luce continues to rant and rave into the muggy midday air, her voice becoming nothing more than an irritated mouse squeak the greater the distance she puts between us.

Haedes shrugs, continuing with a sigh and a grimace.

"Actually, I'm pretty sure that's it."

Having sent one final text to Jules asking for a ride home from the airport, I sink back into the plush, duck-egg blue velour of the cabin's seating, exhaling a sigh of relief.

Luce sits on the opposite side of the aisle, facing Haedes with her back to the cockpit, and a pretty air hostess with blonde hair and a fake smile comes and offers me alcohol that I promptly refuse.

Unfortunately, I can't say the same for Haedes.

As we take off into the air, I watch Luce.

She looks different somehow, wearier, black circles ringing her light blue eyes and causing them to pop alarmingly from her face. She's stroking the cover of the book, the thing we've searched the world for over six months to find, and now that we're airborne, heading home, and with said book in tow, I begin to wonder what's next.

Shifting uncomfortably in my seat, I take a handful of pretzels from a bowl on the table in front of me, shoving them into my mouth and letting the salty dry snack turn my mouth arid. Reaching next for a bottle of water, I return to observing Luce, only to realise she is watching me.

"Do you know you chew really loudly?" she asks, pissed, as she continues to stroke the cover of the volume in her palms half-heartedly.

"Hey, don't get cranky with me. It's not my fault the blue-haired one hauled you all the way out here and won't give you a lift home," I snap, tired beyond what I've realised.

Haedes stares between us, sipping casually on the whisky in his glass, his usual two cubes of ice clinking jovially as he swills the dark fluid in hypnotic motion.

"I'm sitting right here you know." He cocks a cobalt eyebrow, eyes dead in his skull, mouth pursed into a hard, serious line.

"I don't think we could possibly overlook that fact. You're like a troll doll with exceptional grooming habits," I quip, causing Luce to smirk. Haedes scowls.

"I don't know what that is, but you better hope when I find out it's complimentary," Haedes threatens, but I shrug, fighting the urge to stick my tongue out at him.

As I do so, it strikes me that this is a very Sephy thing to do.

It makes me miss her, makes me ache deep in my stomach so inescapably that I feel the recurrence of my grief threaten to swallow me whole, pulling me under in an unexpected tidal wave of loss.

Just when I think the waters have calmed, that I'm merely floating in a sea of despair, the waves begin to build again. The slightest scent of cinnamon, someone's sarcastic tone of voice, a flash of red hair, the smell of whisky on someone's breath; anything and everything that could remind me of her does, and it's more painful than I could have ever imagined.

I wallow, lost in loss for what could be several hours as silence blankets everything around us. Luce tentatively opens The Book of The Dead, flicking through its pages, utterly enthralled by each dark strike of ink upon aged parchment. The only sound is that of the whirring jet engines as I catch Haedes watching her too, expression laced only with half interest.

As we sit in a conversationless void, I realise that what comes next is more terrifying. If we do learn how to resurrect Sephy, if we, in fact, *can* do what is demanded of us, what if it still doesn't work?

I'll have to accept that she's really gone, an execution I've stayed for the last six months by the cruel, intangible safety net of hope the mystical provides.

After ordering two more drinks, Haedes finally breaks the silence.

"So?" he demands, looking at Luce with raised eyebrows and wide, expectant eyes.

"So— what?" she replies, raising her gaze from the pages only long enough to give him an irritated half glance.

"What does it say?!" Haedes exclaims, like she's utterly stupid. He gesticulates so violently he almost spills his drink all over the dirtied white cotton of his shirt.

"It's— complicated. There's an entire section on Resurrection," she explains.

Haedes lets out an exasperated breath.

"Have you not read that yet? I would have thought you'd have started there, given that it's why we went looking for that stupid book in the first place," he condemns her, and I'm momentarily confused.

Why is he being so demanding? She's already done more than enough today, certainly more than I could have asked for.

"I already did. I was just reading this section on—" she begins, but Haedes cuts her off.

"Oh, so you already read it? What did it say? Come on, tell me. I've been waiting six months for this!" The pushy troll doll of The Underworld leans forward in his seat, placing his glass on the table between himself and Luce, jiggling his legs like a small child on his way to Disney World.

"Look I—" She appears immediately uncomfortable, but Haedes isn't having any of it.

"Luce, cut the shit. Just tell me what the stupid thing says." He's angry now, his excitement turning edgy and sharp in only seconds.

"Fine. It says that the ritual of resurrection is like a trade." My heart begins to hammer at her words, realising that this is the moment. The moment all my hopes could shatter into a million pieces.

"A trade?" I chip in, and the two of them turn to look at me as though they've forgotten I'm here.

"Yes. As you should both know, energy can't be destroyed or created, only transferred. Getting a soul back into its body requires a large amount of energy. We can't just make it. So, we need to borrow it from somewhere." Luce seems increasingly uneasy as she explains this, though I can't work out why.

"So, what are you saying exactly?" I press her for a clearer answer, almost desperate in my masochistic desire to know for certain whether this entire journey has been for nothing.

"I'm saying that you would need to take the life force from somebody and funnel it into Sephy's body to reconnect it with her soul—and it would need to be someone powerful, too, because she's not just anyone; she's a demi-goddess. That means it can't be you Xion," Luce adds as though she knows that my immediate instinct is to sacrifice myself to save her.

"What about my hourglass?" Haedes suggests.

Luce and I both glance at one another, surprised by the suggestion.

"If we took the energy from there, nothing would be tethering you to this plain anymore. You'd return to what you were before—" Luce sighs. Haedes frowns too.

"Well then, I guess that's out of the question?" he enquires, almost as though he's asking for her permission in writing this off as a viable option.

"Of course, it is! Without you here, the sun will extinguish, and Mortaria will fall. The scales will tip— the entire universe will unravel!" Luce almost shouts this, and I can tell there's something more bothering her than what is on the surface. I know it's been hard for her and Thane with Haedes gone, but is it just that or something deeper?

I ponder this, wondering why it is that ever since she arrived, I haven't been able to stop analysing her. I've known her a long time, and yet she continues to be a mystery in so many ways. She's a being potentially more powerful than anything the universe has ever known, and yet she can seem so fragile, so innocent.

"Alright, keep your hair on. So— I hate to have to even ask this, but what about if you took the power directly from me?" Haedes demands, and I feel myself turn surprised yet again. I suppose I shouldn't be. After all, Sephy is his daughter. Yet, something about this unselfish suggestion seems so— wrong, coming from him.

"It could work— but I don't know what that would do to you," Luce is candid, stern in expression, angry almost.

"Well, would it kill me?" he demands.

I sigh, beginning to feel like this entire resurrection thing is way more complex than I'd originally thought. Something about the way the world is tells me that nothing is ever free or easy, especially when that something is reversing death.

So then— why can't I let her go?

"I don't know what it will do to you— but that's beside the point. You don't have someone to conduct the ritual anyway. So, none of this even matters." Luce puts the book down, closing the cover sharply with a look of pointed irritation on her face. "Can't you just come back to Mortaria? We need you. Things aren't running right without you in residence," she pleads, stare implicative.

"I can't. I just can't. She's my daughter Luce." Haedes gives her the wide eyes, the pout he's so good at, and she shakes her head. "What kind of person do we need to find to conduct this ritual anyway? A priest? Shaman? Kindred? Demon Lord? If it's someone between Mortaria or Aetheria, I'll find them. You know I won't rest—"

"That's the point though, Haedes. You need to rest and let her rest. Let it all go. You can't keep clutching at straws just so you don't have to deal with her death. Life ends— people die. You should understand that more than anyone. Isn't that what Zeus sent you down here to teach you?" At her words, Haedes stiffens in his seat.

"Fuck you," he curses, spitting the words like they're venomous.

50

The two of them fall into silence.

Leaning back into their chairs, conversation ceases entirely for several minutes until Haedes, without trying for eye contact, speaks out into the pressurised air of the cabin. "You didn't answer my question, Luce. Who do I need to threaten, pay off, or fuck to get this ritual underway?" he growls, expression twisted and desperate.

Luce replies, sighing and crushing both mine and Haedes' hearts in one single sentence.

"I'm sorry, but there just isn't anyone left who can bring her back."#

The rest of the flight passes in a depressing, morose blur, and by the time I'm sat in the front seat of a black jeep next to Jules, the silence has said more than any words ever could.

We pull away from the tarmac, Haedes and Luce in the back with an air of unmistakable tension and rage between them as Jules looks in his rear-view mirror. Taking in the two rigid figures, he coughs twice, clearing his throat and looking to me.

"So where have you been?" he asks as the barrier raises, allowing the car passage out of the airport and onto the freeway.

"A little bit of everywhere. Egypt, Berlin, Peru, Greece, Turkey—" I don't give away the nature of the journey, but I suppose I owe the man something.

"Well, I would have known that before now if you'd have picked up your phone," he scolds me, tightening his black leather driving gloves on the steering wheel and accelerating forward as I look away, staring out of the tinted windows and over the skyline of Chicago. With each mile that passes, bringing us closer to the Estate, my stomach ties itself into tighter and tighter knots.

"I'm sorry. It was a busy trip. I barely knew what time zone I was in most of the time." I make the excuse, knowing full well it's hardly an explanation, and he snorts, pushing down even harder on the accelerator and taking out his frustration on the road as we swerve in and out of traffic, switching back and forth between lanes for no discernible reason.

"Right. And what about you two?" He looks over his shoulder, taking his eyes off the line of fast-moving traffic for only a moment and staring back at Luce and Haedes. They perk up, surprised that he's addressed them at all.

Luce still has the book clutched in her hands, not having let it out of her grasp since she first laid her fingers upon it back in Pergamon.

"Oh, we were just there for— the ladies," Haedes adds, and I roll my eyes.

"He's joking—" I stutter, not wanting Jules to think I've forgotten Sephy.

"Oh, am I?" Haedes quips.

I turn around in my seat.

"Just shut up, Haedes. I've had enough!" I snap.

Jules does a double take.

"Wait— Haedes?" he looks behind him, eyes wide.

Haedes nods.

"Long time no see. I thought the blue hair was a dead giveaway," Haedes snorts, and Jules raises his eyebrows in surprise.

"I guess I didn't recognise you; it's been a long time— and we've both aged." He makes this comment as a harmless rationalisation for not recognising the god made flesh, but Haedes doesn't take it that way.

"Hey, I have *not* aged!" he exclaims.

Jules looks immediately apologetic.

"Of course not. I just meant— it's been a long time for me."

"Right— well, that's just fine then." Haedes pouts, a giant manbaby more than a god as he stares out of the window in a brand-new mood.

"And who are you?" Jules asks Luce, who continues to watch Haedes with a smug smile on her face.

"I'm Lucifer. But you can call me Luce. I like you already," she introduces herself, and Jules gets a strange look on his face as his brow creases and his eyes sparkle.

"The devil?" he queries, face full of wonder, and she nods.

"Of course."

"It's a pleasure to meet you. I've— heard a lot about you," he admits, and she smirks, catching his eye from the back seat in the rear-view mirror.

"All bad, I'm sure," she giggles, face relaxing for the first time since Haedes had arrived with her.

"All true?" Jules enquires, picking up the flow of conversation between them. Luce shrugs, looking up as though remembering something funny and smirking.

"Partly true, I suppose," she relinquishes.

Jules lets out a small smile, his eyes glistening as he finds someone, finally, who isn't fond of silence and brooding.

I watch the two of them, as they begin to talk about the bible and her reputation but tune out the rest of the conversation. I let the leather of my seat cup my back as I relax and try to ignore the fact that I'm returning to the place where I found her body.

Finally, we pull up to the electric double gates of the Sinclair Estate, which roll apart as soon as Jules enters the security key into the keypad outside his window.

We travel smoothly down the alabaster gravel, the familiar crackle of it haunting. The trees enclose us on all sides, a pewter grey sky hanging above with foreboding darkness as we journey through the vast lines of trees enclosing the estate.

As the forest begins to thin, the house comes into view, and I'm reminded of the night I had driven Sephy back here when she had been drunk. It was the first night I realised she wasn't like other girls and the first night I also realised she was one of the most stubborn people I'd ever met. So how can it be she was taken in such a seemingly sudden and cruel way? There was no epic fight, no ancient prophecy, only her, alone in the white sheets where I'd held her, fighting against the blade that had changed her life forever.

Somehow that just doesn't seem fair.

We pull up to the front of the house and I swallow hard, turning to Jules and taking a deep breath before my voice crackles against the otherwise silent air filling the car.

I must ask.

"Jules, has there been any progress with the police enquiry?" I demand, letting my gaze run rampant across the vast and pristine lawns, almost as though, even still, I'm expecting her to suddenly appear on horseback.

"No. It's all gone rather quiet on that front, actually. I've been trying to push them into action, but the security footage the police salvaged from the estate has been wiped. They claim they're at a dead end," he explains, and I almost want to laugh at the term. That seems to be the way my entire life has gone.

Reaching dead end after dead end— so much so that I'm reaching the point where I don't know how to recover. I don't have a purpose anymore. I can kill demons forever, but what actual good is that doing anyone? They just keep coming back.

Sephy had been a spitfire, a light, that perhaps indicated, after all this time, change was coming to The Underworld. Now, that spark has been extinguished before it even had a chance to catch.

"On a plus, the contractors left a few days ago. The estate has been fully refurbished, per your instructions," Jules adds. I shrug, not caring at all despite the enormous amounts of money and time I've invested in the place.

I've had him gut and replace Sephy's suite, mainly because I couldn't bear the thought of her coming back and finding her own murder scene or the damage I inflicted in my demonic rage after the event. That all seems rather redundant now, though. The project, which I'd expanded to the entire manor house after I realised I'd be travelling a while, had been nothing if not a way to keep Jules busy.

"Shall we go inside?" Jules asks, pushing me into reluctant motion. I sigh.

"Yes, I suppose we should." I nod, stepping across the gravel, which crunches loudly underfoot, before climbing the front stairs with an utter lack of enthusiasm.

As Jules unlocks the front doors, I feel my heart wither and step forward into the empty house that I know now I will never call home.

I stand in the doorway of Sephy's refurbished suite. Unrecognisable from the childish pinks and creams it had been decked out in before, the room is now painted a deep aubergine, accented with rich black woods carved into a large four poster and various other armoires and storage units. It's dark yet sophisticated, packing quite the aesthetic punch, just like her. I look over the cream bed linen that appears soft, too soft, yet not inviting at all.

The feel is also much more gothic than I'd intended, and yet it still screams Sephy Sinclair. Jules did a good job, and as I walk through the space, which reeks of fresh paint, climbing two small black marble steps into her bathroom, I wonder if he might not know her much better than I ever could.

As I turn to face the line of freshly installed mirrors, finding only my own ragged and exhausted reflection staring back at me, my eyes drift to the back wall where the damage from my grief has been entirely eradicated. Returning to my reflection, I notice my black t-shirt hanging from me a little looser than usual. I've lost weight in my face too, and my eyes are no longer a shimmering gold hue but rather a dull yellowish brown with no light left behind the pupils.

As I examine myself and then the bathroom further, thinking that it's as though I'm in an entirely different room as an entirely different person, I hear a knock at the door.

"Come in," I call, voice weak.

The dark wooden door swings open and Luce enters, Cerb at her heels. He rushes forward to me, and I bury my fingers in the tender spots behind his ears. He looks thinner too, so I guess I'm not the only one who's bereft at the loss of a certain redhead.

"Oh. Hey," I breathe, and Luce looks heartbroken as her eyes settle on my face. I take several quick strides out of the bathroom, urging Cerb to follow and watching as the Leonberger launches himself down the bathroom stairs clumsily. Climbing up onto the pristine sheets of the bed, he makes himself quickly at home, whining, aware she's missing.

Leaning against one of the thick bedposts, I cock my head.

"You okay?" I enquire, noticing that The Book of The Dead is still firmly within her clutches. Luce nods.

"I am. Are you?" She takes a few small steps forward and places the book down on the bed beside Cerb, who shuffles back from it and emits a loud bark. Taking a free hand and placing it on my bicep, she squeezes firmly, sighing gently into the warm air.

"I've been better," I express. She smiles, a kind of sadness overtaking her that appears to run bone deep in its intensity.

"I'm sorry." She seems apologetic, causing my curiosity to pique.

"Why? It's not your fault. You did everything you could," I remind her, partially wondering if this is true as her face contorts with guilt.

"I know—" she exhales heavily again. I wish, now more than ever, that I could read her mind.

"I guess life goes on. I just need to figure out how— without her."

"You barely knew her for long at all, Xion," Luce reminds me, her lips puckering.

"How long did you know Thane before you felt like you couldn't live without her?" I ask, surprising myself at the harsh tone in which the question falls from me.

"I—" Her eyes light up but then diminish quickly as she blinks a few times, frowning. Brushing her white-blonde hair back behind one ear, she turns on one heel, grabbing The Book of The Dead and looking back at me over one shoulder.

"It'll be okay, Xion. You just have to— take one day at a time." Her words fall on deaf ears as I move to sit, petting Cerb on top of his broad head.

"I guess I just don't know how anymore. I've lived a long time, and it's all the same shit, day after day. Me fighting back the demon inside, killing the demons on the outside— I just thought my life could be better, could change. I thought my penance was over. Guess that's pretty stupid, right?" I ask her as she walks across the room to leave, slowing upon the plush cream carpet as she reaches the doorway.

"Not at all," Luce replies, face riddled with pain for me.

I exhale, staring down into Cerb's enormous chocolate eyes.

"Anyway, I better start thinking about what I'm going to do with my life now—" I begin, not able to tear my gaze from the dog, wondering how long I'll be grieving this loss.

When I lift my gaze again, wanting to ask her for ideas, inspiration— anything, she's already gone.

5

GOING TO HELL

LUCE

I AM SO GOING to hell.

No really.

But also— spiritually, I am definitely going to hell.

Fuck.

As I pace across the luscious lawns of The Sinclair Estate, heading back to The Hollow, I turn with hesitation to find Haedes standing at one of the downstairs windows, his face heartbroken.

Yep. Book me into room fucking six hundred and sixty goddamn six in honour of my wretched birthday. I'm checking into hell!

I sigh, exasperated.

Brushing my fingers through my hair with my free hand, I clasp The Book of the Dead in the other; its power unmistakable to anyone with the slightest sense about these things. It's wrapped me firmly in its charms — there can be no mistake — the blackness of the ink whispering to me even now.

My toes bury deep in the soil and I shiver, the dark sky overhead threatening rain. I suppose I could have changed in the estate, but I was so busy trying to get out of there without breaking down and telling both Haedes and Xion the truth, I scurried away without thinking, like the little weasel I am.

My mind flits to the Sanguine forest, and I shudder at the thought of having my feet bathed in blood. Thane already thinks I'm halfway to the deep end, so turning up half-naked and covered in blood probably won't help my case any.

As I reach the edge of the small forest, I make sure to head into an area densely surrounded by trees. Here, I centre myself, letting my mind travel down into the roots of the earth, beyond the walls that separate this dimension from the next, and into Mortaria— into my closet to be exact.

I click my fingers, magic ebbing through my veins, and relish the sensation before I open my eyes to look down at myself. I'm now wearing my favourite black velvet cloak, black velvet leggings, knee-high boots, and a bloody red shirt that hangs low beyond my cleavage. The short dress I had been wearing has been transported back to the laundry hamper in my apartment.

Nodding with a satisfied smile and placing my fingers over Thane's tether, still fastened tight around my throat, I feel powerful at the achievement of something arguably simple. I would have been freezing and bloody, walking through the Sanguine Forest before hitching a carriage back to the city, but like this, I'll be toasty and stylish. A win-win all around.

With a smile on my lips, I pick my way over thick roots and scattered pine needles, enjoying the feel of this earthen forest as it teems silently with life.

Reaching the gargantuan and wicked outline of The Hollow in only a few minutes, I pick up a jagged stone from the ground. Slashing my palm without flinching, I hold it out against the dark grain of the wood.

Gazing behind me one final time and tightening my hold on the book yet again, I step through into the violent whirring of red smoke and scattered lightning forks, not wasting any more time than is necessary in the void between worlds.

Treading out in large strides onto moist ruddy dirt, I feel the eyes of those guarding The Hollow tracing my outline as they creep around in the dense scarlet canopy overhead. I gaze up at the vermillion sky, giving them a clear view of my face so they know who it is they're dealing with. I sigh as the light of the violet sun bathes me, giving me an energy boost after my exposure to the frailties of the mortal sun.

I trudge across the vast breadth of the Sanguine Forest with uncouth haste, catching a gondola down the River Styx as I decide I'd rather be out in the open air than stuffed inside a carriage.

My skin is warm, too warm almost, as the muggy air of Mortaria tugs at me and my stomach begins to churn atop the ebbing current of the ghostly waters. The ferryman doesn't turn to greet me, and I wonder momentarily if he knows who I am as I give serious consideration to throwing up over the side.

I focus on the volume in my lap, trying to distract myself as we creep closer and closer to the Exilia, looking over the crinkled flesh of the leather binding and the heavy metal clasps keeping the entire thing from falling apart under the weight of its own significance. The cover is stamped with ancient dark runes, a message of warning to those without my persuasion toward the corrupting magics within.

I should have known, should have known that upon picking it up, I would be pulled more deeply into the task of resurrecting Sephy Sinclair than I ever wanted.

But how can I say no to Haedes?

My longest-standing friend, the man who stood by me when his entire family thought I was no good, was asking me for my help — and I've lied to him.

I continue to fight back the nausea, but I know now it's not the boat or the motion of the cloudy glowing waters beneath — it's guilt. Unrivalled by that created by any act I have ever committed, the guilt from lying to both Xion and Haedes, claiming the ritual of resurrection is all but lost to them, is eating me alive from the inside.

The problem is, the only person left who can perform the ritual is me, and in tapping into such potent dark magic, I stand to put myself so much at risk that I'm not sure I can justify the act at all.

Sephy survived incredible odds at the Colosseum, only to be murdered in her bed not a month later. Isn't that most likely the universe's way of correcting the mistake of her survival?

Xion's miserable expression floats back into my head, taunting me, as the gondola finally sweeps beneath the hollow crystal arches of the Exilia's foundations.

I exhale heavily, observing the smoky quartz as it catches the sunlight and the hue of the sky, throwing bloody and broken lilac hues bouncing from every surface in a tainted, dark mockery of what it had been.

As the gondola approaches the dock in swift and fluid motion, I stand, readying to step off as quickly and elegantly as possible. However, once I do, finding dry land nothing but comfort, I realise I have absolutely no idea what I'm doing.

I've returned here, but why?

I suppose I should get back to work. I mean, Haedes asked me to get the spare key to his vault, a secret he and I share, and place the book inside, but the thought of parting with it is almost unbearable. Something about it, about the way it's written, feels like the author is speaking directly to me, but more specifically a part of me that's been crushed down and denied for far too long.

Striding forward with my cloak billowing out behind me, I glide through the lobby of the place, past sinners standing guard. As I feel them shudder in my wake, I wonder now if we're really so different.

They're being punished, are trapped in this place, and so to an extent am I.

Climbing the spiral staircase and dreading finally being home as I know I'll have to deal with Thane, something else strikes me. The sinners of Mortaria— they *earned* their places here.

What have I ever done to deserve being outcast like this?

Being born.

Is that my crime?

Simply existing as half pure god and half ancient god?

I've never done anything bad—

Have I?

I fell in love with Thane, so I guess her mother, Nemesis, would say I probably took her daughter away from her, away from her purpose in The Higher Plains, but other than that— all I've ever done is try to help the people around me.

As I reach the top of the staircase, I find myself going back to when I'd been here last, when I was excited and looking forward to finally spending time with the woman who has been by my side through everything. Now though, I find myself filled with dread as I open the door.

Moments later, disappointment replaces the tension in my gut.

The apartment is empty, and Thane is nowhere to be found. She must be out doing recon again, meaning I have no idea when she'll be back, if she comes back at all.

We've fought before but never like this, never to a point where we can find no middle ground, no compromise.

I shed my cloak, letting it fall recklessly to the floor in a puddle of soft darkness before throwing the book onto the unmade bedsheets, bereft as soon as it leaves my grasp. I untie the choker from my throat, allowing it to fall into my open palm as I stare at the indigo stone, at its sheen, trying to distract myself.

Discarding it on the top of the vintage armoire, I'm restless as I drift through the rooms of the apartment, perhaps lonelier now than I have ever been.

I feel it calling to me the further away I tread, as I light the black candles that adorn almost every surface, and as I stare at my reflection in the slick ebony of the kitchen units when I go to pour myself a rare glass of red wine.

Sipping it down faster than I should, my reservations melt away a little just as the wax of the black candles begins to drip, slipping down the sides of their phallic lengths.

My eyes flit between the bed and the alchemy cabinet as I ponder adding a brew to my drink, but then I'm reminded of Thane's harsh words, her overreaction, the way she'd scorned me for half of who I am. She wants me to deny half of myself, always has, but is it really because of the danger? Or is it because she knows she can't love that part? Knows that half of me is simply unlovable?

The thought of this truth makes me angry, furious in fact, so much so that I shatter the glass in my hand as my grip around it automatically tightens. My mother always shunned me, warned others about me, but Thane has always been the one person who I thought could see me for who I am, not who they painted me to be.

Red wine drips to the floor, a bloody puddle, as I let the smashed glass tumble carelessly after it with a sharp tinkle.

I should clean it up, but my mind is racing, heart pounding as truths I've been ignoring for years start to surface.

First the truths, then— the questions.

Would she love me if I was dark?

Would she still feel the same way if she could see the ancient side of me?

These queries don't have answers, not really, but as I lay down among the black velvet sheets, giving in to my urge to read more of The Book of The Dead, I know that maybe it's time I find out.

As I scan the runes, I realise that I'm making the translations more seamlessly than usual, and smile, glad that the hours I've been spending in my alchemy chamber reading have paid off. I've been trying to solidify my foundation of alchemy knowledge, trying to be careful and do the homework to accompany what I've been practising. It's not like I'm totally reckless after all. I know magic is dangerous; I'm not oblivious to that fact. I never have been.

As I let my fingers caress the crinkled pages, I find my anger stirring, restless beneath the surface of my consciousness.

Nobody minds when I put myself at risk to save the lives of those around me, but then after the fact they seem to conveniently forget how I handled said magic without fault or flaw.

Is it possible I could resurrect Sephy Sinclair and walk away unscathed? Am I that powerful?

Yes.

The answer comes as a whisper from the past, as a collection of memories, each with a similar theme. Warnings about how dangerous alchemy is— but more importantly, warnings about how dangerous *I* could potentially become. I remember those lectures, but more seared into my mind is the look in the givers' eyes. The way they had gazed upon me.

I always thought it was disgust, but now I really think about it, it wasn't that at all.

It was fear.

The Gods in the Higher Plains hadn't exiled me out of hate or disgust. They had exiled me out of fear for who I could become if I ever reached my full potential.

I am the sole product of two opposing forces, which had collided in an act of primal lust and violence.

So how the hell have I become so damn downtrodden?

I roll onto my back, looking up at the ceiling, at the black crystal that reflects my image, blanketed by dark facets, back at me.

Thane, The Fates— they're so concerned with the threat I could become; don't they realise I could be an asset? I could use the power, which is my right by birth, harness it, and put it to good use.

It's true I'm half dark, half ancient, but I'm equally light, equally pure.

So why don't they believe in me?

Why don't they trust that I know what I'm doing?

I get to my feet, book under one arm, exhaling heavily and running the fingers of my free hand down the ruched red fabric of my shirt, caressing my stomach. I take a deep breath, narrowing my eyes and gritting my teeth.

I won't be made a victim of my heritage any longer.

With renewed purpose and confidence unlike anything I've felt for years, I pick up my cloak and stride across the apartment, hurrying into the alchemy chamber and slamming the door behind me.

I shed all the guilt I've been carrying ever since the moment I denied not only my ability but my willingness, to fix something which should never have been broken in the first place.

Sephy Sinclair should never have been murdered.

Why?

Because I say so, and I'm the freaking devil.

I get to my feet, stepping over piles of open books and moving back to where I started my research. Leaning across the dark, stained wood of my workbench, I pour over some of the texts which talk about the four founding pillars of alchemy, these being; Divination, Poisons, Healing, and Offensive Magics, letting the information seep into me even though I know it by heart.

Nowhere in the basics does it mention resurrection, but I'm trying to look deeper than mere surface information, trying to perhaps find something that might apply to more complex rituals but can be found in the building blocks of the craft.

Alchemy is one of those arts with a lot of unanswered questions, mainly because a lot of the researchers have met sticky ends, and their research has gone unfinished. The principles are very similar to that of the universe in many respects though, such as that energy cannot be destroyed or made, only recycled, borrowed, or transferred. However, alchemy doesn't work *with* Gaia but against her, turning back natural cycles, opening doors otherwise closed to the mind, and allowing energies to be used in ways they were never intended. Dark magic is infectious whereas light magic aims to be as connected to a single source and as pure as possible.

With this in mind, I find my eyes wandering to a relic I haven't paid any attention for years. A fractured obsidian shard, standing in the corner of the circular room atop a silver pedestal encased in a bell jar. It's the tether I created to extract Xion's darkness all those years ago, keeping him connected to it, only via the pendant I had carved from the very same stone to ensure the continued survival of the demonic part of him.

Haedes had given me the Obsidian for safekeeping, a gift he said, and had never asked me what became of it. Nobody knows, even now, about the ritual I performed on Xion, and I doubt even he remembers. Especially considering the state he'd been in after the murder of his first lover—

I recall his screams, the way the dark part of him had threatened to consume his personality like the moon blocks the sunlight during a solar eclipse— I had saved him from himself.

And I'm fine— aren't I?

I mean, if I could separate him from his darkness, it stands to reason I could funnel Haedes' life force into Sephy's remains—

I just need The Opal Blade— and probably some coffee.

The other thing I recall The Fates saying, many times, is about control, and how the will of the alchemist directly affects the strength and outcome of some spells. This means that if I want badly enough not to kill Haedes in the process it should work.

In theory.

Swallowing hard, I look over the books I've been pondering again, but don't see the information. Instead, I'm gearing up mentally for the toll this kind of magic will take. It's bigger than anything I've ever done before, probably will ever do again, and I need to get it right if I intend to prove to everyone, including Thane, that I can handle the darkness once and for all.

Debating opening The Book of The Dead and going over the section on resurrection for the fourth time this afternoon, the entire space is illuminated by a familiar and not entirely welcome blue flame.

Haedes is revealed, standing atop the pile of books I've been reading that he's just so tactfully succeeded in setting alight.

"Oh shit!" he cusses, hopping from one foot to the other.

Rushing forward I take my cloak from my shoulders, whirling it through the air and extinguishing the cobalt blaze before it has the chance to spread.

"Thanks for that. Good job none of these are— oh I don't know— priceless first editions—" I sigh, picking up *The Mercury Heavens- An Alchemic History,* and finding the section about Leviathan's influence on oceanic poisons completely destroyed.

Awesome. Thanks, Haedes.

"I'll buy you another one." Haedes looks at me with wide, supposedly sorry, eyes and I shake my head, exasperated.

"You really don't get sarcasm, do you?" I snap, throwing the book to the floor and rolling my eyes.

"Oh, so that *was* a first edition? Shit. My bad." Haedes gives me an apologetic grimace, mouth sagging at the edges.

"A first and *Only* edition. What do you want?" I ask, knowing already but wanting to hear him beg because I'm just that petty today.

"Look, I know what you said— but there has to be a way. We're gods, Luce. We're powerful. Arguably some of the most powerful entities this side of The Higher Plains. If we can't do this— who can?" he implores me.

I sigh.

"You're right. I can do it," I admit, breaking his gaze and staring at the floor.

"Look you're not listening— wait— what?" He looks confused, stepping over the scorched books and my cloak, which now lies in a smouldering crumpled heap.

I pout.

I liked that cloak too.

"I can do it. I have the power, well, at least half the power. It stands to reason I should be able to resurrect a half-god." I sound more confident than I feel, but I've told him now, so I know there's no going back.

"But you said—" Haedes still looks confused, and I wonder if he's as brainy as we all think he is. Without me, he'd probably be dead by now— or maimed— or something more ridiculous than I can think of at this current moment.

"I know what I said. It's a big risk on my part. I've never performed anything this complex or involving this much magic—"

"Yeah, you always say that though. And— you're still here. Still Luce. After everything." His eyes are kind, and for a second, I want to hold him to me, to tell him he's the closest thing I've ever had to a brother.

"You really think I can do it?" I press him for the truth with my gaze, and he nods.

"I think if anyone can, you can, Luce. You're powerful; you always have been."

"I know. I mean I've always denied that, but deep down, I know. I want to right this. For you and for Xion. But it's not just my sacrifice, my risk. It's yours too. I'm going to take the energy I need from you. If you're still up for it?" I cock my eyebrow. His smile fades.

"When?" he demands, taking my hand in his — a sign of fear and gratitude wrapped into a single oversimplified gesture between family.

"The book says that we need to use the sun's natural cycle to navigate the ritual," I recite, knowing the passages by heart from merely five readings. It's as though the words have imprinted themselves on my heart, tattooed themselves on my soul.

"And what does that mean?" his voice is rushed, mouth twisting with impatience.

"It means we have to perform the ritual at sunset. She should rise at dawn," I express, and he takes a deep breath, holding it hostage a few seconds before setting it free in a sigh.

Snatching the book off the table, I turn, and Haedes grabs my arm in his strong grip as if I might flee. I look around the place, knowing that when I return, I will either be the threat everyone assumes me to be, or I will have proved them all wrong.

I can only hope for the sake of my relationship with Thane that it will be the latter.

As the flames rise around us, Haedes speaks, more determined yet more terrified than I've heard him in a long time.

"Let's go get our girl back."

The sky swirls overhead, dark and bloody, unnatural, as the sun hovers, stubborn, just above the horizon. I'm shivering, wishing I'd brought my cloak though it's completely ruined, and so cast my mind back to my closet once more, letting myself travel through the roots of the soil before clicking my fingers. A fresh garment blankets me immediately, and Xion's startled tone breaks the silence as I pull the thick, dark fabric around my shoulders.

"I didn't know you could do that—" he comments, staring at me with a half-concerned grimace.

"Well, I don't usually use my powers for such trivial things but seeing as how I'm about to try raising someone from the dead, I figured wanting a cloak wouldn't really make much of an impact. Especially when you consider the scale of things." I shoot him an exasperated look.

He shrugs, shuffling atop the wet grass as spits of rain continue to fall, rolling undeterred off his leather jacket and sticking as whole droplets in his hair. The gentle, natural downpour causes the scent of fresh dirt and lush greenery to be thrown up into the air around us, comforting me.

"Oh— yeah, right. Sorry." He breathes in and out in shallow, bated breaths, staring at the plaque that boasts her name, etched too permanently into black marble. "Are you sure you can do this?" he asks, doubting me even still.

I cock my head, white locks tickling my ears as impatience grows within my chest.

"Nope, but you doubting me isn't making that any more likely." I scowl, letting The Book of The Dead fall open in my palms to the section I'll need.

"Sorry," he mumbles, and I sigh.

"Look, do you want me to resurrect your girlfriend or not? Because if you do, you better start acting a little more supportive. It's a lot of dark magic, blah blah, it could be dangerous, blah blah. We've been over this. Many times. For the past hour. We settled on doing the ritual. So, we're doing it. Happy?" I bite his head off, sick and tired of being underestimated.

"Yes— you're right. Sorry," he apologises yet again, annoying me further. Before I have a chance to go off on a verbal rampage, Haedes appears, erupting at my side in a shock of blue flames. They're quickly extinguished by the rain, saving the moment.

I pull my cloak closer to my body, overly cautious. He's damaged enough of my possessions for one day.

"Did you get it?" I ask, eyebrows rising on my forehead as I pull the hood of my cloak over my head, letting the long blonde locks of my hair gather around my shoulders and spill out over the collar in a shocking damp torrent of contrast.

"Yes, I got everything. The opal blade was in the trunk of my car along with all the other evidence, which was in the garage, and then I made a little trip back to Mortaria for the incense and the— well, sparkly shit." He holds up the glass jar full of aether — also known as angel dust — that shimmers, wrong, in the bloody light. It seems such a pure ingredient for such a dark deed, and yet the dark magic I'll be invoking to start the process must be contained somehow. Without it, it will undoubtedly try to escape, to disperse and infect however it can without mercy or pause.

"Right, Xion. Sprinkle this on the ground in a circle around me. Haedes light the incense and walk in an anticlockwise circle around the gravesite," I order them, increasing my grip on the spine of the book as tension drips, cold and unwanted into the pool of self-doubt forming in my stomach.

Haedes takes a moment, still clutching the objects to him as he stares down at the ground.

I forgot — he didn't come to the funeral, so this will be the first time he's seen her grave.

His eyes empty of substance, his face hollow and void of all emotion. I give him only a moment before shattering the melancholy hold the scene has over him.

"Haedes, we need to hurry. The sun is almost down," I urge him, the orange light of dusk falling too stark over all our faces and turning the pallor of our skin collectively alight.

"Right, yes, sorry." He hands the jar of Aether to Xion, who promptly removes the lid and pours the white glittering dust in a circle around my feet as I instructed him. Haedes uses his power over The Eternal Flame to light the incense sticks, walking around and waving them, spreading the scent of dark plum and cherry throughout the air.

"So, what do I do with this?" Haedes demands, holding the opal blade up to the dying light of day. It catches the last rays of sun, shimmering multi-coloured, as I sigh. It's so beautiful but so deadly. Arguably I could supposedly also be described this same way, and find myself staring at it for longer than I should.

"When I tell you, you drive it down into the ground above the grave as hard as you can," I explain. I've told him this already, but he's just as unsure in all of this as I am, and clearly nervous.

"Okay. Also, I'd really appreciate it if you didn't kill me. Because as we said— Mortarian sun going out — universe unravelling — all bad. No pressure though." He gives me an anxious grin, eyes darting around as his nerves reach obvious fever pitch. I roll my eyes.

Yeah. No pressure.

"The sun is about to set. It's time," Xion informs me, checking his cell phone.

Well, shit. Okay. I guess it's showtime. I muse, recalling the phrase Haedes always uses when serious magic is about to go down.

I look down at the crumpled pages of the book, tracing the damp edges and black ink with my fingers before closing my eyes, allowing the runes to speak to me.

"Nocturna. Hear me. Sanguina. Hear me. Moloch. Hear me. Bone, blood, spirit, breath. I am yours in eternity." Haedes coughs beside me, shuffling from foot to foot. I try my best to ignore him, focusing instead on my breathing, and grounding myself in the earth, in the roots, in the place where all dimensions connect through Gaia.

"Nocturna. Hear Me. Sanguina. Hear Me. Moloch. Hear me. Bone, blood, spirit, breath. I am yours in eternity," I repeat the chant, and then again, and then once more, knowing that this could go on for a while.

It would probably help if I used magic more often, but as it is, I'm more than unprepared for something of this magnitude.

"Nocturna. Hear Me. Sanguina. Hear Me. Moloch. Hear me. Bone, blood, spirit, breath. I am yours in eternity—" I go to inhale, but a sudden and stabbing pain in my chest knocks the wind from me. I drop to my knees, careful not to break the shimmering circle of what has transformed into pure light energy around me as my palms dig, claw-like into the sodden earth.

"NOCTURNA. HEAR ME. SANGUINA. HEAR ME— MOLOCH—" I cry out, trying to carry on despite the fact it feels like my body is being possessed by pure agony and my head is about to split open.

We hear you, child.

I have broken through the wall, at least telepathically, and now they're in my head.

The Gods of Ancient.

Oh. My. Gods.

I feel their power running rampant like acid through my veins, stinging and burning every inch of my insides until I can scarcely stand it.

I reach out, no longer conscious of what I'm doing as my lips begin to move, and I start to speak a language I've never even heard before.

I'm screaming it, bellowing in ancient tongues as the sky above bursts open, bathing the entire event in a gory scarlet splendour, as if the vermillion skies of Mortaria are leaking into this world.

The stir of dark magic in the skies is palpable as my heart races, the surrounding air rippling and vibrating around me so powerfully that I hardly notice the cries of another.

Haedes.

I turn my head and see him standing, screaming, encased in the same blue flames that he usually commands. Now though, they are the master, and he is the unwilling slave who buckles, falling to his knees, knuckles white around the hilt of the opal blade.

My whole body is on fire, screaming, tearing itself apart from the inside, threatening death.

I grit my teeth, clenching my eyes shut against the horrors of primal magic running rampant through my mind, reminding myself who I am.

"STOP!" I scream, sick of the power overwhelming everything around me. It's not the boss of me, *I'm* the boss of it.

I rise slowly to my feet, fighting with every sinew of muscle in my body to remain in control of the darkness which I've brought down on myself, knowing I must prove I can handle this.

For Thane.

I observe Haedes, the blue flames around him whirring and spinning like a firework gone wrong.

The energy from his soul ebbs. I see it. Coursing up through his feet and then his body before it flows down his arm and into the opal blade.

"Haedes *now!*" I scream.

The man, like a rag doll, slams himself forward, face first into the ground, ramming the curved shard of opal into the earth above where she's buried.

It ripples, the scent of burning grass and dead earth seeping through the air and into my nostrils as the blue flames extinguish and all the energy leaves my body.

I fall backwards, not having the strength to stand any longer.

The voices disappear, and the power I've been commanding fizzles into nothing.

Luckily, I find Xion's arms there to catch me just before I hit the ground.

Before my eyes finally close in exhaustion, I look up to the sky, crackling with lightning as the last dying ray of light dissipates.

I almost swear I get a faint whiff of cinnamon before unconsciousness takes hold.

6

STAYIN' ALIVE

SEPHY

AIR FILLS MY LUNGS, burning its way down my oesophagus and causing me to cough, the pain savage. My throat is arid like the desert, and my nostrils fill with the scent of warm, damp mud tinged with the melding of rotting vinegar and ammonia.

I open my mouth, gasping for fresh air, overwhelmed.

With my eyes still squeezed shut, I feel as vulnerable as the day I was born but in far greater pain. A pain I will never be able to forget.

My breathing is rapid, panicked in my chest, the air too moist, too clammy. My tongue is coated in the taste of rust, dried blood no doubt.

I let my eyelids flutter, scared of what I'll find, only to have my worst fear confirmed.

Panic, overwhelming and undeniable, clutches at me.

I struggle against the confines of the coffin surrounding me, legs bound in something far too tight, and find nothing to cling onto but plain white silk above, below, and on either side.

Oh my god. Oh my god.

Help!

I feel my lips part, but no sound comes as I realise I'm buried alive.

What— why? How— Oh God, I can't breathe. I can't fucking breathe! I lash out with my fists, weaker than I thought possible as I smash them into the upholstered lid of the casket, swallowing air too fast. The corners of my vision are blurred, and the noise of my knuckles rapping against the inside of my own coffin is far too loud.

I still, trying to gain some kind of calm, some kind of focus, but the longer I lay in this grave, the more apparent the sounds of the surrounding earth become. Insects tunnelling, crawling around me, where they've been moving in on my rotting corpse.

I reach up, touching my skin, finding it on fire but unmistakably smooth. Mine—

I take a shaky breath, lungs refusing to cool, and use the little strength I manage to gain from the air entering my aching chest to strike out, to get out, to escape from death itself as I claw open the silk lining.

Once exposed, I slam my fist into the wood above. Over and over, my knuckles meet with wood until they split open, the silk lining tinging scarlet. The blood drips down my arm, and I scream, numb to the pain but not the panic that is threatening to steal my every gasping moment as my heart pounds against the insides of my ribs, caged.

As the coffin breaks open, soil falls, damp and sodden, in through the hole I've created, bathing me in darkness. I splutter, trying to sit up but unable to, panicking and thrashing out with my body, trying to make a big enough exit to fit through.

As I smash the wood apart, piece by piece, I finally find the opening wide enough and sit up, latching my arms over the top and pulling myself up through the soil.

It feels like drowning, being smothered by the world, and I can't breathe for the dirt lodging itself in my throat and in my nose. I reach up, desperate, cold, shuddering as my every muscle and sinew tenses, fighting for life in a way I never have, even in the final moments before my unexpected end at the hand of—*him*.

My fingertips claw through the dirt until finally, finally, they break through the grass overhead. A pinprick of light falls upon me from above. It's too bright, burning my eyes, but I know I can't stop now.

Groaning, torso agonisingly tender, I clamber. I try to find footholds in anything I can, even though my legs can barely move in whatever it is I'm wrapped, helpless and writhing like a worm.

I find a root, small and fragile, but it's enough to allow me to gain traction so that my head and shoulders can finally emerge into the world above. I crawl, skin on fire as rain falls upon my aching body, drenching me and causing me to shiver violently as I lie, face down on the ground. I lift my head, stare up then around, vision blurry and entirely disoriented as the world spins and tilts.

I roll over, pulling my legs out of the soil and stare at the sky, shielding my eyes from the too bright rising sun and tasting the inescapable presence of rust on my tongue as I swallow hard, soil and blood coating my gullet.

The chemical smell continues to be overwhelming as are all my senses. Even the prickle of individual strands of grass, which I notice are singed, feel like needles upon my bare skin.

It hurts to breathe, to blink— to exist.

Why am I here?

Why—

I can barely form linear thought, consumed only by my pain, by the intrusion of the world upon my senses and the fact I have no idea who I am.

I sit up, eyes wide, head throbbing now, and I see it.

My name.

Sephy Sinclair.

That's me.

I— I died.

I was murdered.

And now— I'm here?

I gaze around, neck stiff as the rain comes down harder with increased viciousness, my hair becoming so wet it slicks against my skull. I brush it back from my shoulders, arms aching as I raise them, fingertips raw and knuckles bloody, stinging from my battle out of the ground.

Where is everyone?

I twist, not ready to stand, finding a house behind me.

My house.

The rain continues to pour, hitting the grass, each pitter-pat the equivalent of a bullet hitting glass to my newborn ears as I begin to hyperventilate. Shivering and shuddering, the raindrops begin to feel like icy shrapnel too.

I push myself to my feet, balance non-existent as I stumble, my long legs jutting out and trying to be free from my skirt, which is binding them straight.

Fuck this! Is the only thought I can form, reaching down and ripping the skirt haphazardly down one side. It used to be white, but now it's a mix of brown and scarlet, earth and blood.

I stagger across the lawn, left then right, the wind too loud, the light too bright, the smell of dirt, blood and chemicals lacing my every breath like inescapable noxious fumes.

As I reach the driveway, my bare feet hit the gravel and pain shoots up the backs of my legs, each one of the stones mirroring shattered glass as they dig into the soft soles of my feet, unused for— days?

73

Months?

Years?

The rain pours down my back, down the individual dark scarlet strands of my hair, off my eyelashes, chilling me to the bone as I stagger up the mocha-coloured stone steps at the front of the house.

Falling to my knees, I knock on the door with the last of my energy, the pain of my torn-up knuckles hitting the wood stealing the very last of my resolve.

I hear his bark, my good boy, and my heart calms slightly in my chest as I collapse on the floor, letting my eyes close and my limbs splay out against the cool of the rain-speckled stone.

I don't know how long I'm lying, face down on the ground, but I know that I feel like I'm dying all over again.

The door opens after a few moments, and all I can see is a pair of well-polished black shoes as an audible gasp hits the air.

Arms wrap themselves around my limp and shivering body.

"Jules—" I croak, looking up into his torn expression.

He stares down at me, shoulders broad and back stiff as he lifts me across the threshold.

"Hold on; just hold on!" He hushes me, leaving the door wide open behind us as the downpour continues audibly outside.

Cerb snaps around his heels, barking and hurting my head with the piercing echoes from the high ceilings.

I groan, hair dripping rainwater onto the floor as my head lolls over Jules' shoulder, soaking through his suit.

I hear his tread move to the soft thud of the runner and stare up at the chandelier as we ascend the stairs, closing my eyes and focusing on my breathing as another shudder wracks my body.

"It'll be okay. I've got you," Jules promises, taking a left at the top of the landing and holding me closer to his body.

I whimper, throat sore after screaming myself hoarse, after sucking in soil and air too fast in my desperate attempt to be birthed, living, from the earth.

We turn into my suite, or what used to be my suite. It's not the same, not mine anymore, so I close my eyes again, trying to shut out everything that's happening.

This can't be real. This just can't be real. I repeat internally as Jules carries me up two small steps, his heels clicking with a familiar rhythm against marble.

The room spins, making me nauseous as Jules spins with it, kicking open a glass door gently with one foot and backing us into the cubicle. He puts me on the floor, and I slump against the cold honeycomb tiles of the wall, teeth chattering so violently they're making my eyes rattle in my skull. Jules stands over me fully clothed in the shower, as I slump, slipping down so I'm barely sitting, all core strength gone.

After a few hurried motions, he turns on the jets, upping the temperature with the vigorous and repetitive stabbing of his index finger.

He lowers himself onto the floor, dragging me toward him and placing my head in his lap. Stroking his fingers through my hair, he does nothing for minutes but hold me under the jets as hot water pounds down on top of us.

I stare up at him like I'm a baby and he's the first kindness I've ever known. His gaze travels down to my chest, and I frown, blinking a few times as he reaches out. He traces something just beneath my collarbone, pain searing in the wake of his fingertips.

I raise a limp, sodden hand to the place that runs central to my ribcage, finding a horror show instead of my flawless skin.

Staples.

Pinching the skin together and holding me closed from where some mortician sliced me open. I feel the rest of my body, terrified, as I close my eyes and let my fingers wander down over my breast, finding more staples holding together stab wounds from that— night.

"We need to get the staples out. Your skin can't heal quickly, with magic, like this—" Jules looks at me apologetically, and I don't know how to reply, how to form words.

The only thing I can do is close my eyes, letting tears flow, lost too fast amongst the still-rushing hot water.

Jules reaches into the inside pocket of his suit jacket, pulling out a tool I've never seen before and holding it up with a satisfied expression.

I give him a startled look, the most communication I can manage, and he sighs.

"We've been having the furniture reupholstered, luckily for you. I'm sorry. This is going to hurt," he apologises, taking the tool and first using it to rip open the dress I was buried in. I'm laid bare before him as he begins to work, using one leg to keep me pinned to him as I scream out, finding energy I didn't know I had left inside me as I am made to withstand yet more agony.

He pulls out the staples, one by one, letting them tinkle onto the shower tiles as my blood runs scarlet down the drain.

I whimper, and he cries, tears falling down his weathered cheeks and eyes so full of guilt it makes me want to cry harder. I'm shaking physically by the time he gets to the staples in my abdomen and scream bloody murder with each torturous click of the metal device he's using to remove them, tearing open my skin.

"I'm sorry. I'm so sorry. Nearly done. I promise," he's sobbing as he uses his wet sleeve to wipe his tear-stained cheek, an entirely redundant act.

It makes me realise as I stare up, nerves raw and frayed over every inch of my being, that I've never seen him cry before.

Not when my parents had died, not when I was being hunted by demons— never.

He's been my rock, always, through everything. So, as I lie, shaking, broken and bloody, naked on the shower floor, I do what I know.

I cling to him with everything I have left inside me, fighting the chill, dark cold of the grave I've just crawled out of with every single ounce of strength I have.

Being alive has never seemed so brutal.

Jules helps me to my shaking feet, but I'm barely able to stand, so he props me up on the tiled bench beneath one of the jets. I sit, slightly warmer than I had been but not by much, wincing at the sting of my skin as it begins to knit together with agonisingly slow progress.

"What's that smell?" I croak, the whiff of it filling my nostrils over and over, burning my nasal passages with an inescapable intensity.

"Formaldehyde," Jules replies, frowning with a grim look plastered permanently upon his face. "I'll be right back," he promises, exiting the shower cubicle as I sit, slumped and barely functioning, against the wall.

After a few minutes of listening to my slow and troubled breathing, coupled with the pounding of a continual stream of boiling water hitting the tiled floor, Jules returns. He has a bowl of cut lemons in one hand and a scrubbing brush in the other.

I grimace.

"This might sting, a lot. But it's probably the quickest way to get rid of the smell. Again, sorry—" He gives me an apologetic stare, and I exhale in a staccato of pain-laced exhaustion.

Placing the lemons beside me he unbuttons his suit jacket, throwing the sodden mess of black tailored fabric to the floor in a heap beside the white gossamer of my dress.

I stare at it, transfixed and horrified.

Who the fuck is responsible for that monstrosity?

Jules squeezes the lemons onto my skin, trying hard to avoid my wounds, but the juice still finds its way into every nook and crevice of my broken body, stinging and causing me to weep uncontrollably as he scrubs at my skin with as much mercy as he can.

I'm hunched over, exhausted, as he turns off the shower and wraps me in a black towelling robe before hoisting me up into his wet arms yet again. I whimper as the wounds on my chest and abdomen contort with the change of position, wanting nothing more than to be unconscious— to be dead yet again.

He lowers me into a round-backed, cream armchair and shoves it across the carpet so I'm sitting in front of a brand-new vanity. The lights surrounding the mirror are too bright and cast me in an utterly unflattering hue. My face is stained with makeup that hasn't yet been washed away, applied in a gaudy, wrong fashion by someone who isn't me. The patchy rouge lipstick is too bright and the mascara is tacky. The formaldehyde has kept it from disappearing down the drain completely, making me look like a half-dead clown. My red hair isn't helping either.

Jules reaches around me for a black and silver antique-looking hairbrush, and I sit back as he takes my long hair in his hands and begins to methodically brush from the root to tip of each lock, being gentler than anyone I've ever known. It's in these moments, as I wipe the remaining makeup from my skin with the sleeve of my robe, that I'm revealed in my pallor, in my deathly white and traumatised expression. My eyes are bloodshot, skin translucent, and hair shocking against it all as Jules begins to braid it down my spine.

"There." He smiles at me, fastening the braid with a hair tie he procures from seemingly nowhere.

I hear him, still dripping on the carpet, but can't bring myself to say anything, finding even breathing to be too much effort, too painful.

After staring at myself a few minutes more, I watch Jules turn down the bed before he lifts me from the chair and carries me over to the mattress. I sink into the cream linen, still dressed in the towelling robe but unable to find the energy to ask to change, lying back on the pillow and shivering, cold even now.

"I'll bring more blankets and a heater. Do you need anything else, anything at all?" Jules demands, face desperate for something he can do.

I shake my head, words still not escaping me, as Cerb leaps up onto the bed. Jules looks like he might shoo him away, but I raise my arms instinctually, beckoning the animal to me and burying my face into the familiar darkness of his thick fur. The Leonberger blankets me, pressing me down into the soft hold of the bed and warming me, not taking his large brown eyes from my face for a second.

As Jules leaves the room to get more blankets, I close my eyes, just wanting everything to stop for a while.

The noise, the light, the pain.

Sleep comes too slowly, releasing me once again from my prison.

XION

The whirring portal of The Hollow closes behind me as I step through onto the dark, wet, forest floor of The Sinclair Estate once more. Having been in Mortaria for I don't know how long, it's been as much as I could do to bring myself back here at all.

We waited, Haedes and Luce both beyond exhausted, until the sun had risen over the horizon.

But still, nothing.

The ritual has failed, and so as I had returned Haedes to his kingdom with Luce in tow, it had been hard to want to move forward in any respect, let alone one that required coming back to the place where she'd once been but now will never be again.

I trudge through the mud, the rain a drizzle as the sun approaches the height of the sky. The trees cast shadows, long branches silhouetting in arachnid shapes over my face. It reminds me of demons, and as I ball my fists at my sides, I wonder if I shouldn't just go out onto The Ashen Waste and spend the rest of my days murdering the creatures that made Sephy's last months alive a waking nightmare.

I hit the edge of the trees, having walked unknowingly toward the site where she's buried. I wonder if perhaps this is out of some sick, masochistic urge to cause myself yet more pain, or perhaps because I'm seeking solace, though which remains a mystery to me.

As I reach the grave, I see it. The scorched grass where Haedes had fallen to the ground, burning, scattered Aether, glistening amongst the shimmering raindrops and—

A gash in the earth.

I quicken my step, leaning forward over the earth and finding the ground over the grave broken, torn apart— from *beneath*.

My breathing rate heightens, heart suddenly sprinting as I turn on the heel of my boot and begin to run, never having moved with such desperation before in my life. I almost trip over my own feet when I hit the gravel, not ready for the change in turf as I haul ass up the stone steps and burst in through the front doors.

As I stand, panting, daring to hope, I see Jules appear at the top of the staircase.

"Jules—" I gasp, barely able to speak as he descends the staircase quickly, practised, timely footsteps echoing out into the chasmic hall around us, at a cold and calculated pace.

"Is she?" I begin, as he gets closer to me but find myself soon hoisted off the floor and slammed into the door behind me.

My head hits the wood, disorienting me.

Jules' eyes blaze with fury, his knuckles white in the leather of my jacket collar as he holds me off the ground with seemingly inhuman strength.

"Wait— whaa—" I begin, stuttering, but he growls.

"How dare you! *How fucking dare you!*" he bellows in my face, saliva hitting me as the undeniable roar of his voice rings in my ears. "*You brought her back. Didn't you?*" he demands.

I hang there in his grasp, shocked.

"I— I— Haedes and me— and Luce—" I stutter, eyes widening as I wonder whether Jules may well rip me limb from limb. You wouldn't know it, but beneath his finely tailored suit, proper annunciation, and flawless posture, the man is quite the brute.

"What the fuck were you thinking? Huh? How could you do this?!" He shakes me so my head knocks yet again against the wood of the double doors, pain radiating from the back of my skull that I promptly ignore.

"She was trapped Jules— in The Nether— they wouldn't let her become a Titan. She was stuck—" I pant, barely able to breathe as the fabric from my shirt starts to choke me.

79

At this, Jules drops me to the floor where my legs crumple under my own weight, and I take a few seconds to regain my posture. I ball my fists, not willing to be manhandled again.

"*She crawled out of her own grave, Xion!*" he explodes at me.

I've never seen him this angry, he's almost feral.

"—she did?" I breathe, heart filling from the deepest depths with horror-laced ecstasy.

"You know what I just spent my morning doing?" he breathes, voice barely a whisper, turning from me with disgust.

"— Is she okay?" I demand, eyes shooting to the landing.

Jules squares up to me, turning fast and blocking any chance I might have of moving past him.

"I just pulled out over a hundred staples from that girl's *Y incision*. Yes, the incision they made during her *autopsy*. Not to mention having to scrub her raw of *formaldehyde*. She's absolutely fucking traumatised. I've never seen a human being so broken. How could you do this?!" he demands an answer, shoving his balled fists into my chest.

"I just— I couldn't leave her there, Jules! I couldn't!" I exclaim, trying to make him see my point of view.

"That's it though, isn't it? It wasn't your choice to make. You're not God! You don't have the right to just make this kind of decision. How could you go behind my back like this?" He narrows his eyes, pacing in front of me now.

"I didn't think you'd approve," I reply, tone cool.

"Bloody right I don't fucking approve. She might never recover from this! You've got some fucking nerve!" he cusses at me. I straighten my spine.

"So, you're saying that you're not happy I brought her back? Really Jules, is that what you're saying?" I demand, and he shakes his head.

"That's not the point. It doesn't matter what I feel. It's about her. You might very well have—" he begins, but I interrupt him now.

"What? Made her deader?!" I implore him to see reason, and he folds his arms.

"No. You might not know this, but these things have been attempted before by people a lot wiser and older than you— and they go wrong all the time. People come back wrong!" he exclaims, and I frown, cocking my head.

"And how would you know that?" I demand.

"That's classified and beside the point. I just— I can't believe you were so stupid." He shakes his head, the father I never asked for nor want.

"I had Haedes — ruler of Mortaria, and Lucifer, an extremely powerful being, perform the ritual. It's not like I tried it myself. For God's sake, you're overreacting." I raise my voice again, and he shakes his head more vigorously from side to side, pursing his lips and shooting daggers at me with his eyes.

"And where are they now? Huh? You go up those stairs and tell me you did the right thing. You go up those stairs— and you tell me that the girl lying in those sheets is Sephy Sinclair." He stands aside, and I look up the length of the staircase, not waiting more than a second before taking off up at them at full speed.

As I reach the landing, I slow, heart pounding the way it had been the morning I found her, the way it had when I had known something was wrong.

I creep along the hall, each step falling on deaf ears as my rushing blood drowns out all else.

Turning, I face the door, rotating the handle and entering without so much as a pause.

"Who's there?!" her voice, cracked and strained, calls out into the darkness of the room. Terror drips, rancid, from every syllable.

There is a small heater by her bed, emitting a red glow, so I can just see her face despite the drapes being drawn across the high windows.

"Hey, it's okay. It's only me," I whisper, afraid to make a sound.

As I step into the shadow enveloping the room, I hear Cerb growl at my approach. He's never done that before.

I move over to the side of the bed, pulling up a chair and taking a seat beside the heater. Sephy lies, corpse-like and still, flat on her back with Cerb strewn across her body, protecting her. He eyes me suspiciously like he doesn't know me at all, but all I can do is stare at the miraculous rising and falling of her chest.

Her hands are porcelain, bruised and bandaged atop three thick-knitted blankets which cling to the mound of her small form beneath. She looks so fragile, too pale.

Dead almost.

I reach out to touch her hand, to comfort her, but she pulls away, flinching at my proximity as Cerb barks loudly.

"Shhh," she hushes the dog, voice barely a wisp of noise.

"You— you're alive," I comment, and she doesn't reply, merely closing her eyes as though the sound of my voice pains her.

My heart shatters at the expression on her face.

"Did you— did *you* do this?" she asks suddenly, weak as she exhales, like each breath, each word, is taking extreme effort.

"I did, and Luce. Haedes too," I explain. Her eyelids flutter, breath deepening as she stirs.

"I see," she replies, the orange light flickering across her face the only thing distinguishing her from a body.

I sit in silence, watching her, transfixed until she speaks again.

"Xion?" she says my name, and I feel my stomach flip.

"Yes? What is it?" I reply, eager to hear whatever words she has for me.

"Can you— can you go? I want Jules. I just want Jules," she murmurs, frowning as her brow creases. She rolls over, turning her back on me and burrowing down deeper into the pillows.

"Oh, uh— okay," I whisper, heart falling as quickly as I had dared to hope that she would be as she had been.

I get up from the armchair, placing it back in its original position by the window and taking my leave of the room.

When I close the door behind me, I find Jules waiting for me on the other side.

"Well?" he demands, cocking one eyebrow.

"She doesn't want me. She just wants you," I reply, pushing past him without saying another word.

I head directly for The Hollow, unable to bear being so close, and yet so far, any longer.

7

WHAT'S GOING ON

SEPHY

WHO AM I?

This is the question which resonates throughout each moment, each act, each breath, of the next few days. I spend a lot of time sleeping, too exhausted to deal with the realities of being alive, not wanting to listen to the punishing sound of my own lungs, my own heartbeat.

I cocoon myself in the cream sheets atop the four-poster bed of this alien room that isn't mine, trying to escape the pain of the world outside.

Jules brings me soup, tea, hot water with lemon because I'm hungry for nothing. It remains atop the silver tray I used to be accustomed to, untouched as I watch the steam rise into the chill of the early spring air, existing for but a moment before disappearing into nothing.

I stare into space, tossing and turning, sighing deeply as my chest aches, but find myself unable to drift to sleep either. Every time I close my eyes, I see him, flashing, cruel, and merciless in the moonlight of that night. I feel the shadow of the knife slicing through my flesh, penetrating my body against my consent, rupturing the life within me that I'd fought for so desperately.

I thought I'd been fighting and yet what I'm doing now, this, feels like the real battle, the real war.

Finally, in the dead of the night, I pull myself out of bed and into an armchair next to the tall window beside the bed, staring out across the grounds to where I'd crawled out of the earth, been born again, sentient but not fully me.

The moonlight sheens onto the black silk of my pyjamas, illuminating my face as I stare intermittently at my own reflection and then beyond.

I had been spunky, I think. Feisty. But I have no energy for that fire, for that fight, now. Instead, I merely cling to the hope that I'll find peace once again, someday, if I'm lucky.

Hoisting my knees up under my chin, I rock back and forth, staring up at the moon and trying to empty my mind of all thoughts. Thinking has never seemed so dangerous, like a minefield where each one of my memories, or the wisp of a forming thought, can detonate, sending me spiralling into a pit of despair I won't manage to crawl from for several days.

Cerb lies at my feet, only leaving my side occasionally to relieve himself or eat, and I find myself stroking his head. It's one of the only sensations that still holds what it once did; a soothing balm for my ragged, torn nerves and the tattered remains of what had once been an overwhelming sense of self-confidence.

I sit like this until the sun is risen, when finally, I decide I cannot be still any longer. If I cannot find sleep, cannot find peace here, then I will have to go in search of it somewhere else.

I stand in front of the brand-new mirror in what was once my baby-pink walk-in closet.

None of my clothes fit, unsurprising, seeing as how I've been dead for several months and not been able to stomach food for well over four days. I'm wearing leggings because not one pair of my black leather pants fit snug enough to look half decent, and I've put on a long and baggy white t-shirt. It looks like it could belong to a man, but it's comfortable so I don't really care.

My hair is longer than I remember, and I'm still giving off the faint odour of death as formaldehyde lingers on my skin despite the many showers I've taken. The scar on my chest is healing faster than any mortal wound, but I doubt it'll ever fully disappear. In all honesty, I look like Frankenstein's monster if it had been a hot redhead, but I guess that's better than looking like the original.

I pointedly ignore the random arrangement of stab wounds peppered across my torso in a vicious dot-to-dot of unrequited lust and hate.

"Sephy?" Jules calls, anxious.

I open my mouth to speak, but before I can answer, he's standing in the doorway of the closet, silhouette crisp. "You're— up. You look— better." He sighs like the overfilled water balloon that's been puffing his chest has finally sprung an emotional leak.

I smile, nodding as I see the tray in his hands.

"Is that— food?" I whisper, lips cracked and dry.

"No. It's tea, and broth— but I can make food if you like?" I nod slowly, and his eyes widen, a smile spreading across his face. "I'll make you anything you like! Pancakes? Waffles? Sushi? Take-out? What about Lobster? Pizza? Or I could just get a little of everything— oh, hey, that's a better idea! Stay right here!" He's gushing, and I don't want to stop his joy by telling him I'd be completely content with a slice of toast.

I watch him as a small smile, the first since— before, graces my lips. An even smaller flicker of hope catches in my heart as he dashes from the room, tray still in hand.

I wander out of the open door after him, Cerb following at my heels like a necessary and wanted ghost, lingering in the halls with me as I take in the new décor. It's all very stylish and chic. Blacks and whites accented with deep gem hues in modern designs that sprawl onto the main landing. The runner is no longer green but a pure, distinct ebony, falling down each step in a wave of flawless dark luxury.

I peer down the opposite end of the hall, seeing the corner that leads to Peter's office, and I wonder where he is. The flicker of a half memory threatens to overwhelm me, make me panic, so I quash it, turning and descending the stairs in bare feet, rubbing my naked arms to try and keep myself warm, an ongoing effort ever since my return.

I don't know exactly where it is I'm going, but I let my legs take me where they will as I turn left and make my way down past the ballet studio, where I'd been attacked by a Banshee what seems like a lifetime ago. I remember how scared I'd been, of death, of the pain of dying.

Little did I know it is living that is so very painful, not the other way around.

Keeping my thoughts moving swiftly but calmly away from the death to which they always seem to return, I exit through the French doors, toes embedding themselves in grass spattered with the cool dew drops of a new day.

The sun is warm on my face, and I let it bathe me, taking in all warmth it has to offer as Cerb takes off to stretch his legs after such a long period cooped up indoors.

I end up at the stables after a brisk walk across the lawns, blood pounding around my system in a way that makes me feel unfit beyond what I'd thought possible. The destination is not surprising, but it does, nonetheless, make me smile to myself.

Perhaps there is something left of the old Persephone— I mean Sephy, after all.

Inside the wooden building, my feet hit concrete slick with rain as the scent of damp hay and manure fills my nostrils. I breathe a sigh of relief because it's the first scent other than Cerb's fur that's truly calmed me. I don't want to ride today. I'm not strong enough, but I do want to see her.

Nightshade.

Padding forward, I hear her shuffling in her usual nervous manner upon a stranger's approach. I know I probably don't smell like myself, so as I move into full view of her enclosure door, it takes her a few moments longer than usual to warm to me. As she strides closer, hooves clipping the hard floor, I inhale her scent, running my fingers through her mane and focusing on keeping my breathing calm, even, and centred.

I let myself get lost to time as I close my eyes, focusing only on the feel of my fingers on her coat, the inevitable and reliable rhythm of her breath as her nostrils vibrate over and over against my cheek.

My calm is broken, as I suppose is the way of things, by the barking of Cerb, who rushes in through the open doors toward me. Jules follows, looking uncomfortable.

"Sephy—" he calls, voice carried, soft, by the fragrant spring breeze.

"Yes, what is it?" I rasp, forming each word carefully as though precious, like choosing the wrong one may shatter everything.

"You have visitors," he announces, eyes dark.

"Oh— I'll be right in," I reply, turning back to Nightshade and staring into the black sheen of her enormous pupils. I feel Jules stir, awkward at the wide-open doorway, so turn back to look over my shoulder.

"What? What is it?" I ask, wondering why he hasn't departed yet.

"Just— don't let them bully you into doing what they want. You don't have to do anything until you're ready." He's acting like I'm a small child, that I'm about to be offered drugs. I smirk.

"Oh, don't worry. I won't."

"Come on, we best not keep them waiting," he urges me to follow him, so I take one last look into the face of my Percheron mare, wistful, before turning on my heel and exiting the stables, reluctant to say the least.

I follow Jules back across the lawn, feet icy now as they hit the damp earth yet again. Cerb bounds around me, excited that I'm finally upright and outdoors.

I get a whiff of pine from the surrounding trees and inhale fondly, grounded by the aroma I've so often associated with home. My heart speeds slightly as I re-enter the main house and walk through the hallway from which I've come, arriving only moments later in the entrance hall.

By the staircase, leaning on the polished balustrade, Haedes and Xion stand, talking. Hearing me enter, they turn on the spot, immediately dropping the conversation, eyes falling on me and widening in surprise.

"So, it's true," Haedes whispers, awed.

I take this moment to examine him. He doesn't look well. His once blue hair is streaked through with silver and his face has aged by what looks like at least thirty years. I wonder what happened to him as he pushes past Xion, his motion less fluid than it'd once been inside the black and aubergine fabric of his suit.

"You're really back," he breathes. His grey pupils no longer sheen as they once did, but are instead matte and dull, as though an ebbing emotional tide has eroded them soft and smooth.

"I guess so," I reply, not sure what to do with my hands. I don't have any pockets, so as Haedes reaches forward and pulls me into his arms, I'm utterly stunned and awkward in posture.

He releases me after a few moments and I step back, chest twinging from the close contact, not sure what to say as Xion moves closer.

"Sephy, we came to see how you are— but also because we would like you to go and see Luce. She needs to check that everything came back as it should. We don't want anything bad happening to you," he remarks.

I snort, cocking my eyebrow as I feel some semblance of snark return.

"What? Worse than being brutally murdered and then coming back to life six feet under and having to punch my way out of my own coffin?" I snap, anger flaring, weak but unmistakably there within my chest.

"We— we didn't think the ritual had worked. You didn't rise for three whole days— we didn't know." Xion looks heartbroken as both his fractured sentence and sentiment hit the air.

My eyes deaden in my face. It's all very well him being sorry, but that doesn't change anything, doesn't erase my trauma, my suffering.

As he takes a step forward, foot falling too hard from the runner and onto the cold marble of the floor, I'm reminded of that night. The way Brad's tread hadn't matched Xion's at all, but I'd been too swept up in my own emotions to notice.

It got me killed.

I let my guard down, slept with Xion, and it cost me my life. It made me trust the world around me, made me care, and created a hope that something good could really come from all the death in my life, all the pain of my past.

It had been a mistake.

As the two men look at me, Jules coughs at my back. I choose to turn to him, not ready to answer their expectant stares.

"I made food," he announces, but I shake my head, no longer hungry as I'd been less than an hour ago.

"I'm sorry Jules— I lost my appetite I guess," I apologise, and he shrugs.

"It's okay, I can wrap it up. It'll be ready whenever you are," he promises.

"Maybe when I get back," I express, and he nods, face riddled with anxiety.

"Of course. I believe your Uncle is returning this evening from his trip to London," he adds, making my stomach turn. My mind is so foggy at times, so fuzzy until suddenly it isn't, and the horrific memories come flooding back, jagged and dangerous, still broken, yet more shards of glass. I never liked my Uncle, but this dread verging on fury is something different.

I just can't fathom why I'm feeling like this as clarity well and truly evades me.

Maybe it'll come to me.

Either way, I know I don't want to be here when he first arrives. I'm not standing on ceremony while he gawps at my new deathly complexion and exhausted expression. I just don't have the energy to deal with his stupidity.

"Shall we go then?" I sigh, and Haedes nods. Neither he or Xion speak for a moment as Xion zips up his leather jacket with purpose.

"Have you tried convecting since— you got back?" Haedes asks, and I shake my head.

"Well, you can try now. You should be able to convect between here and Mortaria; that way I can take Xion and Cerb— if you want him to tag along?" he enquires, caring, an odd act for him. I nod, looking down at the Leonberger who remains, loyal as ever, at my feet.

"Alright," I whisper, voice as weak as I feel.

I watch Xion and Haedes convect, Cerb in tow, in a roar of red flames and wonder momentarily how Haedes chooses whether to turn the flames red or blue. I've only ever seen him use the resurrection flame to travel before. I turn to Jules, who smiles at me. I don't return the expression as he speaks, voice cracking.

"Be careful."

"I'll be back soon," I promise, balling my fists at my sides and preparing to convect.

I'm hoping this will be like riding a bike.

"I'll be waiting," he vows, as ever, loyal.

As the heat recedes, I open my eyes, flames diminishing as quickly as they came. Immediately lightheaded, I sit down on the armchair closest to me, quickly distracted by raised voices as Cerb pads over to my side. Haedes and Xion turn to stare at the shadows stirring behind the frosted, sliding partition, eyebrows quirking upon their foreheads.

"I don't see what the problem is, I did one ritual, one time— and according to Xion, it *actually worked*! I gave Haedes his daughter back, Thane! Why can't you see the beauty in that?" Luce bellows, voice high-pitched and incredulous.

Xion and Haedes take a seat on the couch beside me, the air between us becoming frosty and stale. Beelz pads through from the kitchen, looking pissed at the disturbance from the other room as she plants herself next to Cerb with a dull thump. I guess even big kitties need naptime.

"It's not about why you did it, Luce. You messed with primal, unnatural forces, forces that have the capacity to chew you up and spit you out. You aren't equipped to handle this kind of magic!" Thane retorts, voice cracking as emotion drips from every syllable.

Haedes looks at me, rolling his eyes, and Xion smirks slightly. I can't bring myself to laugh at the domestic between the two women though, mainly because I'm the cause.

"You don't know what I'm equipped to handle, clearly! If you believed in me a little more, perhaps you would have noticed that I'm fine. I resurrected a human being, brought her back from beyond death— and look at me. I'm practically fucking glowing!" Luce retorts.

"How do you know that she is though? Had it ever occurred to you that you might have brought back something other than what left? Did it ever even cross your tiny, insolent mind that you could be creating an abomination?" Thane demands, and my heart begins to thump even harder.

Am I what I had been?

I don't feel like myself at all.

"I can't even believe I'm having this discussion with you. You just want me meek; want me to deny what I am. This is half of me, Thane— you said you loved me. All of me. That means you have to love this too." I hear Luce's pain, ringing out, an inescapable truth with every word, and feel slightly sorry for her. She's not like the others, and it's not her fault.

Just as the fight reaches its emotional epitome, Haedes has seemingly gained enough amusement from the spat as he raises his hand to his lips and coughs, not at all subtle.

The two silhouettes still behind the glass doors, and after a few silent, awkward seconds, they slide it open. Revealed, their eyes move right past Haedes and Xion, seeking my face.

"Oh my god— it's really true. I really did it," Luce breathes, hands coming up to rest over her heart. She's wearing a frilly white blouse with a black silk necktie and high collar, a cropped black jacket with flared sleeves, and high-waisted slacks that flare as well. It's the first time I've ever seen her wearing pants, and she's remarkable in stature, tall, leggy and, as she had yelled before, absolutely radiant. Her white hair falls in a stream of stark, silken curls over one shoulder and her wide eyes are full of a joy I'd like to smack right out of her.

"You look like— well, death." Thane purses her lips, brow furrowing in concern. I've never properly spoken to her before, but I recall Xion telling me she can transform into a raven. Looking at her in a buttoned-down, white shirt and black skinny jeans it's not hard to see it. Her frame is so jagged, edgy, and androgynous that it would be hard to imagine she'd transform into anything else.

"Thanks for that," I exhale, depressed, before continuing, "I don't smell much better, I can't get the stench of embalming fluid off my skin." Luce's eyes light up.

"I have something that should take care of that!" She's excited at being able to help, overlooking my suffering in place of her success.

Thane frowns, pressing her lips into a thin line of disapproval as Luce heads over to a coffin-shaped cabinet. From inside she pulls a vial, staring up at it against the light and grinning.

"Any other problems?" she demands.

I shrug.

"I have no appetite."

It's the only physical thing I can think of worth mentioning because physically, I'm practically brand spanking new compared to how I feel on the inside. How can I tell her I feel like I've been put back into an identity that isn't mine, of someone that died and didn't come back?

"I'm going to take a flight," Thane mumbles, turning from the group and stripping her shirt from her jagged frame. I stare at her spine jutting through her pale white skin, noticing two black swirling tattoos etched upon her shoulder blades where I imagine wings sprout when she transforms.

"Go and fetch Muerta and Anubis. I want them to check her out," Haedes demands, but Thane doesn't reply, opening the balcony doors and disappearing through them. I flinch as they slam shut behind her, trying to ignore the mangled cries that follow.

"So, how are you?" Luce saunters toward me, gentle in her step, passing me the two vials she has in her palm. They clink as they fall, cool, into my palm.

"Fine," I lie, not wanting to be interrogated. How can I tell her that I wish she'd just left me be? That I'm so traumatised by what has happened that every single breath is a struggle, a conscious effort. After all, my life was stolen from me so mercilessly, so suddenly, that nothing seems to have any point at all.

"Are you sure?" Xion asks, voice deep.

I find his eyes, full of concern, something I'd been careful not to take in the other night when he'd visited my bedside.

I melt into their gold depths, remembering the way his pupils had dilated as he climaxed inside me.

Fuck.

Don't go there. I warn myself, crossing my legs.

"How am I supposed to feel? After being brought back from the dead?" I ask him, cocking my head and feeling slightly stronger in myself.

"I'm sorry I didn't—" Xion exhales, falling into silence, and Haedes frowns.

"None of us have much experience with something like this. We want to help." Haedes gives me a look I've never seen from him. He's genuinely trying to be supportive, but I just can't help but feel angry at every single one of them. If he had wanted me alive so badly, why didn't he act before when I had been in the Colosseum, alone and fighting for my life?

"I'm fine. Really," I respond, not wanting to be pried open and laid before them. I have never felt so vulnerable or so alone. "I'm tired, though. I'd like to sleep," I decide, done with the conversation.

Grasping the two vials in my palm, I get to my feet.

"You can use my bed. Muerta will want to examine your aura once she arrives, but you don't have to be awake for that if you want to rest. You should start to feel a little more alive soon, especially with the help of the Mortarian sun," Luce informs me as I pass the sofa where Xion is sitting. I feel his gaze on me and my skin burns unwillingly hotter than it has since my lungs first refilled, icy in my chest.

"Do you have a bathroom?" I enquire, and Luce nods.

"Sure, right through there." She gestures through the bedroom as I make my way across the threshold and scurry, still in bare feet, through to the bathroom.

It's grand, in a monochrome theme with a silver tub sunken into the floor. The toilet is silver too, and the basins, with fluorescent lights that bounce mercilessly from each reflective surface. In fact, it's almost sterile.

Just like a morgue.

Closing the door behind me and placing the vials on the edge of the basin, I brace the rim of the sink, turning on the shiny faucet and letting the hot water run, scalding, as I splash it over my face and try out the fragrant dark plum hand soap. The lather froths between my fingers as the water reaches a point where it's almost boiling, flushing my palms scarlet. At least they're not cold like the rest of me I suppose.

I stand for at least five minutes, trying to work out exactly why I feel so distant from everyone in the next room. I can't come up with anything, so I simply take the vials back in my palm and exit the cruelly beautiful and stark exposure of the space.

Back in the bedroom, I find the partition has been closed. Xion is standing, awkward, in the middle of the room.

"Hi," he breathes, eyes dropping to his too-big feet as he stiffens at my presence.

"Hi," I sigh, unsure what to say. Part of me wants to melt into him, to let him hold me so I can cry, be weak, but the rest of me knows I can never open myself that way again, not if I want to survive in this place.

"I'm sorry." He takes a step toward me, and I take a step back in turn, trying to maintain the distance between us.

"Why?" I ask, confused. I can't ignore the spark in his eyes whenever he sees me, whenever he finds me thriving against my will.

"I'm sorry— I shouldn't have left you, that night. I should have been there to protect you." He takes another step, and I try to move back, finding myself closed in now against the wall.

"I don't want to talk about it," I whisper, voice shaking as the images begin to rush back and my blood pressure skyrockets, newly invigorated fluid shooting around my circulatory system, ravaging me as it begins to heat at his proximity.

"I know. I just want you to know I'm sorry. If I could go back— I would never have left your arms," I cringe internally at the overly romantic sentiment, a smile creeping across my lips against my will as his fingers come up to stroke my chin. It's the first sensation, the first touch, that I haven't been somewhat repulsed by.

"You're a soppy asshole. What happened?" I demand, acting a little as I sass him, trying to get out of this overly emotional entrapment with my boundaries and heart fully intact. He laughs, eyes full of precious metals melding together under the heat of his desire for me. It unmistakably lingers.

His expression is infectious, and I can't help but smile too, despite the fact my heart is wilting at what can just never be.

"Finding your lover in a puddle of her own blood will do that to a person," Xion admits, and I flinch. "I'm sorry— I didn't—" he looks immediately scared, like I might run.

"Do you wanna get out of here?" I demand, looking up into the molten glory of his gaze. I don't want to let him in, but he's like a fucking magnet with that face.

"I thought you'd never ask," he puts his arms around me, and I stiffen against my own volition, finding his embrace what I have unknowingly been seeking.

Warmth, finally, radiates throughout my core.

Reluctantly I rest my head above his chest, listening to the steady, comforting beat of his heart instead of the punishing rhythm of my own.

Gripping him, I close my eyes and convect, taking us far away.

We reappear in the dark confines of his apartment.

The torches have extinguished, so I wave a hand, relighting them and throwing the room into a warm light instead of its usual cool blue.

I let go of him, taking a step back and feeling the persistence of the glass vials in my hand. I don't look at the contents of either one, my stomach turning at the memory of Luce's last draft.

Unstopping the vials, I upend the contents, feeling it slither down my throat in a wet, slow, and sloppy goop.

"Bleurgh." I shake my head, blinking once and then twice as the taste refuses to go away.

I stand a few moments, waiting for the effects to take hold, and as reliable as I had hoped them to be, my pores begin to weep the scent of cinnamon out into the air as my stomach gives an audible rumble.

"God, I'm starving!" I exclaim, and Xion moves through the living space and over to the kitchen, opening the fridge with a jerk.

"Luckily for us, the gluttony sinners kept stocking my fridge despite the fact I haven't been here in months," he comments, grabbing several boxes and turning to me. "What do you fancy?" he asks, and I shrug.

"Anything— am I about to see your epic microwaving skills in action again?" I cock an eyebrow, and he smirks.

"Of course." He spins on his heel, throwing a box of food into the microwave and pressing several buttons in quick succession. Turning back, he takes off his leather jacket and throws it over the counter. It lands on the arm of the couch as I take a seat next to it, breathing a sigh of relief. Whether or not I feel safe at the prospect of Xion's affection, I can't deny his apartment, the intimacy of it, makes my vulnerability recede.

"So— how have you been?" I ask, trying to break the tension forming so easily between us as I twizzle my hair between two fingers, absentminded.

"Busy— travelling with Haedes," he admonishes.

I give him a look of utter amusement.

"You went on a road trip with Haedes?" I ask him, doubting the honesty of his words. Haedes doesn't seem like the 'boy's trip' type.

"Well— we had to track down this book to find out how to bring you back," Xion relinquishes as the microwave pings behind him. He grabs a fork from the closest drawer, opening the microwave and handing me a plastic container full of beef stew as he rounds the counter with enormous, hurried strides.

It smells orgasmic.

I dig in, barely breathing between bites as the ravenous emptiness of my stomach takes and takes. I can hardly chew fast enough, the thick meaty juices slicking my throat and warming me further as I chew on tender steak, my mouth flooding over and over with saliva. I reach the bottom of the container far too quickly and so, spotting the disappointment on my face, Xion pops another plastic box into the microwave.

"Book?" I ask, wiping my mouth on the back of my hand and licking my lips.

"Yes, The Book of The Dead. We went all over the place. Peru, Egypt, Greece, Turkey, Germany—" I picture him and Haedes in the various locations he lists off, and I frown.

"How was that— travelling with him?" I ask, licking the fork clean of remaining gravy.

"How do you think?" Xion asks as the microwave pings again. He rounds the counter, bringing me a container of Italian meat sauce this time. The scent wafts to me, making me drool as I remain unsatisfied.

Xion sits down beside me, watching me eat with fascination.

"I'm really glad you're back," he says, voice soft.

"I can tell," is the only way I can think to reply as I continue to shovel food into my mouth, not wanting to think about how hard everything is, how complicated.

In this moment, it's just me and my food.

Xion feeds me four more containers full of perfectly prepared cuisine until I'm ready to burst and my eyelids begin to droop.

I yawn, and Xion eyes the bed.

"Do you want to sleep?" he asks, and I nod, mind filling with fog and becoming slow for which I'm grateful.

As I approach the bed though, fear crawls into my chest. I'm worried the nightmares will return.

"Will— will you hold me until I fall asleep?" I turn, looking at Xion. He raises his eyebrows, surprised.

I climb into the bed, limbs heavy and stomach full, as he comes closer. He doesn't reply to my request even still, as if any serious conversation between us may ruin the calm that's been created.

Taking his shirt off, he gets under the thick, midnight blue velvet of the freshly laid sheets, wrapping his enormous arms around my skeletal form and pulling me close.

Letting the scent of pomegranate mist over my thoughts and the warmth of his body chase the last chill of the grave, I fall into what I hope will be a peaceful sleep.

8

ORDINARY WORLD

LUCE

"I CAN'T BELIEVE SHE'S back," Haedes breathes, leaning back on my sofa and crossing his legs, expression weary but, nonetheless, happier than I've seen him in a while.

My heart, however, is halfway between breaking at Thane's lack of support and overflowing with gratitude to unorthodox gods for the gift I've been able to give Haedes. I can't deny, despite what Thane said, despite her condemnation, that I'm not sorry about what I did. It was revolutionary. It's primal, unnatural, and yet it's what I *should* be doing. Using this darkness inside me to make the world a better place.

"I know, she seems— alright, don't you think?" I enquire, my doubts struggling to surface above the tall tide of my own ego.

"I think she's as okay as anyone can be. We fucked up. We should have exhumed the body before we attempted the ritual," Haedes bites his bottom lip.

I exhale.

"I mean, let's be honest; we didn't really think it would work— I think if we'd have known this was going to be successful, we'd have done lots of things differently," I speak the truth of it all. We've been playing with fire, sure, but none of us expected to see a Phoenix rise from the ashes.

"That is true I suppose," Haedes grimaces, placing his hand over where whatever semblance of a heart he has left resides.

I cross my legs, mirroring his relaxed posture, leaning back into the armchair where Sephy had been sat not ten minutes ago— alive— because of me.

"You alright there, Gramps?" I tease him, trying to maintain a light-hearted mood but unable to keep my worries silent any longer. He'd been a mess after the ritual, more so than I had, and the toll it's taken on him physically is inescapably apparent, even if I wish it wasn't.

"Just tired and with aching joints. It could have been much worse, wouldn't you say?" he asks. I nod, realising now that perhaps what I'd done could have gone very badly wrong indeed.

I could have caused Mortaria to fall.

But it didn't. It worked. My confidence screams at me, trying to repel the negativity I've been saturated with ever since Thane returned to find me passed out with Xion at my bedside.

I exhale, steadying my resolve on the matter, as a knock rings out through the apartment.

"Come in!" I call, turning to face the door as it swings open without a second's pause.

Anubis and Muerta step through, followed by The Fates, who bustle across the threshold, doddery as ever.

I frown.

I didn't know they'd be coming to lecture me too.

I get up from the armchair I'm sitting in, offering Anubis my seat as Haedes steps out of the way so The Fates may sit in his place. His eyes flash a warning at me, so I brace myself for an onslaught of unnecessary critique.

"That was fast," I comment.

Muerta shrugs, her monochromatic, skeletal makeup stark against the low-cut and vibrant scarlet of her dress. Her raven hair is braided, threaded through with wilting wildflowers as it tumbles down her spine in a luscious waterfall of glossy chocolate sheen.

"Well, it would appear the matter at hand is of some urgency. Wouldn't you agree?" she enquires, stare condemning me far too easily.

I look away, not replying.

"So?" Anubis looks at me expectantly, and I raise an eyebrow, sick of her imminent spiel before it's even begun. She crosses her legs beneath her gown, black silk embroidered with hundreds of glistening silver beads that cling to her sparse curvature.

"Yes, Anubis?" I demand, folding my arms across my chest momentarily before moving my fingers to beneath the high collar of my shirt. I twiddle the indigo stone hanging from the choker, which once again adorns my neck, as Thane's familiar cries reach my ears from the balcony. My stomach is turned into a pit of nervous tumult at the sound of her return.

"Well, where is she then?" Anubis snaps, irritated.

"She's resting," I inform them.

Haedes nods, collaborating my story.

"I see. And she's— alive?" Anubis cocks a perfectly threaded brow, her golden skin glistening as every single word she utters makes me feel like a complete invalid.

Compared to her, I *am* younger, and yet I feel like she needs reminding of just how powerful I really am.

"Very much so," I nod, and Haedes shoots a hard stare at Anubis before he meets my gaze. I know he senses my irritation as he fidgets from one foot to the other, expression stony.

Silence falls, and a million judgemental thoughts swarm in the air between us like angry hornets.

"You should have seen her, Nu. It was seriously incredible. She's got more power than any of us give her credit for," Haedes vouches for me, going on to explain in detail how the ritual was performed and what we did. The group listens, but after the tale is told, Muerta clears her throat, striding around the edge of the sitting area and planting herself on the arm of Anubis' chair, crossing her dainty ankles just beneath the frayed hem of her skirt.

"Nobody here has the intention of questioning that Luce has power, Haedes. It is the way in which it is used which concerns us all," Muerta speaks, large brown eyes burning into my flesh with contempt.

I straighten my spine.

"I'm fine, I'm practically glowing. I feel amazing. Thanks for asking," I bite out.

Muerta laughs.

"You can't see your aura, child, or you would not make such claims. You have tainted yourself, and now I fear there is no going back," she warns me as The Fates harness a powerful collective stare, their withered faces judgemental too. I feel utterly cornered.

Watching Thane's shadow behind the doors as she dresses, I hope she doesn't disturb Sephy. I exhale a sigh, ready to begin defending my choices yet again.

I don't know why we're even having this stupid discussion. It's done now. Over. There's no going back as Muerta so correctly just said.

"Yes, let's all ignore the fact that Sephy Sinclair is alive because of me. That Haedes has his daughter back," I gripe, feeling less than underappreciated. As my words fall into awkward silence, the doors to the other room slide apart once again.

"Hey, quiet. Don't wake Sephy," I warn Thane. Her gaze is distant, skimming over me as though she's trying to pretend I, and the problem I apparently present, don't exist.

"What do you mean? She's not even here." Thane frowns as I take several steps around the sofa and peer into the depths of our bedroom.

"Well, shit. She and Xion must have convected out. Yet another sign that she's fine," I continue to make my case, turning on the balls of my stiletto heels as I twist back to face the others.

Thane snorts behind me.

"So, it would seem I'm not the only one who thinks what you did is wrong." She smiles at Muerta, Anubis, and then moves around the couch to greet The Fates as she tucks her shirt into a fresh pair of pants.

She sits down on the rug by the dead hearth, petting Beelz between the ears and giving a swift nod of greeting toward Cerb. The panther gives an audible purr of approval as the group's eyes linger on me, expectant.

What do they want me to do?

Apologise?

Feel bad for giving Sephy her life back?

Haedes shoots me a look, and I sigh. It seems he's the only one who's happy about the choice I made. Not that I should be surprised. Anubis has always been power-hungry if you ask me. Any more competition, other than Haedes, was never going to go down well. As for Muerta— I don't know what the hell her problem is.

"Would you like a cup of tea?" Thane asks The Fates, who shake their heads collectively.

"No, this is not a casual visit. We're here on official business," Layla announces, pulling the loose weave of her lilac shawl tighter around her shoulders with trembling fingers.

"Which is?" Haedes enquires, curious as he shuffles uncomfortably on his feet and crosses his arms across the rich purple silk of his waistcoat.

"This act has many, far-reaching, consequences. More so than any of you can imagine. We are here to give a final warning. A warning to you, Lucifer. Tread any further down this path, and you will prove beyond our reach." Moira answers instead as Layla's unseeing gaze becomes sad, her wispy eyebrows falling low upon her wrinkled brow.

I bite my bottom lip, afraid of what that might mean, despite the fact I should be celebrating. I've done the impossible, done what no individual has been able to achieve since the fall of the ancient gods, and yet I'm standing here being treated like an insolent child.

"Thank you for the warning, but I am fine," I assure them, smiling politely despite the fact my temper is getting out of hand.

"And what makes you think it is only you who will suffer because of this?" Layla asks.

At the close of the sentence, I hear an audible groan as heads snap, turning to Haedes. He's gone white as the River Styx and I observe, adrenaline shooting through my system, as his eyes roll back in his skull and he crumples to the floor.

Shit.

I look to the fates, who smile, contented.

All I can think is, *what the hell are you grinning about? He's the one sustaining us all.*

As though she can hear my thoughts, Moira gives a toothless smile.

"And therein, darling Lucifer, lies your biggest mistake."

I sit at Haedes' bedside long after everyone has left, the scent of bergamot and sandalwood rife in the air as the tall candles around the bed burn, warming the room around us.

I look down at the book in my hand, having been over the same passage several times in the last hour. It's cryptic at best on the aftereffects of the resurrection ritual, and as I watch the sleeping god before me visibly age by the minute, I'm afraid I might have ruined life as we know it.

As I'm beginning to ponder how Mortaria will carry on functioning without Haedes, I hear him inhale sharply and so raise my gaze to his face. His blue-grey eyelashes flutter before his eyes open, and he stares at the ceiling, looking exhausted but unmistakably annoyed. Blinking a few times, he turns his head upon the plump, dander-stuffed pillow of black velvet that cups his neck and skull.

"Hey, you're awake," I whisper, reaching over to touch his skin that's lost a lot of its youthful elasticity. His brow is damp with perspiration as I gently massage his forehead.

"What happened?" he demands, sitting bolt upright like he's been electrocuted.

101

"You collapsed. Muerta says that your aura is still being drained of some of your life energy. I guess now Sephy is back under the Mortarian sun, the ritual completed itself. It explains why she's been so weak, so fatigued," I explain. Haedes' hands immediately climb his body before landing on his face.

Partially dressed in an untucked white shirt and black suit pants, he climbs out from beneath the sheets and hurries over to the enormous mirror adorning the wall opposite his bed. It hangs over the fireplace, which is extinguished, rimmed in an art deco style silver frame.

"Shit!" Haedes cusses, looking at his reflection. His hair is now entirely silver, his skin deeply indented by creases and wrinkles. He looks slightly hunched, his steps incrementally slower, more carefully placed as his stiffening joints hinder his usual rhythmic swagger.

"Yes, I thought you might be less than pleased. I personally think you look quite the silver fox— but I'm probably not the best judge," I try to calm him, as I know how attached he is to his looks.

"I suppose it could be worse," he exhales, taking the reality of his ageing better than I expect.

"Yes. You could be dead—" I voice my fear aloud.

"Are you alright, Luce?" Haedes demands, padding back into bed and covering himself with thick velvet sheets.

"I just— you don't think—" I feel the truth of the last few hours crawling over my skin, an inescapable itch that I can't quite scratch. I don't want to acknowledge it, and yet it continues to niggle at me, irk me on a level soul-deep.

"What?" he asks, voice soft. Placing his hand atop my own, resting softly on the blankets, he tilts his angular but weathered face toward me, curious.

"You don't think what we did was reckless, do you?" I ask.

He smirks.

"Of course, it was, Luce. That doesn't make it wrong," he adds, but I snatch my hand away from his as I realise that perhaps I'd been mistaking his desperation to have Sephy return for belief in my skills.

Have I been so self-absorbed that I didn't see what a huge risk I was taking? If he'd died— it would have been the end of life as we know it for so many.

Muerta had been right all along.

Nobody doubted I have power— they just doubted I know how to wield it without tearing our world apart.

A doubt that I have just entirely justified.

I guess I owe Thane another apology.

"We need to talk about a plan for what happens if you return to The Higher Plains, Haedes. I don't think this weakening of you physically warrants anything less." I'm stern now, afraid I've done more damage than I'll ever be able to repair.

"I'd rather wait until I feel less like utter shit to discuss my demise if you don't mind," he retorts. My mouth twist into a frustrated grimace.

Knowing that this is not the time to broach the subject, I change to something more casual, trying to take my mind off the dark consequences that could still result from my actions.

"Hey, would you mind if I threw a party? I think I have some making up to do with Thane—" I ask Haedes, remembering how good things had been for us back in the fifties. It had been one of our most romantic decades in recent history, so maybe I can recreate those memories to remind her what she loves in me, to get her to forgive me.

"A party? Are you sure that's wise? What with Pandora running around, I don't like the idea of advertising The Nexus as gathered in one room. You know that makes us vulnerable." Haedes frowns, and I startle him as a hysterical laugh escapes my lips.

"Are you fucking kidding me? Mister— *oh hey look, let me just erect this neon sign to announce where my daughter is that you're all looking for?!*" I exclaim, reminding him of us having this exact same argument not seven months ago. He hadn't listened to me then, so I wonder why I'm expecting him to cave now.

Surprisingly, he sighs, leaning back against his pillow.

"Fine, have at it. I think I need a nap," he complains, and I smile at him, moving in and laying a kiss on his left cheek.

"Don't worry. I'll have Dolly lay on an early bird special just for you," I tease him, and he rolls his eyes.

"Can't you leave an old man in peace?"

"Never."

PANDORA

"Anubis, what a pleasant surprise!" I exclaim, entirely fake in my joy as the leggy tan Goddess appears in the doorway of the dark colosseum.

I hear skeletal jackals beyond her silhouette, jawbones snapping together, the hollow sound of bone-on-bone chilling as they yelp, and know she must have come here via the chariot she so favours.

"I come with news. Lucifer— she did it. Sephy Sinclair is back." My eyebrows rise sharply on my forehead as I watch her flick ash from her shoulders with long fingernails lacquered jade.

"Really? *Lucifer*?" I'm dumbstruck. How had she managed to pull off such a feat? Must be her lineage. Having Moloch as a father— as I had proposed to Gorgon before, only to be shot down. I smile, smug.

"Yes, she performed the ritual, used Haedes' life force to bring her back and the opal blade as a funnel to transfer it. Apparently, she's up and walking around, right as rain—" Anubis looks mildly irritated by this, and I wonder why she's here. After all, it's she who has been consistently telling me how impossible the idea of resurrection is.

I pace across the slick, scorched cobbles, the heels of my boots clicking against them at a metronomic pace, indicating I am in no rush to get to any kind of point. I'm wearing pants again as I've only just returned from the mortal world, and I watch as Anubis takes in my modern attire with interest.

"So— why are you here? Didn't you say this would be quite impossible?" I demand, keeping my expression cold as I finally allow my interest to pique.

Her dark eyes narrow and she exhales, trying to be inaudible in her surrender to my way of thinking. Unfortunately for her, the heavily beaded silver of her dress gives her away, tinkling into the surrounding silence as her chest rises and falls with slight over-dramatism.

"Well, I still stand by that. After all, we have no way of performing the ritual, considering that I highly doubt Lucifer is going to be offering her services to you. Even if you could find a way to make her help us, we don't have the forces for a siege on the city. I've seen your demons, they're dwindling, Pandora." I smirk at the assumption, and her previously calm, cold features twist into an affronted look, turning her cruel beauty even harder in the shadow of the hallway.

"Something you're not telling me?" she demands.

"Come with me." I turn on my heel, not waiting to see if she follows or not before taking a right and heading up a set of crumbling uneven steps toward the viewing galleries of the Colosseum.

As I reach the top of the staircase, I feel the sultry Mortarian air encase me and inhale the scent of burning from a recently passed spark shower, relishing the connotations of destruction it strikes within.

"What is this?" Anubis asks as she reaches the gallery and strides so she's standing beside me, looking down over the crumbling railing and into the pit that lies beneath, central to it all.

Below us, Lilliana stands beside Katerina, the two of them instructing a group of bedraggled mortals, pale faces sensing my presence and looking up momentarily with fear lacing their collective stare. Many of them have bloodstained clothes, muddy faces, scratched skin, and black circles around their eyes, and yet they stand perfectly rigid, erect as ancient trees in their acute vertical posture, terrified.

The Banshees circle them, and Succubi slobber loudly onto the ground covered in a fine gravel of small bones and the remains of prior victims. I wonder if Anubis will pick up what I've been working on for the last several months.

"Recruits," I announce. She frowns, confused, as I cross my arms atop my corset-bound breasts.

"Explain," Anubis demands, and I smile, pleased with myself.

"We've been vetting mortals. I'm using the box to take several Demons at a time to feed on the living, to get their strength up. Those mortals, who put up a fairly good fight, show potential as warriors, I've been saving. I brought them here, and now they will fight for us, from the inside," I explain.

Anubis cocks her head, fascinated as she turns to me.

"And— you're going to sneak them into the city with the sinners returning from battle? That's— genius." I smirk at the compliment and shrug, pleased she understands just how serious I am about taking Mortaria for myself. "How many?" she demands.

"Currently, several thousand. I've been able to get greater numbers than I expected, especially because I've been taking them from all over the globe, not just one location," I express, smiling to myself.

"Wow," is all she says in reply, narrowing her eyes as her mind works out what exactly this means for her.

"I told you. I'm serious about getting my revenge. No matter how long it takes. I won't rest until I show Zeus he underestimated the wrong woman," I grit my teeth, rage becoming less and less controllable with every day that passes.

Anubis nods, running a long fingernail down her jawbone as she ponders the predicament. Her skin is fiery, glowing under the violet sun overhead, and I wonder if she knows how truly intimidating she looks. Though, I muse, it was clearly not enough to give her any kind of power in The Higher Plains.

"I may have underestimated you. Not surprising, seeing as you did let Sephy Sinclair slip so easily from within your grasp, but nonetheless true." She attempts the compliment, failing dismally, but with her ego I know it's as close to one as I'm getting.

I take it.

"We all make mistakes. Wouldn't you agree?" I refer in tone to her betrayal of Ra in exchange for his resurrection by Cronus. I wonder now how he had managed that, as it appears resurrection seems to lie solely with the Gods of Ancient, to those with whom a darker persuasion is inherent.

Licking my bottom lip, I watch as the mortals below tremble, staring up at the odd colour of the sky, no doubt missing their ordinary world.

I let a smile twist my lips, turning my expression cruel.

Fear is a useful tool, to say the least, but not the only tool that I'm employing to keep them in line. Only a fool would trust that fear alone brings loyalty, and so I've had them informed that upon taking Mortaria, they will live eternally. Many of them were easily swayed by the thought of immortality, proving just how much of a burden death has become on the human persona.

When I was alive, people died young all the time. You prayed, and you behaved, preparing through the whole of life for death. Now, morals are looser, skirts shorter, tempers more frayed, and ethics questionable as people live in the only too fleeting present. Most have given up on the idea of an afterlife at all, trading the purity of their souls for bodily pleasures and instant gratification. I suppose that discovering the afterlife does, in fact, exist then packs quite the influential punch. Of course, this directs the current of their psychology only in my favour.

"Indeed, we do," Anubis finally relinquishes, her eyes trained, hawk-like, on the recruits below being handed spears made from bone.

"You know you could help me. I need some of those pendants. Abraxis' Kindred informed me that's how Xion recognised them as imposters last time. They weren't wearing the sinstones," I suggest, and she nods.

"Consider it done. What if these mortals— what if they're killed, won't that cause dissension among the others? I'm assuming they don't think they're invulnerable. You know that's a common misconception about immortality among humans," she reminds me, causing me to smile further.

"That's the beauty though. They've been informed that should they die; we won't make them move on, won't make them give up their identity and return to The Crucible. So, the majority are willing to work for us from the inside, even as sinners," I reveal. Anubis looks surprised.

"That is clever. Your idea, all of this?" she interrogates me as if she can't believe the plan is mine and mine alone.

"Of course. Everybody wins. The mortals get immortality, the demons get fresh kills, and I get an army that respects and wants to fight for me. It's perfect."

"I see. Well, given that you've come up with all this, I don't doubt you'll find a way to work out what exactly we need and how we're going to attempt to resurrect Ra." My head turns sideways sharply, to face her satisfied expression.

"You want to try?" I come across as awed, which is how I want to, raising my eyebrows and widening my lilac eyes.

"I do. I don't know if it'll work. We have a long way to go before we're ready to even try. Everything must fall into place exactly at the right time. I intend to keep my plans hidden from the other Nexus members until the last possible moment. You never know when my connections there may come into play," she announces, keeping her sentences clipped and her intent shrouded.

My paranoia rears its head.

Could it be she's playing both sides to try and see which is more favourable in the long run?

Perhaps.

I hear the cries of mortals facing off against demons and turn my back on the arena below, heading back to the staircase to make my exit, bored by the spectacle.

I never did have much of a taste for watching a fight, at least not one where there is a clear winner from the beginning. I lust after the tension, the thrill of not knowing who will triumph until the very last second.

"You'll want to be on your way. I expect you'll be gathering information for a while. I'll be working here, building the forces as best I can," I assure her, pleased beyond measure at this little partnership we've got going on.

"Indeed. Once an opportunity presents itself, be that in the coming days or months, I will return, and we will begin to plot for Ra's return. I'll be on my way for now though. Good day, Pandora." Anubis takes her leave as I pace in her wake, leaning against the arch of the colosseum's front doors and watching her climb atop the golden chariot she drives fearlessly. Unhooking a whip from the inside of the cart, she raises it into the air, bringing it down and lashing it hard against the hip bones of the jackals she always keeps so close. They pull away across the barren expanse of The Ashen Waste, lost in the pewter grey of ash falling like snow.

"Made a friend, did you?" Abraxis' voice startles me as I turn to find him directly behind me, looking over my shoulder.

"I did. What's it to you?" I demand, keeping my expression cold and unfeeling.

I hate talking with Abraxis, never sure how much of my motives he has figured out. He has shoulder-length black hair, thick and wild around his face, gold pupils that glow orange when he's enraged, and a stocky build which I wouldn't mind riding into the early hours of the dawn. He's not a bad looking guy but, then again, if I could choose to wear any face, I wouldn't make it an ugly one.

"Oh nothing, I was just wondering when the other Demon Lords are going to realise that you don't give a shit about them?" Abraxis smirks, reaching out and twizzling a lock of my black hair around his finger as I twist, jerking my head away from him.

"Says you," I retort, pursing my lips and widening my stance. I keep my arms crossed, fingering the box within the inside pocket of my sharp-cut military jacket.

"Says Delyria, sweetheart. You've got selfish motives. Nothing wrong with that, but I can see what you're trying to pull here. It's all very well you are contemplating revenge, but did you ever think about the bigger picture?" he enquires, face cast in an odd light by the sky as the purple sun shines directly upon him. We stand beneath the ruined arch, unmoving.

"There is no bigger picture than my revenge," I spit.

"That's where you're wrong. Demons are an opposing force to mortals. It's true we counteract the light imbued in them upon creation.

However, did you ever think about what happens if that balance tips? Like really think? Either way, darkness and light must balance somehow. Tipping that balance for your personal ends might let loose the Gods of Ancient, but did you ever think about what that'll do to everything else? You won't have anything left to rule over once you're done with the universe. You're not powerful enough to have a place in a world of Ancient Gods— trust me." His expression is serious, and I wonder why he cares.

"Why does that matter to you? You serve a God of Ancient. Don't you want to be powerful again? Don't you want your Kindred to be plentiful and thriving?" My voice takes on a high-pitched and incredulous tone, making me wonder why I'm beginning to sound rattled. The Demon Lord before me shakes his head, a smile marring his beauty.

"My Kindred, if you haven't noticed, are fine. We don't thrive off blood or bone. We need only Mount Mallum to remain strong, and for your information, I am powerful. I don't need a whole throng of worshippers to know that. I have everything I need already," he expresses, eyes blazing now. "And I'll have you know, I was doing a fine job of getting sustenance enough for all the Kindred around here to survive before you came along," he sneers.

"That's just it though, isn't it? You're happy to just survive. The others, including myself, no longer are. Maybe you should think about that before you go running your mouth about things you don't understand," I scold him, reaching into my pocket.

This conversation is over.

"You just can't see the truth of this. The bigger truth. It's not about good or evil, it's about balance." Abraxis looks like he's on the verge of begging me to see his side of things, which is hilarious. A few months ago, it was me trying to get him to see mine. Unfortunately for him, his pride gets in the way, causing him to merely write me off as ignorant rather than correct.

"You're the Demon Lord of lies and illusion. What the hell do you know about universal truths?" I slip open a panel on the box, deciding to go and check in on Banshee numbers, maybe take some of them hunting after the mortal sun sets.

"I'm the Demon Lord of everything which is not true. So, what makes you think I can't see what is?" Abraxis counters.

I shrug.

It doesn't matter what he says, he's just scared of losing what little power he has left.

"I have demons to feed," I call over my shoulder, opening the portal and stepping through, leaving him and his stupid so-called truths behind me as I take my leave to an ordinary world.

9

I HEARD IT THROUGH THE GRAPEVINE

SEPHY

MY EYES FLY OPEN, heat crawling over my skin in a fresh blaze. I'm alert, awake, veins full of fire and muscles crawling with tendrils of unspent energy. I move from Xion's slack grasp and he grumbles, rolling over to face the window overlooking the city and falling promptly back asleep.

I wonder how long it's been since he slept. Probably forever. He's always putting everyone else's needs before his own, or so it would seem.

Standing in the middle of his bedroom, I feel like a spare part, wired and agitated. It's like someone has flicked a switch, and now every single fibre of me is humming, restored, alive.

I tread quietly to the bathroom, shaking my arms out to try and dispel some of this new life, and yet it doesn't work, not even close.

I ponder staying, hanging around, or waking Xion and trying to get him to take me out to fight, or run— or dance. Anything.

However, I don't. As I stand in the high, cool walls of his bathroom, I find myself afraid to wake him at all. I had caved, let him hold me; let him get close. Another mistake because I'm weak.

That weakness must end. It's just not fair to him.

But the thought of fighting those urges is exhausting, even though I'm alert, so instead I simply ball my fists and calm myself before convecting from his bathroom and heading back home amongst a bouquet of fresh flames.

I reappear, flames dissipating upon the new black marble floor of my bathroom. I planned it this way, not wanting to scorch the carpet, and I'm enveloped in the smell of home too fast. Cinnamon mixed in with the scent of Cerb's fur and the aroma of violets that have been placed gracefully on a few surfaces around the bathroom, no doubt by Jules. I smile. He's been amazing, more than a butler, more than a parent in a lot of ways, and certainly more than I could have ever asked for.

I'm lucky to have him.

Padding past the newly refurbished shower, I take this chance to admire the sheen of the honeycomb tiling and the matching golden showerheads I'd been too out of it to notice before, trying not to think about the pulling of staples from my chest as the ghosts of screams echo inside my skull.

Feet hitting the carpet after a quick descent down the bathroom steps, I move into my closet, looking for something to go out in.

I need to get out, go into the real world, be among actual people who don't know me, and try to assimilate back into mortality. Being part god had always seemed like the hard part, but now I'm seeing that being mortal is just as difficult. Everything is so frail, so temporary—it's making me paranoid, making the hairs rise on the back of my neck, every time the temperature drops by one or two degrees, or the wind pounds against the outside of the windowpanes.

The closet feels safe, as much as anywhere can, with deep black walls and an aubergine carpet replacing what had once been juvenile. The gold racks and coat hangers are filled with mainly black attire, though the occasional pop of white, grey, red, or purple does occur every few items.

Nothing has been moved since I died, which is weird if you ask me. Then again, we have so much space it wasn't necessary to move it at all, or maybe Jules just couldn't bear to pack it away into boxes.

I walk along the rack, brushing each garment with my fingertips and selecting things at random. I'm still thin, too thin to wear leather, so I pick out another pair of velvet leggings in black, a matching cotton camisole and one of my favourite jackets. It has a wide hood and is corseted at the back with flared sleeves. A waterfall of fabric, which covers my ass, falls gracefully to mid-thigh. I top off the look with knee-high leather boots, the heel excessive.

Getting dressed in a hurry, I don't want to waste any time. I have no idea what the hour is, but if I only have a little of the night left, I want to make the most of it. Spinning away from a cream loveseat as I pull the jacket over my shoulders, I see myself in the floor-to-ceiling mirror on the opposing wall, my face pale and hair ratty.

I scurry through to the vanity, pulling the antique brush through my hair and yanking it up into a high ponytail so it looks at least presentable. I'm shocked to find my skin ghostly pale but undeniably aglow.

Next, I go on the hunt for my makeup, the thing that makes Sephy badass and fiery to the outside world. I don't find it in the vanity, all the drawers being barren, or in the closet— and I wonder where it could be. Maybe it was thrown away—

I eye the bedside table and figure I might as well check there, but as I yank open the top drawer with careless speed, I find something I don't expect staring back up at me, glinting in the light.

The opal blade.

I feel sick, closing my eyes and tilting my chin upward and to the left as though the incline will allow the memories to slip back into the recesses of my mind where they belong.

Beneath the blade my makeup bag sits, so I tentatively grab the hilt, feeling a rush of power run up my arm. I have forgotten the hold this weapon has over me, only remembering the sting of it tearing skin and muscle from bone.

I don't want to take it, but I'm also too scared to leave it here, so I slip it into the back of my waistband and try to forget about the serrated edge pushing mercilessly into my spine.

Makeup bag retrieved, I pace quickly to the vanity and begin to apply my war paint, my mask.

Once the eyeliner wings have been successfully and precisely tipped, the deep plum lipstick painted on, and my skin given new life with concealer, highlighter, and blusher, I put on the killer; my mascara. It lengthens my already long lashes, priming the trap I so often use to bait and take down my sexual prey.

Sitting in front of the mirror, I give myself one final glance of half-approval before getting to my feet and heading back into the bathroom. I stand beside the bathtub, remembering the nights before Xion, the nights with many different strangers among the bubbles. It had been so simple, easy, not like now.

I want to go back, to rediscover that Sephy, not the Sephy who is vulnerable, scared, a demi-god who's been hunted and humiliated by the Demon Lords.

Balling my fists, I feel as though staying in one place for too long may be a thing of the past — it's addictive, this freedom to go anywhere with a simple blaze of the fire burning within my chest.

Closing my eyes, I picture Retropolis and disappear among the raging flames once more.

I reappear, feet touching down in an alleyway at the side of a building, the club located on its topmost floor. The scent of rot, of too-sweet alcohol like alcopops and hard fruit cider, sears my nostrils as I realise I'm standing in a pile of broken glass next to a dumpster. Flames from my convection find fuel in small puddles of leftover spirits.

"Ugh," I cuss, stamping on the flame as it singes the edge of my boot.

I might have just come from Mortaria, a place where the soil is coated in blood and fields are sewn with bodily fluids, but there's something about the scent of humanity that sends my stomach reeling in a nauseous spiral. I've never had this reaction to the smell of garbage before, and I wonder why now, after I've been to hell and back — beyond the grave and back— even, that it bothers me so much. Perhaps it's because I've just trashed a basically flawless pair of three-hundred-dollar shoes.

Yeah, that could be it, I muse, stepping over several more glass bottles strewn in puddles of pearlescent rain laced with engine fluid.

Then again, money isn't an issue for me, never has been, so maybe it's not the shoes; maybe it's something else altogether.

I pull my hood off my neck and over my head as a brisk wind chills the sides of my face, wrapping the thick fabric around me in an effort to fight off the inner-city chill.

As I turn the corner of the building's slick brick exterior, I see my favourite bouncer, Barry, in his usual dark suit and Rubik's cube style tie. I don't go to join the queue, instead walking straight over to him, swinging my hips the way I used to.

"Name?" he demands.

I smirk, pulling back my hood and staring him straight in the face.

"Sephy Sinclair," I announce as his eyes dart up from the clipboard in his hands. His eyes widen, and I smile at him as he cocks his head, confused.

"Weren't you—" he begins.

I raise one of my eyebrows.

"What?" I demand, enjoying playing with the man far too much.

"I thought you were dead. It said in the papers—" he stutters, and I give him a quizzical look.

"Me? Dead?" I hold up a hand to my face and wiggle my fingers. "Nope. Not dead. I'm thirsty though— can you do a corpse a favour and let me in?" I ask, flashing him my most brilliant smile.

He nods, unable to speak, transfixed as he moves forward to pull back the neon blue velvet rope, moonlight bouncing vicariously off his dark, bald head. I walk past him with purpose, raising my hood back over my head and stepping inside.

Well, that was fun, I snort to myself, shaking my head and finding myself feeling more like Sephy than I have in a while.

I think about checking my coat, but I don't, instead turning right and climbing the glass staircase that fits into the building at a neat ninety-degree angle as it ascends to the club.

Flashing neon lights greet me, and the familiar scents of perspiration and spirits fill my nose as I ball my jacket sleeves around my fists. I tread, acting more confident than I feel, over to the bar, where I take my usual seat on a neon lime swivel stool. Perching, I keep my face shrouded until a bartender with a familiar face comes over to take my order.

"Hey, Simon," I greet him, looking up from the hypnotic colour change of the flashing bar where I'm resting my elbows. Simon, seeing me clearly as the multihued light shines up onto my face, drops the glass he's cleaning. I hear it smash on the floor at his feet, audibly crude amid the DJ's latest retro spin.

"Sephy?!" He looks incredulous, hand still curved as though holding a glass.

"Yes. Can I get the usual please?" I ask him. His mouth pops open in a tiny 'o' shape.

"But— but—"

"Yeah, yeah, I was dead. Now I'm not— can I get a damn drink, please?" I demand, impatient as I slam my balled fist against the counter absent-mindedly.

"But— *how*?!" he asks.

I exhale in a sigh. I could give him the truth, but what would be the fun in that?

"Can you keep a secret?" I demand, and he nods, leaning forward. He's so close to me now I could reach out and kiss him if I wanted.

Hanging on my every word, he swallows hard.

"Of course."

"I witnessed a murder. So, they put me in the witness protection program," I lie, watching his face.

"A murder? Jesus, Seph, what happened?!"

"Some guy murdered this other guy over front row seats to see *Wicked* on Broadway. It was traumatic," I fabricate, having fun with it. I mean, after the last few days, I at least deserve to get something out of coming back from the dead.

"Jesus Christ. Over *Wicked*? I prefer *Mamma Mia*," he comments.

I smirk.

"I'm pretty sure the dead guy would agree with you after what happened," I add.

Simon frowns.

"But wait— isn't the witness protection program for people who like are high-profile killers and stuff?"

He's got me there, so I take a moment, letting my imagination run wild.

"Oh yeah, the guy who killed for the tickets was the son of this big mafia boss. Scary stuff," I admit, nodding my head and pressing my lips together in an entirely fake grimace.

"Jesus. You'd think the son of a mafia boss could get his own front-row tickets to *Wicked*— right?" He looks at me, eyes shimmering and wide.

I shrug.

"Right?! That's what I said!" I exclaim. Simon shakes his head.

God, he's so gullible. Fucking hell.

"Well, I'm glad you're okay. I was worried you got into trouble with whoever is responsible for all those unsolved murders and disappearances downtown," he expresses.

"What murders? Sorry, I mean, I only just got back. I'm kind of out of the loop," I explain, and he opens his mouth to begin telling the story. Throat arid, I decide to interrupt him. "Explain while you pour me the usual? I'm gagging for some booze," I beg him, fluttering my lashes beneath the shadow of my hood.

"Of course." Turning toward the mosaic mirror behind the bar, he picks up a bottle of the club's finest whisky and pours me a glass. I take it in my fingers and down the entire contents, relishing the sweet, hot burn it leaves behind.

"Another," I demand, and he continues to pour, adjusting his crooked Rubik's cube bow tie with his free hand.

"So, it all started— what— six months ago?" Simon begins.

It's just a coincidence. I remind myself. This couldn't possibly have anything to do with Brad. "At first it was the bodies, turning up all mauled and bloody— well— some were bloody, others were drained of blood apparently. I don't know. It was like some kind of wild animal. But then, people started disappearing and there was no trace of a body at all— so the Police think they're looking for some psychopath with a rabid dog or something," Simon explains.

I frown, deathly uncomfortable.

That doesn't sound like how I was murdered at all.

I shrug, dismissing the story as the unfortunate and random bloody act it is. As I have learned recently, there doesn't have to be a reason, or even an injustice, to make someone murder another human being. It comes from nowhere, it can happen to anyone, at any time, in any place. Nothing in this world is sacred. Nowhere is safe.

Security is an illusion at best, just like justice.

I down my second drink of the night, depressing thoughts weighing me down as my senses prickle at the overwhelming auditory and visual overload of my surroundings.

I'm wary every second, unable to relax, hence why I feel the need to drink myself careless.

I sit for a while, watching people, observing them. It's interesting because even from this distance, I can see a stark difference in some from others by their eyes alone. The young, the dreamers, have a spark of hope alight behind their eyes, and yet those who are cynical, those who have seen brutality and felt the relentless sting of suffering have had that light snuffed out without pause, leaving only desolation within.

My own spark had found a home in the idea of a future with Xion, but it was extinguished before it had even had a chance to become anything real, and now I can't allow myself to try to kindle it again. It's just too much to hope for in a world where loss is an ever-lengthening shadow that eventually falls over everything, turning light to dark and life to death.

Sipping on another glass of whisky, I wonder why Xion had been so reckless, so hopeful in bringing me back. Doesn't he realise that I was finally safe from the cruel clutches of the two worlds I'm now forced to live between?

Being in The Nether, as much as I can remember, hadn't been ecstasy, but it hadn't been pain either. Right now, nothingness seems like bliss compared to this.

My legs begin to jiggle on the stool, and as I finish off my third drink, I decide that dancing is probably best for my sanity. At least if I'm moving, feeling the music, then my thoughts will cease threatening to bring a dark cloud over everything.

I take down my hood, letting the fiery red curls fall loose from my ponytail and down over one shoulder as I shake out my hair. I twizzle on the stool, moving to face the room as the song changes to '*I heard it through the Grapevine*' by Marvin Gaye.

I smirk, the song instantly reminding me of Xion as I look around, wondering if he'll suddenly appear at the call of his favourite artist in the world.

He doesn't, so I get to my feet, sauntering with rhythm into the middle of the flashing dancefloor as the provocative, slow rhythm of the song takes hold of my body. I raise my arms above my head, swirling my hips as I let my arms sway and my head hang back. I bite my bottom lip, getting reacquainted with the fact my body can bring pleasure and not only pain as the disco-ball overhead shimmers, speckling pure white flecks of light down onto my face.

My feet move from side to side as I bring my hands down and run them down my body, twisting and gyrating to the music as a smile spreads over my lips. Closing my eyes, I let myself get lost in the voice of Marvin Gaye, finally relaxing, when suddenly, my heart is pounding again.

Hands creep, curling around my waist, dancing with me.

I turn, expecting to see Xion— hoping beyond hope that I'll spin and be caught in the molten glaze of his irises.

Instead, I find a stranger with dark hair and brown eyes, face too close to mine as he tries to move in and kiss me without my consent.

Oh no you fucking don't!

I pull back my fist and throw a punch that lands right between the guy's eyes. He turns feral, not backing off as I had hoped, and I start to panic, Brad's eyes flash across the forefront of my mind as that same male rage, the red mist, descends upon the asshole in front of me.

Cupping his bleeding nose, he lurches forward to grab me, to put me in what he thinks is my place.

I don't think, I just react.

Blue flame explodes from my palm as a ball forms in my grip, crackling and causing him to stop mid-stride, confused, but more importantly deterred.

The club around us halts, turning to watch the spectacle as what had been just some girl getting set upon by a creep becomes something far more interesting. The man's eyes widen, and I see the fear on his face grow as it takes root in his pupils. It sprawls out across his flesh as his face drains white in the cobalt glow of my fire, cementing its hold before his mouth falls open.

"Fuck off," I growl, threatening to throw the fireball at him as I become feral in stance.

"You're fucking crazy!" he exclaims, turning and rushing through the crowd toward the staircase to make his escape, humiliated.

I could go after him, but as I stand there, the eyes of the entire establishment on me, my demi-goddess-ness exposed for all to see, I realise that it's not him I'm angry at.

Realising that the cat is out of the bag, I extinguish the flame in my palm in an instant and pull the hood over my head, hoping to God nobody had gotten a picture, or worse video, of me going badass.

Convecting from the middle of the dancefloor, I leave only smoke behind.

I rematerialize at the edge of the Sinclair Estate, fury coursing through my veins.

When the fuck did my body become goddamn public property? I wonder, disappointed by what it seems to mean to be a woman in this world.

More importantly, as I begin to pick my way through the over-growth of the forest, I realise something I'd been too caught up in before to notice.

Blue.

That flame had been fucking blue!

It was the resurrection flame. I know it. I've seen Haedes use it a hundred times and now I'm producing it myself? Is this a by-product of the resurrection ritual? Or something else entirely?

I frown as I continue to wonder, heel catching a root and causing me to fall, hands flying forward into the dirt.

God fucking dammit!

I sit, splayed in the earth, ready to scream, to smash my fists into the soil beneath me.

I'm so angry. Every fibre of what makes me who I am is knotted and laced with rage.

It's not hard to figure out why.

As I get to my feet and brush myself down, I realise now why I've been feeling this way.

I was murdered.

But more importantly, I was *betrayed*. Betrayed by someone who's supposed to be my family. I reach around to where the opal dagger presses, warm now, against my lower spine.

I hold it up in the broken moonlight falling intermittently through the thick and newly lush branches of the trees, watching as the flash of the lunar glow against the opal of the blade takes me back to that night.

I had struggled, fought, bled, but more importantly, I had wondered—

Where did you get that?

I remember the thought crossing my mind as I had laid there, fighting for every breath, and I know now why I've been repressing the entire event. It wasn't Brad, though I'd quite like to give him a lava facial any day now. It was a deeper cut, a worse betrayal that had me knowing now that family, that love, means nothing.

I grip the hilt of the blade so hard in my fist that my knuckles turn white as I storm through the forest, no longer unsure in my step but practically unstoppable as I manoeuvre the terrain seamlessly as though I'm floating. I reach the edge of the trees and move onto the gravel, finding his stupid little green beetle parked outside the front of *my* goddamn house.

I smirk, remembering how I had left Xion everything, left him penniless yet again.

I'm gonna kiss that lawyer for putting through the paperwork so fast, I vow.

My feet smash into the gravel, leaving tiny pieces of alabaster stone flying up in my wake like earthen shrapnel. I crack my neck to one side, then the other, murderous as every single thing I've suffered, every pain I've felt, culminates in an explosive rage aimed only at one.

Peter.

I fly through the front doors, putting out both fists in front of me, one still clutching the weapon, and sending the heavy wood flying inward with hardly any effort at all.

I race up the stairs, turning right, the direction I'd been afraid to venture not so long ago. Taking the entire corridor in front of me in seconds, I whirl past the bookcase behind which the opal blade should have remained hidden.

Out of reach of say— I don't know— murdering assholes?

I reach the end of the hall, kicking the door in with the sole of my shoe and leaving mud imprinted on the dark wood as the entire thing flies off its hinges sideways, crashing into the bookshelf lining the left side of the office.

Within, Peter lurches to his feet, looking at me with a terrified and shocked expression.

"But—how—" he breathes as I move through the open doorway and reach out over the desk, grabbing a fistful of his neatly groomed silver hair and slamming his head into the wood. I hear his glasses break with an audible crunch. This gives me utter and complete satisfaction as I smile.

"Surprise motherfucker!" I yell, pulling his head back up from the grain so he's forced to look at me beyond the fissures running central to both lenses.

"Sephy! Stop!" Peter cries out, eyes wide and full of fear. I raise the blade to his throat as I round the side of the desk, not letting him slip from my grasp for even a second.

"Maybe we should see if you can handle how it feels to have this knife slice you open six ways from fucking Sunday!? Huh?" I exclaim, breathing ragged as I squeeze my fingers against his skull.

"But I—" he begins, but I roll my eyes.

"Don't give me that shit. I know you gave Brad the knife— or told him where to find it at least! Didn't you?" I yell in his face, spit coating his skin.

"You knew there was no way to kill a demi-god like me without it. Didn't you?!" I shake him in my hand, letting the blade bite into his skin ever so slightly. The first drop of blood is let loose, falling from the mere flesh wound in a drab trickle. It's not as satisfying as I know watching it spray from his carotid will be.

"I—I—" Peter begins, but before he can answer we're both interrupted.

"Sephy. Stop." Jules is standing in the doorway, not panicked but calm, his arms neatly behind his back. His voice is even, not the slightest bit shaken.

"Oh Jules, thank God. She's gone insane!" Peter yells. I let him go, a ball of scorching red flame filling my palm.

"Jules, I have to know, I need to know how Brad got this knife. Peter was the only one who knew where it was hidden except you," I explain.

Jules doesn't say anything, looking at Peter with almost an eerie tranquillity.

"Answer her," he says simply. Still as calm as I've ever seen him, eyes serene and expression void of emotion, the sentiment is not expressed as a request.

"Well? Was it you?!" I demand. I bring the flame right up to his face so sweat begins to bead on his forehead, the flickering of the flames reflected at me in the broken lenses hanging only inches from his eyes.

"I—I saw him, one day. He was outside— I let him in that night—" He gasps for air as the flames crackle against his skin, threatening only more heat with each passing second.

"And you gave him the blade?!" I coax his confession, and Peter, unable to speak, simply nods.

"I knew I would never get this fortune with you discovering your lineage. You're immortal! What chance did a mere mortal like me stand of having any kind of life without that money?" he asks me, his excuse pathetic.

I frown, utterly confused by his logic, or lack thereof.

I go limp at the confirmation of his betrayal as it sinks in, continuing to hold the blade to his throat, but letting the flame near his face extinguish as quickly as it had come.

"Sephy. Don't," Jules warns.

I turn to him, finding his expression not angry but scared.

As I let his loving gaze burn into me, I know he only wants what's best for me.

I do trust that.

So— I lower the knife.

Peter breathes out a sigh of relief as Jules takes a step forward, arms still folded at his spine.

"Thank you, Jules— I—" Peter begins, but Jules cocks his head. Pulling out a shotgun from behind his back and pointing it directly at Peter's smug ass face.

"Oh, that wasn't for you. You're a piece of shit, whom I'm about to escort off the property and threaten to kill if I ever see you again. It was for *her*. I'm not having her become a killer over someone as pathetic as you. She deserves better." My heart swells as he loads the barrel of the gun with an audible click, causing Peter to startle.

"I'm the only family you have left Persephone— this is a mistake!" Peter exclaims as I shove him toward Jules, who continues to hold him at gunpoint.

"It's Sephy. And no, you're not." I inform him with a shrug, winking at Jules. Smiling back at me, Jules places the barrel of the shotgun firmly between Peter's shoulders.

"March," he orders.

The two of them exit through the open doorway.

Taking a seat in the leather of his chair, I put my feet up on his desk, cleaning my nails with the tip of the opal blade and watching as Jules, my real family, goes with a spring in his step to take out the trash.

AGAINST ALL ODDS

XION

I APPROACH THE SINCLAIR Estate, wondering why it is, of late, that I feel like I haven't stopped running between one dimension and the other. Pushing my fingers through my hair, I try to slow my breathing as the familiar scent of my breath condensing in the air mixes with leather.

Having woken up to find her gone, I'm panicked.

Had she been a dream?

Something I concocted to try and cope with the fact the ritual hadn't worked?

It doesn't seem likely, but then with Morpheus' recent interference with my unconscious mind, I can't be sure.

Balling my fists at my side, I push on through the pitch black of the morning's early hours toward the house's moon-bathed silhouette, exhausted and emotionally fraught. I never thought I'd miss the baking heat of Turkey, but here I am, wishing that it was warming me again.

The smell of damp earth rises into my nostrils as I storm across the gravel driveway, skipping all three of the stone steps in a single bound and rapping on the front door.

After a few moments, Jules is revealed as the door swings open with an audible creak, dressed impeccably as always, despite the late hour.

"Oh, it's you. Come in." He steps aside, and I exhale. I guess I need to address things with him. He's important to Sephy. That's never been more evident than in the last few days.

"Yes, I woke up and she was gone— is she here?" I ask, breathing a sigh of relief as Jules nods, expression stony.

"Yes, she's upstairs taking a shower," he informs me, statuesque on the spot as he stands perfectly upright.

"Right. Well, look. I never apologised to you. I put you in a god-aw-ful position. I should have told you. Should have spoken to you before we attempted the resurrection. You deserved a say. You're the closest thing she has to family," I exhale, raising a hand and rubbing the back of my neck as I stare down at my reflection in his toecaps.

"She's practically my daughter, though I'd never tell her I feel that way," Jules breathes.

I give him a slight, hopeful smile.

"I don't think you have to. She knows," I assure him.

"It's lucky for her she has someone. After the entire episode with Peter this afternoon. *Rat bastard.*" Jules' gaze turns disgusted and I frown, straightening as I scan the space for any sign of him.

"Peter?" I enquire, cocking my head as I shuffle on the spot and lean closer to him so I can listen. I'm intrigued, but also worried Peter might be lurking nearby.

"You didn't know?" Jules raises an eyebrow, a slight smirk twisting the side of his mouth.

I guess now it's my turn to be clueless.

"Know what?" My stomach starts to churn.

"He let that psycho in here. Brad. Gave him the opal blade," Jules relinquishes. The room starts to spin around me as red mist descends across my vision.

"Brad? He was the one who—" I begin, recalling my fist impacting his face with a delightful crunch the night he had tried to take advan-tage of Sephy. The first night I met her.

It seems like forever ago—

Why would he do that?

More importantly— *why would Peter help him?*

"According to Sephy. Peter admitted to letting him in. It also ex-plains why the security tapes from that night were wiped clean. Cun-ning prick," Jules sighs. My body coils like steel cable under duress.

"Where is he?" I demand, growling.

"Oh, don't worry. I had the immense pleasure of escorting him off the property at gunpoint. It was, might I say, quite the highlight of my time here at the estate." He smirks, and I can't help but quell my anger for a moment at his clear and undeniable satisfaction.

"I would have paid to see that," I joke, feeling like the bad atmos-phere between us has finally passed.

"I can get the security footage if you like. I've already watched it several times, I even made popcorn." He flushes, and I laugh.

"I knew there was something up with that guy. I'm guessing he wanted the Sinclair fortune?" I conclude.

Jules exhales with a pissed-off look that confirms my theory, face turning grim.

"I think so. It's surprising to me that Sephy trusts anyone at this point, I mean, everyone in her life seems to want to use her." Jules and I exchange an awkward look, and I wonder if he's referring to the night we spent together.

"I don't— I wouldn't still be here if I was just looking for a good time. Resurrection for the sake of getting laid is a little bit of an overkill don't you think?" I demand, and Jules shrugs.

"Good. That's what I want to hear. She's fragile right now. I don't want her hurting." His expression remains stern, and I nod, wanting nothing more than to appease him and be there for her.

"I promise," I vow, and he smiles.

"Go on. I'm sure you want to see her, assuming that's why you're here?" Jules steps aside, and I take off past him, clapping him on the shoulder and finding solid muscle beneath his suit jacket, relaxed now that I know I have his blessing. I really don't want to be on the wrong end of his shotgun.

I enter her room after roaming the newly decorated landing, finding a trolley full of food, half-eaten, beside the bed. Her clothes are strewn on the floor in a trail leading up into the bathroom and the air is rich with the scent of cinnamon. I inhale like the addict I am becoming.

"Sephy?" I call out, climbing the stairs in quick time and finding her in the shower, eyes closed as the jets pound down on her naked body.

Arousal ripples through me as I see the curves of her, soapy, and steam billows up in the air. I open my mouth to speak, and yet I can't help but be speechless as I stand, staring at her.

She opens her eyes, catching me behind the misted glass of the cubicle. Her face turns white as a sheet, blood draining in an instant, and she jumps, screaming at an ear-shattering high pitch.

Shit.

"Hey, hey! It's me!" I call out, realising she must not have heard me the first time I called. She turns off the jets almost immediately, and steps out of the shower, pissed.

"What the fuck! Have we not *just* discussed you standing just staring at me!? *Jesus, Xion!*" she yells, hand rising to cover the place where her heart is pounding beneath her breast. I stare at her, tilting my head as my eyes widen, gaze falling over her bare skin like cold water.

I've not seen what he did before, not seen the damage.

Her torso is covered in stab wounds, still healing, red and raw. I see the enormous Y incision Jules had mentioned but have been too enraptured with her face to notice.

She catches me staring and covers herself with one arm, more self-conscious than I've ever seen her as she reaches over and pulls a large black towel around herself with the other.

"You scared the crap out of me," she sighs. Goosebumps rise on her arms, rippling into existence in a wave of chill that coats her skin as the cinnamon-scented steam dissipates and the air around us cools.

She stands, staring at me as I trace the marring of her skin that remains only too visible, mouth hanging open.

"I'm sorry—" I breathe, expression turning unstoppably sad as my gaze refuses to fall from her scars.

She stands, vulnerable, dripping water onto the floor.

"It's fine— just— *Christ*. Being murdered— not great for the nerves, ya know?" she asks, smirking. My body relaxes immediately at the humour in her tone.

It's like she's the old Sephy. Just for a moment.

"You got your sass back," I comment, and she shrugs.

"I'd forgotten what a great device humour is for avoiding actually dealing with shit," she chuckles, walking past me in just her towel and padding back down into the main room.

She pulls a slice of pizza out from under a silver cloche, placing it in her mouth and groaning as she closes her eyes, savouring the moment as she'd once savoured me.

"I woke up, and you were gone," I comment, trailing after her as I skip down the bathroom steps, my full weight coming down on the carpet with a thud as my heartbeat becomes as heavy as my tread.

"I wanted to go out," she shrugs, licking cheese off her bottom lip.

I bite my own, doubt and hurt pooling in my stomach as I let my lids hood my eyes. I rub my forearm through the leather of my jacket with my opposing hand.

"I was worried about you. I thought— I thought you coming back was a dream." I can't help but let a nervous laugh escape me as I admit this, realising how pathetic I must seem to her. How pathetic I've become because of her.

"No offence, but even you don't have the imagination to make me up," she quips, taking another mouthful of pizza and smirking as she chews.

"I have a perfectly fine imagination thank you very much," I grumble, frowning. She crosses her legs underneath her, tightening the towel around her breasts, and surveys me.

"You own the same outfit fifty times over!"

"Better than being constantly naked. I mean seriously, I think half the time I've known you you've spent totally butt nude, and you have an entire room for your clothes!" I try to insult her, failing as she rolls her eyes, getting off the bed and dropping her towel so it pools around her ankles.

"Ooooh, and I'm sure you're *so* sad about that. I saw you staring in the shower. I should get you a clamp, so you can keep your jaw from hitting the floor next time," she teases me, coming close, but all I can see is the cuts on her skin, the way *he* destroyed her, traumatised her.

As I stand here, I realise I've been stupid. I've been worried about the resurrection, about what that had done to her, about what it could do to the rest of the universe. But I hadn't considered what she would have to deal with after going through such a brutal and sudden loss of life.

Stupid. Stupid. Stupid. I cuss internally, wondering how I can fix it.

I don't know how exactly, but I must do something—

"It was Brad, wasn't it?" I ask her, reaching out to touch her but finding my fingers falling through thin air as she steps back, walking through to her closet and giving me a perfect view of how the stab wounds had gone all the way through her tiny torso, slicing her apart— front and back.

I shudder.

"Yes," she replies from the other room, voice laden with raw and unsolved turmoil.

"Why?" I ask, feeling her fear from even this distance.

"He wanted me to be his and only his, I guess. He took a piece of my hair too— I guess he'd been stalking me for a while, and I was so wrapped up in everything with the Demon Lords I didn't notice," she sighs, voice cracking. The fact she's broken by the entire debacle becomes so entirely apparent; I wonder how it had never occurred to me.

"He needs to pay," I growl to myself. My breathing turns rabid and my muscles tense, furl, ready to break bones and stop his blackened heart from ever causing anyone pain ever again.

I know I can't undo what has happened, can't erase those memories— but the man responsible for her death won't walk around free— not if I have anything to do with it.

Turning on the spot, I pull out my cell phone and exit the room with determined purpose and speed, not wanting to waste a minute more.

I hear her calling after me, confused and alarmed, but I'm too far gone, too far down the rabbit hole of my own rage and desperation to fix the injustice of her murder or to respond to anything but my burning desire for revenge.

SEPHY

Wrangling my wet hair up into a knot on top of my head, I wonder why men are so shit at communicating. One minute, we're having a perfectly uncomfortable and traumatic conversation, the next minute *boom.*

Gone.

Bye bye.

I sigh, pulling on a pair of black denim jeans with rips in the knees and metal studs around the waistband, trying to quell my irritation at Xion's flying visit. I wanted to talk to him about the resurrection flame, tell him that after everything we just can't be together, but now he's gone. Stormed off back to Mortaria no doubt to kill some demons and disperse some of his pointless rage.

That was what I realised in those moments, holding the blade to Peter's throat.

Killing Peter, or Brad for that matter, won't erase what they've done, it won't make anything in my life any easier. You'd think at the thought of killing them, I'd feel safer, but it's not like that. It wasn't Brad who had traumatised me— not really— he was just the individual who had happened to be holding the knife. It was the fact that I hadn't seen it coming, that it had happened suddenly, out of nowhere, and made no

129

sense to me at all. It was the fact that any illusion of safety, of peace or a definitive and happy ending, had been undeniably shattered. I realise now this life is as fragile as a single fraying thread.

It doesn't matter who holds the scissors; the point is they're there.

Taking the lives of those who had taken mine doesn't make me feel safer. It makes me just like them, and it proves I've learned nothing from the experience of dying.

I'm not going through that and coming out unchanged. I just— I can't be who I was before.

It can't have all been for nothing.

Pulling a black, high-necked sweater over my lacy bra, I hear someone enter through the door in the next room. Hoping it's Xion, I pad across the carpet with soft delicate steps.

"Xion?" I call as I turn the corner out of the closet, finding not the uncouth gait I expect but Jules' perfect stance instead. He looks concerned.

"What?" I ask, tilting my head and feeling the weight of my wet hair shifting on top of my head in a mass of sopping tangles.

"What did you say to Xion?" Jules asks me, and I blink a few times. "Uh— why?"

"Well, he just took off in your favourite car— it was my observation that speed limits were not high on his priority list either. I'm pretty sure he's left the windows chipped from the way he was spinning the tyres on the gravel. It's possible we may have to have the entire pane replaced on the left side," he looks agitated, but I feel my heart falter despite the petty matter of a chipped window.

"Did he say where he was going?" I demand, crossing my arms.

"No. He just stormed out of the front doors. Didn't even respond when I called after him," Jules elaborates.

Shit. Shit. Shit.

"Sephy, what did you say to him?" Jules presses me for an answer.

"Nothing really, he was asking me about Brad. He— he kept staring at my scars," I stammer, the look of his pity scorched into my memory. I never want anyone to look at me like that again.

"We need to go after him," Jules announces, moving to turn away. I reach out, grabbing a fistful of his black suit sleeve in my desperate palm.

"What? Why? He's probably just going to rage drive off some of his anger!" I exclaim, wondering why Jules is overreacting like this.

"No, Sephy. He's going to try to kill Brad. You should have seen him. That was the walk of a man with a vendetta," Jules argues, and I stammer, struggling to put my racing thoughts into linear order.

"Look, I don't get why he would do that. I'm alive, aren't I? Why do we need to go and dig up the asshole that murdered me? What good does that even do? It doesn't take back what he did to me. It'll just put blood on Xion's hands!" I express.

Jules breaks character, quickly moving from prim and proper to serious as he places both hands on my shoulders and shakes me slightly.

"Sephy, come on. You can't be this stupid. Xion has feelings for you!" Jules exclaims. I shake my head, denying everything inside me that says he's right.

"We slept together *one time*, Jules; it didn't even mean anything! We're just friends who happened to fall into bed after a hell of a lot of champagne!" I deny it all, and Jules shakes his head.

"How many guys do you know who go and resurrect their fuck buddy?" The language doesn't sound right coming from him, and it strikes horror in me. What if he's right? What if my reliance on Xion has come across as something I didn't intend? It's true, that night, I felt things I've never felt with anyone, but it's a choice to pursue those feelings, and it's a choice I just can't justify after everything I've been through.

I'm just not strong enough.

I don't want to have to break Xion's heart either though. He brought me back expecting— *something*— clearly.

I just can't. I can't be with him, can't be with anybody. I barely feel strong enough to trust my own body, my own mind, let alone someone else.

"Sephy, if we let him do this, he might never forgive himself. Murder is something not everyone can carry— I should know. It's not like killing demons— it's different," Jules begs me with his tone as he stares down into my eyes, impatient. I recall Xion telling me the same thing, telling me that he had never been the same after what had happened with his first lover—

It hits me as I realise what this could do to him, how it could blacken his soul. let part of him loose which will be hard to once again contain.

I can't let him become the demon he's always believed he is, the brutal monster he has so convinced himself he can be, because of me.

I'm just not worth it.

"Come on, Jules. We better hurry."

IN THE AIR TONIGHT

LUCE

I TRUDGE UP THE stairs to my apartment, undeniably exhausted.
What I have done is utterly reckless.
I see that now.
Why had I been so damn ignorant of the risks?
Perhaps not ignorant by situation, but by choice?

Reaching the top of the staircase, I exhale, knowing what I need to do. The thing is, now I think back, I realise something equally terrifying. I *loved* the dark magic coursing through my veins. It made me glow, made me vibrant, made me more alive than I've felt in forever.

I feel the urge to click my fingers, snap apart the wings of an Aetherial Sprite, to smell the scent of simmering magic as it fills my alchemy chamber. It infects every part of me until I'm considering turning around and entering the brewing chamber instead of falling into bed and succumbing to the fatigue I've been fighting.

Before I have a chance to make the decision though, I'm greeted by Thane as I automatically open the apartment door. She's watching Cerb and Beelz tussle on the rug at her feet. The fireplace is set ablaze, and she's sat on the couch, seemingly unoccupied but obviously lost in deep thought to anyone who knows her.

Her eyes rise to mine, weary, dull, the storm within dormant. Her angular features slacken, and she bites her bottom lip, breath coming quick in her chest as she stares up at me, expectant.

"I don't want to fight," she warns, placing her palms up as a sign of surrender.

I sigh, relieved.

"Me neither," I breathe, running my long nails back through my hair and letting them dig into my skull. The pain is a welcome interlude from the nagging itch of untapped power welling over in my soul and drowning out the logic of my mind. I drop my hand, letting it stroke my thigh nervously, allowing my thick lips to twist before I exhale heavily.

"Thane— I'm sorry." The words escape me in a torrent of sudden emotion, like a dam breaking, and she gets to her feet. Stepping over the furry pile of animals, just as Cerb nips Beelz on the ear and is rewarded with a slack, soft paw to the muzzle, she comes close.

"I'm sorry too," she says, but I doubt her sincerity.

"Really?" I demand, and she frowns, looking up before letting a small smile spread across her lips.

"No— not really. I can't be sorry. If caring about you is my crime, then I'm guilty as any of the sinners down in the Indicatus Courts— but I can't repent. I won't." Her proximity doesn't send arousal through me but need, deep and raw, just to be close to her. It's an emotional, clawing desperation, which I've been quelling only through pure rage at her condemnation.

I blink once, my feathered dark eyelashes coming away from one another damp as I feel my eyes fill with tears.

"I'm so afraid—" I whisper, reaching up to her jaw and placing a gentle hand on the rough skin of her cheek.

"Tell me—" Thane orders, taking my hand from her cheek and gripping it in her own, lacing her fingers through mine and leading me over to the sofa. We sit, facing each other, bare to the severity of the situation.

"I didn't hate it— the magic. The ritual— I felt— like I was exactly where I was supposed to be," I admit, terrified of what she'll think of me.

"I know. It's a part of you. Of course, you crave it. We all crave things that aren't good for us." She's understanding, more than I deserve, and I want to break down. Unfortunately, I've been holding on for those around me for so long now I'm not sure how.

"I really screwed up, didn't I?" I ask, needing her honesty now more than ever.

"Very nearly, Luce. But it's not too late. We can fight this— together. You just have to stop. Stop with the magic. No more. I know it'll be tough, but Haedes is back now. Hopefully, things will start to get back to normal, right?" She raises her eyebrows, hopeful, and I shrug.

"I don't know about that. He's not in great shape. Though the ageing seems to have finally stopped, which is good I suppose," I relinquish, and she nods, eyes turning concerned.

"You've just admitted to me you have a problem. That's your first step right there. Now— what can I do to help?" she enquires, wiping a tear from my cheek as it falls slow and hot down over my trembling skin.

"I just— I miss you. I know how pathetic that sounds. But it's hard, being alone all the time. I'm struggling— I guess that's why I leaned on the alchemy side of things. I just needed to be in control for a second," I admit, biting my bottom lip.

Thane sidles closer to me, placing an arm around my waist and pulling me so I'm sitting across her lap. She gazes up at me, adoring every inch of my face as her jagged cheekbones approach the softness of my silhouette.

"You want time together?" she asks, voice soft like brushed velvet. I nod, bottom lip trembling as the tears well up further, threatening to choke all sound from me.

"I do—" I confess, shaking my head as she exhales, smiling.

"Oh, Luce. Don't cry, baby," she hushes me, placing a hand deep in the white roots of my hair and pulling me toward her, caressing my scalp gently. Her lips claim mine as she tilts her chin upward, and I feel her everywhere, the sensation of her open heart taking me into its embrace like a panic room overwhelming everything.

I find relief, letting the tears fall faster as I kiss her back, inhaling the scent of blackberries and pine. I cling to her like a single piece of driftwood in a sea of endless solitude, letting everything dissolve as the world around me becomes weightless and silent.

She is my island in the storm, and I can never forget just how much I need everything she is, everything she makes me.

That is exactly why her rejection is so devastating, so able to break me in more ways than I realise.

"I love you," I breathe, melting into her as I hang in the quiet muted world of her arms for just a moment. The stress of everything over the last six months, the urge to dip into the darkness of alchemy, silence at her touch, and I become deaf to all but her heavy breathing as our chests rise and fall in passionate time.

"And I love you— with everything I am." She pulls back, looking deeply into my eyes. I see fear in the depths of her soul, stirring despite being placated momentarily by our kiss. "Please, if you can't stop the desire to practice magic— think about this moment. Remember this. I never want to lose you to the dark. I couldn't watch you self-destruct like that. I'd rather die," she promises, swallowing hard.

I am utterly overwhelmed by her confession.

I didn't think it was that much of a big deal to her. I just thought she wanted something to nag me about, to take me down a notch.

I guess I was wrong. I muse, letting my hand fall from her neck where it's stroking tenderly against the plump, rapid pulsations of her carotid, and down over her shoulder, caressing the crumpled white silk of her shirt. I watch as her nipples harden visibly beneath, a display of arousal. Her lack of a bra is, as always, erotically evident and desperately hard to ignore.

"You'll think about this moment, won't you Luce?" she insists, pushing me from her lap and back into the luxurious ruby hold of the couch corner, standing, turning to face me and removing her shirt in a ripping of black buttons from white eyelets.

She reaches to take my hand, and I grab her, letting her pull me to my feet as Cerb and Beelz vacate the vicinity, moving with little grace into our bedroom in a scraping of claws against the hard, stone floor.

The heat from the fire coats the side of my body as Thane removes my jacket, untying the black silk bow that hangs around my neck and letting the high collar of my blouse fall open. The indigo stone, the remains of her power, hangs against my throat, a deep aubergine in the light from the hungry tongues of nearby flames. I see the stone reflected in her gaze as she takes it in, eyes rising to find mine only seconds before she pulls my blouse out of my pants and runs her hands up my spine.

We don't speak anymore because every single touch laid upon flesh does the talking instead. I inhale her like a drug, barely able to catch a breath between furious kissing as her warm tongue laps at mine, causing me to moan, helpless as I become limp and only too pliable in her grasp.

I kick off my shoes, sick of bending to reach her face, suddenly finding myself shorter than her, as it should be. She kisses down my throat, getting onto her knees in front of me and unzipping my pants. Her gaze smoulders, smoky, up at me as the garment falls unapologetically around my ankles and firelight flickers on bare flesh.

She doesn't let me step out of them, instead grabbing me by the ankles and licking up the inside of my thighs, kissing my groin over the top of my pewter grey thong. She's making me wet, dripping in fact, with dire need for her uninterrupted closeness.

I take back control of the situation as I pant, falling to my knees before her, ready to worship, or indeed, be worshipped. Two Goddesses, raw and bare in front of a raging hearth, bathed in the glory of a lust-fuelled blaze that can no longer be contained.

She gazes into my eyes again, renewing our connection, making even the inches between our hot and sensitive skin seem painful and unnecessarily far.

I grab the metal studded belt hanging asymmetrically off one belt loop, cupping the curve of her ass, pulling her to me and moaning at nothing more than the sensation of her full, flush torso, pushing heavy into mine as she lays me down on the rug beneath us.

Unbuttoning my shirt with slow and deliberate care, I feel the heat from the fire rush over the right side of my body like an ebbing and welcome tide. My nipples harden, pushing into her body as she works the fabric off me without shifting her weight.

Pressing me down into the carpet, she throws my shirt to one side and wraps her fingers around the curves of my shoulders. Taking me in beneath her, the firelight teases one side of my face, setting the pool of my splaying curls white hot with the hearth's proximity.

The moment soon passes and she's kissing me again, reclaiming me as hers despite the fact I could never imagine being anyone else's. Ever since I first saw her, ever since my glacial gaze met with her stormy one, we've been trapped in a blizzard of intense love and equally intense destruction. We disappointed everyone we cared about and, yet, when I'm here in her arms, I wonder how anyone who truly cared about either of us could deny us a love like this, a love unmistakably divine.

Her fingers crawl down my naked chest, hips undulating into me and placing pressure on my pelvis in all the right places. She kisses my throat, slipping her hand into the inside of my thong, exploring the extent of my physical need.

She inhales as her fingers splay out against my skin, seeking to be inside me, to remind me that I'm hers, that we're good, *great* in fact.

As she enters me, I gasp, eyes fluttering and heart racing against not only my ribs but hers. She uses her free hand to caress my breast, bringing her teeth around the outside of my nipple, teasing me. Looking up, she sees my desperate eyes, my desire for more, so ups the pace with her fingers, relentless in her passion. Crawling back up my body so we're face to face, I get lost in her eyes, in the need and desire that call me to return to her every night, no matter what.

She stares back at me, watching me so intensely I feel as if I can see into her soul, see the cracks, the chips, the immense power, and love. I'm not deterred, but enthralled, as she takes in my every moan, my every gyration, feeling me on a spiritual level as well as a physical one.

When I think I can't take any more, she presses her forehead to mine.

"Come," she commands, General of my heart.

Her voice, the breathless and sincere gasp that it is, unravels me.

My body tenses, and I clutch her as she slams down on my mouth, stifling my cries of ecstasy. I climax beneath her, not able to remember the last time I orgasmed with this kind of emotional intensity.

As she stills, working out the last of the sweet ache between my thighs, she holds me and I cry.

I've missed her, missed this.

Missed us.

The realisation that she is the only thing I want— need, replaces the craving for the dark, and as she rolls over, pulling me close to her scorching skin, we stare into the flames together, finding peace, if just for a moment.

SEPHY

I stand at the foot of the stairs, hopping from one black ankle boot to the other. Exhaling with impatience, I call to the kitchen through the shadow cast by the immense landing overhead.

"Jules, hurry up!" I call, feeling utterly useless as I stand here.

Convecting is making me short-tempered and causing me to develop a real hatred for mortal transport.

"Alright, I'm here!" Jules comes rushing from the shadows, a thick black overcoat over the top of his suit. The lines of the coat hang, clean and crisp from his silhouette, and I wonder where he gets his clothes. Maybe I should suggest he take Xion shopping—

In one hand he's holding his shotgun and in the other his cell phone. As he reaches me, he stills, staring down at his phone screen.

I watch him, curious.

"What took you so long?" I demand.

He shakes his head, exasperated.

"I had to track Xion's cell phone. How exactly did you think we were going to track him down when we have an entire city to comb through?" he asks, looking into the chamber of his shotgun as he holds it up, checking it's fully loaded. He clicks the barrel back straight against the hilt of the weapon, slinging it over one shoulder.

"You track his cell phone?" I ask, incredulous.

Jules cocks one eyebrow.

"Of course." He doesn't even blink as we walk, side by side, across the gleaming chequered marble floor and toward the front doors.

"That's such an invasion of privacy—" I mumble, and he smirks. "What?" I demand. He grins at me.

"I track yours too, you know. The cars are all fitted with tracking devices; even the plane has one. You don't think I'd ever truly let you out of my sight, do you?" My mouth falls open, shock and irritation mixing in the mother of all glares as I cock my hip.

"You do *what*?!" I growl, watching his pupils dance jovial circles inside his skull.

"Come on, Sephy, it's for your protection. Without the technology, we'd be at a loss for where to find Xion. Just be grateful for the precaution." He places a hand on my shoulder, ushering me out of the immense double doors and locking them behind us.

"My goddamn hero," I mutter, just loud enough for him to hear, as my hair bounces off the shoulders of my leather jacket, adorned with gold zippers and matching studs. Jules rolls his eyes at my sarcasm though I can't help but notice the corners of his mouth turn up.

"Well, I do make a kickass coq au vin, so if you want to go with hero, I suppose that would be acceptable."

Cheeky bugger. I scoff at him as we pace across the gravel. Jules opens the garage door, pulling the remote swiftly from his pocket.

We step inside the mechanically ascending door, and I note that my Vanquish is missing.

For god's sake, why did he have to take THAT car, I huff as Jules and I stand in front of the row of cars. I select Goldfinger, examining the hood with interested amusement.

"You didn't have the hood fixed on this yet? You're slacking!" I tease Jules who cocks an eyebrow.

"Well, I thought you might be sentimental about it. I don't know. You never have been before but with Xion it's different, isn't it?" The comment is so honest that my mouth pops open as I slip into the passenger seat. Jules takes his place next to me on the driver's side, painfully self-satisfied in expression.

"Excuse me? You work for me, remember?" I scowl, narrowing my eyes, and he twists his lips.

"Excuse me, ma'am, but I'm calling this a personal favour if you don't mind. There isn't enough money in the world for you to be able to afford to pay me to go racing off into the night after your psycho murderer and possibly more psycho half-demon— buddy. Not exactly what I'd consider a fun night in," he sasses me back, turning my argument against me as I roll my eyes.

"And what is that exactly? Shining your shoes? Polishing the silver?" I scoff, crossing my arms. The engine of the Aston Martin roars to life under his efficient fingers.

"Bloody cheek. I'll have you know I like a bit of feather dusting as much as the next man." Jules twists his mouth, trying not to laugh as we pull forward and onto the gravel, garage door closing automatically in our wake.

"Kinky," I retort, staring at him with hooded eyes.

The rain starts to pour from the sky, another early spring shower that Chicago seems to be favouring lately. We race off into the onslaught, windscreen wipers frantically working as the gate to the estate rattles closed at a steady, automated pace after we've pulled through.

It's true though, what Jules said. There isn't enough money in the world to justify him accompanying me. I mean, I could go alone, but the thought of seeing Brad chills me, making me feel dead inside all over again.

I sigh out into the heated air of the car's interior, looking out of the window and wishing the miles would pass faster as the road begins to blur and raindrops trail, like veins, across the flawless tinted glass of the pane.

Saving souls isn't easy, but then again, Haedes has never given any indication that it is.

"I'm glad you're letting me drive you. All jokes aside, you showing up in a blaze of glory isn't exactly good for keeping a low profile,"

Jules comments out into the silence, breaking my internal monologue. I recall the night that's seemingly lasted forever, cringing slightly.

"About that— I might have convected out of the middle of a crowded club after threatening some creep with a fistful of fire." I sigh, watching as he stiffens in his seat beside me, pressing on the brake as we pull to a standstill before a set of high-hanging red lights.

"No harm done— but you should be more careful," Jules scolds me. My brow furrows.

"*No harm done?* Literally, any of those people could have been recording me." I sound incredulous as the lights change and he pushes down hard on the gas. Feeling the speed push me back into my seat against my will, I continue to stare at him.

"Don't stress yourself over it. I've got you covered. I'll make some calls," Jules replies. I continue to frown, staring at him with narrow eyes and a suspicion I can no longer ignore.

"Okay, excuse me for how this is going to come across, but who the hell are you? I mean— you've been my butler for what, my entire life— and recently, I don't know. You're starting to become an actual person. With secrets and a background and everything," I complain. He cocks an eyebrow, clearly amused.

"I hate to break this to you, but I am more than a robot in a suit Sephy," he announces, and I give a dramatic but utterly fake look of shock.

"What? Not a robot!? Wait— wait a minute— does this mean I've been plugging you in wrong at night— because I've been putting the socket— oh god Jules— why didn't you tell me?" I smirk, and he stifles a laugh.

"Look, I'll keep this short and sweet. I was part of a privatised military unit called the A.D.A.M— Alternate Dimensions And Magic— division. Your father was one of the many millionaires with money invested in the project thanks to your other father— I mean— Haedes. You know what I mean— Anyway, I was hired to work for your family from within that unit. They're responsible for the protection of this world from outside dimensions and magic, and for keeping the public in the dark about the existence of such things. I've had them keeping an eye on local media for your face; so hopefully they should catch any stories on you before they hit the newsstands. Don't worry." I gape at him as he exhales a sigh from the weight of this new and slightly unbelievable information.

"So, you're like— *James Bond*— for real?" I demand as we pull onto the freeway that will take us right into the heart of Chicago.

"Not really. I hate a martini," he jokes. I scowl, concerned he's not taking this seriously. "Look, Sephy, it was a long time ago. I don't like to talk about it, and technically I'm not supposed to either. It's classified." He straightens in his seat, and I roll my eyes.

"Oh— dear lord. *Classified*? Next, you're going to blow my mind by telling me that The Underworld is— oh I don't know— real? And demons too. I might fucking lose it, dude." I shake my head, putting one foot up on the seat and resting my chin on my bare knee peeping through the rip in my jeans. Jules coughs and, once again, we both fall into silence as I wonder just how many people he's killed.

I ponder this for a while; eventually determining that I guess it doesn't matter.

After all, he really does make the best coq au vin I've ever had.

We pull up outside a shabby block of apartments in downtown Chicago. Having been in close pursuit of a glowing green dot— a nimble little fucker, I might add — which I wish was resonant of its subject, we finally find ourselves with a permanent destination.

How did he even find Brad? I wonder as the car pulls to a standstill beneath the shadow cast, intermittent, by forks of lightning slicing through the thick darkness of the night sky.

"Ready?" I ask Jules. He sighs.

"Yes, let's go." He's not wasting any time, so we step out into the rain, locking the car behind us.

Treading across a cracked and crooked concrete path that's been laid about as evenly as the Alps, my stomach starts to churn. When we reach the doorway, a flash of lightning illuminates where he's been, making me even more nervous.

The door's been smashed in and is hanging off a single hinge.

Well damn.

I remember how mad I'd been kicking in the door of Peter's study and continue with only forward motion, knowing that if I stop and think about who I'm about to come face to face with, I might just convect to the Bahamas and not come back.

I climb steel steps slick with the rainwater dripping from my heels as I race upward, the blood in my body cold yet rabid as my senses slip into overdrive. Jules follows, and I wonder how I'm going to locate exactly which apartment I'm looking for.

Luckily for me, I hear fists hitting flesh long before I have to ask that question.

Following the sound of grunts and quick, violent breathing down the dark corridor, I turn. Intermittent brightness from the lightning forks outside the shabby window straight ahead reveal the door to the crappy apartment is wide open, lock busted and dangling from the splintered frame.

I step through, the air becoming suddenly rich with the scent—

Of *my* perfume.

Straight ahead, behind a cheap television that's been purposefully smashed to pieces, a shrine of Sephy Sinclair photographs are taped crudely to the wall. It's all fucked up though, pictures of me sleeping, possibly after the night we'd spent together.

So not flattering.

Fluttering in the sharp breeze from the smashed window to my right, a single lock of hair is taped alongside the collection of images, making me want to throw up.

What the fuck?

What the fuck?

WHAT THE FUCK?

These are the only thoughts I can form as horror threatens to overwhelm my forward momentum.

No. I need to stop Xion from killing Brad. I remind myself that it's not about me. It's about him.

It stinks in here; the fragrance having been used too freely, and my nostrils burn, but it's all too soon forgotten as I turn in dramatically slow time, setting my eyes on him pinning the one person I'd hoped never to see again to a kitchen island holding a single meat cleaver.

His skin is blackened, blazing. It illuminates the terrified face of Brad orange as the molten citrus glow of his tattoos spin rapidly, demonstrating the racing of his heart.

"Xion," I say his name, not yelling, just speaking as calmly as I can, taking a lesson from Jules' book.

Xion's demon form has its hands clamped firmly around Brad's throat, and it honestly looks like he's about to turn purple and die.

Boo. Me so sad. I roll my eyes.

I can't believe I'm about to save this fucker's life.

"What?!" Xion's voice is deep as he spins, realising as he does so that it's me.

"Xion— you need to stop. Don't do this," I plead, widening my eyes and feeling Jules stir at my spine on arrival as he takes in the sick wall of fame behind me.

"Sephy, this man *murdered* you in your bed! He *must* die!" Xion growls, his deep voice feral and inhuman. I nod, taking a single step forward as I place my hands up, signalling my intention to keep things calm.

"I know— I *know* he did. But— I don't want you to become a killer too. That makes you no better than him, and I know you're a million times the man he'll ever be. Even if you are half demon—" I add with a small smirk.

Xion stills.

"Sephy, what if he does this to another girl? What if I can save—" he begins, but I cock an eyebrow.

"What? Save me? You *did* save me." I reach out again, taking another step toward him, rain dripping to the floor from my jacket sleeve. I make contact, placing my fingers gently onto the arm he's using to throttle Brad. I can feel his blood pulsing, hot and angry, beneath the surface, each muscle turned to steel. "I'm right here. See?" I use my free hand to tilt his chin towards me. I watch as he relaxes, our eyes meeting, and steps back before I have to try using any more forceful tactics.

I exhale, relief flooding me.

As he releases Brad, the prick sits up and sputters, trying to suck air into his damaged windpipe. I try to ignore him, but it becomes increasingly difficult as he starts stammering, eyes wide and staring at the side of my face like I'm the ghost of fucking Christmas past.

"Oh, hey Brad." I cock my head at him as he straightens, looking momentarily like he might fall forward and try to grab at me.

Fear rises within me, but I know I need to appear strong for Xion, so instead of doing what I want to and running, I bring my knee up solidly into his crotch, feeling his testicles explode against my kneecap in a way that's oh so satisfying. In fact, it's kind of like getting into a hot bath at the end of a long night's partying.

I watch, smiling as he crumples to the linoleum, and walk away.

"You're not going to kill him for what he did to you?" Xion whispers in my ear as I pull him after me, treading heavily over the mess of blubbering human I've just floored.

"What good would that do? It doesn't make him sorry. It makes me less human." I shrug, proceeding out of the kitchen and past Jules, moving into the other room.

I jump as the sound of a gunshot rings out, shattering the silence around us.

Spinning on one foot, I find Jules holding a smoking gun, as cliché as that is.

On the floor of the kitchen, Brad lies, head blown open by an absolute bullseye shot. There's blood dripping from the crummy kitchen cabinets and down onto the crappy blue and white chequered linoleum of the floor.

I stare at Jules, who takes a moment to blow the smoke from the end of the shotgun before turning to me.

"Right— shall we go then?" he asks, and I cock an eyebrow.

"Shall— *shall we go then*?" I repeat, horrified. "You just shot—" I begin, but Jules rolls his eyes.

"Oh, don't worry about that. Xion is absolutely right. We can't let this psycho just walk around free, but I'm not having either of you do it. He was going to reach for that knife anyway, and I've got enough blood on my hands already. One more isn't going to make much difference. Besides, he hurt you. He doesn't get to live for that." Jules doesn't wait for my response but merely walks past me. "Oh, and you should probably use that flame of yours, don't want him coming back to haunt you in Mortaria," he suggests.

I shrug, flicking my wrist absentmindedly and watching as scarlet flames engulf the body, casting Jules' slick form into shadow as he partially eclipses the blaze.

"I'm going to convect back to the Estate— you go ahead and take the car. I need to talk with Xion," I call after him, raising my voice over the crackling flames as he exits the room. He doesn't reply, so I can only assume he's heard me.

The smell of burning flesh fills the apartment, making me crinkle my nose as I turn back to Xion, taking in the face of his demon.

As the rain continues to pound down upon the jagged edges of the smashed windowpane, its sharp edges catch the lightning and shatter it, turning the flash sharper, more wicked. We stand in the middle of Brad's sitting room, staring at one another in the natural strobe effect of the passing storm.

"You shouldn't have come." Xion's face is black, charred skin covering his entire body. His tattoos have diminished considerably, but his eyes are still full of rage.

I step closer to him, looking up and giving him an earnest look.

"No. I *should* have. I can't have you going around killing for me. You have enough on your conscience as it is," I retort, sighing and shaking my head.

"I just— I can't bear the thought of him touching you— of him cutting you up." Xion's eyes turn meek, diminishing with a mix of cold anger and shame.

"But Xion, you already saved me. Isn't that enough? I'm right here— right now." I raise a hand and let it light with The Eternal Flame as I kiss him tenderly on the lips, letting myself be weak one last time. He groans into my mouth as I let my body melt into his, and he lifts me off my feet, deepening the kiss and giving me more than I bargained for.

As we stand, hanging between heaven and hell in the vice of passion, I convect us out of the apartment.

Away from the burning flesh of the killer's murder scene, of the shabby chapel where obsession and violent lust had been both worshipped and brought to life, we travel back, enthralled in the taste of one another, to somewhere I can finally be honest with Xion.

Unfortunately, it's about everything that I know is going to break him.

There's that saying, echoing through my head—

Life's a bitch, and then you die.

Turns out it doesn't get any better if someone brings you back either.

WANNABE

LUCE

THE HEELS OF MY stiletto pumps chime out against the solid gold floors of The Icon as I climb to the height of the pyramid. I pass the curious, collective gaze of sinners as the flared Lolita skirt in black lace flutters against my knees. My fishnets, which are studded with silver crystals, catch the light with every step as my hair bounces vibrant on my shoulders.

The scent of red Honeycrisp apples follows in my wake, wafting softly from my skin and into the warm surrounding air, melding with the existing scent of myrrh. Thane and I enjoyed a long bath together after talking, inducing an overwhelming and inescapable state of much-needed relaxation. This is the first time in months I've felt like my old self.

As I turn the corner into The Icon's decadent dining room, I find Anubis sitting with crossed legs on the edge of the long golden table. The white train of her dress falls around her ankles, and sinners bustle across the room with large silver platters filled with glistening treasures enough to make any mortal man lose his morals. The sound of the swinging pendulum remains, constant and metronomic in its consistency as it cuts through the air with merciless precision over and over, casting moving shadows over the hieroglyphs on the wall behind.

"Lucifer, what brings you up to The Ashen Waste?" Anubis looks surprised, and so I straighten my spine as I stroke the envelope in my fingers, silver parchment silken to touch.

"I'm here to extend an invitation, actually. I'm throwing a little party." I take several steps toward her, weaving in and out of sinners who continue to work as though I'm not even here. The scent of their body odour irks me, as does the heat coming from their bare, perspiring skin as I pass. I wish they were more adequately clothed, but I guess this is Anubis' home so if she wants Doppels half indecent then that's her right.

Reaching her, I pass the envelope and she cocks an eyebrow as her long freshly French-tipped nails snatch it from me, the smell of nail polish wafting right under my nose.

"A party? Whatever for?" She looks at me like the mere idea of a party is perhaps the most affronting thing I could have concocted before slipping her fingernail beneath the seal and yanking out the invitation.

"I think we've all been a little tense lately. Can't hurt to have a little fun, right?" I pull out a chair, taking a seat on the plush midnight blue cushions and staring up at her expectantly.

"I suppose— did you and Thane mend things?" she pries, not turning to make eye contact as she uncrosses her thighs and hooks one ankle around the other.

She summons a passing sinner with a wave of her long fingers, demanding a bottle of wine and two glasses in no polite tone.

"Mend?" I ask, wondering what she knows.

"Well, she flew over here and began shouting at me while I was dining with my son. I assumed it was because you two had been in an argument?" She shoots a look over her shoulder at me, pushing a beaded lock of dark hair behind her ear, gaze unforgiving and unimpressed.

"She did?" My heart begins to beat faster. I had no idea she was taking our problems to the other Nexus members.

"Indeed. She's worried about you, clearly. As am I," she relinquishes, staring at me earnestly as the sinner returns, scurrying in bare feet across the gilded floor with a trembling silver platter, this time it holds wine and two luxuriously adorned glasses.

Clattering, the platter is laid down on the table and Anubis uncorks the wine with a provided crystal screw, pouring us both a glass of sumptuous merlot.

Reaching for the glass she passes me, I take it. Sipping it down too fast, the sweet bite of the wine causes my mouth to flood with saliva and my nostrils to flare.

"You needn't be worried. I'm cutting out the magic, going cold turkey. Thane made me see I was being reckless—" I sigh.

Anubis laughs.

"You're not a stallion, Luce. I mean I know that Thane wants you to stop cold turkey, but that's not the only way." Anubis surprises me as I raise the glass back to my lips before pausing, watching her with interest over the rim.

"A stallion?" I enquire, confused. Licking my bottom lip, I take in more wine, blinking slowly.

"Yes— beautiful horses, right? Stunning in fact," Anubis voices this fact, which seems random at best, as she sucks down some wine with an absent-minded expression. Her eyes don't wander from the platters of precious metals being continuously hauled to and fro.

"I suppose—" I shrug.

"But that's the thing about stallions, they're beautiful— and yet, the most beloved stallions, the ones who find homes with mortals, who are cared for and treated as royalty— they're broken. Tamed."

"Hmm. Well, I'm not even sure there's much to be tamed. I'm only half God of Ancient remember? I'm pretty sure I only just had enough power to resurrect Sephy, and that's only because she's a demi-god." I don't know how to reply, simply sipping more of the sweet wine and trying not to let my ego run away with me. Thane and I have agreed it isn't good for me, so I need to stick to that.

"You are very much a stallion Lucifer, don't let anyone convince you otherwise. You just need to make sure you harness your power in the right way, and gradually. Not just jump in the deep end by performing something as extreme as a resurrection," she scolds me, swallowing hard. I watch her gullet ripple beneath the flawless, ageless gold of her skin. "Then again, I suppose dark magic *is* addictive, and dabbling is a gateway to the shadows. I guess everyone is worried that a taste for it will lead you to seek out a more potent source," she muses.

I frown.

More potent? What the hell is she talking about? What's more potent than using the magics described in the Book of The Dead?

"What's all this for anyway?" I gesture to the hoard of treasure being shifted, the lit torches of the walls turning the mass blinding with multiple, fiery reflections as the odd coin or bangle falls with a slight tinkle to the floor. Anubis scowls whenever this happens, watching as sinners scramble to retrieve every penny lost.

"I'm just having some of the underground vaults emptied, taking stock. It's easy to forget what's down there after so many years," she replies, gesturing for one of the larger silver trays being carried by two sinners, one at either end, to be brought closer.

They shuffle toward us, the sound of jingling metal ringing out against the precious walls of the room. As they get within arm's reach, Anubis opens a small wooden chest that's caught her eye. It's out of place, rustic and nothing special, so I'm intrigued by the appeal. I peer over the rim, finding only two objects inside.

"What's that?" I ask, peering at the silver chalice with bloody red and onyx stones that she pulls out first.

"I don't know. Must be important, being separated from the other chalices." She shrugs, placing it back from where it came before pulling out something far more unusual.

"I do know what this is though. Ra's temporary tether. He broke it, killed himself at the thought of working under Cronus," she explains, holding up a broken citrine ankh— which comprises now of two jagged crystal shards— into the light. It's beautiful, with sweeping canary facets glistening with the effortlessness resonant of luxurious power.

"I'm surprised you kept it," I comment, recalling Thane's story about how Anubis had resurrected her God by sacrificing her husband. It's always irked me, that fact. "Did you love him?" I ask, letting my curiosity get the better of me.

"Who, Ra?" she asks, placing the shards of crystal back into the depths of the wooden chest before nodding to the sinners, indicating they should whisk it away.

"No. Horus," I elaborate, running the tip of my finger around the rim of my glass and tapping my foot absentmindedly to the unending click of the swinging pendulum.

I stare up at her, and she smirks.

"You must understand. Marriage and love in the mortal world, at least back then, was not as you know it. I was married to Horus because my father wanted me to be looked after, wanted me in the Pharaoh's inner circle. I didn't love Horus. I barely knew him when we married. I was a— distraction to him. A shiny toy I suppose," she replies, and I frown. That sounds awful.

"Thane and I weren't exactly encouraged to be together, remember?" I comment, remembering those days, how I'd fought with everything I was to stay with her. We've both given up so much to be in each other's lives, I wonder why I'm so upset about giving up alchemy. After all, isn't it just another thing that simply pales in comparison to our connection?

"True, but at least you knew what love was. I was taken from being a child to a wife in only one night. My father's choice, not mine. It wasn't until I found Ra— truly found him, that I realised what I had with Horus wasn't love," Anubis recalls, eyes turning misty.

I can't help but feel sorry for her, it seems that wherever she's been, life has told her she isn't worthy of real love or appreciation.

"I'm sorry you went through that," I reply.

"I'm not. It made me who I am. It made me a good mother. I protect my own, and I'm not sorry for that either," she states, looking away from me as if eye contact is painful for her. I exhale.

"That's what I kept thinking when I was using the dark arts. I mean, I have all this power, and most of the time I feel utterly helpless to do anything to aid those around me. I guess it just got frustrating—" I explain, and Anubis shrugs.

"I once worshipped a god who was selling what you're buying into Luce, I've seen what happens to people consumed by those magics. It's something I think you're honestly best to use but only with caution and when absolutely necessary. After all, it *is* half of who you are. Thane can't expect that to just disappear because she doesn't like it. Still, caution should always be exercised in these matters. Always," she responds.

I reach out, placing a hand over the top of hers.

At the touch, she turns, looking back over her glistening, tan shoulder and meeting my gaze. The dark mahogany irises of her eyes recede as her pupils dilate and she takes me in, surprised by the gesture.

"Thank you," I breathe, knowing now that perhaps I hadn't been crazy in thinking Thane was being unreasonable wanting to ignore that part of my lineage.

I'm so torn, so utterly broken in half by what I want and what my soul fears it needs. It's easy to forget when Thane's right in front of me, when she's touching me, but then once she takes flight into the bloody skies once more, I seem, always, to be left wondering.

"Anyway, I had better get going. I've got more invites to hand out," I inform her, placing the half-finished glass of wine down on the table beside me and getting to my feet.

"Thane not helping you?" she demands, cocking one eyebrow.

When did she get so interested in my relationship?

"No, she's out on recon again, Annie and Dolly are helping me do the rest." I sigh, and Anubis frowns.

"You don't sound happy about that—" she pries, and I shrug, taking a step forward and pivoting back to face her.

"I just hate it when she's out there. She's most vulnerable in raven form, and it's only so long until the Demon Lords catch onto that fact, especially with Pandora throwing them all into a frenzy," I sigh.

Anubis purses her lips tightly, the mere mention of the name putting her on visible edge.

"I assume you will have tight security at this event?" she enquires, no humour in her tone, her gaze condescending.

"Of course, can't have a repeat of our last little gathering. That was a complete disaster," I recall, and she gives a small jerk of her chin, indicating she agrees.

"You might want to pass Haedes on the invite list if you're looking for peace and quiet," she smirks, but I'm annoyed at the comment. She hasn't even asked how he is.

"I don't think he'll be up for it anyway. He's not looking that great, to be honest. Thanks for your concern though," I snap, turning on my heel and moving to exit the room.

"What a shame." I hear Anubis call after me, tone snide.

She's starting to get on my nerves, despite her seeming to understand my call to the dark better than anyone, and that is not a place anyone wants to be.

PANDORA

I return from the mortal world, the stench of fear still uncanny in my nostrils and the sound of screams forever ringing in my ears. Banshees explode back into existence on either side of me seconds before the portal closes, jaws dripping with cold bone jelly from their latest kill. It spatters down onto the blackened cobbles as their paws contact the ground.

Standing on the main street of what had once been a kingdom of ancient gods, of suffering, I look up to Mount Mallum. It, as always, dwarfs everything in its shadow; a reminder that even the Demon

Lords, their Kindred, are a part of something bigger, and that in the larger scheme are but specks.

The aroma of molten rock and sulphur overcomes me as I tear my gaze from the mighty height of the volcano and begin to stride ever onwards, placing the box back into my innermost pocket, Banshees at my heels.

I have their loyalty now because I am the one feeding them, but I know in an instant they could turn on me, especially if it means the harvest of their next meal.

I tread past raised stone platforms, displaying the outlines of veins of blood long since licked dry by desperate, hungry Succubi. There had once been puddles of it, dripping down from the rusted guillotines, stocks, and the frayed rope of the hangman's noose that still dangles, motionless and empty now, in the still air of the Mortarian day. The streets once ran red with blood, with death, but now only the memories of those last breaths, of those most fruitful ends, remain.

I up my pace, the breathing of the Banshee becoming frantic, excited. I don't want to deal with them when the energy from the ichor they've just consumed takes hold, so hurry to one of the many identical stone huts that used to house sinners between torture sessions.

Entering through the gaping doorway, I find only warm, muggy shadow and the scent of flesh— of bone, lingering in the air. I hear slow, snarling breaths as tiny primal minds fill with dreams of carnage, of murder.

She stirs, sensing me, among the pile of matted fur, white eyes glowing out from the dark as she signals for me to venture deeper into her den.

"Pandora—" The Demon Lord's voice is dreamy as she treads, barefoot, over tangled paws and twitching tails, coming close and clutching my wrists in her bony, warm fingers.

"It was a successful trip," I inform her, and she smiles.

"We know. We saw," she sighs with nostalgic longing, breath rich with the scent of death. The hairs on the back of my neck stand on end.

"I'll be back later," I promise her, watching as the Banshees who accompanied me collapse atop the pile, damp muzzles sporting nostrils that flare, taking in breaths laced with the stench of butchered meat. In the claustrophobic and warm darkness of the hut, the scent quickly becomes overwhelming.

"Farewell Pandora—" Lilliana waves, slow and eerie like a ghost as her wild and unkempt outline disappears into the far depths of the room.

Making my way out into the street once more, I take my leisurely time, taking in the crumbling stone ruins, the bleached bones strewn across the cracked and charred sidewalks with sick satisfaction. I wonder what the fall of this place looked like, wonder whether the sinners had flailed or cheered at the defeat of those gods and goddesses that had made their afterlife a living misery.

What's worse when you're in that position, the unknown terror of new masters or the grating cruelty of those you already know?

"Pandora," My name is called as I move past a wilting garden centred around a stone monument to Delyria. The stone is always liquid in the way it's been carved, smoke billowing from the base to form the silhouette of a woman with many faces, each one blank with not a single feature to be seen.

I spin, caught off guard, finding her propped atop a metal railing laced through with withered ivy and crisp, dead, black roses.

"Anubis," I voice my surprise, eyebrows rising on my forehead. I hadn't expected to see her for at least a week, if not longer. "What are you doing here?" I demand, stepping under a twisted iron archway draped thick in decorative spider webbing. The stench of floral rot grows stronger; the antithesis to what had once been delectable dark blooms and shadow-casting succulents.

Treading onto the garden's knifelike and charred blades of grass, I stare at her, ignoring the audible crunch of decay beneath my soles.

"An opportunity has presented itself, so I have returned as promised. I thought we should discuss it," she announces.

I keep my expression still, unfeeling.

"We should— with the Demon Lords," I add, watching her with half interest as she leaps, feline in her elegant and agile posture, from where she's leaning and onto the grass opposite me.

"You're sure?" she asks, and I smile, batting my lashes in innocent plight.

"Oh yes, whatever you have to share you need to share with them too. After all, without their Kindred, their alliance, we cannot hope to achieve our goals," I remind her. She looks uncomfortable at the suggestion; the violet velvet of her cloak pulled closer around her as she fiddles with the gold ties which close around her throat. Her eyes drop, two rich and knowing pools of dark cocoa, to the ground.

"Very well. Shall we?" she asks, eyes darting in decisive motion to my face as she shakes out her lustrous dark hair.

"I'll go and get Lilliana; you gather the others. I believe they're playing poker in the main room. Though I don't know why; nobody can beat Abraxis anyway—" I comment.

She smiles, though the expression is as forced as they come, like a puppeteer is yanking her strings far too hard and with obvious disdain.

As I turn to exit the rotting monumental garden, I ponder Anubis' character. She's a strange entity to be sure, betraying those closest to her, and yet seemingly averted, repulsed even, by the implications of her actions.

It is possible that she and I will one day face-off, as our motives will not align forever. However, that is tomorrow's problem, and today, she's proving quite the ally.

In the central meeting chamber of The Halls of Antiqua, I arrive, finding all the Demon Lords gathered except one. Lilliana moves from my side, taking her seat at the table as Anubis looks down on the Lords from her immense height, imposing her shadow upon Katerina's gaunt face.

"So, why the intrusion on poker?" Gorgon asks, putting his arms behind his head. Abraxis snorts, smirking to himself with devilishly contoured lips.

"What?" he demands, glaring daggers at Abraxis across the table as his chest inflates inside the bottle-green linen of his suit. It's crinkled, reminding me of snakeskin right before it sheds.

"Why do you care, you were getting slaughtered anyway, *as usual*," Abraxis taunts him, and Gorgon slams his fist down on the already cracked table, rising in a sudden jerk of momentum to his feet. Tiny stones skitter from beneath his knuckles, tumbling down the crack central to the table, now forever lost.

I lean against the mirror on the wall behind me, watching them with a semi-amused fixation bordering on unwarranted obsession.

"Hey, I almost had your guts for garters, Abraxis!" Gorgon exclaims, and I roll my eyes.

Boys. So goddamn predictable.

"Yes, well, I have an opportunity. I think I know how we can obtain the items we will need to resurrect Ra," Anubis relinquishes the information, ignoring the two bickering men as inconsequential, and turning her attention only to the silent members of the group.

"How?" Barbas demands immediately, speaking up as he slicks his long grey hair back against his skull with one hand. His suit is dusted with webs, noticeable in stark and glistening silver contrast against the thick black material of his jacket and pants.

Anubis reaches into the inside of her cloak, pulling out a silver envelope and dropping it onto the table between them. Abraxis reaches forward, swiping it up before anyone else has the chance, pulling out a thick piece of card, and eyeing the typeface.

"A party?" he laughs, and Anubis nods.

"Yes—"

"We've been here before. We tried infiltrating The Exilia using a large-scale event last time—" Gorgon sighs, exasperated.

Anubis exhales, sassing him right back.

"Yes, but this is different. We don't want to kill or kidnap anyone; we just want to get in and out while everyone is distracted. It's called *subtlety*. You might have heard of it, Abraxis?" Anubis purses her lips and Katerina stirs at her left side.

"What do you want to steal exactly?" she enquires, ribcage expanding and contracting with an audible creak as her ribs protrude against her thin white flesh. Anubis crosses her arms over her breasts, authoritative in every sense of the word. It is a wonder to me sometimes that she let Haedes take Mortaria from her without a fight.

"Well, we need The Book of The Dead for a start," Anubis reminds them. Gorgon smirks, rolling his sleeves up and leaning back in his chair.

"And what are you going to do with that? Use it as a paperweight?" he demands. She rolls her eyes yet again at his lack of faith, pushing a beaded lock behind her shoulder as she leans forward, both hands palm down on the table. Her fingernails scratch against the stone, grinding down with her irritation.

"Don't be so dense! Of course not. While you're getting the book, I'll be stealing Thanatos' tether."

Now it is my turn to be confused.

I stare at Anubis, straining my neck.

"What good is that? Thanatos can't resurrect anyone," I remind her, wondering if she's lost it.

"Because we're going to capture Thanatos and use her life force—she's the only one powerful enough. You know her heritage—" Anubis cocks an eyebrow. I shrug, wondering why that's important.

"Excuse me?" I demand, and she sighs, exasperated.

"How the *hell* did you manage to capture a demi-god? You're hopeless!" she scowls, and I give her a look of warning, violet irises flashing dangerously in the half-light.

She calms herself as the Demon Lords visibly tense; remembering who it is she's surrounded by. "Thanatos is pure— *very* pure. As I'm sure was Erebus' intention when he seduced his own daughter, Nemesis. Thanatos and her twin Hypnos are the result, it was his wish to try and keep his bloodline as pure as possible. We can use that. You'll need someone with that kind of energy to bring back another pure god—"

"Yes— but without Lucifer—" I begin.

Anubis shoots me a glare this time, silencing me.

"Lucifer will be persuaded. Once we capture Thanatos in her weakened raven form, we will give Lucifer an ultimatum. If Luce refuses to take the energy from Thane's living body and resurrect Ra, we will smash the tether and release Thanatos to The Higher Plains."

I feel my eyes widen.

It's *genius.*

Lucifer would never let Thanatos die. She'll have to perform the ritual.

"The only problem we have is that Lucifer isn't as powerful as she needs to be to bring back a full-blown god," Anubis adds.

Lilliana shifts, the bird's nest of her tangled dark hair an indistinguishable onyx mass around her head and shoulders, like an inescapable shadow she carries everywhere she goes.

"So— why are we having this discussion?" she demands, impatient as her voice echoes out in a husky yet hollow echo. Anubis reaches into her cloak once more, pulling out a silver chalice and slamming it down onto the table.

"Is that?" Barbas leans forward, squinting at the cup.

"The chalice of Uranus," Anubis declares, smug. I watch as she quickly takes it back up off the table, clearly concerned one of the Demon Lords is going to try and take it.

After watching Abraxis swipe that invitation off the table, I'm not surprised.

"So, you're going to take her to the—" I ask and Anubis smirks, interrupting me.

"Well, first things first— we need to pull off stealing the book. It's not going to be easy. Haedes' vault is protected by all kinds of spells, I doubt your box will work, at least inside," Anubis informs me, and I wonder why she hadn't mentioned Haedes' vault before. I didn't even know he had a vault.

I wonder what kind of artefacts he keeps in there—

"So, what do you need from us?" Barbas demands, seemingly contented with Anubis' plan. I'm surprised. Usually, he's the one resisting all ideas that don't originate between his own oversized ears.

"A distraction. You've been growing Banshee and Succubi forces. Maybe it's time to display that to The Nexus, make them aware that you've not just been sitting idle. We also need to bait Thane close to the Kingdom if we're going to capture her in raven form. Pandora, I'd expect you to use your box in this instance, to unleash the demons in The Exilia," Anubis instructs.

"I see, and who will be going in for the book?" I ask her, and she frowns.

"I was thinking about that. I'd like to take in some of your recruits as personal security. They won't be recognisable like demons. I got those pendants you asked for too," she announces, and I wonder how long she's had to think about this. "It won't be an immediate theft. That would be too obvious. After things have calmed down for a few hours the recruits will lift the book and drop it off with you Pandora at an agreed time and place. Hopefully, it'll be a while before anyone notices it's gone."

"You really think this might work?" I ask her.

"I do. I think if you'd have had me on your side last time at the Exilia, you'd have succeeded in killing Sephy Sinclair as well." I feel this comment is slight overkill, a little cocky even, but then knowing who she is and where she's been, it's hardly surprising.

"And what— dare say, would you think if I asked you why you're helping us?" Barbas demands.

Anubis smiles, the white of her long skirt coming up filthy as she circles the table, moving closer to Barbas.

Bending down close to him, she gets within inches of his acutely angled nose, a brave move to be sure.

"I'd tell you to look into me and know my fear. My fear that my son will never reach his rightful place as ruler of Mortaria with Haedes on the throne. With Ra, at least he stands a chance." Barbas blinks, eyes turning white momentarily before he smiles at her, reaching out to touch her cheek, transfixed. She moves back before he can lay a finger on her, elegant in even this swift act.

"I see," is his only response as he relaxes back into the uncomfortable stone of his seat. If he's contented, then she must be telling the truth.

Barbas is certainly no fool.

"And what makes you think that with us in charge, you'll get that chance?" Abraxis asks, shrewd as always.

"Ra is more powerful than you can imagine. I've served him my entire life. I do not doubt that his resurrection will escalate my son to his rightful position, or at least gain him more power than he has now." Anubis seems so sure of this, and I wonder why.

Is it a flaw in her logic?

After all, after resurrecting Ra last time, he killed himself out of disgust at her alliance with Cronus.

The Demon Lords don't reply, nodding collectively, but I can tell what they're thinking.

They don't want her ruling over them, no more than they want Haedes. I have proven my loyalty to them and their kindred, having no stake in Mortaria other than using it to get my revenge on Zeus. Is Anubis so stupid that she's under the impression we're doing this for her benefit?

Perhaps.

I suppose only time will tell.

13

ETERNAL FLAME

SEPHY

WE REAPPEAR, WRAPPED IN one another's arms, kissing desperately against the wide trunk of a tree bathed in the dim light of dawn.

"Xion, stop," I breathe against his lips, feeling his erection grow against me as the heat between us consumes him. I resist as the flames flicker into nothingness from my convection, placing my hands on his chest and pushing him away.

"What? What's wrong?" he enquires, face glowing orange in the persistent fire of sunrise.

"I can't do this," I whisper, eyes beginning to prick with tears. His eyes become concerned, caring, so I turn away, unable to hold his gaze.

"Do what? Was I too— was I hurting you?" he asks, sweeter than I deserve.

"No. I just can't do this with you. It's too hard. I'm not strong enough," I admit, heart hammering inside my chest as the last taste of pomegranate and fire dissipates from my bottom lip and the burn from his stubble against my cheek fades.

"Sephy— you're the strongest person I know. I don't understand—" He stands, palms open, bereft from where before they were clutching my face. I exhale, pain radiating through my chest unlike anything I've ever experienced.

"I just— I don't know what you expect from me. You brought me back from the dead, but we only spent one night together. I'm not looking for a relationship, for feelings. The only thing that leads to is pain. Especially when it's you and me." I straighten my spine against the ridges of bark that press into my skin, knowing I have to be firm. I need to kill any and all hope within him. I can't leave him hanging on by even a single thread; it's just not fair.

"What's that supposed to mean? That night we spent together— it was the best night of my life, Persephone," he confesses, using my full name. He knows I wouldn't let anyone else get away with calling me that, and I feel the tears coming faster, threatening to choke me out because he sounds so goddamn honest, so vulnerable.

He takes a step toward me, and I want to back away, cursing internally at the solid trunk preventing my escape.

His rugged features, the almond curves of his eyes, the definitive line of his jaw and his sculpted lips beckon to everything in me, everything weak— and yet, I put out a hand, stopping him before he can get too close.

"You and I aren't good for each other, Xion. We had— amazing sex. Out of this world sex. But— I'm the daughter of a god, and you're the son of a Demon Lord. We have prophecies to consider; we have people who would use those feelings to tear us apart. It's better to stop this before it begins," I whisper, barely able to make my voice louder than the surrounding breeze.

"But I thought—" Xion begins, and I cock an eyebrow.

"That we'd fall in love and have babies? Settle down in a little house on the edge of The River Styx?" I demand, tears unrelenting as they continue to trickle silently down my cheeks.

"I— I—" Xion stutters, eyes wildly searching mine for some sense of how he can change my mind. I feel cruel, dirty, knowing that what I'm saying is a lie. I felt that same hope that night, felt the almost irresistible pull to stand by his side and never leave.

"I thought he was you!" I blurt, voice exploding from me in a burst of unexpected volume as I turn away from him, tilting my head sideways and letting a single red lock blow across my cheek. It sticks, becoming damp with hot, salty tears.

"What? I don't understand—" Xion demands, voice gruff, void of emotion despite the fact I know he's anything but. He places rough fingertips on my wrist, but I pull away, afraid to be weak. Afraid to hope. Especially when it comes to someone who had given me something I had thought was lost to me forever. True and unmistakable happiness.

"Brad. I never would have let him get on top of me if I didn't think he was you. I— I let my guard down. I hoped— and I was killed for it. There's no place in my life for anything that makes me that vulnerable, Xion. Not ever. I can't go through that again," I implore him, and he drops his gaze now, looking at his feet as he finally understands.

"You're not strong enough— to lose this. That's what you're saying, isn't it?" he asks me, and I nod, feeling pathetic as I close my eyes and let loose another torrent of rapid-falling tears. "So, you'd rather not have anything to do with me?" he demands. I open my eyes, shaking my head.

"It's not like that. I want to be friends— I want you in my life. I can't imagine not knowing you," I reach out, trying to touch him now, but instead, he steps away.

"It's okay Sephy. No need to explain. Sorry about the misunderstanding." He pulls the collar of his jacket up, so it crowds his throat like armour, and turns to move away.

"Xion, wait—" I call after him as he turns, desperation clutching at me as our friendship slips through my fingers. He's becoming yet more sand in the hourglass of my life, weighted lead-like with misery.

He doesn't reply, and I simply watch him walk away, not moving to go after him. Too afraid to be weak, to move, and yet too shattered to be brave.

Rooted to the spot, I fall down the length of the tree trunk and onto my knees, quivering as nausea rises quickly in my throat. I cry silently as the fresh rising sun turns everything around me ablaze. I've never had this kind of reaction to someone leaving before, and I'd honestly give anything for it to stop, but I can't go after him, can't hurt him that way when I have nothing to offer.

No heart to give, no words left to comfort.

I'm just too fucking broken to be any good to anyone.

Especially him. The one person who constantly makes me feel pale by comparison with his permanent and righteous plight to do what's noble.

Even if I had an open heart, emotions to give, and dreams of a future to share with someone, I have no choice now but to face the truth.

Xion is just too good for me.

It's been two days, two days of too much ice cream and not enough sleep. I've been awake all night.

Stupid, stupid, stupid.

This is my own damn fault of course because I destroy everything I touch. Some people were made for relationships, for flowers and boxes of shitty Belgian chocolates, for wedding vows, for inspirational montages set to *Eternal Flame* by The Bangles.

Not me. The only eternal flame I'm interested in is the one in my hand, which will burn your fucking white picket fence and gardenias right to the goddamn ground.

I'm not your average girl. But then again, he knew that.

As I raise a spoonful of Ben and Jerry's *Chunky Monkey* to my lips, this being the healthiest breakfast I could stomach — because bananas — I let my teeth clamp down hard on the spoon, anger washing over me and trying to drown out the sound of my guilt.

He knew that. The thought occurs to me again, echoing out in a haunting realisation as I wonder why I'm blaming myself in all this.

I haven't done anything wrong.

He knew me, knew who I was. It's not my stupid fault he's suddenly all wide-eyed, and his heart has turned the consistency of fucking tapioca.

He's supposed to be a freaking badass, a demon, and instead he's walked off like what— a kicked puppy?

A basset hound, no less.

The thought of his sad eyes makes me want to hurl.

Asshole, I cuss, shoving more ice cream into my face and chomping too hard on a walnut coated in chocolate.

I'm wearing a black silk camisole and matching shorts, and my hair is pulled up in the same top knot it had been thrown into right before Jules and I had been unceremoniously called by some stupid moral obligation to stop Xion committing murder on my behalf.

He brought me back, he risked the universe and put me through the infinite pain of resurrection, so what? So, I could be his *girlfriend*? A lesser woman, a woman not half hellfire, would think that was sweet I suppose.

Oh fuck no.

At least I've been clear with him, made it a clean fracture between us. Sure, I'll miss him, but I'd been just fine without him— hadn't I?

I think back to those days as I lean back against a landslide of fluffy pillows stacked against the dark wood of the headboard. I'd been fierce, unstoppable. It wasn't until this crap with the Demon Lords and being hunted made me vulnerable, made me need him, that the real problems had begun to snowball. What is it about him and his presence, those eyes, that make my sanity and logic run in the other direction? Why is it that he's turned me into a complete and utter emotional car wreck?

As I hear a knock at the door, I realise that perhaps I'm not forgetting my place at all. Perhaps he's forgetting his.

It's time I remind him of who I am.

"Come in," I call, watching as Jules enters my suite at a brisk pace.

"How's it going? The moping? Need another pint to go with the sunrise?" he asks me, face serious.

"Nope. I think I'm about done being a hot mess. Thanks though," I reply. He smiles, green eyes catching the rising sun and reflecting it at me as he stands opposite the window.

"I was hoping you'd say that. You have a visitor," he reveals. My heart drops right through to my ass.

"Is—" I begin, but he shakes his head, reading my panicked expression like an open book he has memorised by heart.

"The lovely Miss Lucifer— she's waiting for you downstairs," he explains, blushing before he dismisses himself.

"I'll be down in a minute," I call after him, reaching over to the bedside table and plonking the tub of mostly eaten ice cream down on the surface, spoon protruding up like a flag of surrender from its depths.

I haul my ass out of bed, pacing across the room and proceeding to pull a black silk robe, which has been draped across the armchair by the window, over my shoulders. The early morning sunlight has fallen, dappled, upon it, and I hum slightly as I tie it around my waist and the warm fabric caresses my skin.

Padding out of the room, my bare feet kissing the runner gently as I find more spring in my step than I've had for a while.

I don't need a man, don't need anyone. I'm fine being my own support. Totally fine.

As I pass under the archway partitioning the hallway to my bedroom from the landing, I see her. She's standing in the entrance hall at the foot of the staircase, all six feet of legs and fabulously radiant skin pulling all light from the room and spotlighting it on her face. It's almost as if she has her own gravitational pull, which is easy to forget when she's surrounded by the other gods in Mortaria.

"Hey, Luce. What brings you to this side of The Hollow?" I query, taking the steps in quick time as I descend toward her. I catch her eyes tracing the scar on my chest where my robe is falling open, and so pull it closed as quickly as I can.

"Uh— I wanted to give you this." She hands me a silver envelope, pale blue eyes rising quickly to my face.

"Coupon for twenty percent off my next resurrection? Buy one get one free?" I cock my head, smirking, and she laughs, smiling up at me. Her face is so beautiful, so almost cruel in its perfection; I can't help but forget where I am for a moment as I stand on the bottom step, envelope still clutched in my motionless fingers.

"I would hope you won't be needing one! Aren't you going to open it?" she urges as I lower myself off the step and tear my gaze from her. I'm instantly meek as she towers head and shoulders over me, her crimson stiletto heels giving her even more height than usual.

I gesture for her to take a seat on one of the newly upholstered sofas in the small waiting area by the left side of the balustrade, which she does with a kind of grace that can only be described as wholly unnatural.

As I round the edge of the sofa, black mottled fabric beckoning my weary soul, I slip my fingernail underneath the seal and tear open the envelope.

Inside, there's an invitation to a party at the Exilia.

You've got to be kidding me. I give her a quizzical expression.

"You're throwing a party? And you want *me* to come— after last time? Really?" I demand, wondering momentarily if she wants to use my being alive as some sort of party trick.

"Yes, I thought you could come and work security, but also attend as a guest if you want. I thought it would be good to show you're back on your feet. Stop anyone getting any ideas. I mean, the Demon Lords will probably be watching somehow as they always seem to be. I want them to know you're not a viable target for any future schemes." When she's finished, I nod slowly, her plan makes a lot of sense. Except for the fact I have no desire to return to Mortaria any time soon.

"Well, I don't really belong in that world anymore. I don't exactly know what I'm doing with my life yet. I'm still adjusting, but I'm sure I'll work it out. I think I've had enough danger for a lifetime, I just want to be on my own and have fun," I express. She looks surprised.

"What about Xion?" she demands.

I sigh.

"What about him?"

"Well, aren't you two— you know?" She makes a rude gesture with both hands and I scowl.

"He told you?!" I exclaim, and she nods.

165

"The night you were murdered, he came to me looking for a solution to that little prophecy The Fates had warned you about," she elaborates, and I sigh out, placing my hand to my forehead.

"Oh, Jesus. I didn't know— it was just one night," I exclaim, brushing the idea of romance away entirely.

She squints at me.

"I don't think he saw it that way," she replies, face stony.

"Really, I hadn't noticed that! What with him staring at me like I'm the fucking sun!" I begin to roll my eyes but can't complete the gesture as my head falls too easily into my hands. Luce frowns at me as she crosses her legs and presses her hands together atop her knee.

"Did you break it off?" she enquires. I nod vigorously, unable to look at her.

"Of course! It's not like I love him; it was just sex. I mean we're friends but—" I feel myself start to ramble. Luce raises a hand.

"No need to explain. I get it. If you're not in that place with someone, you just aren't. I wouldn't know. I've only ever been with one woman," she reveals, and I feel myself unable to hide my surprise or my awe.

"What's that like?" I ask, and she smiles.

"Pleasurably consistent. We all need good sex, right?" she demands, and I smirk.

"Of course, I mean the sex Xion and I had was the best I've ever— it was phenomenal. Boy's got stamina," I compliment him unknowingly, and she licks her bottom lip, eyes glinting wicked.

"Well, I'm sure you'll be glad of those memories when you find your next conquest. After all, I'm sure supernatural sex is hard to compete with, again, not that I'd know. It's so good with Thane I can't imagine anyone else in that way," she admits.

"Well, I mean we're still friends— me and Xion. It's not like I'm cutting out of my life totally," I add, a flicker of panic bursting into life within my gut.

"I'm sure it'll all turn out fine. After all, you might have just given him the confidence to realise he's worthy of love after all. It wouldn't surprise me if he found someone to settle down with after what you did. He owes you a great deal." She gets to her feet, the dark lace of her dress hugging the curves of her lithe body.

"I owe him too— I mean, still being alive and all— plus he did that thing with the car and the suicidal drive across The Ashen Waste. That was pretty cool," I recall, a feeling of urgency pulling at me in a way entirely unnatural.

"True. True. So, you'll be at the party? It's tonight. You're the last person on my list left to invite. I'm actually about to go back and start getting things ready," she adds. I get to my feet, rubbing my now sweaty palms down the front of my bare legs.

"Um— is Xion going to be there?" I ask, trying to be subtle, but she smiles, a look of satisfaction on her face that makes me wholly suspicious.

"Of course, you both have plus ones too, so if you want to bring someone, I guess he might be bringing a friend or something. Maybe you could bring that butler of yours? He's pretty cute." She gives me a wicked grin, and I wonder if she realises what she's doing.

Probably. I mean, she is the devil after all.

"Oh. I'll be there. I'll even get there early to scope out the guests before the event. Can't be too careful after last time, right?" I exclaim, overly enthused, and she grins.

"Of course not. Awesome! Thanks, Sephy!" She turns on her heel, striding across the lobby as her black gossamer skirt billows out, an elegant shadow in her wake.

After a second, she pauses and turns back. "Oh, while I think of it, you might want to visit Haedes on your way there too. He's looking pretty— *withered* since the ritual. I think a visit from you would cheer him up." At her words, I'm surprised to find myself concerned. Haedes risked a lot to bring me back, which means he really does care about me in a selfless way.

I vow to go and drop in on him before the festivities begin, but first I have a more pressing problem.

I have nothing to wear, and Xion might be bringing a 'friend'.

Over my dead goddamn fucking body—

I mean— next time.

"*Jules!*" I bellow, voice ringing out violently against the walls of the room and causing the crystals of the chandelier to tinkle.

"What?! What is it?" He comes running from the kitchen, face red, eyes wide and alarmed.

"Get your goddamn coat. We're going shopping."

"Do I look okay?" I demand, looking at myself in the mirror and then back through the open closet doors.

Jules is sitting on the edge of my bed, bored.

I sigh; I'm paying him for his time, so he can at least pretend to be interested. There are hundreds of bags strewn across the floor, half of them still unopened with crepe paper ripped and receipts sprinkled on the carpet like ridiculously expensive confetti.

"For the fiftieth time today. Yes. You look magnificent. Radiant. You shine with the light of a thousand suns."

At this last comment, I scowl.

"Don't say that. I'm serious. Do you think this is too— *obvious*?" I ask, looking down at the floor-length gown. It's black velvet; plain, classy even as it hugs me from head to toe. It's off the shoulder as Luce had said the theme was the fifties, and my hair is curled against my head, held in place with a million grips courtesy of Jules and a whole lot of complaining on my behalf. My lips are red, my eyeliner applied in vintage fashion, and I can see my shoes peeping out through the high slit in the side of my skirt.

I'm wearing a dress.

And I never wear dresses, at least not in my right mind.

Ever.

"Sephy why are you doing this? This isn't— you. I mean you look gorgeous but— why a dress? Aren't you always saying how you can't kick ass in a skirt?" Jules demands, reaching over and picking up a flute of champagne off the tray in front of him. He downs the entire contents, gasping for air when he's done.

"I'm doing this, Jules, because if *he* brings some freaking gorgeous woman, *I* don't want to look like last season's reject bin!" I scowl. He shakes his head.

"But you don't even *like* Xion!" he exclaims, looking at me like I've gone utterly mad.

"So? So, what?! That doesn't mean I want him wrapped up in some other harlot. I'm the only harlot around here. You got that?!" I stomp my foot.

"Don't scowl like that. You look like an evil clown with that lipstick in a frown," Jules taunts me, face deadpan, and I twirl once more.

"You know, this would have been over a lot faster if you hadn't got drunk off all the free booze they coax you with in designer stores. You're always warning me about those— what the hell happened?" I gape at him.

"You were three hours in one store! I was bored!"

"Well, I've never bought a dress before! I was nervous!" I scowl, and he rolls his eyes.

"I am well aware. I have had the pleasure of listening, for the entirety of today, to your internal monologue, which sadly resembles that of a fourteen-year-old going to prom. I just want to go downstairs and knock myself unconscious with one of the industrial-sized rolling pins— please, Sephy. I'm *begging*—"

"Then tell me, for the fifty-first time today, that I look alright!" I cock my hip and then an eyebrow to match, sticking my leg out and showing him the most flattering angles of my silhouette.

"Yes, oh annoyingly sarcastic queen of leather and sass, I approve of the dress. Can I go now?" he demands, slamming the champagne flute back down on the tray in front of him so it rings in a ghastly high pitch. I huff.

"Fine! Get out! It's not like you have any style anyway. You and Xion, between you, are like an advert for freaking outfit cloning!" I shout as I hear him chuckle, scurrying away down the hall.

Our relationship has certainly become a lot less formal these last few weeks; then again, the guy pulled staples out of my y incision, so I guess you could say we're past the whole handshake phase.

I take one final look in the mirror, taking as deep of a breath as I can manage in the corset negligee I'm wearing underneath the gown. I must be crazy. I'm wearing a dress for a man I don't love, who I just dumped, and who probably wants nothing to do with me— just so I don't have to suffer watching him all over some other woman.

Xion might be driving me crazy.

But why?

You have feelings for him— duh!

That's what everyone would say, but this is me. I don't get feelings. In fact, I flee from feelings like they're the plague— batting them off left and right with my baseball bat made entirely of sarcasm and sass. So— what the hell is up with me?

Sephy Sinclair doesn't get jealous. Especially not of imaginary women.

And yet, here I am, dressed to the nines—

I'm too afraid to feel for him, but too attached to let him go.

That's the truth of all this.

A truth I'll most certainly be too stubborn to admit. A truth I'll deny until the day I die—

Again, I mean.

I arrive in a torrent of unexpected blue flames, finding Haedes playing checkers with Yama in front of the dead hearth.

"Not on the rug, not on the rug!" he yells, leaping to his feet and grabbing a blanket hung over the back of his chair. He swoops in at my feet, smothering the flame before I have the chance to leap out of the way.

"Oh shit. Sorry!" I exclaim, and he looks up at me, quizzical in expression, from where he's crouched by my feet, patting down the potential blaze.

"It's fine. Karma. I did the same thing to Luce recently. You'd think I'd know better by now—" he mutters, shaking his head as his eyes widen suddenly at my appearance.

"You look—" he breathes, and I roll my eyes, giving him a hand and pulling him to his feet as I hear his knee joints give a noticeable click. As we reach eye level, I can see immediately what Luce meant. His hair is almost entirely silver, his skin thin and beginning to wrinkle with old age. I stare at him, and he stares back at me before simply saying, "—just like your mother." He swallows hard, and I wonder what he's thinking as his eyebrows knit together too fast.

"Wait a minute— did you just convect here using the resurrection flame?" he demands, conveniently changing the subject.

"Yeah, I've been meaning to talk to someone about that—" I express, shifting uncomfortably in front of him atop my heels. Yama stares between us, his long silver robe blanketing his form as his golden cornrows and periwinkle skin glow cold in the light of the room.

"That explains why I can't seem to summon so much as a blue spark lately I suppose—" he grumbles. I look at him, wondering what he wants me to say.

Does he want me to be sorry?

Because you know, I didn't ask to be brought back to life.

From behind him, Yama clears his throat, uncrossing his legs beneath the stark monochrome stone of the free-standing game board.

"You know, Haedes, this might be a solution to that little problem we've been discussing while I've been annihilating you at checkers," he adds, smirking.

Haedes shoots him a look.

"Solution to what problem?" I demand.

Haedes sighs, clearly irritated Yama brought this up.

"Yama, can we rain check? I need some time to talk with my daughter," he demands, and Yama exhales heavily before getting to his feet.

"If we're checking for rain, it'll be a long break. I'm not sure I can wait that long to beat you again." He smirks, passing Haedes by and patting him gently on the shoulder before departing. Haedes ignores him and doesn't say goodbye, turning straight to me.

"Come with me," he demands, taking me over to the far side of the room. Here, amongst the thick black stone of the walls, I watch him push open a door I never would have noticed. It's barely a door at all really, just a moving slab of rock leading into a stone passage on the other side.

"Ooooh— let me guess— this is your red room of pain?" I ask him, joking, and he cocks one eyebrow, lips pressing into a serious line.

"Red? No— *black*. Black is the only respectable colour for a torture chamber, Sephy. God, I have so much to teach you. Do you know how hard it is to get blood stains— like proper arterial blood stains out of red paint? You can never get the shade exactly right to cover it. Bloody nightmare. Quite literally," he huffs, shaking his head like he's remembering something truly horrific.

"Jeez, keep your hair on. It was only a joke," I reply, walking through the opening as my velvet puddle train trails along the floor behind me.

Haedes doesn't reply, shutting the panel behind me and leading me with a gentle hand up the spiral staircase made of cold, smoky quartz, the air chilly from lack of presence. The stairs twist tightly inside the apparent tower, rising into the floor of a small room with an entirely transparent ceiling and walls.

"What is this place?" I ask, staring up at the sky, distorted by the clear quartz facets of the roof. From here, a magnified view of not only the sky but of the entire city can be found. I see my mother's gardens; those Haedes keeps locked to all but himself, beneath us, a noticeable vibrant green among the dark scarlets and blacks of the sprawling city that disappears into an ashen horizon.

In the ceiling, a golden model of some kind of solar system is slowly spinning, but it's not the solar system I grew up learning about.

"This is my solarium. It's where I struck my original deal with Erebus and created the Mortarian sun. I keep an eye on it from here. It's an artificial sun, hence the spark showers and the ash clouds further north, so it needs monitoring," he explains, moving around the centrepiece of the room and swinging it toward me.

"What is that thing?" I ask him, gesturing to the spinning model overhead.

"That's a map of the Celestials."

I catch the telescope as it rotates, swinging toward me, almost falling off my feet under the immense weight of the thing.

"The Celestials?" I demand.

"Yes, greatest mystery in the universe. The gods of gods, so to speak. Not even Gaia herself knew much about it. The only thing we know is that it's where universes are born. It's where the energy for everything, you, me, magic, those shoes you're wearing, came from. It's not even really one entity, just lots of pinpoints of energy— or we *think*. Like I said, we don't know. Nemesis is the closest person to ever find out what's out there, and she refuses to talk about it. When she returned, she uttered only one word— '*Chaos*,' and has been silent on the matter ever since." He watches the spinning golden orbs overhead with wonder, face turning from old to adolescent for just a moment. I'm uncomfortable as he gapes, staring down at the floor and finding not the quartz I'm so used to, but a dark midnight blue stone speckled through with gold flecks catching in the enhanced and exaggerated lilac light of the sun.

"Take a look," he suggests, breaking the silence. I bend so I can peer through the gargantuan gold telescope, finding my retinas burned as I stare directly into bright purple light enough to blind any regular person.

"Jesus! My eyes!" I exclaim, and Haedes laughs, reaching inside his pyjama pocket and pulling out a pair of sunglasses.

"Sorry— I uh, forgot to give you these," he smirks, not sorry at all, and I scowl, blotches of black floating across my vision.

Asshole.

I take the glasses, placing them over my eyes, and look down the telescope again.

"It's very purple," I compliment, not sure exactly what I'm supposed to be doing.

What, does he want me to grade him or something?

"It's made from the restoration flame. A flame that can only be created by melding the eternal and resurrection flames together. There's no actual report on what the flame does if it consumes a person. I've only ever managed to create it once myself, and the result is what you're staring at," he explains, and I cock my head, straightening as I let my fingers rest delicately on the eyepiece.

"Why are you telling me all this?" I demand, worry pooling in my gut as I remove the sunglasses before passing them back to him.

He sighs, straightening inside his clothes. They no longer fit him as they should.

"Sephy—" he breathes, and I scowl.

"Oh, *fuck* no. If you're about to go all Mufasa on me and tell me that '*everything the light touches will one day be yours.*' I'm fucking out of here!" I exclaim, horror consuming me.

He slouches visibly in his silk pyjamas.

"Look, I don't know how long I've got left. The ageing has slowed down, but I no longer have control over the resurrection flame. Something I sorely need to run this place. If something happens to me, if everything goes to shit— I need to know that you'll—" he begins, but I hold up a hand and interrupt him.

"What? *Rule fucking Mortaria*? Are you insane? I can barely remember to walk my goddamn dog!" I turn on my heel, hearing him call after me as I storm down the spiral staircase and out of the passageway, utterly and completely done with the conversation.

I think, if it's possible, my resurrection has made Haedes even more mad than he was before.

LUCE

Leeah brushes her fingers through my hair, massaging my scalp with her long, pointed nails as she finishes blow-drying my hair. My own nails have been lacquered ombre, fading from red to black, by her expert touch, and I stare at her as she works over my shoulder in the vanity mirror. Her pale skin is radiant, nose smattered with freckles and set between deep brown eyes that remind me of the colour of hot chocolate with added cinnamon sprinkles.

Her hair is fire engine red, contrasting starkly against her pallid face, tied up in pin curls against her head and wrapped up off her elegant neck with a fifties style bandana. She's the only sinner in the whole of Mortaria allowed to lay a finger on me, and it was only after

173

years of searching that I finally found a stylist who I trusted enough to make it so.

"So how have you been since I last saw you?" I ask her, having given her a rundown of my latest news already. I take a sip of my coffee out of the mug clutched delicately between my freshly manicured nails. The ceramic reads: '*I have an angel on one shoulder and a devil on the other. I'm also deaf in one ear.*'

"Well, I had a colour consultation with Haedes—" she replies, giving me a shifty look.

"Oh, and I suppose that was a barrel of laughs?" I guess. Her gaze turns awkward as her posture stiffens.

"I'm grateful for the recommendation and all, but he got so mad when I told him that I wouldn't be able to make his hair change colour like it used to. He was all '*My hair is my signature, woman!*' - It was stressful," she adds, and I laugh.

"My hair is my signature? Oh, good lord, he's more of a diva than a god." Leeah laughs at this, beginning to style my hair into curls that will frame my face before swooping back into an elaborate bun at the back of my skull.

"Yes well, I know it's not my place to ask, but well, the other sinners are curious. Is it true? Did you really bring his daughter back from the dead?" she asks. I purse my lips, nervous suddenly. I need to be careful, or I'll end up with a line of sinners at my door, asking to be put back in their bodies.

"It is true. There were special circumstances. It's not something I could ever do again. It was stretching the limits of my power," I admit, humble. She nods, eyes wide, awed by my skills. I'm a little smug inside but keep my face straight; not wanting to admit her admiration makes me feel good.

"So, the other sinners have been talking then? What's the latest news down in the city?" I demand, and she shrugs.

"Lots of unrest about the lack of demon presence in The Ashen Waste. People think it's too much to hope for to think they might have retreated. There seems to be a lot of respect for Sephy though, I mean the story of what she did in the dark colosseum is still being told down at the club on a nightly basis. And the guys telling it weren't even there." She rolls her eyes, placing a grip between her teeth and curling a lock of my hair tightly around a hot iron.

"That night was certainly eventful," I reply, and as she finishes curling, before locking the hair to my head with the grip, she continues.

"Well, if you ask me, what's more remarkable is the demon half-ling— Xion— I think that's his name? Two guys from The Icon security team say he was out of his mind in love going after her, trying to save her life. He crashed out and almost ended up getting himself killed in the process, but that's goddamn heroism if you ask me. My Matt, he would've done that for me before all this happened of course," she remembers her husband, the one who I know is still alive and a thought suddenly occurs to me.

"Hey, uh— how would you like to meet Xion?" I ask her, and her eyes widen, lighting up and losing their previous sorrow.

"Really? Me?" she asks, and I smile.

"Yes, why don't you come along to this party? I'll lend you something to wear. He could use the company. He was complaining to me he didn't have a date just yesterday," I express, and she claps her hands together, nodding wildly, bracelets jingling as her pumice sin stone bounces up and down on the exposed skin of her chest.

"That's perfect then. You two will go just great together!" I exclaim, and she smiles, red lips parting with excitement.

I wonder if she'd smile so much if she knew just exactly what I've been planning. Or if she knew she was going to be on the receiving end of one very pissed-off Miss Sephy Sinclair.

14

VINES

XION

THE CARRIAGE SHIFTS; THE hooves of phantasmal, white steeds clipping the road with a deep and repetitive click. The sound is inescapable inside the padded interior as we jolt over an uneven piece of ground separating the road to The Exilia from the surrounding city.

My heart is in tatters.

There's no denying it. And yet, it's probably my fault.

I took this too far.

We slept together once and my mind, riddled with grief, ran to all kinds of insane conclusions about a future that was probably impossible.

Am I so lonely, so desperate to be loved, to be seen as something light instead of dark, that I'm making up connections where they don't belong?

She'd been clear, so I've drawn a line in the ruddy earth between us, simply returning to my prior existence. Eating, sleeping, fighting, training— reading. It's not as simple as I remember it to be, and yet I still hold out for a return to normal after a less-than-regular couple of months.

I can't regret what I did. Can't regret bringing her back to life, even if that life is spent with some other poor fool.

She really does know how to drive a man to his knees.

Sighing, I feel my bowtie strain against the stubble around my throat as I exhale. I wasn't sure what to wear, not wanting to overdress for the occasion, so I've styled my hair in a pompadour and gone with the only tuxedo I own.

I can't help but wonder, as we pass under the arches of smoky quartz and into the Exilia, if Sephy will be in attendance. The building

Xion!" A voice I don't recognise calls, and I turn on the spot,
king down as I'm greeted by a redhead who's seemingly appeared
n nowhere. Luckily for me, it's not the one I'm dreading seeing
in.

exhale, relief flooding me.

he's dressed in a gothic floor-length lacy gown with elbow-length
ves that continue to fall, dramatically unhindered, to the ground.
throat is bound by a leather choker, which weaves around the pale
that covers her ever-still carotid. Fire engine red hair falls, some
ld say as a warning, curled, over one shoulder from where it is
led by a black metal broach centred with an enormous diamond.
seen Luce wearing the same thing before, so narrow my eyes,
lediately suspicious.

he woman takes strides, the mermaid silhouette of her gown pud-
g behind her in an elegant train that drags up each step silently
he approaches, chocolate eyes glinting warm in the flickering of
rby sconces alight with The Eternal Flame. She's tall, curvy, but
, and I swallow hard, trying to place her face as she gets closer
closer.

m I supposed to know who this is?

er face is long, jaw curved as if a sculptor had a hand in her design,
her scarlet-painted lips spread too easily across perfectly white
h. Arching her brow, she's understandably expectant as she smiles
e.

Jh— yes, that's me," I respond, smiling with awkward and stiff
ure, a lack of welcome horribly evident in my forced expression.
uce— she didn't tell you I was coming?" she asks.

hake my head, embarrassed.

don't know, who are you?" I enquire, placing both hands in my
ets as I'm unsure what to do with them.

'm Leeah. She asked me to accompany you this evening," she
ains, a look on her face like she's hopeful I've just forgotten her
tation to join me.

ce— what the hell are you playing at? I wonder, inhaling sharply and
ing one hand absent-mindedly on the balustrade. It's cool to the
h, offering a sweet contrast to the heat radiating inside my tux.

Oh, no she didn't, but it's lovely to meet you." I offer her a stiff
d, which she stares at momentarily before taking it in her palm.
long fingers, adorned with many silver rings and ending in long
nails, clutch mine as a look of admiration overtakes her.

looms overhead, smouldering and smoky, melancho
nence against the bloody sky. As I peer out of the an
carriage window, I realise the place has never seemed
a woman. But not just any woman, the woman I'm h
entirely for the foreseeable future.

Luce said she doubted her attendance and told me I
plus one to keep me company, but I refused, finding the
at best.

I'm too attached to her, have been ever since that
not even physically, but the idea of someone as beauti
witty and funny finding me of all people worthy.

I'm a murderer. A killer. A demon.

What did I expect?

A woman like that isn't just out of my reach; she's o
plain of existence.

I am utterly over being an emotional wreck, so it's
time I toughen my shell once again and return to the s
The enforcer, the disciplinarian, the silent, dark justi
coming.

I need to remember who I am, who I was before sh
sass unravelled me at my fraying, bursting seams.

Demons don't get to be happy. I've always known th
about her that's given me the illusion of anything oth
hard truth?

The carriage stills as I pull my bowtie away from my
centimetres, struggling to breathe inside the warm
velvet box.

Stepping out onto the slick floor of the entrance hal
thud, I find the place buzzing with energy as security a
staff skitter like insects from one end of the dark cr
other, making last-minute preparations.

The warm air is sickly with the unmistakable rich
apple, making me wrinkle my nose. It's far too pungen
my taste. I prefer something spicier, hotter, and with

I step forward, fast approaching the staircase rising
crystal to the doors of the cavernous throne room, the
evening's oddly out-of-place celebration of what seem
more than a return to normality.

I'm halfway up the steps when I find myself coming
unexpected halt.

177

looms overhead, smouldering and smoky, melancholy in its imminence against the bloody sky. As I peer out of the annoyingly small carriage window, I realise the place has never seemed so resonant of a woman. But not just any woman, the woman I'm hoping to avoid entirely for the foreseeable future.

Luce said she doubted her attendance and told me I should bring a plus one to keep me company, but I refused, finding the idea abhorrent at best.

I'm too attached to her, have been ever since that night, perhaps not even physically, but the idea of someone as beautiful, someone as witty and funny finding me of all people worthy.

I'm a murderer. A killer. A demon.

What did I expect?

A woman like that isn't just out of my reach; she's on a whole other plain of existence.

I am utterly over being an emotional wreck, so it's time I man up, time I toughen my shell once again and return to the stoic entity I am. The enforcer, the disciplinarian, the silent, dark justice nobody sees coming.

I need to remember who I am, who I was before she and her feisty sass unravelled me at my fraying, bursting seams.

Demons don't get to be happy. I've always known this. So, what is it about her that's given me the illusion of anything other than the cold hard truth?

The carriage stills as I pull my bowtie away from my throat by a few centimetres, struggling to breathe inside the warm confines of the velvet box.

Stepping out onto the slick floor of the entrance hall with a familiar thud, I find the place buzzing with energy as security and the in-house staff skitter like insects from one end of the dark crystal hive to the other, making last-minute preparations.

The warm air is sickly with the unmistakable rich odour of cherry apple, making me wrinkle my nose. It's far too pungent, too sweet, for my taste. I prefer something spicier, hotter, and with more depth.

I step forward, fast approaching the staircase rising in precisely cut crystal to the doors of the cavernous throne room, the location for the evening's oddly out-of-place celebration of what seems to be nothing more than a return to normality.

I'm halfway up the steps when I find myself coming to a sudden and unexpected halt.

177

"Xion!" A voice I don't recognise calls, and I turn on the spot, looking down as I'm greeted by a redhead who's seemingly appeared from nowhere. Luckily for me, it's not the one I'm dreading seeing again.

I exhale, relief flooding me.

She's dressed in a gothic floor-length lacy gown with elbow-length sleeves that continue to fall, dramatically unhindered, to the ground. Her throat is bound by a leather choker, which weaves around the pale skin that covers her ever-still carotid. Fire engine red hair falls, some would say as a warning, curled, over one shoulder from where it is pinned by a black metal broach centred with an enormous diamond. I've seen Luce wearing the same thing before, so narrow my eyes, immediately suspicious.

The woman takes strides, the mermaid silhouette of her gown puddling behind her in an elegant train that drags up each step silently as she approaches, chocolate eyes glinting warm in the flickering of nearby sconces alight with The Eternal Flame. She's tall, curvy, but thin, and I swallow hard, trying to place her face as she gets closer and closer.

Am I supposed to know who this is?

Her face is long, jaw curved as if a sculptor had a hand in her design, and her scarlet-painted lips spread too easily across perfectly white teeth. Arching her brow, she's understandably expectant as she smiles at me.

"Uh— yes, that's me," I respond, smiling with awkward and stiff posture, a lack of welcome horribly evident in my forced expression.

"Luce— she didn't tell you I was coming?" she asks.

I shake my head, embarrassed.

"I don't know, who are you?" I enquire, placing both hands in my pockets as I'm unsure what to do with them.

"I'm Leeah. She asked me to accompany you this evening," she explains, a look on her face like she's hopeful I've just forgotten her invitation to join me.

Luce— what the hell are you playing at? I wonder, inhaling sharply and placing one hand absent-mindedly on the balustrade. It's cool to the touch, offering a sweet contrast to the heat radiating inside my tux.

"Oh, no she didn't, but it's lovely to meet you." I offer her a stiff hand, which she stares at momentarily before taking it in her palm. Her long fingers, adorned with many silver rings and ending in long dark nails, clutch mine as a look of admiration overtakes her.

"You look rather dapper," she compliments, giggling. I smile at her, trying as hard as I can to seem grateful for her presence.

"Thank you, you're stunning," I compliment, reaching forward to place a hand on her shoulder and kissing her on the cheek, trying to remember my manners as she flushes a similar colour to the hair surrounding her face.

Hearing the opening of a door, I pull away, finding none other than Sephy standing at the height of the staircase, looking down at us.

Have I done something that's pissed off The Fates? I wonder, wishing the floor would open up and swallow me whole.

My heart falls through my chest as my breath is stolen out of my lungs, the pain at her proximity more crippling than I expect.

The light from the hall behind eclipses her, but I can soon tell she's wearing a dress from only her outline. I gape, craning my neck to get a better view as she stills, silhouetted, curvaceous, by the warm glow at her back.

"Dolly, we need more candles!" she bellows, turning and slamming the doors behind her.

Shit.

I frown.

She can't possibly be pissed at me?

Can she?

She broke it off. She told me it was over, whatever it was. She has no right to be angry.

Then again, this is Sephy we're talking about. Since when has she ever needed my permission to be irrational?

"Shall we?" I gesture up the staircase with one arm, offering Leeah the other so she can loop the crook of her elbow inside mine.

"Why thank you, good sir," she giggles again. I smile.

At least if I have to see Sephy, I won't be alone.

Maybe I owe Luce a bunch of flowers or something.

We enter the hall, which is empty of guests but full of staff. The ceiling has been turned into an intimate, tent-like construction with large crimson drapes suspended at a single central point. Each enormous piece of silk billows and trails, fastened to one of the many-faceted walls before puddling on the ground. The floor is still smoky with its usual slick yet textured quartz, but the entire space, apart from this one detail, is basically unrecognisable. The dancefloor is central and cordoned off with red and gold velvet ropes, and the tables, which are also gold with matching chairs, are dressed in monochrome. Centrepieces made from velvety alabaster roses and slick ebony candles trapped inside tall glass vases stand central to each table, creating mood lighting on a macrocosmic scale. The floor at my feet is scattered with similar white petals, breaking up the dark textured sheen.

Leeah inhales deeply, taking it all in with wide eyes.

Luce really went all out.

"This is amazing! Oh my God!" Leeah claps her hands together, rings clinking as she hops up and down on the balls of her peep toe stilettoes.

"Haven't you ever been to one of The Exilia parties before?" I ask, surprised, and she shakes her head.

"No, vanity sinners aren't supposed to dress up for things like this. I'm Luce's stylist. She invited me to be your date last minute," she explains, almost cringing at her social status. I don't know why she should be embarrassed. She's standing next to a demon half-breed.

"You're a stylist?" I look down at myself, embarrassed now I hadn't tried to be more original with my fifties style attire.

"Yes. So, if you ever need a haircut, I'd be happy to be of assistance," she offers. I smile, grateful for her easy-going attitude.

As we stand, looking at one another before falling into awkward silence, I sense someone watching me from the opposite side of the hall.

I turn, eyes finding her as she stands in the doorway of the room, stone still, with glass vases in hand, no doubt for the candles she was yelling for. She doesn't look like herself, more like a dream. A black velvet, off-the-shoulder gown accentuates all the curves I keep imagining caressing, and her red hair is swept up making her beauty a radiant focal point of the now pallid surroundings.

My heart stops, time stops, as our eyes meet and I take her in.

What the hell are you doing to me, woman? I cuss internally, unable to look away until the sound of smashing glass breaks the inescapable hold she has over me.

The glass vase has shattered in her hands, causing her to swear loudly before turning back on her heel and storming off into the prep area at the back of the hall. Tiny shards of glass hitting the floor in her wake are the only sign that anything has happened between us at all.

"I guess it might be a while until everyone gets here," Leeah concludes, and I sigh, awkward even still. I know it's not Leeah's fault.

Only one particular temptress could have this kind of impact on me from across a crowded room.

"Should we take a walk or something?" I offer, the thought of staying in the hall never so unappealing.

"That would be lovely."

We've avoided returning to the party for as long as possible, but as I see the carriages and gondolas start to dwindle on the third lap around the Exilia, I realise it might be time to head inside.

Leeah is nice, *really* nice, but I can also tell her heart belongs somewhere else. Somewhere with rain and not spark showers.

"So, your husband— he's a millionaire?" I ask, trying to remember the conversation we've been having. I haven't been paying attention, too preoccupied with dread at the thought of returning to the party.

"Yeah, he's pretty business savvy. We had an amazing life." Her eyes go glassy, and I can see a haze fall over her as memories begin to surface.

"I guess we'd better go back inside; looks like the party is about to start," I suggest.

"Okay," she replies, not argumentative or stubborn, simply compliant. It's funny. She's the kind of girl any man would be lucky to have, laid back, funny, attractive, witty, and smart, but all I see is that she's not Sephy.

My life might very possibly be completely and utterly ruined, I muse, wondering what the hell is wrong with me.

This chick has even revealed she knows I'm a half-demon and she's okay with it. Instead of being excited— I'm merely uninterested.

Fucking typical.

We make our way back through the lobby, her arm still looped through mine, strides matching step for step as we head up the staircase and through the open double doors. I rush, deciding it's best to rip off the band-aid with careless and idiotic abandon as her heels click rapidly against the floor.

The hall is full on arrival beneath the deep red fabric canopy, and Thane waves to me, dressed in cropped black slacks, braces, and a shirt. Her hair is slicked back, and she looks like a teddy boy in a blazer with cropped sleeves. She's talking to Anubis about something, who is surrounded by sinners that look utterly overwhelmed. I stare at her, wearing a baby pink cocktail dressed over the top of too many thick petticoats.

181

Since when did she start bringing personal security? I wonder, but then remember the last event we attended in this hall.

I guess it's not surprising.

I find Yama and Muerta dancing to the jazz band, which is playing their first song in a grandiose yet unpredictably delicious melody. It's sweet, considering they're divorced. They both look magnificent, divine even, with Muerta wearing a white, knee-length tea dress, adorned with a black lace overlay spattering the pale canvas of fabric with contrasting sugar skulls, and Yama in a matching monochromatic white suit with a black waistcoat and trilby cocked over his golden dreadlocks.

I find myself searching the crowd for her, but I don't even have to look as her too-loud laugh overtakes the room from my left. My head snap sideways, discovering her surrounded by not one, but *five* men. She's letting them take turns twirling her, placing their hands on her waist as she sips champagne from multiple glasses that they pass her in turn. She's giggling with an over-the-top high pitch, not a real Sephy laugh.

I roll my eyes.

Jesus Christ, she's actually jealous. I smirk.

Utterly ridiculous woman.

I decide to ignore her and focus on having a good time. After all, I've spent the last two days feeling like complete crap because of her, so I deserve to have at least some fun.

"Would you like to dance?" I ask Leeah, holding out a hand.

"It would be my pleasure," she replies, taking my hand as I lead her out to the centre of the dancefloor. As I do so, the crowd parts and Sephy's voice gets louder and louder.

"Oh, Jack— that's *hilarious!*" she chortles, pushing her ass into his crotch.

I watch her over Leeah's shoulder, deciding to let her get on with it, and instead focus on the woman in my arms.

Placing my hand around my date's waist, I move her with the music. She's a good dancer, and the jazz of the night soon takes me away from the awkwardness of the situation going on behind her. I stare, unwavering and determined, into her genteel face, take in her radiant smile, and enjoy for just a moment not being completely and utterly vexed by the woman in front of me.

If only things could always be so simple.

"You know, my Matt, he could dance too," she whispers, and suddenly I'm reminded why it can't be that simple. The woman I'm finding so simply lovely is probably still shredding the heartstrings of some other poor sucker from beyond the grave.

I guess love is always hard, no matter who it's with.

As the song changes, we continue to sway, feet chasing petals caught up in our dance as if it were an easy-going early spring breeze.

Sephy and her boy posse move closer, getting on my last nerve, and the sound of her overly amorous giggle sets my teeth on edge as my muscles bulge inside my suit. Soon, she's so close to us that one of the guys surrounding her 'accidentally' trips Leeah. Luckily, I catch her.

"Hey, watch it!" I grunt, glaring at her and the Neanderthal she's dancing with without a second thought.

"Hey, you got a problem buddy?" One of the sinners squares up to me, sliding his hand from where it's hovering over Sephy's ass before balling it at his side.

"Yes, you actually just almost knocked my date over," I comment, letting my hands fall from Leeah's waist as I prop her upright and square my shoulders.

"Should have been watching where she's going then, shouldn't she? Though with tits like those, I doubt she needs a brain. Ain't that right honey?" He glowers at Leeah, dark eyes rife with malice.

I push her behind me, immediately defensive.

"Hey, back the hell off!" The warning explodes from my chest in an epic rumble, and the eyes of the crowd turn to me. My voice echoes, drowning out the sounds of jazz and the subtle but ever-present fizz of freshly poured champagne, before dying out and leaving only silence behind. The sinner looks to his buddies, first left, then right, shoving Sephy sideways as two of them crack their knuckles.

People still crack their knuckles?

Seriously?

I knew they were Neanderthals.

I shake my head, rolling my eyes.

"Come on mate, let's fucking rumble then if you're so sure your missus there has had whatever honour she has left compromised," he goads me.

I smirk.

As you please, fuckwit.

Clenching my fists, I let my skin ripple beneath my suit from pale olive to the charred shade of coal. My suit creaks at the seams as my muscles pulsate against the material, my heart rate heightening.

I watch the man's eyes turn wide in surprise, and his fellow sinners back up, stiffening visibly in posture as I transform in front of them.

They cower beneath the glowing orange fury of my gaze.

Pussies.

"Oh uh— sorry, mate. Come on, honey." He turns on his heel, grabbing Sephy's ass with one hand and then promptly proceeding to spank it to get her to move. She glares at him, tipping me over the edge.

No, you don't. I act without thinking, reaching forward and grabbing his wrist before reeling back my free hand and landing a punch on the side of his jaw.

Leeah gasps behind me as I set to hitting him in the face over and over. Lost in a sea of red mist, rage courses through me at the thought of his hands touching her, disrespecting her.

The bones crack beneath my fists and I ignore the scent of blood as it hits my nostrils.

I don't know when it happens, but suddenly, there's a tight female grip on my arm, right before I'm consumed, fighting, in a torrent of scarlet flames.

SEPHY

"What the fuck was that?!" I exclaim, flames receding and leaving us both standing on top of white gravel, surrounded by the dark cover and lush depths of my mother's garden.

"Are you fucking *kidding* me?" Xion exclaims, still demonic, eyes wild, hair puffed up in a pompadour. If I wasn't so pissed, I'd probably laugh because as a demon he really can't pull off the whole hair thing. Instead, I merely scowl, taking a step forward onto the grass and kicking off my shoes, the scent of thorny roses enveloping me.

"You just fucking went all Mike Tyson on my goddamn date! You could have killed him! What the hell is your problem?!" I cross my arms over my breasts, the velvet of my dress caressing the pale skin of my wrists as I do so. The grass is cool and wet beneath my toes, a welcome relief from the torment of my stilettos as I stand, glaring at him for far longer than I intend. Finally, after a few deep and ragged breaths, he retorts.

"He was an asshole! And besides, why do you care? You have four other assholes just like him lining up to drool all over your stupid shoes anyway!" He clenches his blood-stained fists, stepping onto the grass and following me with a predictable and uncouth thud.

"I care because I don't understand why you're pissy about me seeing other guys when you're all wrapped up in that piece of skank you showed up with!" I yell, rage building as I continue to storm away from him.

That girl *really* isn't his type.

Like— a redhead with a love for black, long legs, and great taste in shoes. Puh-lease!

"Sephy Sinclair, you told me you wanted nothing to do with me romantically. You have no right to act like a jealous brat!" Xion retorts as I spin on the spot, the ball of my foot making a moist imprint in the dirt.

"Excuse me? *Jealous*?! Get over your goddamn self!" I exclaim, watching as he rolls his eyes, a smirk overtaking his face as he morphs back to his human self, expression cocky.

"So— you really liked those guys you were dancing with?" he demands, placing his hands into his pockets and tilting his head sideways.

I want to lie, to say yes, but I know he's got me pegged. He's one of the only people I've ever met who can rival me when it comes to playing mind games.

So instead, I stay silent.

"I see. Well come on, we better get you back to the party then. I have my date to get back to," he baits me, and my temper flares, formidable beneath the petite glamour of my gown.

"So, it's that easy for you? Just walking off with another woman?" I call after him, hating that he knows me so well, knows how to make me desperate.

"Isn't it for you? You had men all over you back there. Clearly, our little encounter wasn't as memorable for you as it was for me. If you could settle for those losers," he spits, and I wonder if I've actually hurt his pride, his confidence.

"Yeah well, that loser is now going home with a bloody nose and a broken face thanks to you," I retort, unsure how to counter anything he's saying. He's not wrong.

"He touched you," Xion replies, and I scowl, refusing to let the fragrant scent of familiar yet deadly greenery from nearby soften my expression. Standing here, amongst the deceptive dark beauty that my mother made from nothing, I'm reminded that she made me too, and I wonder if she would be proud.

"So, that girl had her hands all over you too," I mutter, voice diminishing in power as I'm taken back to the sick feeling I got in my stomach watching them dance together, laugh together.

Xion takes a step towards me, eyes full of rage.

"Ah, and therein lies the problem, doesn't it, Sephy? I want you. You don't want me. And yet you're getting jealous of other women putting their hands on me. That doesn't make sense now, does it?"

"You shouldn't have hit him." I ignore what he's saying altogether this time, feeling his proximity even though I wish I didn't.

"He touched what's mine," Xion growls, feral now as desire pools in my stomach. It's wrong, and yet when he claims me, I feel more powerful than I ever have before.

"I'm not yours. I told you that. I can't do this with you. I can't. It'll hurt too much," My emotions spill at the seams as I turn and take a few paces away from him, covering my face. I don't want him to see me cry, and for some stupid reason, he's turning me into one of those weak weepy women.

Encasing myself in the shadow of a nearby pomegranate tree, surrounded by leaves of nightshade and belladonna, I keep my back turned to him, aware with every single step he's getting closer and closer.

"Doesn't it hurt now?" he asks. I shrug.

"I lost my friend, of course it hurts," I admit, stomach churning.

"That's all I am, a friend? After everything— that night?" He sounds broken almost, so I turn to face him, only to find him directly at my back, too close.

"And what if you *were* more? What difference would my admitting that make? It just makes me weak, gives something else for people to take away from me," I exhale, a sad tear running down one cheek.

"You wore a dress," he comments, placing a hand on my bare shoulder and stroking down towards the velvet of the sleeve.

I want to pull away, but I'm rooted to the spot, just like the other poisonous plants nearby. They seem so beautiful, but I know, as I know of myself, they too hold the power to silently bring a man to his knees and leave him gasping for air.

"I won't be upstaged," I bite out, furious with myself for allowing him to see me this way.

"Nobody could, even if they were trying." He's being sweet now, so I wrap my arms around myself, trying to protect what little personal space I have left.

"Don't say that. You sound so— enamoured," I sigh, frustrated.

"So, let me get this straight. You don't want to be with me— and yet, you don't want me to be with anyone else either?" he asks, smirking, though his eyes fill with sadness.

"I know that makes me an asshole," I admit, sniffling as I brush a loose curl of red hair behind my ear before drying my cheek with my palm.

"No, it makes you attached. It means you felt those same feelings I did before—" I watch his eyes trace down to my scar, peeping unapologetically above the sweetheart neckline of my dress.

"That doesn't matter, Xion. I can't. I can't love you!" I blurt the words and clap my hand over my mouth, shocked.

"Come here." He melts, eyebrows rising on his forehead, and before I know it, his lips and body are crushing me to the trunk of the tree.

He kisses me sweetly, chastely, pressing his warm body against mine as the scent of pomegranates and the temptation of their low-hanging proximity, the mere fantasy of such taboo juices spilling from each orb, threatens to overwhelm everything. When the kiss is over, he stands, holding me close to him as though scared I might run away, looking deeply into my eyes. All I can do is silently weep in his grasp, pathetic and broken, exposed.

"I know why you don't want to get into a serious commitment with me; I understand. But— maybe we could just try and have fun, be casual? No flowers, or chocolates or anything like that— just maybe, we make our own rules?" he suggests.

I feel my heart flutter.

"So, what, like demon friends with benefits?" I ask him, breaking the tension and giving a tiny giggle.

"If you want. Whatever you want. I just— I can't imagine never kissing you again. Or watching someone else put their hands on you—" His breathing is fast in his chest, heart pounding as I rest a gentle hand against the white cotton of his shirt. I undo the bowtie from around his neck, noticing that the top three buttons of his shirt have popped clean off.

"But— what about you? What about your feelings?" I ask him, and he sighs, taking a free hand and running it back through his styled hair as I toss the loose bowtie to one side.

"Nothing lasts forever. If I've learned anything, anything at all from living this long, it's that the only things we can count on are change and loss. But I can't not take this chance, not see where it goes with you, not try. Even if I end up getting hurt." His words mean more to me than he can know, but they also fill me with fear. I don't want to hurt him, and I know I'm being utterly unfair, selfish even, in even considering this.

It just feels too damn good to resist, and I'm no saint.

"Okay, let's— see where things go. But I can't promise I won't get scared, or bored—and run, or get killed—" I admit.

Xion smirks.

"I brought you back from death once already, I'm pretty sure you getting in your car and blitzing it to Retropolis for a binge drinking session is going to be easier to deal with than that," he admits, lips spreading wide.

I do what I dared not, what I swore against, letting myself hope as I see the embers of what had been flicker back to life in his eyes.

I kiss him, placing my fingertips on his cheekbones on either side of his face and holding him to me, desperately terrified with each passing second that something terrible will happen, that I'll be pulled from the familiar warmth of him and taken kicking and screaming back to the grave.

"Xion—" I murmur against his lips, and he smiles, inhaling the scent of me with unrestrained fondness as he pulls back only slightly.

"Yes?" he asks.

I lean back, letting my head fall against the tree.

"If I hurt you— I *am* sorry. I don't want to be this way. But— loving someone, anyone— it's just not who I am."

"I am entering into this with full awareness of who you are Sephy Sinclair. If you weren't as you are, I'm not sure I'd be so desperate to keep you. I promise you, I can handle this," he vows, stroking my hair as it falls down the side of my neck.

He's stronger than I'll ever be. I know that now. He knows that love can hurt, can destroy a person, and yet he's still coming at me with arms wide open, heart bare and exposed.

I'll never understand why, but I don't have the strength to fight this thing, whatever it is, between us any longer.

15

1 PUT A SPELL ON YOU

LUCE

THE FLUTTERING OF A red velvet curtain is all that separates me from the buzz of the crowd. It's been a long time since I performed, so it's no wonder I'm nervous.

Dolly is rushing from the left side of the stage to the right, her heels click-clacking on my last damn nerve.

"Dolly! Calm down; you're putting me on edge!" I snap, flattening the red velvet of my off-the-shoulder gown against my stomach, inhaling deeply and preparing my lungs for the performance ahead.

"Sorry!" she calls, breathing rapid in her dead Doppel chest as she disappears around the corner yet again.

The vintage microphone beckons, both terrifying and alluring as I go to take a step forward toward it. Unfortunately, before I can do this, I feel someone with cold hands grab my arm, pulling me back.

"Luce! Luce!" It's Haedes, dressed in his silk pyjamas, eyes wide with something between rage and horror.

"Haedes, I'm a tad busy. What is it?" I demand, turning to look over my shoulder at him. Pressing my thick red lips together, I feel the moist gloss of my lipstick, still slick on my lips.

"You have to come and see! Right now! Sephy and Xion— you won't believe what they're doing!" He's frantic, with eyes wide, hand clamping down on my arm as he tries to tug me away from the curtains, which will soon open, revealing me.

"I can imagine what they're doing— and no I don't want to come and see. I'm not perverted like you. That's your daughter! Have some respect!" I scold him, temper fraying as a mixture of anxiety and exasperation meld fast into fury.

"You know?! How do you know what they're doing? They're— Luce! Oh, it's horrendous; he's nailing her against a fucking tree! A tree in *my* garden! I feel *violated*!" he yells, putting his hands on his head in horrified surrender.

I roll my eyes, impatient.

"Yes, I know, I thought you did too? You didn't think Xion went on that little road trip with you because he wanted to help *you*, did you?" I cock my head and his jaw falls open.

"But— wait— *what*? When did this happen?!" he demands, shaking me slightly so the thick curls of my white hair tickle my bare upper spine.

"Haedes, I don't have time for this! I thought you knew they were seeing one another, why are you so shocked? He wrecked your car trying to save her!" I exclaim. He shakes his head, stilling as he thinks, which actually looks painful if you ask me.

"But he was her bodyguard! He was charged to protect her— I mean I knew Morpheus said something about them being lovers that night, but I thought— I thought he was trying to screw with my head," he mutters, and this time, it's my turn to be surprised as I cock my head.

"Wait— *Morpheus*? You saw Morpheus? What happened? Why didn't you tell me?" I demand, watching as his lips part to explain, but then he stalls.

"Uh— nothing. Never mind. I'm just going to go and find a bucket of ice water to throw on them out of the Solarium window—" he turns on his heel, storming off.

"Haedes, no! Leave them alone! This is none of your business!" I yell after him, a mother calling after her rebellious adolescent.

Sighing, I turn, finding Dolly waving to me from the wings of the makeshift stage. She's looking for me to give her a thumbs-up, so I turn back to face the microphone, taking it in my palm like it's the ripest most delicious apple I've ever seen.

As I do so, I signal her, and she makes a hand gesture to someone else. After only a few seconds, the curtains part, revealing me in the stark glory of an unhindered single spotlight. As I'm exposed to the crowd, the torches within the hall dim, casting the mass of expectant guests in a bloody and intimate light. They turn to me, putting their hands together in a round of applause.

"Put your hands together for the one, the only, the fabulously luscious, Miss Lucifer!" Dolly speaks into her headset as I smile, picking out Thane's face in the crowd far quicker than I expect.

191

She looks hot, just as she had done for the entirety of the generation I'm trying to capture, and so I take a deep breath, voice coming across husky as I breathe, sultry, into the microphone.

"Good evening, ladies and gentlemen. I wanted to kick things off with a number dedicated to that wonderful lady in my life— Thanatos, this is for you baby." I gesture to her, nodding to Dolly as a signal that I'm ready for the orchestra at my spine to begin the agreed song list for the evening.

I lean forward, taking a half step directly into the spotlight and pushing my body flush against the microphone stand. My lips part and the lyrics of Nina Simone's *I Put A spell On You* spill from me.

I raise a hand, splaying my fingers apart and then running it down the side of my body, sensual, as I sing, voice filling the room as the band reaches an epitome of delicious rhythmic cacophony.

I sway, keeping one hand on the microphone, caressing it, and not dropping my gaze from Thane's face for even a second. Her eyes are wide, awed, almost like she's forgotten who I am, and she's seeing me again for the first time. The memories of us fill my head as I continue to croon, annunciating with sexual purpose as the crowd parts and a second spotlight follows her as she treads, step by purposeful step, toward the stage. She holds out a hand, and I feel myself drawn to her with the same magnetic attraction I've known ever since I was a little girl.

Abandoning the microphone as the crowd of people watching us disappears, I take several steps forward, placing my hand in her palm and feeling the magic of us running up my arm.

I bend, shoes kissing the edge of the stage as I fall forward into her open arms.

Dolly comes in to replace me on the vocals.

I stare into her eyes as she whirls me in a three-hundred-and-six-ty-degree spin on the edge of the dancefloor before placing me back on my feet. I'm dizzy, hundreds of eyes watching us, but she steadies me, putting her strong arm around my waist and pulling me to her.

The crowd parts as the spotlight tracks us and we float across the dancefloor, white petals swept up in our wake like fallen, natural stars, laced with the magic of our attraction. My skirt flares out as she pushes me away from her warm torso and spins me beneath the spotlight. I keep my eyes locked on hers, the moment more intimate than anyone can imagine as her rugged alluring scent envelops me and she pulls me back so we're flush against one another, lips only millimetres apart as my own part in a seductive smile.

"I love you," she whispers in my ear, cheek pressing against mine. My heart pounds, blood hot beneath my skin.

"I love you," I reply, not hesitating.

When I'm with her, the world dissolves, and we become a dream, a fantasy. That's the thing about being banished from The Higher Plains. They had sought to deny me heaven, and yet, somehow, heaven had followed me right down to hell.

As the final few notes of the song ring out, Thane bends me backwards and kisses me in true Hollywood style. The crowd claps as the band falls into silence and we both take a bow.

"Have a wonderful night!" I exclaim as the rest of the crowd floods out onto the dancefloor and the musicians begin to play *Feeling Good*, filling the entire room with a relaxed but sensual vibe.

I stare into the throngs of partygoers abuzz with conversation and the slurping of drinks, finding The Furies at the edge of the room, scouring the crowd for disturbances. Continuing my surveillance, I locate Haedes by the bar amongst guests adorned with feather boas, sparkling jewellery, and sharp pinstriped suits, still clad in his pyjamas with an uncomfortable-looking Annie serving him. I move to intervene, but Thane grabs my arm, pulling my attention back to the present moment, where Muerta and Yama stand, staring at us.

"Oh Luce, we've been so worried, but you're really alright!" Muerta places her bony arms around me and the scent of too-sweet roses overtakes the more welcome aroma of Thane, her proximity chilling my rabid, hot skin.

"I told you! It's all going to be fine," I express.

Then, Thane speaks up.

"Luce and I have discussed it, and she's decided to give up the alchemy. Isn't that right, honey?" she asks, and I feel a slight pang of irritation muddy the waters of my joy.

"Yes. That's right," I nod, voice diminishing as the confirmation falls from me.

"Well, that is good to hear. You don't need it. I can see you have everything you need right beside you," Muerta gushes, causing Thane to grip me a little tighter. The raven-haired and wide-eyed Goddess turns, sensing Anubis' arrival, Osiris at her side, before I even realise she's heading toward us.

"Luce, what a wonderful little diddy!" Osiris compliments me, offering a hand. I take him in; he's wearing a white suit with a black bowtie. Unoriginal, but it does suit him.

"Thank you. What's all this?" I gesture to the accompanying posse of sinners dressed in crude white fabric wrapped around their bodies. It's not exactly party attire.

"I decided to bring personal security. I hope you don't mind," Anubis announces. I can only shrug.

"Well, we have The Furies on duty, but whatever makes you feel comfortable. Sephy and Xion were also supposed to be working security, but I guess they got— busy—" I express. Anubis swallows hard at this, cocking an eyebrow as the coil of her solid gold spiral choker visibly undulates.

"Aren't you concerned about that?" Yama enquires.

I shrug yet again.

Why is everyone looking to me like I'm in charge? Aren't they the same ones telling me I don't know how to handle power?

"It's none of my business—" I interject, but Anubis chips in.

"It is every *bit* our business. We're responsible for the sinners down here, how and when they move on, for the balance of the universe. If their union could put that in jeopardy, it must be stopped."

"Jesus, Nu. It's a party. Can you just get off the soap box for one night?" Thane interjects, and Anubis' Egyptian features turn harsh, her beauty morphed cruel before my very eyes.

"You forget the times we live in, Thanatos. The Demon Lords are still out there, and so is Pandora. If we can avoid yet another threat, I say we do it and quickly."

I sigh, her condemnation threatening to quash my happy buzz.

"What do you want us to do? Lock them up?? Put a chastity belt on her? Castrate him? The more we fight this, the harder they'll fight to be together. You know what they say about making something forbidden—" I retort, looking at Thane with a knowing gaze. I remember only too well how much more exciting being forbidden from seeing one another had made our relationship once upon a time. Anubis shakes her head, glass-beaded locks of thick hair clinking together with undeterred fury.

"The mortal condition from which they both suffer isn't an excuse. Weakness isn't an excuse. Not when the outcome will be to doom us all." She turns on her heel, pink dress flowering out around her waist in petals of soft contrast to her flint and steel attitude. Osiris trails after her and her security entourage, a lost little boy turned god.

"What's got her panties in a bunch?" Thane demands.

Yama shrugs, placing his hands in his suit pockets.

"I don't know. She's been tense lately. Something is bothering her. I know she doesn't approve of Sephy and Xion— but as we all know, we can only do so much. If Sephy and Xion want to be together, want to copulate, they'll find a way. After all, she's half god, and he's half demon. They're not helpless or powerless by any means," Yama says, and Muerta looks up at him, eyes full of admiration and unrequited love. I cringe at the clinical nature of his language, but she seems to find it adorable.

"That was actually romantic— for you." She blushes, the blood rushing to her cheeks in an only too noticeable way beneath the skull facade of her makeup.

"I'm merely being logical, Muerta," he mumbles, and the two of them share a wistful glance as the memories of their marriage visibly fly up like disturbed shrapnel from an only too-fatal bomb blast.

I grab a glass of champagne off a passing tray, feeling the sudden need to get unceremoniously drunk. Taking it to my lips, I watch Anubis, who towers over many of the sinners around her, as she makes her way toward the back of the room, whispering something to Osiris. I wonder what she's saying, but before I can think any further on this Erin taps me on the shoulder.

Spinning on the spot, I turn to face the three Furies, their features equally stoic, each as hard as the next. In fact, they almost remind me of white marble statues in their flawless beauty, only marred by an ever-impenetrable emotionlessness.

Erin's dark skin is in harsh contrast to her shiny silver armour which ripples, each piece of chainmail formed to mimic dragon scales, a trick taught to the blacksmiths here by Thane, who had learned it from her mother, Nemesis. Ericka straightens her spine, visibly uncomfortable as the crowd of people having a good time shifts around her. Her dark eyes dart from left to right with paranoid vigour as her caramel skin shines with light perspiration and her pupils become chasmic, taking in all signs of danger. The final Fury, Erlea, steps forward, harsh Asian features and pale skin unforgiving in their beauty as the hand she uses to draw her long sword twitches at her side, every sinew in her body tightening with unspent energy.

"Yes?" I ask them, and they look at me with a collectively tense expression.

"Ma'am, we are happily performing our security duties— but—" Erlea's eyes drop, nervous. I thought that was an impossible look for any of the Furies.

I'm immediately curious as to what has them so wily.

"It's just Haedes— he is making advances— unwanted advances, on Ericka," she explains.

I exhale.

"I was going to cut off his manhood for my suffering, but Erlea informs me this would be a mistake?" Ericka suggests, with an unsmiling and unamused expression. I almost laugh, but then I realise she's serious. The Furies are unpredictable; mix that with a drunk Haedes, and someone is going to end up dead or maimed at best.

"Oh Jesus, I'm sorry. Hold on." Downing the entire contents of my glass and passing it to Erin, I pull Thane behind me as we weave in and out of happy chatter and dancing couples. I find Haedes, unsurprisingly, still at the bar.

"Haedes!" I bark, exhaling heavily as I approach his slumped form. Still wearing pyjamas and sitting upon one of the shiny gold stools with red velvet padding, he jumps slightly, turning to me.

"Oh look, it's the happy couple," he sneers.

"You've had too much to drink— come on." I try to pull him down off his seat, but he shakes his head, yanking his arm out of my grasp.

"No, Luce! I can't go back up there! I can hear them— there's a demon fucking my little girl, and it sounds like a pair of goddamn porn stars going at it! What did I ever do to deserve this? I'm a good person— right?" he asks, and I shake my head.

"Um, no. Whatever gave you that idea? Besides, she's not your *little girl*. She's a fully-grown woman— and you didn't even know she existed until like a whole five seconds ago. Come on—" I reach out to take his hand, trying to make him go without a fight. He slaps me away.

Before I can summon the energy to yell at him, I'm startled by an ear-shattering and high-pitched scream.

Shit.

I spin on my heel, discovering the stage full of Banshees and Succubi. The band scatters in a clatter of falling brass and rattling drumsticks as the entire room is thrown into chaos. There must be twenty of them, looking out over the space with teeth bared and jaws dripping. They've appeared from seemingly nowhere. I, however, know better.

Pandora.

Thane stiffens at my side as The Furies push through the crowd, which is rushing against them like salmon swimming relentlessly upstream. The lethal trifecta upends guests without care as they draw sharp blades which glint, merciless, in the low light. They cry out like heathens, battle ready, and the only thing I can feel is a kind of twisted relief— at least this might make them a little less twitchy.

The guards surrounding Anubis rush the stage at her command, unceasing in their post-mortem loyalty as she reaches out a graceful arm, pointing to the beasts and identifying them, quite unnecessarily, as targets. I watch as the throngs of party guests, collectively fleeing toward the doors in an unorganised and what would be a potentially fatal bottleneck, panic. They descend into a predictable and entirely human every man for himself mentality. They shove, push, yell, and cuss, showing perhaps they have learned nothing from their time here at all.

Well, that'll teach me to throw a party, I huff, as Thane shoves me behind her like I'm a damsel who needs saving.

Haedes gives me one look of utter drunken carelessness and convects out in a burst of what seems to be sputtering red flames without pause.

His powers are certainly weakening.

Awesome. The one guy with the flame that can permanently kill these sons of bitches flees like a toddler in a tantrum. And his daughter is away pissing off The Nexus by screwing a demon-halfling— apparently against a tree and with a lack of care for volume control— Perfect.

My eyes dart from one end of the room to the other as the chaotic events unfold like a disturbed line of dominoes. Thane pulls out a knife from the inside pocket of her jacket, causing my eyes to widen as I take in the sharp serrated edge. She doesn't usually carry a weapon.

She suspected trouble just as everyone else in The Nexus had, so perhaps I'm the one at fault in fast becoming an ignorant and apparently fatal optimist.

She rushes forward, long legs making quick nimble work of the space between her and the demons, looking over her shoulder to me as though I should stay put, but I refuse.

Edging forward, I find the snarling pack of Banshees meeting head-on with The Furies in a smashing of blade against bone.

The Succubi launch themselves from the edges of the stage, dividing the demons into their species as they act a separate force entirely, knocking over freshly set tables and sending crockery flying into the walls. Ceramic explodes in fragile and sharp alabaster supernovas as the entire dining area is upended.

I can only stand, watching in horror and trying to work out how I can fight without alchemy, in heels and a dress no less.

The Furies are magnificent as I stand there, watching them, transfixed but nonetheless struggling for tactical inspiration. My gaze bounces from wall to wall, ceiling to floor, finding Thane, The Furies, sinner guards, and myself the only remaining entities amid the tatters of what I had intended to be a great night. Anubis and the other Nexus council members are nowhere to be seen, making me an obvious and vulnerable target.

"Luce!" Thane shouts.

Before I can respond, standing at a complete loss for what to do, I'm knocked to the floor, cringing as my wrists meet with the hard stone beneath me. I'd been too distracted making sure everyone else got out unscathed, trying to work out how to fight myself, and now I'm paying for it.

I twist onto my spine, writhing, trying to crawl back behind the bar, but the Banshee pins me beneath its matted furry body, enormous paws coming down on my chest and knocking all breath from my lungs. Its white eyes bore down into mine, breath rancid with the too-sweet aroma of stolen marrow. After a moment, I stop struggling, realising that I cannot escape.

The Banshee is breathing heavily, breathing me in and staring into my eyes with unwavering and hungry intensity bordering on soul-deep starvation. I relax beneath it, too scared to move, to blink, staring back into the milky depths of its barren soul. Its thick black eyelids close once, then twice, severing our connection, before it backs away from me and takes off toward the doors, letting me live.

I sit up, the sleeve of my gown hanging loosely from the garment, torn asunder. Erlea catches me in her sights as she skewers a Banshee with her sword, pulling it from the body and launching the blade in a bullseye trajectory with a single swift motion of her left arm. The Banshee, which has just shown me mercy, crumples to the floor as the long sword lodges itself in its skull, speckling the white rose petals on the floor dark with blood.

I simply watch on, confused.

Why hadn't it killed me?

Demons don't have souls. They don't feel mercy. Don't have a conscience— so what the hell was that?

"Luce!" I hear Thane bellow as she pulls her knife from the skull of a Banshee she's just ended, her agility nothing but an asset despite her willowy build. "Are you alright?" she demands, rushing across the dance floor and grabbing me by my upper arm as she skids to a halt on the balls of her feet. Her hand comes away bloody, and I look down to find my shoulder weeping scarlet where the Banshee's claw had caught my pale skin, ripping it wide open with ease.

"Yes, I'm fine— I don't understand—" I murmur, and she frowns.

"What do you mean? Understand what?"

"That demon— it— *let me live*—" I express, and she shakes her head.

"Go and wait for me in the room— I can't fight with you here. I need to focus," she orders me.

I scowl.

I'm not the little woman. I'm not a damsel. I'm the goddamn devil. I don't sit out of fights; I cause them.

"But—" I protest, and Thane shoots me a warning glare.

"Luce, just go!" she yells, breathing ragged.

I turn, angry but not sure what else I can do without magic or even a weapon at my disposal other than to become a mere liability.

I feel so helpless as I flee, making my way across the lobby full of the echoes of sinners screaming and toward the spiral staircase. The sound of pounding footsteps on crystal echoes out through the halls as I ascend, feeling castrated, caged, tamed— she told me to give up the magic— so what, now I'm supposed to sit back and let her fight for me, like some princess?

Oh fuck no.

By the time I've reached the top of the staircase, I'm furious. However, as I'm about to turn left into my alchemy chamber, I'm distracted by the fact that the door to my apartment has been left ajar.

I tread forward slowly, pushing open the door with caution and hearing low purring yowls.

Beelz.

As I take in the room before me, I'm surprised.

Anubis, strewn on the carpet, leg bloody and mauled, is crying in pain as Beelzebub glares at her, tail erect and orange eyes narrowed, posture alert.

"Anubis what happened?" I whisper, wondering what on earth she's doing here and if we're alone.

"I came— to protect The Book of The Dead. To set Beelz loose on the demons, and to get to safety— that stupid beast went crazy and attacked me!" she accuses, and I frown.

"But— The Book of The Dead is in Haedes' vault—" I reveal. She sighs, rolling her eyes and brings her hand up, limp, to her moist and furrowed brow.

"Of course, it is! I don't know why I thought you'd have it—" she pants, thigh spilling blood all over my vintage rug.

"Anyone could come in here and take it. Of course, I wouldn't keep it here." I cock my head, assessing her but not rushing forward to help, hesitant despite the obvious pain betrayed by her watery dark eyes.

"I should've known that. I guess I underestimated your common sense," she sighs as her head lolls back against the arm of my couch, surrendering to the mortal sensation that plagues her.

"I'd say that's true. Not surprising though; you tend to underestimate most people," I add, gesturing for Beelz to move to my side.

The panther doesn't look sorry or remorseful, instead scared, which I suppose I should expect. She can probably sense the Demons downstairs. I stand aside, pointing out of the door and giving her a firm glare right in the eyes.

"Go, help Thane," I order, and the Panther takes off, velvet paw pads slapping against the crystal stairs as she descends the spiral staircase at high speed.

Turning from the open doorway, I take in the rest of the apartment, only to find Cerb cowering in the corner. I gesture for him to come close, whistling at a low volume. Padding over to me, I let him chase my heels as I move to get bandages and antiseptic from the kitchen cupboards, knowing he's rattled too.

"I'm not using magic, so we'll have to do this the old-fashioned way—" I explain. She winces as I fall to my knees, moving the petticoats from her leg and exposing the wound.

"You can't just fix this with alchemy?" She raises an eyebrow, irritated, and I shake my head.

"I told Thane I wouldn't."

She groans, putting her hand on her forehead as though she's getting a headache.

"Can't you make an exception?" she asks, entitled as ever.

I shake my head.

"No. I can't. Sorry," I apologise, setting to cleaning the wound with gentle fingers.

She winces.

"You should put that thing on a goddamn leash, Lucifer. What are you thinking? It's a wild animal for Ra's sake!" she condemns me, and I give her a wary look.

"Beelz only attacks like this when she feels threatened. So, either you were threatening her, or she could sense the demons— either way, it's not my fault," I retort in a calm, even tone, looking her square in the face. I watch her hesitate, narrowing my eyes.

"You know— you couldn't touch The Book of The Dead even if you wanted to. You're too pure. So even if I had been keeping it in here, you wouldn't have been able to do anything. I thought you'd know that— being that you've seen a resurrection before?" I query her, but she only shrugs.

"I don't like your tone, Lucifer. You sound like you're accusing me of something." She winces as I begin to wrap a bandage around her upper thigh, attempting to stop the bleeding from three enormous claw-shaped gashes.

"I'm not accusing you of anything. I just find it amazing how little you know about something you feel so strongly against. After all, you really got in my face about resurrecting Sephy Sinclair." I exhale heavily, and she glares at me, pursing her lips.

"I'm sorry. I am. I guess I just worry too much. What with Haedes being so weak and everything with the Demon Lords. I'm a control freak, and I've never felt more out of control in my entire existence," she admits.

"I can agree with you on that. I can't help but feel like something bad is coming— and yet, I also feel helpless to do anything, even though I'm a goddess." She stares at me, blinking slowly as I finish dressing the wound on her leg.

"I guess we just must wait and see— I suppose that's the curse of mortality. Little control and no foresight." Anubis' breath hitches and she presses her hand to her chest as if she's struggling to breathe before pulling herself up onto the couch behind her.

"I'm sorry about the leg— by the way," I add, depressed as the night moves ever onward, having become a total disaster only too fast despite my precautions.

"It's fine. I guess I was pretty stupid coming in here in a fluster and spooking a Panther— I'm more of a dog person, and I just wasn't thinking. This demon attack isn't unexpected, but did you see how strong they look? How many there were? It's like they've been growing stronger right under our noses— and yet— I haven't seen hide nor hair of any of them in The Ashen Waste for weeks, so they aren't feeding on Doppels." she exhales, pain stealing her breath as she places her foot on the floor tenderly. She gets up; hopping on the spot with the least grace I've ever seen her exude. She looks so vulnerable like this, an unusual state for her to be sure. She'll be healed up within hours with the Mortarian sun, of course, but I bet that still stings like a bitch.

"Maybe it's time Thane went and had a closer look at The Fallen Kingdom—" she suggests, careful to maintain her balance as she turns to look at me.

"As much as I hate that idea— it's probably necessary," I admit, kicking off my heels and moving over to the phone to call for assistance so she can return to The Icon to rest.

"Unfortunately for you and me, necessary is what we do," she grimaces.

16

MEMPHIS IN JUNE

LUCE

I SIT FACING THE fire, basking in its warmth, still wearing the red velvet gown from this evening's party, shoulder throbbing. I'm entranced by the flickering of each red flame upon the hot coals of the hearth, the fragrant smoke filling my nostrils as my attention shifts, hypnosis broken only by the turning of a key in the lock of the door.

She enters, a visible cut on the otherwise flawless edge of her cheekbone, blazer hanging over one arm. Her shirt is untucked from her cropped pants, her face weary, and her hair dishevelled. Beelz trails in through the open door behind her, licking her lips as though she's been offered a lifetime supply of cream.

"Finally. I've been waiting ages!" I leap up off the couch, startling Cerb who is lying next to me, curled up on the ruby velvet of several couch cushions.

"I had to help with the clean-up— lots of dead bodies—" She shakes her head, white shirt visibly peppered with a fine mist of crimson.

"Demon bodies I hope—" I express. Again, she only shakes her head.

"Both. I'm guessing we're going to be getting an earful from Barry when he reanimates— he had his leg torn off by one of those Banshees. There was blood everywhere!" she sighs.

I tread around the couch, watching her every movement as she places her jacket on the coat rack beside the door, half dreamy in her expression as she turns to face me.

"I'm glad you're okay—" I breathe, placing my arms around her neck. She smells like death, like demons, but I don't care. She's still my Thane.

"I am— the Exilia's main hall has looked better though. Haedes' vault door has been knocked clean off its hinges— I've had to station those guards Anubis left behind as extra security until we can get it fixed. At least I know they're good at their job though. I don't see her hiring numbskulls as personal security, do you?" she asks, grey eyes stormy with turmoil.

"True— I found her bleeding on the rug after I left you. Beelz took a nice chunk out of her thigh," I explain.

Thane's expression turns quizzical.

"Beelz attacked her? What was she even doing up here?" she demands.

I shrug, shoulder twinging.

"Supposedly she was coming to grab The Book of The Dead— she figured that might be what the Demon Lords were after. I'm guessing that we're lucky she was here; I can't think of any other reason that those demons would attack other than as a distraction at this point. Were they looking for something? Someone?" I demand, wondering perhaps if they were sent to finish the job with regards to Sephy.

"I have no idea. None of the demons managed to escape, me and The Furies got every last one— it seems odd though doesn't it, how strong they were," Thane muses.

"Anubis said the same thing. She said The Ashen Waste has been desolate for a while now. She suggested you go and look in on The Fallen Kingdom," I recall.

"Yes, I'll just get patched up and be on my way." I feel my heart wilt at the thought of her leaving so soon again.

Pushing my hand into the tangle of her hair, I move closer to her, breathing her in deep.

"I was so scared," I whisper. Her eyes widen, adoring every inch of my face with the utmost scrutiny.

"I can handle myself. You know that," she replies, kissing me lightly on the lips as her hands come around my waist.

"I do— I just, I can't lose you. It would kill me." My voice thickens and tears well in my eyes, the shock at what has happened hitting me as I crumble in her presence.

She's my safe harbour, and now I'm in her arms again, I feel myself falling apart, the lack of control over everything around me never more evident than it has been tonight.

"I know— but it's okay; everything will be okay," she hushes me, kissing me again and again.

I feel myself freefalling, so I open my eyes, taking back control the only way I'm allowed.

"Let me take you to bed—" I whisper, running my long fingers up her back as I reach underneath the crinkled cotton of her shirt.

"But—" she begins to protest, eyes flickering to the window, but I place a finger to her lips.

"No buts— *please*," I implore her, and she exhales heavily, lurching forward and pulling me through the apartment in a burst of impatience. I follow, helpless to resist, my skirt trailing behind me as she closes the partition, sealing us inside our bedroom.

"Let me show you how much you mean to me—" I purr, unzipping the back of my gown and letting it fall to the floor in a bloody red puddle around my ankles. Thane falls back onto the end of the bed, legs falling apart as she leans back on her elbows, surrendering to my wishes.

I tread out of the fabric, my lingerie a strapless red corset, matching thong, and suspender belt. "Let me worship you— *please*, Thane," I beg, falling to my knees, wanting to watch her unravel beneath my hands, beneath my tongue.

"Anything for you." She bends forward, taking my lips into hers and tasting me—

"You taste so damn delicious—" she moans, relinquishing control as I take my fingers and unzip her pants, pulling them off and throwing them into the corner of the room. She's commando underneath, making me gnaw on my bottom lip.

I place my hands on her knees, running my fingernails up her inner thighs, inhaling her scent, and watch as her breath catches, aroused, in her throat. She takes off the shirt she's still wearing, and lies back, placing her palms under her head, staring down the length of her naked body at me.

I gaze at her, taking in every curve, every fold, every peak and dip, the way she glistens, wet in the dim candlelight of the room.

Leaning in, I kiss her skin, making love to her slowly, deliberately, watching as she unravels with every single motion of my mouth.

I take control back, her cries of pleasure only driving me harder to command her.

Forbidden fruit has never tasted so sweet.

I return to consciousness in her arms, warm, content, spent, and yet— I'm awake.

Sitting upright, there's a niggling urge in the back of my mind, one I cannot quiet. I move from her slumbering form, trying not to wake her as I wrap myself in a robe and make my way out onto the balcony for some fresh air.

My whole body is humming, radiant, raw from stimulation, and as I close the balcony doors behind me a welcome but warm breeze caresses my bare legs and feet, lifting my hair from my face.

It's desperate right now, whatever it is between me and Thane; clawing and uncontrollable, as it had been in the early days, when everything we did was scrutinised— but why? Why is it that every-thing seems so suddenly fragile, so completely and utterly temporary? She has always vowed forever, so why now does it seem like every embrace, every kiss, might be the last? I feel the need to tell her how I'd break if she was taken from me, something I've not felt necessary to voice since when we had been forbidden.

I sigh, staring out over the city, to the ashen horizon where the sun hovers, lilac and omniscient, above everything.

Is it the Demon Lords? The mystery of not knowing when they'll strike next or who they'll attack?

No. They've always been a threat. I deduce, wondering then if it's not to do with them but something about me that has changed— or rather, been taken away.

I feel so helpless, and that is because I am. I can't use magic, can't use my power— so what am I other than another mortal waiting to be picked off? I have never felt this vulnerable, this human— and I'm sick to my stomach with it.

It calls to me through the doors, now that I realise what exactly it is that's making me feel so useless, so unworthy of a place at her side. It's not the magical part of me that's the problem. It's the mortal side, the weak side, which has me flailing. I'm terrified I'll be killed, or she'll be killed— and I'll be helpless to stop it.

I can't give up the magic. Can't let us be weak that way. I can't risk losing her— I realise, leaning over the balcony as my heart hammers in my chest. Thane won't like it, won't understand, but I need to have some kind of defence at my disposal, for us.

I turn, re-opening the balcony doors to find her still slumbering inside. Tiptoeing across the room, I exit the apartment, excitement building and mixing with fear as I enter my alchemy chamber for the first time in too long.

The scent of dragon heartstrings, of crushed sprite's wings and powdered unicorn horn, of kelpie's mane, call to me, beckoning, alluring as any woman I've ever known.

I pace over to the shelves, running my fingers along the rows of vials, taking in the contents one by one and remembering the day I'd felt the Gods of Ancient inside my head. Such power— such security was to be found in their way of life, in their collection and hoarding of magic. That, I suppose, is the beautiful thing about dark magic. You don't have to be born with it, don't have to fit into some insane caste system to possess it. It's the kind of magic that anyone with enough desire can master, something unbiased in whom it seeks to attach to, in whom it imbues with its protective power.

I pull down a jar of aether, recalling the way it had surrounded me during the resurrection, my heart pounding frantically at the mere memory of the pain, of the excruciating yet delicious power that supercharged my veins, possessing me so completely.

I open it, wondering what I should make first— a draft for Xion and Sephy, perhaps? To avoid conception? Or something protective for Thane on her flight? I stand, thinking on this before I realise I should be looking for something to help Haedes get stronger first.

I pick up the feather of a Sephilim, glistening gold, and feel the immortal rays of the Aetherial sun absorbed into its every fibre, smiling. I turn back to my workspace, clearing the books I'd been looking at before the ritual and setting a flame burning beneath the cauldron I've missed so much.

I am careful, methodical, respectful in how I work with alchemy, knowing it's dangerous, but inevitably get caught in an inescapable dance with the magic itself. It pulls at my soul, calling and embracing me without question as I add ingredient after ingredient to the pewter pot, scanning over recipes for rejuvenation drafts— deciding to make a hybrid of three different potions to try and reverse Haedes ageing, if only a little.

The scent of it, of burning feathers, powdered unicorn horn, and the scale from a mermaid's tail simmer satisfactorily before me when suddenly I'm interrupted as the door opens wide, casting stark light on the cosy, mythic atmosphere of the chamber and breaking my alchemic trance.

"I thought I could smell burning—" is all that Thane can say as she turns on her heel and storms from the doorway.

I rush into the hall after her, panicking, guilt overtaking me.

"Thane— wait!" I exclaim, grabbing her arm.

She pulls it away from me, eyes furious as she shoves me back and slams the apartment door in my face.

"Thane, I'm sorry!" I cry through the wood, resting my head on the grain as my white hair falls forward. The aether dust on my fingertips leaves sparkling trails on the inside of my palms as I form a fist, banging for her to come back, to let me in voluntarily, to forgive me.

She doesn't, and when I finally stop crying and muster the courage to enter the apartment, to defend my actions, I find only the wide-open balcony doors and the dark, gossamer curtains blowing in the stifling breeze of yet another Mortarian spark shower.

SEPHY

"Ow! Careful! Mr. Featherlight touch! Do you have any finesse? Like at all?!" I cuss, cringing as Xion pulls yet another splinter out of my back. I'm sat in the bath with him, bubbles frothing high around us both as his spa tub works out the kinks in my muscles from our little run-in with nature earlier. The splinters, however, are not so easy to remove.

"I'm sorry, these tweezers are tiny and my hands— well, not so tiny. On the plus side, I feel kind of like a giant—" He sighs, running his fingers down the skin of my back, tracing the outlines of my scars. I shudder beneath the graze of his touch, causing him to stop immediately.

"Well, I'm glad this is fun for one of us—" I mutter, rolling my eyes and crossing my arms over my naked breasts, causing bubbles to fly up and engulf me in a fresh wave of bergamot and Himalayan rock salt.

"You should have told me to stop!" he complains.

I turn, looking over my shoulder as tangled wet knots of fiery, red hair fall down my spine and over his hand.

"And what fun, dare say you, would that have been?" I demand, cocking my eyebrow and biting my bottom lip.

"Do you want me to stab you with the tweezers again? Because distracting me with that face is making that more than likely—" Xion smirks, his body shimmering with hot water. His hair is even darker wet, and it's slicked back against his skull as individual droplets of water catch in his stubble. I examine him, letting my head hang back as I arch my spine, pushing my ass toward his crotch.

"Who said anything about tweezers?" I demand, and he gives me a deadpan expression.

"You know most people would find the whole stabbing metaphor a turn-on— with our history— not so much," he explains.

I huff, turning back as he continues to pull splinters from my skin. "I think that's the last one," he says after five more minutes of eye-watering tweaks, putting his flat palm against my spine and running it from my neck to my tailbone, feeling for anything more.

"I don't know why I was worried about a romantic involvement with you— having splinters pulled out of my spine just about sums us up, and it isn't goddamn romantic." I spin in the water, leaning back against the opposite side of the tub and resting my bare feet on his legs. My knees bend, coming out of the water as I scrunch up to fully submerge my torso, relishing the hot water on my skin and the steam opening my pores.

"Well, I am a half-demon. What did you expect?" he asks, placing the tweezers back on the edge of the tub and resting both arms along its wide rim.

"Death, mayhem, a bouquet of half-rotting corpses. Getting fucked against a tree and getting splinters in my ass— not on the list, but it's original I'll give you that. I've never had the guy stay around long enough to pull them out either— so that's also a win for you," I tease him, and he blinks once, then twice, an innocent compared to me despite his demonic tendencies.

"I thought you were going to say it was the first time you'd had sex outside—" he mumbles, looking disappointed.

"Uh, I went to a boarding school in the middle of the English Countryside. Not even close." I smirk, remembering those days when I'd been inexperienced and happy with whatever half-assed job a guy had been willing to do while he tried not to finish all over my leg.

"Oh—" Xion looks half amused and half interested at my response. My eyebrows knit together, immediately suspicious.

"Wait— was that the first time you've?" I ask him, and he nods before I can finish, pressing his lips together in a semi-embarrassed smile.

"I've only had sex with one other person than you, and that only lasted as long as I could control myself before going full demon and killing her."

That's right. I had totally forgotten. He's not a normal guy, not a player. Not in this for the thrill of the chase and catch. This, for him, has an entirely deeper, more profound meaning.

And I'm the selfish asshole who can't commit; who's scared to make this into something meaningful, something serious, I muse, the guilt at what I've done by letting him sleep with me again hurtling toward me in a wave of unwanted emotion.

The loss of control I feel with him is terrifying, and yet it's so fucking addictive, better than any drug, better than any drink. His touch on my skin is like heroin, taking me to a place of bliss and ecstasy I never want to leave.

It's perhaps the only time I've felt truly alive since crawling from my own grave.

So why am I so afraid to embrace it? To take it as mine? To allow myself to feel for him? I wonder, staring at him as I bite my bottom lip once again.

Oh yeah, because I'm me, and good shit doesn't happen to me. Ever. If I let this turn into something wonderful, it's just going to crash and burn, destroying everything in its path as it does. Why bother hoping for something that just isn't going to work out?

He's a half demon, and I'm a half-god. He's murdered. I've been hunted. What on earth could we possibly have to offer one another besides pain— and splinters in the ass?

Still, we have time before the inevitable, before the pain. So maybe I should just be grateful for him, right now, in this moment.

"What are you thinking about?" he asks me, taking my foot in his hand and massaging the ball of it with his thumb.

"I was just wondering if you've ever had sex in a bathtub before—" I let my eyelids drop so they hood the cognac depths of my irises.

"What do you think?" he demands as I crawl onto my knees. He lurches forward, grabbing me and pulling me into his broad lap.

"Have you ever been on the bottom before?" I whisper in his ear as I run my fingers through the thick damp curls of his hair, drawing him in toward my throat. Here, he kisses me, inhaling my scent as his hands push my torso flush to his, the warm water sloshing between us.

"What do you think?" he murmurs against my carotid as he pushes me back from him, taking my nipple into his mouth and tugging generously. A moan escapes me as I straddle him, and his hands move down to my ass, squeezing and tugging in all the right places.

"Are you sure you've never done this before?" I smirk.

He winks, giving an innocent look as he flutters his too-long, too-dark eyelashes.

"I promise."

I feel his erection pulsing between my thighs and so let him enter me, moving rhythmically as the jets pound repetitively against my knees.

As I begin to ride him, he groans, looking up at me with wonder.

"Can you promise me it won't be the last?" he demands, a chuckle forming deep in his throat and erupting in a half laugh, half moan as I increase the pace, wishing to silence him immediately.

"Oh, now I know I've got a practically blank sexual slate to play with, I can guarantee you it won't be the last," I vow, moaning too as he stretches the deepest parts of me with a delicious and firm rhythm.

"I'd never thought of inexperience as a turn-on before— but I guess I can live with that," Xion admits, breathing in ragged wisps as he grows larger and hotter with each passing second.

"I'd never thought I'd get splinters in my ass from fucking a half-demon against a tree— guess we should prepare ourselves for the unexpected when it comes to each other," I realise, glad now I agreed to this.

My life is so painful at times. I deserve a little relief, a little something for me. I just hope Xion doesn't get hurt in the process— then again, he has a naked chick riding him in his spa tub— so why should he complain?

We fall into silence as I ride him with the most punishing rhythm I can muster, muscles burning with every movement as my body is re-submerged in the bubbles over and over. I can barely speak as I feel him pushing me to the point of climax, letting my head hang back as I push his mouth onto my breast. He digs his fingers into my ass as he thrusts, unable to stop himself beneath me as we both become utterly lost in a frenzy of drawn-out, savoured pleasure. I wonder which one of us will break first, but I don't want it to be him, so I yank his head back, digging my nails into his skull and buying myself a few more seconds.

I orgasm loudly on top of him, clenching around him and pushing him over the edge as he cries out against my skin, grazing me with his teeth. I hold him to me as I ride out the wave of pleasure between us, not faltering for even a second as I want him to experience his release to the fullest, aware now more than ever that he's practically untouched.

Looking down into his eyes, I kiss him gently, feeling his heartbeat rapid against my palm.

We sit like this, me in his arms, straddling him, for a while, simply staring into one another— trying not to feel. Despite it all and against my volition, I can't deny that in the heat of this moment, I'm burning soul-deep for him.

I'll never admit it, never give in to it, but I wonder, just for a moment, if Xion knows he's not alone in this instance, being scorched raw right through.

For both our sakes, I can only hope he remains oblivious and that the flames which threaten to consume us both, turning my touch ashen and fatal, die before it gets that far.

17

PANDORA

PANDORA

THE DRIPPING OF STAGNANT water upon already damp cobble-stones echoes out through the labyrinthian corridors of the Exilia dungeons. Breathing in, the scent of stale blood and rot penetrates my personal space, causing me to take in only shallow wisps of the chill, stale air.

I wonder how long it's been since the weak excuses for gods and goddesses who make up the Nexus put anyone down here.

As I wait, I satiate my curiosity, peeking in between the rusting iron bars of hundreds of tiny cells. I am disappointed, finding only empty shackles hanging down against the slick brick walls and the stench of human excrement and urine which, even after all this time, has not entirely dissipated from the air. It seems, however, that the ghosts of screams, of pain and misery, have been all but lost from this once great example of terrorising the inferior.

Hurry up. I growl internally, patience running out as I feel the sting of the empty cells, of the lack of justice against those who have sinned, those who are not worthy. I don't know why, but after seeing how there is no such thing as justice in The Higher Plains of all places, it seems that people who haven't earned their place, who have fritted their lives away on chasing bodily pleasures and chemical escape, deserve everything that they get.

The fact that sinners are walking around, partying, drinking with The Nexus and living what could be considered blessed lives makes what happened to me even worse. I never did anything but serve my gods, be chaste and good and pure, and I was still damned to hell. It just isn't right.

Just as I'm about to check my watch, which doesn't exist because clocks honestly serve no purpose in this godforsaken place, a shadow appears, scurrying and meagre, moments after the sound of panicked footsteps fills the hollow halls.

Finally, I breathe, relieved.

"Pandora?" the mortal male queries, and I roll my eyes.

Who else is it going to be? Idiot.

I nod, not gracing him with a response, eyes dropping to the red velvet bundled in his arms.

"That doesn't look like a book," I assert, voice dry in the old air of these long-abandoned passages.

"We had to wrap it in something. Three of the others had their hands severely burned by the cover," he explains, and I frown. Anubis hadn't mentioned anything about that.

I examine him a moment, his body shivering as he's simply dressed in a thin burlap tunic and tights, his feet covered by simple leather sandals. His face is narrow, chin pointed, and eyes almond-shaped, a stark contrast to the acuteness of his other features. I look deeply into him and see nothing I don't expect – fear, anxiety, desperation— he's the walking equivalent of a Phobia's favourite meal.

"Give it to me," I demand, not wasting any time as my fingers begin to itch at the book's proximity. He passes me the bundle like it's hot, and I wonder if he realises what he's in possession of or knows the power he's just handed over so willingly.

"There's something else," he adds, dark eyes sheening with moisture in the flickering torchlight. His breath condenses in the chill air in front of his face, exposing his breathing as being too fast. He's panicked, or perhaps even excited, though I highly doubt it.

"Yes?" I bark, and he bites his bottom lip.

"Some of the mortals— they said that I should mention it, but I don't see the relevance—" He's babbling, and I feel my tolerance for his mortality waning fast. I readjust the bundle of red velvet in my arms, the book heavier than I was expecting, glowering at him.

"You'd better spit it out, or stop wasting my time," I threaten, and he gives a visible shudder, running a hand back through his greasy and unmoving dark hair.

"There's something inside that vault— something more valuable than any of the other objects. It's in a secret room right at the back. Some of the sinners, the ones who have been working here for a while, they say it houses an enormous hourglass—" he explains, and I cock my head.

"Well, of course, every sinner in this place has an hourglass. It helps Haedes keep track of how much time they have left on their penance," I blurt, exasperated at his lack of knowledge about Mortaria. I don't have time for his stupidity. I move to turn, reaching for the box inside my pocket as I hear him stutter.

I turn back, amazed at the audacity of this man who knows nothing. Compared to me, he is a worm in the dirt; blind, deaf, helpless, squirming— and yet he continues to babble on about a completely non-sensical rumour.

"No. This is different— it's black. Apparently. You can't see into it," he adds, and I feel my forehead crease as I frown.

What good is an hourglass you can't see inside? I wonder, shrugging and waving him away.

"Hurry back. Someone will notice you're missing," I shoo him, licking my top row of teeth with my tongue as my brain whirs.

After a few moments, the sound of his footsteps and the outline of his form, cast in shadow, disappears.

Balancing the red velvet against my hip, I open a portal. Clutching the box, hot, in my palm, I step through, curious as ever.

I reappear inside The Icon, not wanting to waste any time. Now I have the book in my possession, things can start progressing, making the waiting and the uncertainty seem finally worthwhile.

I tread, heels clicking against the hard and cold floor of the dining room, echoing out around me with a hint of grandeur. The place is deserted, an unusual state for The Icon. Usually, guards litter every doorway and corridor.

I can hear chatter coming from upstairs, and so I swallow my reservations about the last time I'd entered Anubis' room and make my way up the steep staircase.

Halfway up, I am almost knocked sideways by a slew of servants whipped into a flurry of motion, no doubt by Anubis' short and ever-growing temper.

Reaching the top of the staircase with a scowl, I cannot help but wonder why everyone is rushing around like lunatics.

"Anubis?" I call through the open doorway, bathed in a rich light from the crystal chandeliers of the sprawling suite.

"Come." I hear her bark, knowing immediately she's not in the mood for small talk. As I weave in and out of staff carrying various platters of steaming water bowls and hot, scented towels, I find her sprawled out on the bed, gossamer drapes drawn.

I catch her dark eyes in my gaze, noting Osiris at her bedside in a wide-backed, plush armchair as he turns to me, looking uncomfortable. As I tread toward them, I'm greeted by the growls of three feral jackals resting at the end of the four-poster bed, protecting their mistress.

"Set, Tut, Imhotep, hush!" Anubis scolds, causing them to fall into immediate silence as three identical fur-covered skulls drop once more upon their petite paws.

"What's going on?" I demand, observing her nudity. Wrapped only in the Egyptian cotton of the sheets, her right leg is propped up on a pillow, exposed and bare. I take in the bandage around her upper thigh and cock my head, seeking answers.

Surely her pets hadn't caused such an injury—

"Nothing major, I just had a little run-in with a panther," she explains. I visibly wince.

"Ouch."

She rolls her eyes, pursing her lips in distaste.

"It was my fault. I forgot that Luce keeps that ridiculous wild animal as a pet," she grumbles, propping herself up against a pile of gold and violet velvet cushions. Osiris shifts in his seat; clearly deeply affected by his mother's pain, tan skin glistening more vibrant than hers. She now seems pale in comparison from blood loss.

"Is it healing?" I ask her, and she nods, running her fingers back through her dark lustrous hair, tumbling poker straight and loose over her shoulders.

"Yes, it's just taking longer than I'd like," she complains. I shuffle from foot to foot, trying not to seem exasperated by her lack of appreciation for her healing powers. She's lucky. Any mortal would be dead or at least permanently maimed after a run-in with a pissed-off panther.

"So, I'm assuming you got what you went searching for?" I query, impatient even still. She nods, eyes fixated now on the fabric in my arms.

"I did, and I see the mortals followed through on their end," she expresses, sighing as she shifts, wincing.

"Indeed," I reply, giving the book to Osiris without pause, hoping to inspire confidence in our alliance, even now.

"Don't touch that Si; it'll burn you," Anubis warns him, and he nods, simply leaving the object resting on his knee. "Give Pandora the tether— and the other thing," she instructs, sounding hesitant, though I can't work out if that's because she's in pain or if she's having second thoughts.

Osiris places a hand inside his white linen jacket, pulling out a piece of black velvet. He passes it to me, and I take it in my palm, examining the choker as the central indigo stone catches in the light, purple-ish blue facets promising a kind of powerful allure that comes only from knowing the worth of what lies within. As I'm staring, Osiris gestures for a nearby sinner to come forward. I'm presented with the chalice of Uranus, which I take while giving Anubis a quizzical look.

"I thought you were going to take her to the—" I begin, but Anubis shakes her head.

"No, you should do it. I have some preparations to make with Horus' body down in the sinstone mines before the ritual can take place. It'll need to be ready by the time you arrive with her," she explains.

I smile, relishing the prospect of being close to such ancient power.

"I assume you know the conditions for this kind of ritual?" Anubis enquires, and I nod, scouring my memories for something similar.

"I want to say we need the spilling of innocent blood— is that correct?" I demand.

"Yes, that's right. The traditional sacrifice should do it," she elaborates.

Keeping hold of the chalice, I return to examining the tether, wonder filling me.

"So small—" I comment, wondering who would make something so crucial, so easily lost or crushed.

"Tethers should be small. Small and easily hidden— I was always telling Haedes that— of course, neither he nor his brother ever listened." Anubis rolls her eyes, and I feel my heart skip a beat.

"Wait— Haedes has a tether?" I demand, and she nods.

"Of course, every single Nexus member has one, including myself. We can't take mortal form without funnelling off some of our power. A mortal body could never fully contain the power of a god or even a titan. Zeus created Haedes when he banished him here. I thought you knew that?" She looks uncertain, worried even, as she speaks.

"I didn't. So Haedes— his tether is large and not easily hidden I take it?" I ask her, and she nods.

"It is," she replies, scrutinising me as her eyes narrow. "Not that it matters. You won't kill Haedes, that would be extraordinarily stupid," she announces, and I cock my head.

"How so?" I demand. She looks more uncomfortable by the second, and I wonder what she's so scared of.

"Because he is responsible for powering the Mortarian sun. It would dramatically decrease everybody's life expectancy that resides here. Yours and mine— we'd be pretty much mortal," she warns me.

I cock my head.

"Ah yes, of course. I didn't think of it that way. So, we should aim to capture him and keep him alive indefinitely then?" I suggest.

"That's what I would suggest. It won't be hard, he's weak from the resurrection ritual," I smile at this small revelation.

"Weak? Is that something we should expect to happen to Thanatos once Ra has returned?" I ask, and she nods.

"Yes. It's transferring life force from one person to another according to Lucifer, she will weaken afterwards," Anubis informs me, and I cannot help but feel glee stirring in my stomach.

"Perfect." I clutch the tether in my palm, placing it inside my jacket pocket without pause. "So, I'm going to head out to The Fallen Kingdom and prepare everyone to capture Thanatos," I add, and her expression seems serious as Osiris presses his hand atop hers.

"Keep your eyes trained on the skies. After tonight's events, I don't doubt she'll be taking to the air anytime now—" Anubis guesses as I turn on my heel.

"Get well soon," I call back over my shoulder, storming from the suite, purposeful in every motion.

Descending the stairs from her chambers, I wait only until I reach the dining room to open my box once again and disappear inside.

SEPHY

I stare out over the city, the sky stormy overhead, as Xion slumbers in the bed behind me. We've had our fun, and now that I've surfaced from the sea of his far too addictive touch, I'm restless, wondering now whether, if I wanted a future with him, one would even be possible.

Taking in my reflection in the window beside me, I find my long bare legs and torso are blanketed by his too-large white shirt. I breathe him in unwillingly, looking beyond my wide, alert gaze and out to the city beyond.

The skeletal skyscrapers pierce the vermillion sky ablaze with falling sparks. They take on the overwhelming appearance of a burning galaxy as every tumbling ember becomes star-like in its illuminative, macrocosmic glory. Staring at them, at the infinity of fire blanketing the city, I'm taken back to when the sky had been eclipsed to me by the earth, to when I had been dead and buried.

I bite my bottom lip, concerned. Did either Haedes or Lucifer know what they were doing when they brought me back? What does this mean for me? Am I perfectly fine now? Am I different? Has my soul changed? My body? Am I exactly as I was, or I have I returned as something less— something more broken than I had been upon my death?

Careful— someone might think you're planning on having a future with that kind of thinking, I muse, wondering why it is that I can't just let myself live. I'd been on the cusp of change that night, on the edge of something meaningful and evolutionary in my personal development, but it's as if the world had conspired to snuff out that hope, to remind me that people like me, we just don't end up happy. All that happens to people like me is pain, bloodshed, and death.

Anyone would think I'm depressed with the way I'm thinking, but I'm not. I'm contented, almost, with only the niggling of questions I want answered but don't dare ask dancing on the tip of my tongue.

I turn from the window, stripping off the shirt and tiptoeing across the room before scouring the bottom of Xion's closet. I find the trousers I wore the night I'd been attacked at my welcome party by two Abraxians. Slipping them on, I pull one of Xion's identical, black, round-neck t-shirts over my head and sling an unremarkable and loose-fitting leather jacket of his over my shoulders. I inhale the scent of pomegranate mixed with leather, closing my eyes and indulging myself for only a moment, remembering being enveloped in that same scent for the past few hours, the carelessness I felt, the surrender to everything including him.

Stupid. Stupid. Stupid. I cuss at myself. The fear of being close to him, of letting him in, engulfs me in a complete yet momentary instance of panic.

Heartbeat rapid in my chest and palms sweaty, I slip out of the apartment, slightly guilty but not guilty enough to make me want to stay. I tread lightly even though I could probably tap dance out and not wake him after how much energy he's expended in the last couple of hours keeping me happy. I could have even convected out I suppose, but there's something appealing about fresh air and stretching my legs, working out the kinks in my muscles from the short yet deep slumber I'd fallen into during my post-sex haze.

Flicking my hair out from under the collar of the leather jacket as I descend the million stairs, a comfortable burn in my thighs and calves begins to mount, making me realise I've missed working out. Thinking about this, I exit through the glass revolving doors of the alabaster stone building spattered with red flecks — Xion has told me the name of the stone before, but I can't remember.

I begin walking toward the sharp silhouette of the Exilia, which rises in a way nobody can ignore over the entire city, casting shadow over everything. Staring down at the slick black crystal of the side-walk, I discover it alight with the glistening of embedded garnets and the reflections of falling overhead sparks.

This place almost feels like home— I ponder, looking up to the sky and finding a raven silhouetting against the lilac glower of the sun. It's Thane, I'm sure of it, and I wonder as I see her soaring off into the smoky horizon if I'm so different.

I don't feel like I belong anywhere.

Except when I'm with him.

But Xion isn't my home, and neither is Mortaria. Ever since I came back, I don't feel like The Sinclair Estate has anything to offer me either. It's different than when I left, and it's not just the décor.

I'm a nomad without a future, without a purpose, just floating around between dimensions looking for what can only be described as a good time with no strings attached.

But Haedes said— I hear the voice in the back of my mind and slap that bitch back down to where she belongs.

Me— rule Mortaria?

Pfft.

Absolutely not. I'll put Haedes on life support before I let that happen.

And yet I wonder— would I take the throne given no other choice, or would I simply shrug my shoulders and let the world burn as I watch with a glass of fine whisky, gyrating in my half-demon lover's arms, engulfed by the shadow of Ragnarok's flickering flames?

The truth is, I don't know.

I'm no hero; that's for sure.

Oh well. That's never going to be an issue, I remind myself. So, I guess I shouldn't worry about it.

By the time I stop wondering about this and conclude that I'm better served not wasting my energy, I'm convecting the last hundred or so feet inside The Exilia on my approach towards the spitefully sharp main gates, not wanting to deal with security.

I have enough problems accepting that I'm Haedes' daughter, brought back from the freaking dead no less. I'm not about to spend three hours trying to convince some boneheaded Doppel guard.

As I reappear in an onslaught of flickering blue flames, I'm staring down at the exact person I want to see, in exactly the mood I wished never to see anyone in. I'm crap at comforting people, especially women, and particularly when that woman is none other than Lucifer.

"Hi—" I announce, watching as the shuddering form, sat on the floor in front of a raging fire, looks up, Beelz at her side. Her eyes are rimmed red, and her cheeks are stained with mascara.

Well. Shit.

I don't have time for drama today. I just want to ask my questions that I don't really want to ask at all and be done with it. As I'm pondering this, Cerb comes bounding toward me, wagging his large fluffy tail. I bend at the knee, fussing him between the ears. I've missed his company.

"Oh, hello—" Luce sniffs, her face puffy. This isn't a great look on her.

I rise, moving to take a seat on the sofa beside her, hoping this will be over quickly.

"What's wrong?" I ask, not caring but knowing if I don't ask her then this may well take forever.

"Me and Thane just had a fight. It'll be fine—" She manages to exhale the words in between tiny, silent sobs that rob her of all sound.

I frown.

Well, I'm extra crap with relationship advice so this should be fun.

"What happened?" I ask, and she shakes her head, white locks ratty and dishevelled, more so than I've ever seen them.

"She caught me using magic, I told her I'd stop, but I just— I can't be defenceless. Can't leave us so open, so vulnerable— you know? I just hate being this way—" she exclaims, getting passionate as she wipes her eyes on the back of her hand and gives yet another heavy exhale, trying to calm herself.

"Way?" I ask, my voice making me sound like I'm actually interested.

"Human. Mortal. In this crappy body— I've never hated it this much before. Never felt so vulnerable—" She begins to cry again, and I blink a few times, surprised that I know exactly how she feels.

"I don't blame you for wanting to use magic to protect yourself. If I could have stopped my murder using magic, I would have in a heartbeat. No matter the consequences," I express. She stops crying a moment, long enough to stare me square in the face.

"Really?" she asks, and I nod with ultimate sincerity as I find myself caught off guard entirely by my empathy for her.

"Really. Besides, if it weren't for your magic, I wouldn't be here. I'd be dead still, and even before the resurrection, I would have been demon food without you—" I remind her.

She throws her arms around my neck.

"Thank you—" she breathes. My nostrils fill with the scent of sweet apple.

"It's just the truth, Luce. That's all," I mumble, not into the overly emotional nature of the conversation. I've had enough emotion tonight already.

"So— why are you here? I thought Xion and you were—" she trails off, and I cock an eyebrow, staring at her.

"What? Killing each other's dates? I wanted to thank you for that by the way—" I scowl at her; well aware she'd orchestrated the entire thing.

"I'm sorry. I just— you two need to get over yourselves. Love like this doesn't come around except maybe once in a lifetime—" she explains, imploring my forgiveness with wide blue eyes.

"Love is a strong word, Lucifer. I thought I made myself clear. Even now, Xion and I are just having fun. It's not a serious thing—" I express, and she shakes her head.

"You can deny it all you want, but it won't keep your heart safe, Sephy Sinclair— don't you think I tried? Tried not to love Thane when her mother came to me and told me to stay away or I'd lose everything— my home, my family— my people? Of course, I wished I had never set eyes on her. I didn't want to be exiled, but pain is temporary— regret isn't." She's so serious now I can't help but look away, trying not to hear what she's saying.

"I'm not big into regret actually. But I am into answers. So, I was hoping you would have some for me—" I change the subject fast, looking at her as she cocks her head, eyes glassy.

"Answers, about what?" she asks, crossing her legs and leaning forward with interest as Beelz shifts at her side.

"I need to know what happens now. To me— do I just walk away from death unscathed? Are there consequences? What about that prophecy— the one about the Chimera of all souls? Does that have anything to do with this? Does this make that redundant?" The queries spill out in a single unhindered torrent, and she leans back, looking exhausted.

"Those are some serious questions. Are you worried about you know— getting pregnant? Because I have potions which should prevent that from happening. I gave one to Xion right before you were murdered—" she reminds me.

"I know. He and I took some a while ago— just to be safe." I remind myself unwillingly of the taste, of the revulsion mixed with the desperation to continue kissing him. I had taken that nasty liquid into my body, the thought of which now makes me shudder, but back then, I was so aroused I would have downed a molten lava cocktail if it had meant I could stop worrying about ending the world by sleeping with him.

"I'll make you some more— have you seen a doctor since you got back?" she asks as Cerb comes closer, licking my outstretched hand. I move to pet him, trying to distract myself from Lucifer's emotionally fraught face.

"Of course not! You can't exactly walk into a mortal hospital and ask for a post-mortem check-up—" I say with a scowl. She sighs, shaking her head as if she should have known this.

"Of course, sorry, well— I don't know much about the after-effects of the ritual. I wish I knew more, but if the answers are anywhere, they'll be in the Book of The Dead. It's in Haedes' vault. We can go now, and I'll take a look if you've got time. Is Xion with you?" she enquires, looking to the door as if he might magically appear.

"No, I came alone. I thought he'd like to sleep. He's been running himself ragged lately," I lie.

Me sneaking out in the middle of the night— or day, or whatever time it is, has nothing to do with him getting his rest and more to do with the fact that I can't bear to let myself sleep in his arms for longer than an hour. Terrified that if I sink too deep into ecstasy, I'll never want to leave.

"I see. Well, let me get dressed and we'll go." She gets to her feet, gliding around the sofa and back into the bedroom, closing the frosted partition behind her.

"I'll just pop Cerb back to the estate while you change. I'll be two seconds." I call, standing to grip the Leonberger's collar between my forefinger and thumb as he remains, loyal, at my feet. Truth be told, I feel uncomfortable waiting in an apartment still rife with the negative energy from whatever argument had passed between Luce and Thane, especially because Xion has already caused me emotional exhaustion.

Consequently, I don't wait for Luce's reply before disappearing in a torrent of blue flames.

When I return, Cerb having been taken for grooming by Jules, Luce is still in the bedroom.

"Do we need Haedes for this?" I call after a few minutes of silence, alerting her that I've reappeared.

Sliding open the partition once more, she reveals that she's now dressed in a pure white, floor-length, clingy silk gown before shaking her head. I've never seen her wearing white before, and it does nothing but exaggerate her pallid skin and hair, causing her light blue eyes to pop, glowing out of her face, vivid against the deep bloody red of her lipstick.

"No, according to Thane, the door of his vault was knocked clean off by the Banshees during the attack." I feel my eyebrows rise on my forehead as I get to my own feet, moving after her as she sweeps right past me and opens the door. Closing the distance between us, I pass beneath the crook of her arm, taking in her pure, flawless aesthetic as I do so, confused.

"Wait, attack? There was an attack?" I demand.

She looks over her shoulder as she closes the door behind us, locking it with a key she procures from her cleavage.

"Oh yes, you missed that— *great* job with security by the way." Her tone is dripping with sarcasm as she recovers her usual flawless composure, emotional angst seamlessly tucked just beneath the pore-free velvet of her alabaster complexion.

"Oh uh, yeah, sorry about that. Guess I kind of missed the party. Though next time if you want reliable security, you might try not pissing them off with skanky redheads called— what was her name— Leia?" I cock my eyebrow as the two of us hurry down the spiral staircase, footsteps ringing out in painfully obvious and unsynchronised time.

"Leeah. She's my stylist, and a lovely woman if you'd get to know her—" Lucifer gives me a judgemental stare, and I roll my eyes as we reach the floor of the main lobby, striding fast past sinners whose faces blur into a single morose expression.

"Nah, I think I'll take a rain check—" I remember Haedes' words as I speak, smirking, but she doesn't reply.

We pass the rest of the journey to the vault in comfortable silence, both content with saying nothing at all for once. I see more sinners than I remember, semi-invisible against the walls of every room, standing stoic and still. Their eyes flit collectively in a domino effect as we pass, each as curious about what it is we're not saying as the next.

When we finally reach the vault, I discover the door knocked clean off its hinges and lying dented to one side where a group of sinners are trying to prop it up. They're not doing a very good job, which isn't surprising. It looks heavier than a lead elephant.

We step past them, over puddles of blood being mopped by sinners in blasé garments that attract absolutely no attention whatsoever. In fact, if it weren't for the blood, I may very well not have noticed them at all.

I can smell the familiar scent of ichor as we pass into the vault through the chasmic open doorway, and I know that Banshees have been here recently. It's not a smell I'll ever forget as it's one I'd been overcome with as I'd stared into the white, hungry eyes of death.

As we stride past the many shelves of audibly trickling hourglasses, each containing different types of sinstone, and then three urns with their lids off, we turn a corner to where the innermost chamber of the vault is sealed, containing Haedes' hourglass.

I look around a moment, finding nothing else in the space other than an empty pedestal and the still-closed high-security door, locking the hourglass away from public view.

"Wait— *what*?!" Luce startles me as I snap my head to face her. She takes a few running steps forward toward the pedestal, her hands slamming down hard on the top of the stand and causing sand to fly up from where it's fallen from what I assume was the book.

"This can't be happening—" Luce's breath turns frantic.

Spinning to me with eyes wide and full of horror, hands visibly shaking, she speaks.

"It's gone. The Book of The Dead is gone."

18

DANCING IN THE DARK

PANDORA

RETURNING TO THE FALLEN Kingdom, I'm slightly giddy as the cogs of my mind whir into motion, slick with new information as they glide against one another, forming not only one plan but two.

My stride takes on the rhythm of my joy, light and full of spirit, reminding me of how I had once walked, head held high and full of divine purpose, around the halls of the Solis Castra.

Entering the central meeting room, my reflection is cast back at me from every angle as the mirrored walls alert the two Demon Lords occupying the space to my arrival.

"Pandora, did it go well?" Abraxis demands, cocking a dark eyebrow at me with an undeserved superiority in his gaze.

"Very. In fact, I have come to ask you for your help. Both of you," I look to Barbas, who appears utterly bored as he leans back in the way he always favours, seeming careless and untouchable as he runs his arachnid fingers through his long silver hair. His pet tarantula, Mr Skinny Legs, crawls from beneath his collar and walks slowly and purposefully down his sleeve before resting lazily in his pale palm.

"I'm intrigued, go on—" Barbas coaxes me, letting the spider crawl slowly between his fingers and causing mine to unwillingly twitch.

"I'm thinking of putting together a two-pronged attack. So, we have a backup plan just in case the resurrection doesn't go as planned. I mean, The Nexus are spread thin; apparently, Haedes has been weakened significantly in bringing his daughter back," I announce, and Abraxis opens his mouth. I wonder if he'll interject, but instead, he takes pause for a moment before his expression hardens.

"That seems sensible," he replies. My expression turns surprised. Could it be I've changed his mind about my cause? Made him see reason through the recruitment of Anubis and the solidity of my plan?

Perhaps— or perhaps not. I muse, wondering if he has another agenda. You never can tell with Abraxis. He's slippery at best.

After the plans have been laid, I make my way with haste over to the fields of volcanic soil. This is where the dark Kindred who are killed find themselves reborn under the will of their Demon Lords. I know this is where I'll find Lilliana and, considering she's by far the best with a bow and arrow, I also know I'll be needing her, and soon.

The sky is ablaze with sparks, mixing in with ash blown north from the waste of land strewn with Doppel warriors and the odd demon charged with holding them back while we build forces.

It was a genius idea to recruit mortals, and an even more genius idea to lessen our presence in The Ashen Waste, making the Nexus believe I've been thwarted, that they have triumphed, perhaps once and for all.

They will never see this coming, never see the two-pronged attack, and by the time they know what is happening, it will be too late. Mortaria will be mine— I mean ours— for the taking.

My hair blows from my shoulders, winding around my face in thin tendrils as I climb the shattered stone steps leading toward a crumbling wall surrounding the most fertile volcanic soil at Mount Mallum's base. I cannot help but glare up at it as I feel the ground tremor slightly beneath me, reminded that I am fragile, small and, as ever, that nature rules all.

As I take an exaggerated step over the wall, head held high and spine forced straight, I find Lilliana and Katerina standing upon the earth, jagged knives made from bone clutched in their palms. They have closed eyes, making them look frail, weak even, as they mumble, entranced in a half-dream state. I know, however, that they are anything but, and so wait as they loom over the graves. What they're waiting for I'm not sure of, but I guess it has something to do with how they bring back their children.

Lilliana's eyes jerk open only seconds after the bloody puddles of Katerina's hollow eye sockets are revealed beneath the pallid curtains of her eyelids. They both look down at the identical knives in their palms, lips falling silent of ancient whispers as they slice the skin of their free hands in unison. Holding them out, palm down, the blood drips fast into the soil, a quick running, scarlet trickle from each of them takes on a life of its own as it hits the dirt. The fluid contorts like a flailing insect, writhing, and then disappears after a few moments as though it had never been there at all.

I watch on, fascinated.

Opening my mouth to speak, to ask what I must of Lilliana as I know we have little time before Thane is in the skies overhead, I'm startled when she raises a hand. The gash on her palm flashes wide and exposed before it heals in front of my very eyes, imploring silence.

Katerina stands, bronze gown blowing around her ankles in a sharp wind seemingly strong enough to knock her off her feet entirely. Lilliana gets down on her knees, tucking the black, free-flowing but threadbare tulle beneath her as she watches the soil.

After a few moments, I see why.

The smell is the first thing to hit me, the smell of decay, of rot, of old musty blood. As the soil before both Demon Lords begins to shift into two discernible masses, my eyes widen. A look of expectation warps the Demon Lords' faces, twisting them anxiously as if someone is in labour in the next room.

After a few moments, a noticeable snout pushes its way from the undergrowth, a wet hungry nose with trembling nostrils protruding out into the air, hungry like a newborn. These Kindred don't appear to be helpless at all though, as the pile of dirt next to Lilliana erupts in a sudden and unexpected plume of black earth, scattered over us like dark rain. In its place, as the Banshee beside it is brushed free of the same dark soil by its mother, the Succubus stands, lanky, with pale skin and too-large teeth, a thing of nightmares.

Katerina smiles, taking a step forward and raising a hand to its face before laying a scarlet kiss on the side of its thin, widespread lips, making me want to throw up.

I suppose all children are beautiful in the eyes of their parents— even if they do look like an albino bat that's been run over by several cars and left for dead before becoming the victim of bad taxidermy and horrendous post-mortem dental work.

As the Banshee scrambles free of its birthing grounds, it shakes its fur, full-sized and just as vicious as before it had been slaughtered. The Succubus takes off behind it, leaving Katerina looking bereft as her dark hair is blown back from her face.

Lilliana smiles, gesturing for the beast to head back down to the ruins of what had once been the main city streets. Here, it will once again join its packmates.

"Can we help you, Pandora?" Katerina demands, her shoulders creaking as she folds her hands in front of her corset.

"Yes, I need Lilliana for something of the utmost importance," I inform her. Lilliana cocks one eyebrow, looking more present in this moment than I've ever seen her as she pulls her thick lips back over her teeth.

"I'm intrigued," she relinquishes, stepping toward me and beckoning for Katerina to follow us both. We walk as a threesome back across the seemingly barren fields, stepping over the low wall and taking the cracked stairs in our feminine, agile strides.

"So, what exactly do you need me for?" Lilliana asks, the light skirt of her gown billowing around her. I turn back to her, Katerina mimicking me, and smile.

"I need you to come and shoot down a raven for me," I elaborate, and she gets a playful look like I've presented her with a brand-new chew toy.

"A raven? We don't have any raven— well not any *real* raven around here. I assume we're talking about Thanatos?" Katerina isn't the brightest spark, as I've come to conclude about any creature truly fuelled by bloodlust.

Looking to the sky, barren of all life but full of fire, I merely nod. I've always thought it obvious Katerina is more concerned with what she can sink her teeth into than using her brain.

"That is correct," I smile at her politely, fighting the urge to roll my eyes.

Lilliana gets a wicked glint in her eye.

"Very well, it would certainly break up an otherwise boring afternoon. I'll get my bow."

"I'll meet you in the Colosseum. We'll have a good vantage point from there," I suggest, and she merely stills, dreamy looking yet again, as though she's no longer checked into the conversation.

I stand awkwardly with Katerina as Lilliana departs, skirt billowing out behind her like an untameable cloud of polluted smoke.

"Would you like to take a little detour on the way round to the colosseum, stop in at the mortal encampment? I'm sure they'd love to see you," Katerina suggests. I can't help but snort slightly. I doubt, sincerely, that any of the mortals would love to see anyone responsible for getting them stuck here. As I said, Katerina is far from the brightest crayon in the pack— in fact, I'm pretty sure she's the black.

"You laugh, but many of the mortals look at you as a God made flesh Pandora— truly. You've offered them immortality. They're afraid, so naturally they cling to what they know, and what they know is that you have power, have offered them absolution and freedom from their penance. You should take a walk with me if you doubt the validity of my claim." She blinks once, then twice, eyes shining like a galaxy bleeding bright orange falling stars as they capture the burning sky above.

"Very well." I shrug, still not sure I believe her, but the encampment is on the way to the Colosseum anyway, so I may as well look in as I'm passing.

Katerina and I take off down the rough path, made only by many-layered demon tracks that have impacted the earth flat beneath our feet. She's tall, willowy, and her long legs make quick work of the distance as we hurry beneath the weeping fire of the sky. I wonder as we do so, as I take in her slim silhouette and we turn a corner towards the bustling outline of the mortal encampment, what it must be like to be her—

Everyone knows the story of how Katerina became the Demon Lord of the Succubi, servant of Sanguina, and while many of the Lords are still shrouded in mystery, Katerina's tale is legend.

Why?

She was made by Dracula.

As I'm pondering her in all her pallidity, we come nearer with every step to the encampment of mortal recruits, hidden from the view of Mortaria by Mount Mallum.

As I approach, the humanity of this place penetrates my senses like noxious gas. The way the flaps of their tents blow, the silhouetted bodies within giving glimpses into the intimacies of life in progress. I smell cooking meat, sweat, bodies that haven't bathed in days all mingled together in the symphony of basic aromatic desperation for life, reminding me only too clearly of how it had been when I was alive. Scrambling to survive, never having the resources to thrive, the bated breath that came between meals as if every mouthful may be your last. Mortality had been waiting, slowly, for luck to turn on me and snatch the bread and stew right from my calloused fingers. For the hunger pangs to return, or the money to run out. For who could deny the justice in trading the right to live for cold metal coins?

We pass the entryway, which is little more than burlap sacks filled with dirt and piled high, creating a low, make-shift wall around the place. The tents line the outside of the crude territory, showing that no matter how fragile their defences, this place has been claimed.

As if they have any real right to it at all.

Taking step after careful step, I find myself enveloped by the collective anxious— and what could even be considered awed— gazes of the people I've abducted. I am surprised as they emerge from their tents, seeing my imminent outline pass, heavy leather skirt falling dark around me and creating an adequate boundary to keep their mortal stench at bay. They peer around the fabric of their meagre homes, eyes wide as they unfold outwards and into the street like origami. They're fragile seeming, and come closer, forming a circle around me.

"Yes?" I demand, cocking an eyebrow as the breeze takes my dark veil up in its gentle caress. They look at one another, not one syllable passing anyone's lips. A man with dark rusty-coloured hair and green eyes stares at me, dead ahead, before dropping to one knee like he's about to propose. As he does so, the rest of the mortals copy him, each man or woman falling to bended knee and gazing up at me. They don't speak, as though they're so infected with melded fear and awe that they dare not shatter the moment.

My heart inflates in my chest as I step amongst them, passing through the encampment with Katerina by my side, surprised at the fact it seems she was correct in her assessment of their loyalties, of their devotion.

As we leave the small settlement only too soon, I look back over my shoulder, finding them rising in my wake and continuing to stare. I smile, waving to them in a stiff and practised motion, like royalty, as they wave back, hypnotised.

"Well, that was— flattering—" I smile, cheeks flushing with rare warmth.

"I told you. You've shown them death is not the end and simultaneously offered to prevent not only their penance but also their arrival at life's final destination. They are devout to you, the perfect mixture of fear and adoration running in their veins. I can practically taste it—" Katerina looks like she might start drooling as she evidently salivates, licking her burgundy bottom lip and wringing her fingers, twitchy in posture at the thought of a queen bee's red nectar.

"Yes. It is pleasing— to be recognised." I don't elaborate much more than this on my feelings toward the matter, sensing an unwanted and enormous rush of pleasure at their adoring eyes. I must not succumb to their worship because if I do, I shall only turn as arrogant as Zeus himself.

As we pace across yet more impacted earth, the Colosseum reveals itself, a stocky black shadow with dark edges, undeniably grand, in the shadow of the volcano that seethes above it.

Nearing the entrance, I hear heavy paws and claws approaching from the rear and soon find myself overtaken by Lilliana, who is riding a Banshee barefoot and with a bow formed of bone and a quiver of alabaster arrows strapped to her spine. Her hair is wild with the momentum of her rabid steed, and as I smile to myself, glad she's hurried, we finally pass under the immense height and darkness of the Colosseum entranceway.

I find Lilliana dismounting the Banshee that's carried her here only too easily as she lands in a crouch, dark skirts pluming around her as she uses a flat palm to stop herself tilting forward. There's a feral look in her eye, a glint, the kind you know is indicative of a lust for the pounding hearts and heaving lungs of the hunt.

She inhales deeply, white pupils retracting as she comes back to herself having dismissed her steed. It takes off past myself and Katerina, leaving the stench of ichor in its wake as matted fur brushes against my shoulder, depositing unwelcome damp.

"Shall we?" Lilliana breathes, taking her bow from her back in one fluid motion. I smile, finding her arrows made entirely of bone as she turns, putting the quiver made of animal hide clearly in view.

"We shall. Just remember do not hit her in the body— we don't want her dead. Just unable to fly," I decree. She nods only slightly, so slightly that if I hadn't been scrutinising her, I would think she hadn't heard me at all.

We march the length of the hallway, still stained with blood from previous victims, climbing the crooked and crumbling dark stone stairs in single file. Rising to the height of the building's cyclical architecture, my eyes rest on the land that sprawls out in all directions.

"So now we wait—" I exhale in a sigh.

Lilliana looks up to the sky, inhaling deeply, a smile pulling her lips apart far too wide.

"Not for long. I can smell her—" she practically growls, bounding from my side and around the edge of the stands, seeking the best vantage point. I sit with Katerina, watching the feral Demon Lord as she takes aim at a target neither of us can see until the very last moment. She pulls back the string of the curved skeletal bow, lining up the nocked arrow with the thick curve of her top lip.

We all inhale, waiting as the rest of the world falls into silence.

She arrives, soaring around the side of the volcano, banking a hard right.

Silent, but unmistakable against the vermillion of the sky, she flies.

The arrow is released, the bone of it piercing through the sky with too great an ease as it soars effortlessly along its trajectory.

We watch on, breath trapped in our chests but only until a single agonised caw rings out into the stagnant air.

I sigh, relieved.

XION

Another carriage, another journey back to the Exilia. You know it's all very well her running off like this, but I'm the poor sucker who can't convect, can't disappear in a flaming inferno. So, I'm left with what? Trailing around Mortaria after her with my super awesome, heavy-footed walking abilities?

Ugh.

She's like water. Vital to me now, but impossible to keep hold of. The moment I think I've quenched my thirst, had enough, she slips through my fingers, leaving my throat once more arid, thirsty for more.

Goddamn woman.

The scent of cinnamon lingers on my tongue, the memory of her eyes staring down into mine as she unravelled beneath my desperate grasp. She'd seemed so present, so *there*— but when I'd woken, it was as though she'd been a ghost of my innermost fantasies, fleeting and more haunting than any terrifying spectre.

Fuck this is hard.

Harder than anything I've ever had to deal with.

No really.

I thought that having her gone had been torture, but it seems having her here, having her so close and yet so far out of reach, is worse.

It's like she's returned, but she's scattered now, torn between two worlds. Between running and fighting. Like she's not got a choice but to live, and yet she's unsure of whether she still holds the desire.

Sighing out into the clammy air of the carriage, I hook my index finger beneath the round neck of my white t-shirt, not my first choice, but it seems Sephy has taken my only other clean black one. I pull the fabric taught away from my body, trying to cool down, trying to breathe as the obsidian pendant cools against my chest.

She's driving me insane, and I'm beginning to feel resentment despite myself. I just want her to stop, to be in my arms for a moment, to still and leave me with no doubt in my mind that she wants to be there. Instead, even when we are intimate, I see the wanderlust, the fear in her eyes, diminishing the once ferocious flame that blazed there for me.

The carriage stills to a halt, the wheels squeaking and in need of oiling, and hastily shove open the door, squeezing through and stepping out yet again into the entrance of the Exilia. As my feet hit the ground, I find myself face to face with a sinner. He has dark hair and dark eyes, tan skin and freckles spattered across the bridge of his nose. His eyes betray no meekness, which is unusual when put in context against his standing here.

"I'm sorry sir, you can't be here. We're on security lockdown," he informs me, straightening his spine and attempting to appear intimidating as he looks up at me. He's wearing clothes made from black burlap, just like those belonging to Anubis' new security posse.

"I'm Haedes' personal security— I think you'd better let me in," I growl, agitated he has no idea who I am. I mean I know I'm not one of The Nexus, but I'm not just some random nobody either.

"Do you have anyone who can verify that for me, sir?" he asks, and I wonder if I should turn demonic on him where I stand. Then again, if they're on lockdown, that might not do me any favours. This guy seems pretty green to me, a freshly cut jade pendant hanging loose around his neck. I mean, he probably thinks a Banshee is some white-skinned woman with the ability to hit high octaves for Christ's sake.

As I'm pondering what possible form of identification he thinks I might be carrying, a familiar flash of red catches my eye from the far end of the hall.

Atop the staircase, Sephy stands.

"Hey, hey! Sephy!" I call out, yelling as loudly as I can.

The sinner in front of me startles, my voice echoing in the high dome of the crystal ceiling.

"Hey! What are you doing here?" Sephy calls as she races down the staircase, taking them two at a time as she jogs toward me, hair bouncing around her.

"Well— you left without saying anything. I was worried," I counter as she waves the sinner away. He glares at me, suspicious, before taking his leave.

"Why? You know I can take care of myself." She cocks her head, smiling, and my eyes widen.

"I do— I just—" I begin and watch as her eyes narrow.

"Look, I won't hold you to what you said before. If the sex thing is too hard for you— if it's too difficult for you to separate your emotions, I get it. It's fine. But I don't need you trailing after me like a puppy. You don't owe me anything, and I'm a big girl. You used to know this," she implores me, and I realise she's right. She was murdered, but she also clawed her way back from beyond death, and she's still standing. I might want her to need me, but that's nothing to do with her and everything to do with me wanting to be needed. She can take care of herself, and I need to remind myself of that. I must, as she says, detach.

"Of course. I guess it's just habit. I'm used to you being in mortal danger." I shrug it off with a hollow laugh, gesturing to the bustling bodies behind her. "What's going on here, anyway?" I demand, changing the subject as quickly as I can.

"Someone has stolen The Book of The Dead," Sephy announces without blinking. My brow furrows.

"What!? How? That was locked up in Haedes' vault, right?" I demand.

"Yup. I'm about to head up to see his mighty blueness right now, wanna come? Could be funny watching him freak out about the vault—" she invites me with a smirk. I give a stoic nod, feeling like a spare part.

She turns on her heel, grabbing my arm in her elegant fingers and gripping me with a hard edge as we convect together, the fire enveloping her and then me as she reaches mid-step. I watch the flames, *blue* flames.

"Hey, wait— you can make the resurrection flame now?" I exclaim as the entryway of the Exilia dissolves in a plume of smoke and we reappear in the high, cold walls of the corridor in front of Haedes' door.

"Oh yeah, old news. Side effect from the ritual." She waves a hand like it's nothing at all, eyes fixed on the door as she raises a fist and knocks three times. I gape at her, wondering how I've been so distracted that I didn't notice something so radical.

The door opens slowly, and as my eyes meet with Haedes, his left eyelid twitches, mouth falling slack as he takes us in. We stand, him with a twitching eye and me with a growing impatience, for several minutes before Sephy breaks the silence in her usual sarcastic drawl.

"So are you going to invite us in or—" She lets the final word drag out as her lips remain parted ever so slightly. Haedes doesn't move even still, so she shoves past him, leaving him standing aside, eyes still fixed on me.

"Are you alright?" I ask, cocking an eyebrow as I enter his suite, utterly perplexed as to why he's giving me such an odd glare.

"Oh. I'm fine. Totally fine," he mumbles, glaring at me and then at Sephy even still. I scowl.

What the hell is up with him?

"We're not here for a social call, Haedes. You need to get dressed. There's been a break-in—someone's been in your vault," Sephy informs him, voice unfeeling as she takes a seat down on the edge of his bed, expression noticeably fatigued.

I know how she feels. Our after-hours activities weren't exactly what I'd call chilled.

"Shit! What did they take? Did they touch—" he begins, but Sephy shakes her head.

"The Book of The Dead. We're not sure if anything else was taken. We need you to come and take inventory if nothing else—" she informs him, tone clipped. Haedes sighs.

"And I was just going to sit down with a nice glossy magazine and attempt to return my hair to its former glory— apparently Kim's new ass is to *die* for — not that I should be surprised, she traded a hell of a lot of years for that booty—" he laughs to himself, striding across the length of the suite in his velour slippers before disappearing behind a black, free-standing screen in the corner of the room. Opening the wardrobe behind it, he begins to change as Sephy picks up something from his bedside table. She stares, the crumpled item clearly fascinating her.

"What is it?" I demand, and she turns the image to me.

"My mother—" She smiles, expression oddly nostalgic but happy. I squint at the image, taking a few steps toward her and bending down.

Her mother is dressed in a floor-length gown, and on her arm, Haedes stands, dressed to the nines. They appear to be at some kind of Day of the Dead celebration. Demi Sinclair's expression is one I've seldom seen on her but one I recognise from her daughter.

"She looks—" I begin, but Sephy interrupts me as we hear the clink of a belt buckle being fastened.

"Happy," she finishes, glancing down at the photograph once more before placing it back on the wood of the bedside table with wistful fingers.

As we hang in the moment, Haedes' arms rise into the air as he puts on a shirt and a knock at the door breaks the momentary calm.

"Can you get that?" Haedes calls.

I turn from Sephy, moving swiftly to the door. Yanking it open, Luce is revealed on the other side.

Pushing past me, the white of her dress makes her appear spectral against the black décor of the room. She looks at Sephy and then at me, calling to Haedes.

"Haedes, you know you don't have to scold them for having sex— they weren't to know that your solarium looked over those gardens. Just get over it already—" she exhales. I feel my heart stop in my chest.

What. The. Fuck.

"What?!" Sephy exclaims, eyes darting to me and then back to Luce.

Well, I guess that explains the look on his face when he opened the door.

"Thank you for that, Luce. Can I help you?" Haedes glowers at her as he steps, fully dressed in a white shirt and indigo suit pants, from behind the black partition.

"Wait— you saw us?" Sephy sputters.

Haedes shoots her an annoyed glare.

"Well, you were fucking a half-demon, very loudly, against my god-damn tree. So yes. I did. Now, can we move on? I'd rather not relive that little moment of hell— which coming from the god of the place says a lot, don't you think?" He scowls, and Sephy rolls her eyes, flushing bright red. I cross my arms, defensive and embarrassed all at once.

"Now, Luce. What is it?" Haedes demands, staring at her with unwavering intensity. Luce shrinks slightly.

"Uh— well, I just wanted to let you know that upon inspection, your hourglass seems untouched. Not so much as a scratch. I assume you know about the theft?" She cocks an eyebrow.

"And what about your tether?" he asks, and I frown. I've heard the term used before but never felt comfortable enough to ask about Luce's personal bind to this plain.

"You know full well that mine is perfectly fine— you stitched it into Beelz yourself—" Her eyes widen slightly at the name of the panther, and before any of us can ask her what's wrong, she's turned on the spot and dashed from the room, expression fraught.

"Well, that was weird—" Haedes exclaims, shrugging inside his freshly pressed cotton shirt. I stare at him as he sighs. "Well, shall we?" He gestures to the door, and I stutter, wondering how exactly to act around him now he's seen me screwing his daughter.

"But— shouldn't we talk about the—" I begin, but Haedes brushes past me, storming off into the corridor outside and calling back over his shoulder, not giving me the privilege of eye contact.

"No, Xion, no we should not."

19

THE SOUND OF SILENCE

<u>PANDORA</u>

SHE CAWS FOR THE fiftieth time, weakening by the second.

Lilliana instructs the Banshee to drop the raven's broken and limp body, twitching, into the bottom of a rust-plagued bird cage she's produced from seemingly nowhere.

"A perfect shot my dear, not even close to the body of the bird, bravo." Katerina applauds. The bones of her fingers hit one another, rattling out into the silence as we stand, surrounded by the mirrors of the main chamber.

Blood dribbles down between the bars of the base, falling into the crack and bridging the gap between the two halves of the table with grim adhesive span.

"There is no time to waste— we must proceed to The Icon. Grab that cage, Katerina— Lilliana, I'll be back for you later," I order them. For a moment the decree hangs between us, and I wait for either one of them to sneer, laugh, or object to my sudden authority. Instead, Katerina and Lilliana merely nod.

As Lilliana's footsteps fade into uneven echoes, showing her excited haste at the prospect of action, a familiar voice slithers through the air, causing both Katerina and me to turn.

"So, you actually did it— interesting, very interesting indeed." Gorgon's thin lips spread into a smirk, his forked tongue caressing the outer edge of his top row of teeth with fervour.

"I think you mean impressive—" I correct him, crossing my arms softly over my chest and running my fingernails down the inside of my bare arm in a light caress.

"You shot a bird. Let's not get too carried away—" His smile vanishes as a serious expression overtakes his face. He hisses something unintelligible, and the air around my ankles shifts.

"What are you doing?" I demand, uncomfortable at his spontaneity.

"Telling my Kindred to reinforce the cage. You can't honestly want to risk her escaping, even if she does have a broken wing. Thanatos has quite the reputation for survival—" Gorgon explains as Katerina watches the cage with fascination. Smaller Gorgonians wrap themselves between the bars, rippling in and out of camouflage as their green eyes glow bright into the dim shadow.

"We had best be going then," I suggest, reaching into my pocket and pulling out the box I'd been holding only moments before.

"Yes, we should—" Gorgon smiles, eyebrows relaxing on his forehead. I watch him with interest, cocking my head.

"Oh, you're coming with us now?" I demand, amused.

"But of course. I wouldn't miss this for the world." He grins, gaze salacious and malicious all at once. He treads across the floor to me, steps definitive but soundless as he closes the space between us.

Katerina grabs the cage and Thanatos exhales a feeble squawk, eliciting a smile from the three of us simultaneously.

"Where to?" Gorgon demands as I press in the required panels on the box.

"The Sinstone Mines—" I reply.

We step through, the only thing left behind the echo of a raven's caw in the dark.

The outside of the Sinstone Mines is abandoned as I had hoped.

Anubis stands, son at her side, looking impatient as grey ash settles in her hair that's slicked back in a wet look, braided against her skull. She's wearing a floor-length black gown adorned with gold embellishments, a simple but flattering cut on her as it falls in a sheath against her slim frame. Her limbs jangle as she shifts to greet me, adorned with their weight in over-the-top chunky jewellery. I smirk, amused that she's dolled herself up for a god. If anything, he will merely see her as what she had started from, the poor wife of a pharaoh who had been sold into marriage.

"Is that her?" Anubis asks, jerking her head to the cage, eyes shifting too fast from left to right.

"No. It's the other raven we were sent to capture. Of course, it's her!" I exclaim, shaking my head and trying to assert my superiority.

She might be dressed to the nines, but I won't have her stealing the show. I'm still the star after all.

Osiris quivers at her side, dark eyes pinpointing the raven body of Thanatos, dwarfed beside the arrow that juts from her left wing in blood-stained alabaster.

Anubis turns, gesturing for us to follow her, but I shake my head.

"I can't, I've got to go and prepare things at the well," I decree.

She smiles, clearly glad for my departure.

"Ah, of course. See you soon— follow the tunnels until you reach where the crystals are mainly unmined. There's a small opening in the wall there; that's where Horus' tomb lies," she instructs me, and I nod, thinking it nothing if not odd that she'd mummified and stored her ex-husband's corpse for a rainy day. Anubis is not exactly a simple creature by any standard.

"Sure— I expect you'll be ready when I return. Lucifer shouldn't be standing around or left to her own devices. I want this done quickly," I express, unblinking as I stare at the group turning to leave me.

"Of course, where will you go next?" Gorgon demands, half turned away, and I smile.

"To procure a sacrifice— and then to her," I inform him, and he smiles.

"Make sure to pick one with white fur, that's always a great puller of heartstrings if I do so recall—" he sneers, enjoying this more than I'd thought. He's usually so reserved in his emotions, but now he's letting them all loose, displaying his dark and wicked underbelly. I can't deny I like it. He seems so unhinged, so ambitious. It's nothing if not a temptation to want to try and tame him.

"I'll be back soon," I vow, turning once more and disappearing through the box, anticipation pooling like sweet nectar in the bloody chambers of my long desolate heart.

LUCE

All I can hear is my heartbeat racing in my chest, my blood pounding in my ears, as the harsh slamming of my feet on the stairs is all but lost amongst the sounds of panic. I reach the top of the stairway, launching myself forward and into the door of my apartment, realising only too fast that I'd locked it behind me. I frantically palm my torso, trying to remember where I'd put the key, before shoving my hand down into my cleavage and pulling out warm steel clasped in my sweaty desperate palm.

Ramming it into the lock and twisting, I burst through the door into the apartment. It's empty, Thane still not having returned from our argument earlier. At her absence, my heart begins to pound even more ferociously, mouth turning dry as my eyes dart from left to right.

Where did I leave it? I think back to the last few days, to the party, to how we'd made love in front of the fireplace—

She'd taken it from me then, placing it—

On top of the mantel. I recall, spinning on the spot and rushing to the cool slab of black marble framing the fireplace.

I look around the ornaments adorning the surface, the antique lamp from the middle east, a brass statue of a raven Haedes had gifted Thane last year on her birthday— I stare at them, around them, finally picking them up one by one and scouring beneath them, my pulse heightening with each fruitless passing second.

It's not here— shit!

Maybe Dolly or Annie moved it? When they came in to clean? Yes— that's probably it.

I storm through the wide-open sliding doors into the bedroom, a whiff of blackberry and pine sending my senses into overdrive as I pass Thane's shirt, strewn on the floor. Grabbing a black ceramic jewellery box off the top of the armoire, I don't even take the time to give the seven-pointed star on the lid the usual stroke with my index finger. Instead, I fling it open, moving over to the bed and tipping the entire contents upside down onto the sheets.

My fingers splay through the crimson velvet, desperate, seeking a twinkle of indigo, a hint of matte jet velvet—

Where is it? Where is it?! I panic, blinking rapidly, hoping I'm just not seeing it, hoping it'll appear suddenly, hidden between the folds of fabric adorning our bed.

After a few moments, I feel a stir at my back. Turning and thinking it must be Thane finally having returned home, my stomach floods with dread. She's going to be furious with me.

Instead, as I look up at an unexpected silhouette towering over me, I find exactly what I'm seeking in the palms of someone I despise.

Black leather skirts billow around her, a buckled corset binding her breasts flat so they're almost spilling out of the top. Her inky hair is curled and twisted into a half-up style and her head crowned with a black tiara, from which an ebony net veil floats, dreamily, in the still air of the room.

I inhale, breath caught in my throat as her feline expression twists into one of pure wicked glee, her dark lips spreading too wide over white teeth.

"Looking for this?"

"How did you get in here?" I demand, caught utterly off guard as my focus remains on the small indigo crystal, which glistens, taunting me as it hangs from Pandora's long pale fingers.

"Really? Come on— I know you aren't that bright, but jeez—" Pandora rolls her eyes as I scramble to my feet, straightening my spine under the scrutiny of her gaze.

"Shut up!" I bark, flustered. I'm tempted to reach out, to try and snatch the choker from her, but something tells me she wouldn't be here unless she had something to prevent that from happening.

As we hang in the moment, staring at each other, I hear an audible yowling, a growl emitting from the lips of Beelz, who pads in, eyes glowing orange. Her eyes are narrowed with only slits for pupils as she takes in the intruder. She steps closer, and Pandora stares, eyes wide.

"You better tell that thing to stay the hell away from me—" she orders.

I cock my head.

"Why should I?" I bark, looking between her and the panther, as I debate letting the beast devour her whole.

"Because—" she purrs, raising a hand above her head in a dramatic flourish, "if you don't—" she pauses, reaching down and plucking something from her cleavage.

I feel my face drain of blood and my heart break as she pulls a long, black feather from between her tightly bound breasts. She holds it up to the light, examining it, before she looks at me with malice in her eyes— "It'll be bye-bye birdie for you."

"What did you do to her?" I whisper, eyes filling with tears, as she hits me square in my metaphorical Achilles heel. Slashing invisible tendon from muscle, she shatters every part of me supported by Thane's presence in my life.

"I'm not telling you anything with that monster in the room—" she barks, appearing even more uneasy by the second.

I turn to Beelz, hands brushing against the white of my gown as I point to the other room.

"Beelz, go," I command, turning back to her and swallowing my tears.

"What do you want, Pandora?" I growl, baring my teeth just as my panther had done moments before.

"The question is not what *I* want, Lucifer. The question is what do *you* want? Do you wish to see Thanatos dead? Or merely weakened?" she asks, and I scowl. Neither of those options are acceptable. My fists ball at my sides, nails biting into the soft skin of my palms.

"I don't understand," I reply, the air deathly still between us. Pandora smiles, brushing her hair behind one ear as she places both the choker and the feather inside invisible pockets hidden by the leather folds of her skirt.

"You see, a little birdie tells me that you brought Sephy Sinclair back from the dead. So, I was thinking you could help me out with a little problem I've got. I want Ra resurrected," she breathes, each syllable laced with triumphant intent.

"Ra? Why would you want to resurrect a God of Ancient?" I demand, and she chuckles.

"That's none of your business. I don't need your approval. I just need you to perform the ritual," she barks, crossing her arms across the low square neck of her corset.

"Pandora— I'm not even sure I *can*—" I plead with her, reduced to a pathetic shell of what I have always thought I would be in a situation like this. It's different this time, different when it's Thane's life in the balance. I'm paralysed.

"Oh, you can. I have it on good authority." Pandora smirks and I shake my head, the white locks of my hair tickling against the silken flesh blanketing my collarbone.

"No— you don't understand. I resurrected Sephy — that is true — but she's only a demi-god— I don't have the power to resurrect an entity as powerful as a full god. I'm only half dark magic. Besides Ra doesn't even have a body to return to—" I stutter, trying to make her see reason, meek now more than I ever thought I could be.

"Oh, you shouldn't worry about such trivial matters, Lucifer. It's all been taken care of. And as for your level of power, I thought I'd take you for a little drink first." From within the deep pocket on the left

side of her skirt, she pulls a small silver chalice. I've seen it before—
yet I could not be certain of its function until now. More horror floods
my insides. Where I thought I had no depth left to sink to, she proves
me wrong, a new torrent of icy terror drenching me and dragging me
downward. I recognise the cup and feel my suspicions to be correct,
crushing me in merely seconds.

I thought Anubis was my friend.

"No. You can't make me," I bite, finally rediscovering my backbone.

"Oh, but I won't have to. You're going to drink willingly. If you
don't, then I'll kill her, send her back up to her family." Pandora isn't
bluffing, and even if she is, I can't tell, and I won't risk misjudging
her. Her jaw is fixed strong and determined, her eyes not betraying a
single ounce of doubt in my compliance.

"So, this is it? You're going to force me to take it in from the source?
Do you know how dangerous that is?" I ask her. She shrugs.

"Not really. Either way, I'm sure you can handle it. You're this big,
bad blonde everyone is so afraid of. Doesn't that just piss you off?"
She cocks her head, and my eyebrows rise on my forehead.

"Why would it?" I demand, swallowing hard.

"Well, if my only crime was being the product of a rapist god and
his victim, I'd be pretty pissed off with how you've been treated. It
hardly seems fair that you got banished for something that isn't your
fault— does it?" she asks.

"It doesn't matter about fair. Fair isn't realistic," I bite out, and she
smiles.

"Right you are. The thing is, I'm going to make it realistic. I'm going
to get revenge and show the blockheads upstairs that they aren't so
high and mighty after all. You should consider joining me, given your
history," she invites me, holding out a hand.

I simply stare at it.

"So, let me get this straight— you've taken the love of my very long
life hostage, and you want me to become your ally? Are you *high*?"
I ask her, channelling Haedes as I find sass to be the only reaction
pertinent to such an utterly ridiculous suggestion.

"You say no now, but I wonder if you'll be so hesitant once you've
had a true taste of your darker nature—" She licks her bottom lip before biting down on it and looking up at the ceiling, over dramatically
pondering this.

"So, what— you're going to kill her if I say no?" I demand, looking
her square in the face.

246

"Oh yes. I'll smash this tether into a million pieces." She nods, smirking and moving to examine her long plum nails.

I stand, rooted to the spot, not sure what to do. Anything I do to stop her could end in losing Thane forever— but doing what she's suggesting and taking Thane's life force to bring Ra back isn't much better. I guess I know now what happened to The Book of The Dead.

I'm torn, fatally, between the love of my existence and potentially ending who I am, who I have always been.

I recall my own words.

"I just— I miss you. I know how pathetic that sounds. But it's hard, being alone all the time. I'm struggling— I guess that's why I leaned on the alchemy side of things."

Would losing Thane not lead me down the same dark path, to the same edge of destruction?

What am I without her?

I don't know.

I don't want to know.

I've loved Thane for as long as I can remember, since before I was even grown, since that day in the Othrysian Orchard, the first day her stormy eyes had seen me. Really seen me.

I can't lose her.

After all, a life without her in it, a life without her love, isn't much of a life at all.

I scrutinise Pandora, mind made up as she stares down at an imaginary watch on her wrist and pulls out the box from her pocket, replacing the chalice as she does so.

"Well, Lucifer? What's it to be?" she demands, holding out her hand once again.

Without pause, I take it.

As we step from the portal, the white of my gown's hem stains scarlet right through.

The sanguine forest is ablaze with the light of the lilac Mortarian sun overhead, and I find myself just outside the entrance to the place where The Well resides. I sigh. This isn't a place I ever wanted to be, let alone under duress.

The tall gothic brick of the mausoleum-esque entryway is crumbling, wrapped intensely with red leafy vines, and I can smell blood, as you would expect from this place, though something about this scent is different.

It's fresh.

Pandora pulls me forward, my feet catching the edge of my long skirt as the heels of my shoes attempt to sink into the ruddy earth. My heart hammers as we pass swiftly beneath the entryway, shadow blanketing us momentarily as my heels ring out, a hollow sound echoing around from the broken concrete of the floor where nature tries unsuccessfully to flourish.

I peer around, finding the rust-laden steel gates smashed open, leaving a gaping vulnerability in the security surrounding such a potent power. Emerging on the inside of the brick walls surrounding the space, I see why. Sinners lay dead, their corpses strewn across the scorched onyx ground, peppered in an imperfect dot to dot of violence around The Well of Eternal Torment, which sits, silent and unremarkable in the centre of the massacre.

"You did this?" I demand of her, looking at the bodies, at the way they've been dismembered. She nods, face rich with self-satisfaction.

"Oh yes. You must not forget I was a warrior of Aetheria long before I ever came to be here. One never quite forgets how to slice and dice—" She gestures to a long brutal looking knife that's been dropped on the ground, bending to pick it up and not bothering to wipe the scarlet-tinged blade before passing it to me.

"What's this for?" I demand, swallowing hard as I momentarily debate running her through with it. I tighten my grip around the handle, wanting so badly to end her but knowing that it'll only result in Thane being taken from me.

"You must first be bathed in the blood of an innocent, baptised in death, before you can drink from The Well. You know all power comes at a price. The Well requires blood, and of course the thievery of true innocence." Pandora reminds me of a fact I'd already known but that I've been repressing, hoping that it wouldn't come to this.

I look down at the ground at the skewered and splayed corpses that flood the already bloody soil an even deeper shade of scarlet, which glistens, fresh and damp beneath my feet. I wrinkle my nose, breathing in deep before letting out a sigh.

"So, who do I have to kill?" I demand, and she smirks.

"You think you'll find any innocent blood around here? Don't be so ridiculous. This is hell. And the question isn't who— but what," she announces, treading delicately over bodies as her skirt trails over them, tracing their unremarkable and now unanimated features as it billows around her, smearing them in a new film of blood from the ground.

I step after her, moving closer toward The Well. That's when I see it.

A baby goat, a kid, tied to a crude wooden stake that's been haphazardly driven into the ground.

Its white fur looks soft, and wide brown eyes with thick lashes look up at us as we approach, assessing Pandora first and then myself. Its tiny horns, not yet anything of a threat, refuse to glint in the stark light from overhead, but its wet nose catches that same light, showing the panic on its breath as its nostrils open and close faster with each step I take.

It's so cute, so small— how can she possibly think I'd murder it?

"No, absolutely not," I object.

This charade has gone far enough.

"Oh, for heaven's sake. It's just a goat. A beast. And you will. You will slaughter it." She sounds firm, but I shake my head.

"Do you have any idea what kind of forces you're playing with here? The last being who tampered with this kind of darkness, this particular source— it didn't end well at all," I announce.

"Oh? Do tell—" Pandora coaxes me, her lips spreading into a deliciously unhindered smile.

"Poseidon screwed around with The Well too, and he ended up with a rogue race of Kindred on his hands. I'm not strong enough to be able to wield this level of power. It may well kill me," I protest, trying to stay logical as I refuse to let my voice shake with fear.

"Don't be so overdramatic. You and I both know that you're the least likely out of anyone to be killed by this kind of dark power because it's half of who you are already," Pandora spits. I sigh again.

"That doesn't mean it won't happen—" I retort, and she smirks.

"Well, if that's the case, I guess you and Thane will be together after all. It just won't be here."

"You know as well as anyone that I won't be allowed back in. I'll end up stuck in The Nether, just like Sephy Sinclair." I feel like screaming as her expression doesn't diminish in joy at all but merely becomes more radiant with it.

"What a shame—" She gives a fake sigh, crossing her ankles beneath her skirt as she tires of standing in the same spot, impatient.

A slight breeze picks up around us, muggy and stifling, giving me the unorthodox desire to strip off all my clothes and stand naked in an effort to free myself from this panic. Silence falls around us, deadly and full of dark promise as Pandora cocks an eyebrow at me, looking between me and the goat with a furious flitting of her irises from left to right.

"Well?" she urges me, and I turn back from her to look once again on the kid, who is jumping slightly, legs not quite in tune with its body yet.

"Well, what? I already told you. I'm not killing a baby goat. No," I protest, and so she reaches down deep into her cleavage, pulling out the long dark feather and handing it to me.

"Really?" she asks.

As I hold the feather in my palm, I realise why she's passed it to me. It's wet, leaving thin scarlet streaks brushed upon my palm like a map of too-delicate veins.

"What did you do to her?!" I cry out now, tired of this game as I teeter on the edge of tears, of crumbling.

"That, Lucifer, is none of your concern. You are either compliant in this matter or you are not. Which is it to be? Because I can smash the tether right now and be done with it!" she barks, becoming short-tempered as she stomps one foot audibly beneath her skirt and crosses her arms over her breasts. I look down at the feather, drawing my gaze from her pinched haughty features, and feel Thane's blood, cold and damp, against my fingertips.

Gripping the knife harder and trying to muster some resolve, I close my eyes, exhaling hard.

I don't have a choice.

I have to do this.

"Fine," I bite out, spinning on my heel and letting the bloody feather fall to the ground, disgusted by it.

I let my stare next focus in on the kid, which is silent, staring up at me with wide eyes as I fall onto my knees in front of it, letting yet more blood seep into the white of my dress and causing the fabric to take on a chill damp that makes me shudder.

"I'm sorry—" I whisper, closing my eyes yet again, wishing that I'd wake up from this nightmare.

Swallowing hard, I keep my grip tight on the knife as I push the pure shade of my hair behind one ear.

I lure it to me, holding out a hand and kissing the air with my lips. It looks excited, coming as close to me as the rope around its neck will allow in small and uncoordinated hops, eyes wide and glistening. Its nose, wet and desperate for new experience, touches my fingertips, its coat soft as a cloud.

I stare at it in the eyes, but then tear my gaze away, knowing that finding it sentient and soulful will only make this worse.

I grab it around the throat as it nears my knees, pulling it close to me as the creature begins to flail; its legs no longer reaching the ground. I yank it into my lap, feeling the pulse in its veins beneath my fingers quicken, panicked. It bleats, the sound high pitched and mangled as its feeble cries hit the air, and my ears, like razor blades, shredding me emotionally and making my stomach turn with nausea.

I take the knife to its throat. Praying this will be quick as it struggles against me, fighting so desperately for the life I am about to steal.

I do it.

I dig the blade into its milky pale flesh.

The skin of its throat is too soft, like butter, the serrated edge snagging on it only momentarily as I feel myself riddled with disgust.

Cries of agony and the terror, of staring into the abyss of death, ring out into the air around me as the scent of iron, of rust, coats the insides of my nostrils like sickly sweet syrup.

I yank the knife across its carotid.

Grimacing, the arterial spray drenches me in a layer of scorching hot scarlet as the blood flies up, coating my individual eyelashes, becoming lodged in the cracks of my lips, even the shell of my ear.

The edge of The Well beside me, which is made from nothing more than stacked charred pebbles, is coated too, delivering a second layer of blood in an audibly horrifying and sick splashback like the kind you'd expect with a high-power garden hose.

The animal cries out, heart pounding against the hand which restrains it even still, being driven faster with every passing second as the dying light in its eyes goes out like a white-hot star meeting an underwhelming and flickering end. The spray of its blood soaks me through. It's hot, spreading too fast like a vermillion plague as it covers my hair, my dress, and my chest, until finally, the sound of silence is all that remains.

She loves me in red— says it's my colour.
There's so much blood.

How can such a small creature contain so much blood?

I look up at Pandora, her silhouette casting me in darkness where I belong.

"Happy now?" I demand, a single tear falling from my eye, dribbling down my cheek and then falling onto a rare patch of the goat's fur that remains white, leaving a pinkish bloody spatter.

"Not yet. Get up." Pandora grabs me by the wrist, pulling me to my feet as the corpse of the kid falls like a sack of potatoes from my lap, hitting the ground with a heavy thud that causes my heart to shatter. "Here." Pandora shoves the silver chalice she'd produced earlier into my palm. I examine it, finding it encrusted with onyx and rubies, the colour of blood and darkness. My hands leave the silver metal scarlet as I examine the runes around the rim of the cup.

I consent to taste the darkest fruit, it reads.

"What do I do?" I ask her, looking down into the endlessness of The Well.

I've seen it before, but I never really took the time to look deeply into its waters. The cylinder made entirely from stacked worn pebbles buries deep into the earth. Inside, water lies motionless. It's a black mirror, so pristine and unmoving that I can see my reflection without so much as a wrinkle upon my bloody face. I discover myself, a mess of pure stark white and deep burgundy as I tear my gaze away from the abyss of it, staring at Pandora.

"I think you drink now—" she suggests, and I scowl.

"You don't know?" I ask her, and she shrugs.

"As you said, this isn't something to take lightly. I don't know of anyone, other than apparently Poseidon, who has drawn from this well since the Gods of Ancient were created. And if they did, I'm pretty sure the darkness consumed them, killed them— maybe even destroyed their souls— who knows? You should know better than anyone that sharing information on this kind of thing isn't exactly a strong suit of the gods. Knowledge is power, and they want it all to themselves," she reminds me, and I roll my eyes, feeling blood trickle in between my lips and onto my tongue. The taste of it is sickening, and it makes me want to take a goddamn drink just to rid myself of the nauseating metallic tinge.

"So, I just dip this in and drink?" I ask her, and she nods.

"Yes, that cup is the only way you can draw directly from The Well— so drink up," she encourages me as I look down at the cup in my hand and then back at her.

Here goes. I sigh, inhaling one large deep breath before plunging the chalice into the still, black fluid.

My hand comes away unscathed as I raise the chalice to my lips, heart pounding as adrenaline spikes through my system. If I'd ever wondered what pure darkness tastes like— I guess I'm about to find out.

I tip back the cup, slowly, waiting as the liquid flows from the silver depths and into my mouth, passing my lips in a kiss of dark ecstasy. The taste of her floods me, overtaking all my senses, blackberry and pine, the smell of her hair filling my nostrils as my veins flare, alight with newborn power.

I down the cup of all contents, desiring another as I begin to buzz, fingers sparking electricity from their tips. I watch as black veins trace up my arms, my fingers scorched black within seconds as excitement clutches at me, extinguishing the dread I've been consumed by almost entirely.

I look at Pandora, veins full of fire, as the world comes alive around me. I can hear her heartbeat, estimate the rate at which blood is coursing from her heart to her brain and back again. I can feel the movement of the individual hairs on the back of my neck as they flatten; calming me as I know now the worst is over.

I look down into the well at my reflection, and where before I was bloody and stark, my hair is ebony, matching my now dilated eyes that have become abyssal pools of onyx. My face is mapped over with veins and so is my chest, my neck— everything, making my body into a sick murderer's work of art.

My work of art.

The darkness spins itself through me within seconds, like a spider's arachnid soft touch, coating everything inside of me with the ability to control each and every aspect of my world in a gossamer weave of black magic.

Inhaling, I smell the air, the scent of energy ripe for transformation catching my attention. It's not wrong, this power, it's *mine*. It's what I'm entitled to.

I look down upon the body of the kid, knowing that if I wished to, I could reanimate the corpse, watch it dance for me again in cute little hops, like a dead puppet for my pleasure. Unfortunately for me, I don't have time for fun and games. I have somewhere else to be.

Pandora watches me with alarm as I step over the baby goat's dead body, grabbing her forearm in my still hot, wet, and bloody palm. I smile at her as I realise that I'm about to see just how powerful I can be, just how unstoppable. The prospect of finally rising above helplessness is addictive, and I relish each passing second as my heart beats, powerful and certain, beneath my breast.

I'm about to resurrect a god and save my beloved with nothing more than the power that is my birthright. Thane will never have to worry about me again, and I will never have to worry that someone will take her away from me, not even Nemesis.

I am the master of my own destiny now, and nothing is going to get in the way of my happy ending.

I turn to Pandora, mouth parting as I lick the blood off my bottom lip carelessly. Staring into her, I feel her become uneasy at the unending and intense depths of my eyes.

"Well, what are you waiting for? We have a god to resurrect."

20

I DON'T WANT TO SET THE WORLD ON FIRE

SEPHY

"WHAT THE HELL IS this? I thought you had *good* taste—" I demand, eyeing up the golden monstrosity as I haul it out of a wooden chest encrusted with emeralds. It's a suit, or what I think is a suit. It would be a lot easier to tell if it wasn't burning my retinas as it reflects the red of my hair back at me in a jaundiced hue.

"Elvis, March 28th, 1957. Chicago's international amphitheatre," Haedes reels off the date like it's nothing as he sits, cross-legged, on the floor at the opposite end of the vault. He peers into the depths of one of the urns from the shelf behind him and dust blows up in his face from the sandstone container, causing him to cough. I want to laugh, but it's far less funny now than when it happened the first time, what seems like forever ago, when he first started checking them. We've been rifling through boxes, chests, and searching the most hidden corners of the vault for hours, and though the tension between Xion and Haedes has diffused somewhat, my temper is fraying rapidly. It would definitely help if Haedes wasn't secretly the world's biggest hoarder of utterly useless shit. I doubt he even knows everything that's in here, let alone has a written record.

"Let me get this straight— you can recall the date some dead guy wore this monstrosity, but you somehow missed that you accidentally had spawn?" I gape at him, cocking an eyebrow in disbelief. He shakes his head.

"Hey, Elvis is more than just some dead guy—" he counters, not looking the least bit guilty for his lack of presence in my childhood.

Not that I needed it. I mean I had enough asshole in my life with Peter at a young age without adding some smurf-headed psycho.

Something else catches my eye at the bottom of the trunk, so I pull it out, holding it up with a triumphant grin.

"Ha! I knew it! I knew you did drag on the side!" I exclaim, looking at the odd asymmetrical cut of the glossy blonde plastic mop.

"Cher, Walking in Memphis, 1995. Single cover," he announces yet again, not even looking up at me.

I roll my eyes, tossing the wig aside.

Shutting the chest, I walk back past many rows of slow-moving crystal hourglasses before hauling out another, this one less decadent and far dustier than the last. As I place it down next to the one I've just emptied, dust flies up out of the crevices in the lid, accompanied by something heavier. Sand.

Yanking open the lid, the scent of musty water hits my nostrils, making me wrinkle my nose.

"What the hell do you need this for?" I demand, hauling up a net off the top of yet more stuff that's been haphazardly shoved inside.

"Oh— that, yeah that— I kept that just in case," he mutters, eyeing the net with a half glance.

"In case of what? Kinky net play?" I demand. He smirks.

"No actually, I was going to use it to piss off my brother, Poseidon, at some point. That's the net his wife got caught in when he banished her in Mermaid form. Nice little tale if you like petty marital disputes that end in yet more petty marital disputes—" he chuckles, and so I throw the net aside. Beneath it I find a velvet bag, which I grab, ripping it open. Inside, a deck of tarot cards falls into my palm.

"Really? Even you can't believe in these cheap magic tricks?" I cock my head at him, brushing a strand of hair back behind my ear as I turn over the top card. I glance at it quickly in half disinterest, it shows the five of swords, whatever the hell that's supposed to mean.

"Oh, I don't. I got those from this woman— what was her name— ugh. Madame— Lola— yeah that was it. Batshit old lady, she did have the sight though," he sighs, thinking back.

As we're discussing this, I hear Xion's heavy and unmistakable footfall encroaching from toward the back of the supposedly secure space. Placing the deck back in the velvet clutches of the bag, I toss it aside with the rest of the other junk.

"Haedes, I'm not sure— what exactly is the mystical value of this?" he demands, holding up a hideously proportioned knitted jumper. It's

256

grey with red and blue flecks running throughout the yarn. On the chest, an enormous 'H' has been adorned in yellow. I look at it, and then him, quizzical and utterly bemused.

"Oh, nothing, the Fates gave me that one Christmas. It's just so ugly I can't bear to look at it and they've messed with it, so I can't set it alight or permanently dispose of it. It just keeps coming back like the knitted plague."

I snigger as Xion tries, unsuccessfully, to stifle a deep rumbling laugh.

Looking down into the chest at my feet, I find something dark and heavy-ish at the bottom. Hoisting it up with both hands, I query why on earth he'd need shackles this size.

"And what exactly are you thinking of restraining with this? A giant elephant?" I demand. He scowls as I stare at the metal restraints and attached thick chains. It's laden with rust, but the size is overkill for any demon I've ever seen.

"Of course not! That's for a Dragon!" he tuts, exasperated.

"Oh right, of course. A *Dragon*," I scoff, dropping the chain and shackle back into the bottom of the chest with a clatter. "Look, we're not getting anywhere. This could take forever— you have so much shit— like jeez, what is your staff doing?" I wonder aloud, and Haedes gets a sly smile. I quickly blurt, "Don't answer that," as a shudder runs up my spine.

"What the fuck!" I hear Xion's voice echo out in a surprised yelp as he comes running back from the shadows encasing the far end of the vault, something long and coiled in his hand.

"What— why— *how*—? Should I be worried about finding dead bodies back here?!" he exclaims, shoving the remarkable severed braid into the warm light of the sconces flickering with The Eternal Flame.

"Oh, don't worry about that. It belonged to an Equinian I met once— he bet me I couldn't beat him in a fight. So, I went and cut off his braid while he was sleeping. Equinians never cut their hair; it's a sign of strength. The longer the hair, the better the fighter," he smirks.

I shake my head.

"It's a wonder someone hasn't had you assassinated yet," I muse, squinting as the caramel hair, which is intricately braided, glistens - individual strands standing out as being coated in gold. "Why didn't you just throw it away?" I demand, and he shrugs again.

"Well, no one would have believed me if I didn't have proof. Besides, Kindred body parts, even the hair, go for a pretty penny to the right alchemist," he explains as Xion throws the braid to one side, face full of disgust.

"I'm done. *So* done. I'm stopping this before I end up digging up some fairy's dentures—" he shudders, making me giggle at the thought of an old woman fairy with a gummy smile. "I'm going to get something to eat. You want anything?" he asks.

Haedes and I shake our heads, food the furthest thing from my mind.

After the loud echoes of Xion's tread dissipate, the silence speaks more than I want it to, so I pick a topic at random, trying to ignite some form of conversation.

"So, you can travel to other dimensions— ones other than here and Earth?" I ask Haedes, suddenly fascinated. I wonder what it would be like to visit other places, other realms that aren't Earth but also aren't saturated in blood and death.

"It depends. Aetheria I've visited in the past, but it got me arrested by the hoity-toity Sephilim guards there. They hate trespassers. Other realms like The Nether and then The Higher Plains are too far out of reach for even my power. You kind of need the help of someone on the other side of the gate to get into The Higher Plains, if you know what I mean—" Haedes expresses and I nod, hair tickling my ears.

"So that's why I didn't make it to Titan status— Zeus denied me access?" I frown, and he looks guilty.

"I'm sorry. If it was me up there, you know you would have been welcome. Unfortunately, your Uncle has this theory that letting you in makes him denying Hercules like this double standard— it's all utterly petulant." Haedes comes across as someone else as he delivers this sentence; he comes across as defensive and highly intelligent like he's been well-educated. I mean he probably was, being a god and all, but you'd never know that from how he usually acts—

"So— you and him, you're seeing each other?" Haedes asks me, coughing as soon as the words leave his lips.

"Well— he's seeing parts of me, and I'm seeing parts of him, if that's what you mean." I shut the lid of the chest with a loud slam, which causes Haedes to startle. Sitting down on top of it and cupping my chin in my hands, I rest my elbows on my knees. Pressing my lips together, I continue to watch his aged expression with interest.

"You know that's not what I meant." Getting to his feet, his joints audibly creak as he exhales, out of breath from the sudden change in posture.

"Look what do you want me to say? We're just— having fun. It's none of your business," I shrug, non-committal in every respect.

"My scarred retinas and permanently traumatised mind would attest otherwise," he takes a few steps forward, the soft pad of his soles barely making a sound. He might have aged, but he's still damn light on his feet.

"Look it doesn't matter—" I breathe, trying to end the conversation, and Haedes cocks an eyebrow.

"But what about—" he begins, but I glare at him.

"Look, no prophecy ever determined what I did before, so I don't see why that should be any different now," I exclaim.

"That wasn't what I was going to say. I was going to say what about if you end up becoming a serious player— universally I mean— there's no place in that role for love. I promise you." His gaze is piercing, intense, and morose as the greys of his irises storm beneath the glass of their reflective surfaces.

"I have no intention of becoming important in any sort of way, so there's really no risk of that. Besides, it's not love; we're just screwing around. Even if it was, you had a full-blown affair with my mother, so you can't exactly talk," I mutter, feeling like a little girl as he looks down over me.

"Your mother would have been the undoing of this universe. A part of me thinks that's why fate took her so soon. If I'd had to choose between her— and my duties as a god, it wouldn't have even been a question in my mind," he explains. I frown.

"So, what you're saying is that the reason you're alone is because you're mystically cursed to be that way?" I demand, snorting. He's so goddamn self-interested it's insane.

"I'm saying that the person who sits on the throne, the person who rules The Nexus, that person must be loyal to only one, and that is Mortaria. There is no room for compromise in this place because we are so vital to maintaining universal order," he elaborates.

I shake my head.

"Well lucky for me, I'm just an heiress with a thing for leather pants and fine whisky," I retort. "And by the way, you could be an inspirational speaker. That was very— *this isn't just a job, it's a lifestyle*—" I put on the corniest motivational accent I can muster as I get to my feet.

"I know you think I'm old and that I don't know you or anything about how you desire to live your life, but honestly— you have to be able to make the hard choices. You're not just an heiress, though you do have a thing for questionable clothing and good taste in fine liquor— you're my daughter. Your fate is wrapped in with Mortaria, and with me, whether loosely or in a binding fashion. This place— your responsibility to it and the balance will never go away. Not ever. You've been given the power, and this is the responsibility part. It's not fair. It's just fate—" he expresses.

Jeez. When did he morph into Ben Parker?

I roll my eyes, but then something occurs to me as I stare him full in the face, realising there may be a faster way to work out what, if anything, has been stolen.

"Fate— you know, it might not be fair, as you said, but it may have answers. We should go and pay them a visit," I suggest.

"Great idea, just uh, don't tell them about the sweater— okay?"

We hurry across the entrance hall floor as a delicious scent wafts through the warm air and into my nostrils.

As Haedes and I turn the corner, heading me to where The Fates are currently staying, I come face to face with the source.

"Holy hell, what is that smell?" I demand.

Xion, who stops abruptly right in front of me has a napkin clutched tightly in his palm.

"Meatball sub—" he mumbles, licking marinara sauce off his bottom lip. I pout, noticing a seemingly bottomless chasm opening where my stomach usually resides. It gives an audible rumble.

"Can I have a—" I ask, but he frowns, a look of completely over-the-top affront twisting his usually stoic features.

"Absolute not," he replies, cutting me off.

"Well, geez. It's not like I was asking for a freaking kidney. You brought me back from the dead without my permission. The least you can do is give me a bite of your stupid sandwich," I complain, crossing my arms over my breasts and pouting. The scent of thick tomato pulp and fragrant spices taunts me.

"I don't share food. And besides, I asked you if you wanted something—" he defends himself while Haedes coughs beside me.

"She's a woman Xion. She can't actually ask for what she wants, so she has to hope you'll guess. And then when you don't, she'll steal yours. It's the way of the world. Now hand over the sandwich so we can get going—" He stares at him, grey hair catching the light from the nearby eternal flames and tinting it gold.

Xion sighs, rolling his eyes.

"This is so unfair!" He scowls at me, handing over the sub. I take it and immediately bite into the buttery roll.

I groan.

"Oh my god, this is amazing!" I exclaim, closing my eyes in delight as we begin to walk again. Xion crosses his arms over his chest, huffing.

"You can go off people you know—" he mutters, but I pretend not to hear him, continuing to eat his sandwich without the slightest inkling of guilt.

By the time we reach The Fates' living quarters, I have finished the sandwich, and the taste of it has completely overcome my senses to the point that I barely noticed where I was going. Food is definitely one of the perks of being alive.

"So, they live here all the time?" I ask Haedes, who shakes his head, straightening the lapels on his suit jacket and taking a deep inhale.

"It depends — if the workload at the courts is high, they'll stay there with Muerta and Yama. But they have a place here too. After all, we have better security," Haedes explains with a sigh, and I nod, feeling questions about The Fates begin to rise to the surface. They're still a mystery to me, even after everything, and I have no idea how they're able to see the future, or even if the future they see is one hundred percent certain. I guess now I can ask. I mean, unless they have some bombshell that is going to send us all running for the exits, which seems likely.

I mean am I the only one who is starting to think things have been far too quiet?

Did Pandora and the Demon Lords just take a six-month vacation after my death?

Something deep inside, something that knows the way of the world, highly freaking doubts it.

"Come in!" Layla's voice rings out and Haedes turns the brass doorknob counterclockwise, letting himself in.

The inside of the suite is like stepping back in time, with too many ticking grandfather clocks, professionally painted canvases of dogs playing snooker, and china plates adorned with glazed cottages sprawled across the walls in a cacophony of clutter. The scent of talcum powder fills my nostrils, and amongst the never-ceasing and

261

nerve-tattering ticking of the clocks comes the unwelcome click-ety-clack of knitting needles, failing to keep either metronomic or synchronised time.

I weave my way in and out of mismatched wooden furniture, finding the three women we seek at the opposite end of the room, sitting in three armchairs, facing one another. They're knitting individually this time, and Anya smiles at me, her perfectly toothless mouth a gaping testament to her age.

"What brings you here?" Moira demands, looking at the three of us as we gather in front of their chairs. I examine them, each upholstered in a different floral fabric.

Looking up into the unseeing eyes of Layla, I lick my lips, chasing away any trace of the marinara before speaking my mind.

"We came to ask you if you had seen anything about the break-in down in the vault—" I enquire.

Moira frowns. Anya signs to her, and it's clear to me that I spoke too quickly for her to read my lips. After a few seconds, Moira nods, her scraggy neck looking fragile as tissue paper as she moves her head vigorously.

"You haven't come about the chalice?" Layla demands, and Haedes scowls.

"Chalice? You can't mean—" he begins, slowing as he grimaces, looking as though thinking is physically hurting him.

"What chalice?" I blurt, and Xion looks troubled.

"The Chalice of Uranus, I think—" he explains as Haedes turns to me, his face etched deeper with lines of anxiety.

"That is correct. It's the only way to drink from The Well of Eternal Torment." Haedes explains and I frown. Doesn't exactly sound like a happy hour cocktail to me.

"So—you mean it's been stolen?" I demand, folding my arms tightly across my torso as I start to feel sick. The idea of more drama, more action, is making me nauseous. I thought the danger was over. I should have known it was too good to be true.

"It is not clear. But it is tied to Lucifer— her fate is evolving—" Moira announces. I open my mouth to speak, confused.

"How can somebody's fate evolve? Isn't fate certain? I thought that was the whole point—" I exhale, wishing that this life came with an instruction manual. Mystical shit is always so goddamn wishy-washy. Where the hell are all the little book nerds in monasteries making records about this spectacularly unbelievable shit? Where are the goddamn monks I ask you?

"Fate is a game of odds child. Like gambling— as time goes on, certain fates become more likely than others, depending on the type of souls involved— their psychology, their choices— weaknesses. We see the most likely fate at the time. We used to run a racket up in The Higher Plains until Zeus got odds he didn't like—" Layla tuts, the sound of her dentures smacking against her lips lost amongst the click of her unceasing needles. The women continue in their tirade of knit one-purl one, surprising me because the subject at hand seems far more important than any jumper or scarf.

"You never did let me in on that little titbit—" Haedes begins and Moira shakes her head, causing his words to fall into silence.

"We do not speak of this. It is what got us banished, our sight fractured. Never again," she spits, and I feel my heartbeat harden against the inside of my ribs. What could be so terrible that Zeus banished three old dears to hell?

"Alright, well— so what are you saying about Lucifer exactly?" Haedes demands/ Layla sighs.

"We have been watching Lucifer for a while— her use of magic has been concerning, to say the least. Now with the appearance of The Chalice of Uranus mixed in with the threads which weave her fate— we are more than concerned."

"But Luce— she would never hurt anybody. She certainly wouldn't willingly drink from The Well, chalice or not," Xion stands up for her, loyal as ever.

Moira pushes a strand of wiry grey hair behind the shrivelled shell of her ear, her milky eyes wide with a kind of fear I never want to see, let alone on the face of a Fate.

"Everyone, child, and I mean *everyone*, has a price— we just must pray to the heavens that someone has not found hers."

21

PAPA DON'T PREACH

LUCE

THE PORTAL, WHICH SPINS from the box before returning too fast like a mythical boomerang, looks different to me now. Where before the colours, the magics, had blurred, bled into one another, now each type of magic is clear as day. I feel as if I could reach out and grab the shimmering, dark tendrils that tempt me as they fly before my eyes, but before I can so much as contemplate manipulating the portal for my own means, we're stepping out on the other side.

Half a mile from the too-bright and ominous outline of The Icon, I wonder what exactly it is we're doing here— could it be— I still don't want to believe it.

Anubis.

I should have known that she wasn't in my suite trying to protect The Book of The Dead. I'd been naïve, too pure and trusting, to want to believe what I know now to be true. She is a traitor. Through and through.

She had stolen Thane's tether.

I ball my fists at my side, the breeze whipping around me as the thin white silk of my gown is peppered grey in the falling ash from the sky. Blood has dried, clinging to the pale dander of my skin, the only hair on my body that remains unchanged by the dark. My black locks billow around me, making me indiscernible in some respects from Pandora, who adjusts the veil atop her head as she trails behind me. Slipping the box back into her pocket, she watches me with intensity as I stand, chilled as the remaining wet blood of the kid dries, blanketing me with gruesome permanence.

I don't have to root myself, don't have to use Gaia's energy to sum-mon clothes to me, instead I merely wave a hand, blinking slowly. The circular motion of my fingers causes the air to heat as I transfigure magic, still rife in my veins from The Well, into adornments suitable for someone of my power. A black military jacket with shimmering brass buttons scattered across the double breast covers my previously scarlet, bare skin. The collar is high, exactly as I had hoped. I don't want Thanatos to know about the goat, to see the murderer I am. It might be true, but seeing it reflected at me through her eyes is sure to hinder me emotionally. I observe the black velvet pants clinging now to my legs, lace panels travelling up both sides adorned with poison ivy's silhouette, my feet rooted solidly in leather knee-high boots, and smile, content. The stifling breeze draws my attention to one shoulder as a heavy cape, that's burgundy on the underside, flutters around the backs of my knees, dangling artfully from one side of my spine. I turn to Pandora and find her startled. "How did you do that?" she demands. I cock an eyebrow at her, bored.

"Magic," I spit, tired of her slow and feeble mind. "Shall we proceed?" I suggest, a slight sigh falling from my lips as I make my dissatisfaction only too evident.

"Of course," she mumbles, treading forward.

We walk for several moments, and I let the hardened toes of my boots kick up ash violently in my wake as I examine my nails, black veins webbing beneath the pallid silk of my flesh, thrumming and rich, just under the surface.

Beneath the vermillion glory of the heavens, we come to the entrance of The Sinstone Mines, surprising me. I haven't been here in forever and wonder why on earth Pandora would bring me to this location specifically. It's not a place of magical power; in fact, it's the opposite. The crystals buried in the earth are far better at storing magical energy than they would ever be at magnifying it.

Strange.

I follow her anyway, admiring the shine of my new shoes as we begin to descend into the mines. Cast iron beams support the vast and sprawling tunnels, with geodes and multifaceted crystals jutting from the dark Mortarian rock of what makes up the bed of The Ashen Waste. It's volcanic, fertile, yet sturdy, not that you'd know it because it is permanently coated in a thick blanket of grey.

We pass through tunnels filled with the bloody glow of garnets, the pink allure of rose quartz, and the deep glower of jade, each crystal catching the light of the hundreds of torches flickering every few hundred yards amid the labyrinthian and never-ending construct. The sound of hard steel on stone rings out in an overload of sharp echoes bouncing with unhindered ease from tunnels on every surrounding side.

We pass sinners, the avarice in their eyes evident as they toil, skin black with dirt and grime. Overalls of patchy matte ebony hide the disrepair of their bodies, but I know the Doppel skin beneath will be dry, maybe even bruised from such heavy labour. This is their punishment, and it is a wonder to me now that I had ever considered we might be the same. We are not the same. I am quite clearly destined for greater things than writhing around, sweating in the earth. The fact I had even thought otherwise is a blatant testament to the fact I've been downtrodden for too fucking long.

We continue to pace down long tunnels, delving deeper and deeper into the mines as I find the crystals in the walls growing gradually larger, with a closer spread and less fragmentation of their surfaces.

It's obvious as we walk on, and my posture remains relaxed, that Pandora is nervous. Her breathing is laboured, her shoulders stiff within the confines of her buckled corset, and I can almost feel her eyes darting from left to right as she leads me slowly deeper into this hell.

Eventually, she slows. We're far beyond any miners now, and as she turns on the spot, pivoting so the leather of her skirt pinwheels around her, she widens her eyes, finally contented.

I let my gaze travel to where she's looking, the dry musk of the surrounding earth filling my nostrils and making me feel somewhat claustrophobic. Being surrounded by absorptive matter isn't exactly where someone of my persuasion longs to be. I find what she's staring at, a sense of underwhelmed confusion mingling with irritation.

"What the hell are we doing here? Is this a joke?" I call her out, crossing my arms as my pupils dilate, and scowl at her. She turns to me, putting her fingers to her lips and slipping through the gap in the tunnel wall. I can see it had been boarded up before, but someone has smashed the wood apart bridging the space, leaving it splintered and scattering the shimmering dirt floor, sharp with crystal dust.

Stepping through, our footsteps echo against the cavernous walls, which sprawl out from the end of the narrow tunnel. The light is dimmer here, softer, and more foreboding. The walls are scrawled with runes, not hieroglyphs as I might have expected with my suspicion of Anubis' involvement.

We turn a corner and as Pandora's wide skirt sways into the farthest edges of the chamber, my view is unobscured.

I take in the scene confronting me.

It steals my breath entirely, which had until this very moment been calmer and more certain than ever before.

"Thanatos—" her name tumbles into the air, no longer jagged as my speech has become, but eroded smooth with unplanned emotion.

She's suspended by what I think are chains at first, but soon I realise the slick glisten of firelight on scales is unmistakable. The Gorgonians wrap around her edgy frame, spiralling around her arms and legs, pinning her to the wall. I notice her upper arm and shoulder are angled wrong, spotting a white projectile protruding from her as my pupils fixate. Blood drips down, caught by the black silk covering her modesty, and she whimpers, the sound harrowing. It's not a cry or a scream. The pitch of it doesn't even produce harsh echoes but merely ripples with despair like a pebble skipping across the still surface of a dark bottomless lake.

"Welcome, Lucifer," Gorgon's familiar hissing tongue fills the space, creating unnecessary pleasantries.

I don't reply, unable to tear my gaze from Thane as fury runs rampant through my veins to fuel the defence of what belongs to me.

"I should've known it was you," I spit, ripping my eyes from my lover and targeting Anubis who, predictably, stands surrounded by Katerina and Gorgon for protection. She never was much of a hero. Not even brave enough to pick a side and stick to it.

The soft orange light of surrounding iron dishes filled with flame flickers on her gold skin, making it considerably more foreboding to the average bystander as her deep eye sockets and high cheekbones become sharp shadow casters. I, however, am not perturbed.

"But you didn't, did you? Instead, you helped me to a carriage and dressed my wounds." She smirks at me, clearly entertained by my goodness, by my weakness.

It's not a mistake I'll make again.

"Why are you doing this?" I implore reason from her.

Staring around the room my eyes focus on an open sarcophagus. Inside, I know what I'll find, but I don't need to see it. The energy surrounding it is almost completely faded from existence, only a lingering sniff of life that had once been remaining in the marrow beneath fallow withered flesh. It's the mummified skeleton of Horus — it must be — and is surrounded by what used to be skin, so dry now it can only be said to consist of little more than dust and dreams of grandeur.

I step forward as Anubis' serrated tone tears through the air, jagged where Thane's had been dull, the predator to her prey.

Who would have thought the Jackal would be a likely match for the Raven?

Not me.

Then again, I've never seen jackals as much as a threat, because I'm the devil.

I fear no one, not anymore, only what they can take from me. Only losing her. So, I step forward, guilt not even tainting the dark waters of my soul with its purifying tonic, ready to do what I must.

"Your father would be proud—" Gorgon announces, and I sneer.

"What would you know of my father? You're nothing but his little bitch boy. You just watch. The day you unleash any of those gods, they'll devour you whole without a moment's pause. Justice— if you will," I purr, tongue caressing the words as I unleash them, watching each of the faces remain unfazed. I wonder now though if they are or if inside, they're questioning if I'm right. It makes me want to crack open their skulls and read the squiggles of medulla and grey matter between their ears, if for no other reason than to satiate such burning curiosity.

At my words, I feel her eyes on me so elevate my gaze to the wall where she's suspended by the snake-like demons in a pose not unlike that of crucifixion.

"Luce— what— what did they do to you?" she whispers, voice hoarse and cracked with the pangs of shock.

"We didn't do anything, Thanatos. Lucifer drank willingly from The Well— you know as well as we do that there is no other way. One cannot be coerced; one must *want* to consume such forbidden fruit. She was not unwilling but beautifully compliant, thanks to you— or perhaps not— perhaps she was craving this all along." Pandora smiles, genteel in expression, calm even, as she turns away from Thanatos who glares at her, a fire lighting in her otherwise extinguished gaze. Pandora gazes next to Anubis, who has a glint in her eye, lips twisting into a deliciously sadistic smile.

"Anyway, I had best be going," Pandora announces without stutter or pause.

Anubis frowns, the simple black of her gown, which is adorned with ridiculously over-the-top gold embellishments, only too resonant of her overly inflated sense of self.

"Wait, you're not staying? This was your plan all along, wasn't it?" she demands. Pandora shrugs.

"I never was one for the ceremony. Besides, I'll be assembling the full mortal and demon forces with the other Lords to present to Ra when he is risen. You cannot think he will be satisfied seeing Haedes on the throne of Mortaria and not a demon in sight? He'll think we've gone mad!" Pandora muses, and I watch Anubis mull this over, jaw ticking as her mind slowly works.

In the corner behind me, I sense something stir. Thinking it may be a demon, I turn quickly, cape flaring from my spine as I spin.

It isn't a demon though.

It's Osiris.

You slimy little mummy's boy— I snarl internally, glowering at him. He flinches under the scorn of my gaze, his white robes dusted over with dark slivers of crystal from the floor.

"Mother, I'll be going too. Pandora will need my order to open the gate for when she returns with the demons— you know the guards may well attack her without it." He clears his throat, eyes shimmering like dark endless pools of bullshit, reflective I'm sure of what lies behind them.

"Of course, good thinking. Ready my chariot as well. I may be in need of it, Si," Anubis instructs him as I turn to look back at her, continuing to not pay me any attention as Pandora passes her Thane's tether. It catches in the light, and I find myself forced to look away yet again, ashamed I've been so careless, so reckless with an object more precious than I realised. They're holding her ability to stay with me, our ability to be together, in their merciless hands.

Osiris nods as my scrutiny bears into him, scurrying from the room like the nauseating cockroach he's become. I know he was born in The Higher Plains, that he's been sheltered, but doesn't he realise what he's doing by putting the universe in jeopardy like this?

As the last of his footsteps die, I turn, only to find Pandora opening a portal and stepping through before I can so much as try to step forward to cuss her out for giving me dark roots I hadn't wanted.

As the portal closes, I shut my eyes against the overwhelming brightness she leaves behind, exhaling and trying to keep my temper under control. I'm deep in the earth, and with every single spike in my blood pressure, I feel the sparks begin to tease the air between my fingertips. The earth is all around, and one careless wave of a hand in rage could potentially bring the entire mine down on top of everyone inside, including Thane and myself.

I stand, rooted to the spot by Thane's heartbroken gaze, by her shattered and disjointed silhouette, as the Gorgonians slither and constrict, keeping her alive but barely. Just enough for the ritual.

I think about trying to steal the tether back, but I know why that's not possible. It's too powerful of an object to be moved by magic, which is exactly why Anubis had been forced to steal it in person.

I really wish Beelz had taken her leg off right now— I muse, reminding myself to give her an extra steak later after this is all over, when Thane and I are back drinking red wine and laughing the whole thing off.

As the room around us descends into silence for only a moment, I am not given the reprieve I'd hoped for. I am not given the mercy of a second to compile a plan of escape, a kind of bargain I might strike, or a sacrifice I might make. Instead, Gorgon simply steps forward and shoves a bundle of red fabric at me.

I hold it in my hands, unravelling the weight that lies inside.

I uncover the book, the object that had started me down this long and winding path, an unlikely road to the destruction of everything I have loved. The thing is, it matters not, though, what I have loved, what I have done. It matters only who I do love even still, and that is her, has always been her. So, for her, I will do anything, even if that something is dooming the universe.

After all, what has the universe ever done for me?

22

DOES YOUR MOTHER KNOW

XION

MY TEMPER FLARES, ANGER rising just beneath the surface of my skin and threatening to scorch it black.

"I can't believe we're actually having this conversation!" I bark. Layla's head snaps sideways, fingers tightening visibly around her knitting needles.

"Who are you to say that she is immune to the darkness, halfling? You yourself are evidence that even the noblest hearts can be made dark, made susceptible by the frenzy of passion— by the vice grip of love." Her poetry doesn't placate me; the beauteous spilling of vernacular from her lips nothing but an affront. I wish she'd speak frankly. Wish she'd simply say, *she's still weak for Thane; she'd doom us all.*

But would she?

Lucifer?

The woman who had saved my soul. Who delivered me from evil.

Sephy exhales heavily, looking between me and The Fates as her tongue comes out to stroke the crack at the edge of her lips. I fixate on it, being taken back to how it had warmed my flesh and melted my better judgement. She opens her mouth to speak, but Haedes interrupts, running his fingers through increasingly dishevelled silver strands of hair. My eyes catch hers across him but quickly dart away, afraid of finding conflicting opinions within.

"Luce— I mean, you three know her. She's not stupid. She wouldn't just—" he stutters, but before he can make another excuse, I look to Sephy.

"We know her in a far more personal way than you do, Sephy. What do you think?" I ask, hoping she'll be more impartial.

"I think she loves Thane. Love can make us do stupid things." She sighs, and my heart breaks.

Then a thought occurs to me, something that gives me a glimmer of hope. If she's acknowledging that love can make one do stupid things, is she perhaps considering that she loves me? Is that how she's able to jump to such a conclusion?

I'm being ridiculous, soft, weak, pathetic. I need to toughen up.

She doesn't love me.

But— I know now that I irrevocably love her. Even the darkest parts of me are pulled to her like a magnet to cold steel. Seeking comfort, pain, and pleasure melded together. She's like fire itself, warm but burning, consuming, blinding all those who look upon her and yet a shining light in the dark.

What the fuck is happening to me?

I sound like a goddamn schoolboy.

Is she killing the demon within? Is it falling in love too?

Why do I continue to ponder, continue down this path when I know the ending will come down in a torrent of pain and heartbreak?

I don't know.

I just don't.

The only thing I know— is that letting her go before she rips herself from me is more than I can bear. As sad as that is.

Who knew I would end up being a fucking martyr over a goddamn woman?

If I met me now, I wouldn't know me; that's for sure.

Silence falls over the six of us as eyes flit from one face to the next, grim expressions taking over each, one by one. Lucifer loves Thanatos— more than the world. It's the purest love I've ever seen, the most obvious connection I've ever had the pleasure of witnessing— threaten that, threaten a woman of Luce's potential power—

I shudder unwillingly.

"We're all overlooking one simple fact though— we have no reason to believe that Thane is in any kind of danger, or that their relationship is in trouble," Sephy reasons. I watch her, smiling despite my better judgement at her attempt at optimism.

"Besides, you can't just kill a god. You have to destroy the tether binding them to this plain. If not, they can be killed, but not easily—" Haedes announces. I query him with a glance.

"So, you mean to say that even with your tether intact, you can die?" I enquire, and he nods.

272

"Of course. If this body didn't serve my needs, for example, because of age, or if I was beheaded or something instantaneously fatal, which I had no chance at healing from— I couldn't return to The Higher Plains without my full life force though— so until my tether was broken, I'd remain in The Nether—" Haedes explains. Sephy scowls, the porcelain of her face refusing to wrinkle.

"I don't get it— my tether, that's the opal blade, right?" she asks, and he nods.

"Kind of— it's what your goddess half was tethered to before you reabsorbed it," he explains. Sephy scowls deeper even still.

"But that wasn't destroyed— so how come I ended up in The Nether?"

"That's easy. The blade reabsorbed your Goddess power when you were stabbed with it, but your life force isn't in that power. That's just a by-product of the more powerful energy that makes up your immortal half. Because it's intertwined with your mortality, when your mortal life was over— you were able to move on to await entry into The Higher Plains—" Haedes explains, and I feel my mind melt.

"That made absolutely no sense—" I cuss, impatient and annoyed at the complexity of it all.

"Of course it didn't. It's the goddamn way of the universe— if it was simple, any moron could go in, understand how it works, and fuck shit up! You're only a halfling. It took me hundreds of years of schooling to understand the intricacies of life energy— of magic. You wouldn't put your money in a bank with a simple lock and key now, would you?" Haedes snaps and I shrug, wondering why he seems so impatient suddenly. Then again, he's arguably closer to Lucifer than any of us, so I guess he's probably worried sick.

"I kind of get it— I think—" Sephy's eyes narrow, and Haedes smiles.

"Well, you got my brains, clearly," he quips. As I'm about to open my mouth to retort, a knock at the door disturbs us.

"Would you go and get that Xion, dear?" Moira asks, voice shaking as her lips tremble, a limp pink tongue flicking out to wet them as she speaks.

I turn from the group, wondering why I'm here at all. They clearly don't need me for this, the intellectual part. I'm only good for hitting shit and opening the door.

I cross the room, suspecting the person on the other side to be a servant. This is why, when I yank the door open toward me, I simply bark, "What?" in a blunt exclamation.

As the door swings back toward me, the person revealed is not who I expect at all, causing me to blink a few times, mouth hanging slightly open.

"Osiris?" I query, looking into the wide gaping darkness of his chocolate irises and knowing immediately that something is wrong.

"I need to come inside—" he blurts. Shoving past me, the white cotton of his long robe ripples around his upper thighs like lukewarm milk as he rushes across the space.

"What is it?" Sephy demands, gaze accusatory as he stills behind the armchair where Layla sits, using her as a human shield.

"It's my mother—" I hear him state, voice shaking and unsure.

Closing the door and restoring our privacy, I return to the group, my tread breaking apart the tension, which is thick in the pause between Sephy and Osiris. His breathing can be seen, rapid beneath the thin material of his tunic, and I realise he's nervous, terrified even.

"What happened?" Sephy presses him, shifting from foot to foot, impatient.

"She— she's got Thane, she's trying to make Luce resurrect Ra. She threatened to kill Thane, to smash her tether and send her back up to The Higher Plains if Lucifer doesn't do as she asked. Just like she did with you— Pandora— she— she took Luce to The Well. Made her drink—" His words ring out, riddled with insecurity, as though he's not sure whether he's doing the right thing. He brings a tan hand up to knead the back of his neck, gaze unfaltering in its desperation for any kind of guidance.

"Lucifer drank from The Well? *Willingly*?" Layla queries him, her voice soft as Anya's eyes widen, turning back to stare at Osiris full in the face. He paces around the side of her armchair, fleeing her gaze with unperceivably soft footsteps as if he's merely floating across the deep jade crystal of the floor.

"Yes," he replies.

Moira looks from him to Sephy, then to Haedes, and then back to me again.

"Well? What are you waiting for? Somebody go and stop her!" Moira exclaims, and Sephy frowns.

"Stop her? How exactly do you propose we do that?" she exclaims, throwing her tangled mess of red hair over one shoulder with a swift jerk of her chin. "She's powerful without The Well— that's the source of all darkness, right? Where Uranus funnelled his life force after he retired from The Higher Plains?" she asks, and we all nod in unison, not having the words for more of a history lesson.

"So, she's been supercharged? And you want us to what, exactly? Go and tell her to let Thane die? Somehow, I doubt that's going to go down well—" Sephy is cynical as ever, and it makes me wonder why. She's survived incredible odds herself, so why does she doubt the same of other people?

I continue to look to The Fates, as if three old women will provide a failsafe among this madness.

"Reason with her, capture her, knock her unconscious— kill her if you must. Ra *cannot* be resurrected," Layla finishes Moira's implication, her unseeing eyes becoming narrow with anxiety. "If Ra is resurrected, he will release the other Gods of Ancient from The Island of The Blessed. They will return here, and we will all be at the mercy of their wrath. They will multiply the demon numbers, perhaps even turn out the sun. The universe will be thrown into chaos. We cannot allow that to happen."

"Kill her?!" I exclaim, looking to Haedes for reassurance that this is absurdity, that this is madness spoken by an old woman. Haedes doesn't laugh it off though. Instead, he looks grim.

"That's all you've got? Go, and hope she doesn't do it— and if she does, kill her?" Sephy scowls.

"Child, you cannot simply separate a soul from darkness once it has been absorbed. It's infectious— like a parasite almost. The only thing with the power to draw off such darkness is long since lost— and thank goodness for that. Such weapons should never have existed in the first place," Moira gets a look of distaste, her spindled fingers wringing nervously, as Sephy stomps her foot.

"Okay, enough of the riddle me this bullshit, stop with the inferences— what the hell are you talking about now?" she barks. Haedes answers this time.

"The weapons which were used to create Demon Kindred and before them the Demon Lords— obsidian forged by the Gods of Ancient, they held the ability to deliver and store dark power. I had them destroyed when I took over this place. I couldn't risk the Demon Lords using Doppel bodies as weapons against us— they could have infected them. You know that's where zombies come from," Haedes explains. Sephy nods, seemingly unphased by the zombie comment.

"I mean technically, even broken, they can still store dark magic, but we don't have time to go gallivanting around Mortaria, praying for fragments of weapons which I made sure to incinerate— I mean they're gone. I used The Eternal Flame and decimated the lot," Haedes explains. I shift on the balls of my feet, heart hammering as more moments pass without so much as a step towards the door from any of them.

"I should get changed— this isn't exactly save the world attire—" Sephy sighs, looking down at herself. She's wearing my leather jacket and an oversized black t-shirt with super baggy slacks.

"Your room is still fully stocked as you left it—" Haedes reminds her, but she doesn't reply to this, simply looking at me with a grimace.

"Okay, I'll go and get changed, then I'll meet you down in the vault in a few minutes. We can decide where we go from there— and I'm going to need weapons," she says, decisive in the way she turns sharply on the spot and heads for the door.

I trail after her, leaving Haedes with Osiris as my long strides make short work of closing the distance between us out in the corridor.

"What exactly are you planning to do?" I demand.

She looks up at me, biting her bottom lip without so much as a pause in her stride as we hurry away from The Fates' suite.

"Whatever I have to." The threat of her words makes me suddenly angry at her.

"What the hell is that supposed to mean?" I snap as we storm through the entrance, each one of us increasing pace for seemingly no reason, as if we're suddenly competing.

"Look, if something happens to Haedes, I'm screwed with responsibility for this place— supposedly. I'm not letting that happen. I don't care if Luce is your friend. She's not worth the whole universe. I mean, she's nice, and she saved my life— twice, but I like being able to get in my nice cars and go out and party. I don't need this crap!" She's boisterous as her step quickens even still, and we ascend the ramp that leads to her suite. I gape at her.

"So, you can kill her— someone you know— a friend to you, just like that?" My tone is accusatory, breath catching in my throat at the thought of her laying a finger on Luce.

"Not just like that— but there's more at stake than her life. Isn't Ra like bad with a capital B? Surely her life isn't worth the suffering that he'll cause? And do you really think she's going to let them kill Thane?" she asks me, taking a deep inhale and continuing before

I can answer. "Isn't everyone always saying that the universe is so important? That there's a bigger picture here? Well, it's convenient that never seems to get mentioned when it's your loved ones on the line— funny that." She's sarcastic, and bile rises in my throat as I struggle to keep my inner demon under control.

"Well, I find it funny that you suddenly give a crap. Aren't you always trying to run off back to your life in that big old, empty house you seem to love so much?" I spit. Her eyes widen, surprised at me as her cognac irises blaze. "She risked herself to save your life, Sephy. We all did," I protest, and she shakes her head.

"And what? I'm supposed to be so grateful for that I let her fuck everything up for everyone? I let her resurrect this god everyone is so terrified of, so she can keep her girlfriend? What about other people? What about us? You and me? You want to risk my life? Because you know I'm related to Haedes— if someone wants control over this place, I'm not a loose end they're going to just let go—" she's yelling now, and I can tell she's been thinking about this more than I thought.

"I just— I feel like you owe her—" I begin, but she cuts me off again.

"I don't owe her shit. I didn't ask to be brought back. I was perfectly content being nowhere. It was a nice fucking break from getting my heart yanked out and stamped on." Her words cut me deeper than I want to admit, so much so that my rage diminishes and I'm left simply with my mouth hanging open.

I didn't break her heart.

She's breaking mine.

"So, you're saying you would rather I'd left you dead?" I ask, the power in my voice gone. I cross my arms, raising my defensive walls and letting them close in around my heart once again, a fortress from the verbal attack she's launching on me.

"I'm saying— life fucking *hurts*— okay? Everything with us— it's painful, but I can't seem to stay away— so I bear it. This universe— this place— it's not built for happily ever after. It's built to maintain the balance, and for that to happen, the people with power, the people who matter— the people like Haedes— don't get to be happy. He gets to be a pawn, to make the hard decisions. No matter the personal cost to him. I won't let that be me. I've given up enough already." She turns on her heel, and I wonder where the hell this is coming from as she walks away.

I stand there in the hallway, confused as all hell, melancholy and fury rolling into a single, too-tight knot beneath the steel muscles of my chest.

How the hell does she do that?

I thought we were good— I thought it was fine—

But now it's not just her that's fucked up; it's the universe?

She's always been cynical, always, but hell— that was bordering on the talk of someone who's completely lost the will to live.

She says she's given up enough already, but I know, and unfortunately so does she, that life just doesn't work that way.

There is no enough.

I stand outside her door for a few minutes, trying to regain my cool, before I cave into the reality of what I really want to do.

I knock on the brass sliding door to her suite.

She answers, dressed only in underwear, eyes dead in her skull.

"If you're here to tell me not to kill Luce, I got it. You don't want her dead. I'll make sure to consider that when weighing up whether to doom the world or not to make you happy." She turns, taking an elastic band off her wrist and yanking her hair up into a high ponytail. The red of her hair catches the light seeping from the fireplace and into the chocolate diamond and tourmaline décor of the room, warming her face as it does. I examine her almost naked back, the hourglass curve of her tall body, the way her ass swings from left to right with all the arrogance of a queen. She says she's not cut out to make the big decisions, but she seems ruthless to me.

"Why are you taking this upon yourself at all? I mean if you don't want anything to do with Mortaria?" I ask her, suddenly curious, as she rifles through a standing wardrobe on the far side of the room.

"Maybe because Haedes is weak as shit— because of me. You guys unearthed that stupid book which allowed all this to happen— because of me. Lucifer proved she could do the ritual to bring me back. So, when the world goes to shit, I want to say I did everything I could. I have enough of a guilty conscience where my parents are concerned; I don't need the rest of the universe on there too— I might just throw myself off the top of the Sinclair Estate." She rolls her eyes at me, and I frown.

"You honestly think this is your fault?" I demand.

"You should've just left me dead, Xion. It would have been better for everyone," she says, back turned to me even still as she selects several black garments and lays them out on the bed beside a crumpled pile of her clothes. My leather jacket lies there too, and I can't help but feel my heart hope that she'd stolen it for sentimental reasons, not just to chase away the cold.

"Not for me," I bite out, taking a few steps forward and sliding my hands around her bare waist. It's a bold move, one I instantly regret as she pulls out of my grasp the second my fingers meet over her navel.

"Don't. I don't have time," she mutters, pulling on a pair of black faded jeans. She dresses silently and I watch her, fraying at the seams. Her rejection stings far more than it should, far more than mine would ever sting her.

As she's pulling on an armoured corset and a chainmail bolero, I decide I've had enough. Enough of the mixed signals, enough of the self-pitying crap. Enough of her wickedness and of her stubborn-minded mean streak. I had once found it attractive, arousing, the friction between us, but now it's merely exhausting.

Feeling the demon stir beneath my skin, rearing its head as unspent anger begins to gnaw at my insides, I leave her to prepare to make the choices she never wanted to.

PANDORA

"Is it done?" Abraxis' voice echoes out against the mirrors of the room. If it were as sharp as it sounds, they'd be sure to shatter.

"Indeed." I smile, foot contacting the stone of the floor as arachnids scatter out from beneath my impending shadow. The skitter of them alerts me to the presence of their master, leaning against the corner of the room, half cloaked in darkness. His long, silver hair cuts through the air, proceeding him as he takes a step forward into the light cast down from the half-ruined ceiling overhead.

"You persuaded Lucifer to resurrect Ra?" I hear him ask, voice dulled with what seems to be disappointment, or perhaps it's an underwhelming attempt at surprise.

"I did. Though you shouldn't be surprised. We exposed her biggest fear. You know better than anyone the impact that can have. I was surprised she didn't put up more of a fight against the invasion of dark magic into her soul— then again, perhaps it was something she was looking to surrender to." I shrug, looking at them with sly eyes.

"It is possible. She is half Moloch; it would make sense that the darkness is something she's pulled to. Isn't the fact she's got an inherent affinity for the darkness exactly why Zeus banished her?" Gorgon presumes, but I smirk.

"Is it? Was it that she's inherently evil? Or could it be that the mixing of light and dark could present a power rivalling his own? Darkness tempts you— but you don't have to oblige it. I didn't. I resisted. It was what made me a Kindred in Hera's eyes. I had so many opportunities during my lifetime to succumb to sin, to harm those around me for my benefit, to take the lives of men sleeping, vulnerable, beside me. But I did not. It is, as ever, a game of will," I remind him, as articulate now as I had been giving speeches to the other Nephilim back at the Solis Castra. The only difference is, back then, I was preaching the word of a god. Now I am pushing an agenda that is purely mine and mine alone.

The air stirs slightly at my back, and I know she's staring at me before I turn. As I do so, Lilliana's white eyes meet mine, unblinking and unphased by my slick motion.

"We are ready—" she purrs, licking her top lip. I take a step forward, placing a calm and cool palm on her cheek.

"Thank you, you have never doubted me—" I bow to her slightly, letting her know that the respect between us is still intact. She is potentially my most powerful asset once I have accomplished what I need to. Lilliana's demon kindred surmount all others in number alone, or from what I know— it's hard to keep tabs on the Gorgonians.

"You will know, either way, when the time is right. Keep your eyes to the skies but also to the wall. Either one may signal our success," I remind her, and she nods, turning promptly on her heel and placing her fingers between her lips. A sharp whistle pierces the humidity before a rumble and the scratching of claws against stone grow closer.

Within moments, Lilliana is straddling a Banshee, a wild woman in an untamed black tulle gown being carried through The Halls of Antiqua and back toward the pack of her children. They wait, jaws dripping hot saliva at the entrance.

"Shall we proceed?" Barbas requests, sweeping past me, his long black coat billowing out behind him before his slim frame is made jagged by it yet again.

"We shall."
I smile.

23

YES SIR, 1 CAN BOOGIE

SEPHY

I STARE AT MYSELF in the mirror, exhaling heavily as I take in my reflection.

Had I been too harsh with Xion about Luce?

Perhaps.

It's not like I care.

If it were anyone else, we wouldn't even be having this discussion.

I don't want to deal with this, with any of this, but the way I see it, Haedes is too vulnerable, Luce and Thane are in trouble, and Anubis is apparently of no use either because she's a traitorous bitch. I could always call on Yama and Muerta, but if anything happens to the rest of The Nexus, they're perhaps the only two left who know how to run things— and my last chance at escaping the shackles of my heritage.

Why am I even considering this?

I look at my outline, made hard by the heavy garments I've chosen from inside the closet. A black armoured corset protects my heart, my lungs, my entrails that had not so long ago been cold, and a chainmail shawl clings to me, each rung of steel cold against my warm skin. I look at the jacket on the bed, feeling bad I had pushed him away. I can't let myself melt, though, because if I let him kiss me, let him make me feel the way I do when I look into those magnetic eyes of his, I would be agreeing to save Luce's life no matter what the cost.

I know my weakness, and that weakness is him, even without a conventional relationship.

Unfortunately for us both, I don't have time for weakness right now. I'm too busy trying to stop everything from falling apart, if not for entirely selfish reasons.

I know I'm selfish. I know wanting to walk away from Mortaria and everyone in it is self-serving, but don't I deserve to do something for myself? I've been through enough, felt enough heartbreak and suffered enough trauma for any single person to endure and want to continue standing. Why is it so wrong I just want to step away from this madness— from the death, the desperate importance of every decision? When does it end? When do I finally find the peace I've been craving, the contentment I seek?

Does it make me a coward to walk away?

Maybe.

I bite my bottom lip, looking into the heated whiskey-coloured depths of my irises. They're sad, weary, tired of it all.

I've been brought back to life and shoved right back into the killing fields, each passing moment one more grain of sand falling into the base of the hourglass counting down to yet another inevitable doom.

We're all doomed. Every single one of us.

Doomed to die, doomed to suffer, doomed to the mercy of this universe.

Luce is no different, except perhaps her fate could have been avoided. She made the choice, she drank from The Well, and now it may well be the end of her.

I cannot deny, in her shoes, I doubt I'd choose to willingly sacrifice the love of my existence either. I mean, it's not like what she'll be saving is a utopia. It's brutal and unfair. Why would anyone give up such a blatantly fated love for that?

I just wish it wasn't me who was having to consider taking her out.

If there were someone stronger, someone less attached, I'd pass this off to them in a heartbeat, but as it stands, there's only me. I'm the only one with control over both the eternal and resurrection flame, and I'm the only one who doesn't care deeply for the woman.

So, it must be me who saves or kills her.

Awesome.

I have no doubt in my mind this will make me the bad guy if it goes south, maybe even destroy how Xion sees me, but maybe it's time I came down off that pedestal anyway, for his sake and for mine.

I sling his jacket over my shoulders, inhaling deeply and knowing that I must not allow him to accompany me to find Luce. I need to protect him, need to protect everyone from themselves. Apparently, I have only been proven correct in my theory that love does nothing but cause pain, heartbreak, and bloodshed.

I hate being right.

Somehow, I've yet again ended up with the weight of a world on my shoulders— and it's not something I'm sure I can carry much longer.

The flames die down quickly as they rose, and the solid smoky crystal of the main hall catches my weight. I bend my knees, steadying myself within only seconds before striding across the length of the hall to where Haedes, Xion, and Osiris stand, staring at three women. Their gazes collectively caress me as I approach.

"Persephone," Erin greets me, the deep cocoa of her skin glinting warm in the glow of the many torches lining the walls. Her dark eyes glint, as flawless in rich dark pigment as her skin. Her wild hair expands out from her skull, untameable as she. I barely know The Furies, having only met them for the first time in passing at Luce's party.

"It's Sephy," I correct her, and she scowls, fingertips brushing the handle of one of the many torturously twisted blades sheathed in her belt. She's wearing leather, scantily dressed, the fabric tight and unmoving as she cocks her head.

"You are not Persephone?" she enquires, and I shake my head, exasperated.

"No, I am— I just prefer— never mind." I wave a hand carelessly, sick of explaining. Haedes looks to Ericka, who is standing at his side. She's watching him like a hawk as her palm rests upon the hilt of her sword, anxiety evident on her face. I notice a wooden bow strapped across her spine, a quiver of arrows stored on her hip, ready to be drawn at a moment's notice. The coffee colour of her skin glistens with light perspiration, dark hair pressed against her skull in two French braids.

"What are they doing here?" I demand.

Haedes cocks an eye at me as Erlea clears her throat. However, before she can speak, Xion replies instead.

"They're here to assist us in getting into The Sinstone Mines," he explains.

"The mines?" I question him, and Haedes nods.

"It would appear, according to Osiris, that's where Anubis had the mummified corpse of Horus, her ex-husband, stored— I mean I personally collect vintage guitars— but each to their own I suppose." He's trying to be funny, but I can't laugh as I gaze at Osiris. He shuffles, shoulders sagging under the scrutiny of my gaze.

"And how do I know that this isn't a trap?" I demand, tone as sharp as broken glass and even less forgiving.

"Why would I come here— why would I tell you all of this? There's nothing in it for me!" Osiris protests, crossing his arms over his chest, outraged. His posture says he's sure, but the way his voice wavers tells me otherwise.

"Because this could be a distraction. Perhaps this is merely a way to— I don't know— get us out of the way? Make us vulnerable maybe?" I suggest, but he shakes his head.

"No, of course not!" He's defiant; dark eyes wild and desperate to be believed.

"I just find it hard to believe that a mummy's boy like you willingly hands over the woman who gave him life." I cock an eyebrow, and his expression hardens, skin creasing around his thick lips.

"Perhaps I'm tired of having my life controlled," he replies, and my lips press into a thin line, doubtful as I narrow my furious gaze.

It's possible— I muse, but then again, so is a betrayal by him equalling that of his mother.

"Look, we don't have time for this. Every second we waste is a second we move closer to Lucifer performing that ritual," Xion speaks out in a rush, my eyes flitting to him, as I exhale loudly.

"Xion, you're not coming," I announce, not so much a quiver of uncertainty in my voice.

"*Excuse me?*" His eyes blaze orange, an obvious demonic rage beginning to build inside him. It doesn't scare me as it once would have, and my fingers twitch, only a whim away from sparking hot and lethal.

"You can't be objective for one. Besides, I need you to stay here with Haedes. In case this is a trap," I remind him, eyes flicking between Osiris and Haedes and back again in only a few seconds.

"So, I can't come either?" Haedes scowls.

"That's right. You're too weak. Sorry, Gramps." I shrug, expecting his hair to turn red at the root. Instead, it merely continues to shine a dull grey. His eyes, however, tell a different story.

"Don't be absurd, Sephy. You can't do this alone," he protests.

"I won't be alone. I'll be with them." I gesture to The Furies who stiffen, spines straightening and stances widening, clearly up to the task.

"How are you going to get there? You can't convect with all three of them. Not even I have that power—" Haedes interjects, and I give him a look of mischievous foreboding, my eyes sparkling as a small smile tugs at my lips.

"No. *Absolutely not.*" Haedes shakes his head, crossing his arms over the lapels of his indigo suit jacket as he grasps my intent.

"Look, you know it'll be faster than a carriage. Faster than any other way we have of getting there with this many people—" I say, trying to stay calm as he narrows his eyes.

"No! Absolutely not! I just had it repaired! The polish is barely dry!"

"Haedes, it's just a car—" I remind him, but he shakes his head vigorously from left to right.

"Yes, but it's *my* car! I already had the spare keys confiscated from Luce for exactly this reason!" He pouts like a small child as I hold out a hand, palm open. I cock my head and stare at him. This isn't a discussion.

"Give," I command, not blinking. He sighs deeply, rolling his eyes and reaching into the innermost pocket of his jacket.

"Fine. But no letting The Furies drive! They have horrendous road rage, and none of them can parallel park!" he barks, shoving a set of keys attached to a pair of blue fluffy dice into my outstretched hand. I clutch them, pulling my hand back immediately, victorious. Then I smile. For what I have in mind with the kind of protection surrounding The Sinstone Mines, I doubt we'll be doing any parking, let alone parallel.

"Weapons— I need weapons too," I demand, and he rolls his eyes yet again.

"You don't want much, do you? Have kids they said— it'll be fun they said— bleeding me goddamn dry— freaking vultures," he mutters, and I smirk, amused, as ever, by him and his utterly ridiculous obsession with the material. Then again, if I know him — and I think I do — it's a mask for his anxiety, for his fear of losing what's really important. "The best weapons I have are down in the dungeons," he adds, turning on his heel. "The entrance is on the way to the garage— come on." He gestures for the group to follow him, so we do, quickly exiting the hall in a cacophony of heels upon flat polished stone.

Passing through the large doors into the entrance hall, I notice the eyes of more sinners than I'm used to boring into us. The security here has certainly tightened, so perhaps I'm being paranoid in leaving Xion behind to protect Haedes. Then again, if he dies, I'm utterly fucked, so perhaps I have a right to be.

After several minutes of fast-paced steps echoing around us, we turn into a more sheltered corridor. The ceiling is still high, but the encroaching walls on either side dampen the echoes of our tread as we pace its vast length in single file. It seems to go on forever, as do most of the corridors in the Exilia. I wonder if it's the crystal, an optical illusion by the reflective surfaces casting the existing corridor back at you.

We turn right, where an oddly archaic wooden door is pushed open, before the group descends a flight of cobblestone steps in silence. It's strange, I muse, the décor being such a stark and downright draconian contrast to the rest of the place.

As we pass cells constructed of rusting wrought iron bars, I find only empty shackles hanging with thick and foreboding shadows against the walls and hay scattering floors. I wonder why a dungeon is even necessary.

What was this used for?

Is it still used?

Curiosity claws at me in a way I wish would stop. I have no desire to know, not really, and yet my mind is restless, gnawing at any old subject matter to prevent me from having to address the fact I may very well be about to murder a woman I had thought was a pillar of goodness. When we first met, I knew she looked far more innocent than she was, but those concerns had been quieted by her persistent plight to keep me alive.

"Here," Haedes says as he hastily pulls open one of the cell doors. I hadn't noticed before, but this cell is different because it's stacked from floor to ceiling with wooden chests. Xion pulls one down, and Osiris aids him, beginning a chain of hands as we begin to hoist the chests out into the central corridor. The Furies kick open the lids, without care for the damage they may cause, behind me.

As the chests fly open, lids slamming against the floor, shimmering silver is revealed, catching the shadow of the place and purifying it so it shines out stark from the blades.

"Ooh shiny!" I exclaim, reaching in and picking up several knives. I stash them in my waistband quickly before picking up a broadsword and testing the weight of it in my palm. Xion stares at me as he treads out of the cell, cocking his head and then an eyebrow, kicking a clump of hay to one side with unwarranted fury.

"No, you want this one. That one is too heavy. It won't balance with your weight correctly." His voice is thick with irritation, anger even, as he takes the sword from me, passing me another which he hastily selects from the chest beside him. Our skin grazes against one another's, a shudder running involuntarily up my arm.

For Christ's sake, I cuss, hatred for the effect he has over me seeping, cold, into my chest like vitriol. Everything would be so much easier if I felt nothing at all, but instead, this attraction, animal or not, is going to be the breaking of me.

"Thanks," I mutter, though our eyes don't meet. Instead, I focus on the sword he's handed to me. It's slightly longer than the other, but slimmer, moving with ease as I swing it from left to right.

Haedes gets a look of alarm on his face.

"Hey! Don't swing that in here. You'll take someone's goddamn eye out!" he cusses, sounding older by the second as I smirk at him.

"Jeez, sorry— *Dad!*" I exclaim, meaning it to come out as a joke. However, the final word gets stuck in my throat as I see his eyes widen. I quickly drop my gaze yet again, turning my back on the group as I adjust my grip on the handle of the sword with a careless flick of my wrist.

"We should hurry." I turn to the three Furies, who nod, synchronised in their precise motion.

We mobilise as a collective, ascending back up the stairs in a hurried flurry of both punishing and nimble footsteps.

"Where now?" I demand, looking to Haedes as he's cast in the stark light of the hallway, shutting the wooden door of the dungeons behind him.

"The garage. Come on, this way," he sighs, clearly unhappy about the entire arrangement but moving forward regardless. That seems to be pretty much a theme of his position, whereby he's very seldom able to act as he wishes to but instead, acts as he must. It makes sense to me now, his small acts of rebellion; fucking the help, drinking himself stupid, buying fast cars— it's all his way of maintaining his autonomy, of keeping a small part of his existence his.

I know this because that was how I avoided succumbing to the weight of my heritage back before I'd known the truth.

As Haedes leads me down an almost invisible corridor that runs back against the wall, descending rapidly into the basement, I realise he and I have perhaps never been so comparable.

We reach the garage, and as Osiris' footsteps are the last to fall silent from the staircase behind us, I see it. In all its restored glory,

The Mean Machine stands upon a revolving platform, centre stage under the stark scrutiny of harsh fluorescent lighting.

Haedes whimpers beside me as my eyes widen, taking in the slick black and cobalt blue of the flames that adorn the wheel arches and bonnet.

It's a beautiful car, and no matter what anyone says about Haedes, you can't deny the guy's got style mixed with good taste. However, I don't have time to stand around admiring the hot rod like I want to. Instead, I have to keep moving.

"Come on, let's get going." I gesture to The Furies who jog forward, climbing up onto the platform. I throw Erlea the keys, who catches them without visible effort. Unlocking the door and pulling the passenger seat forward, she lets Erin and Ericka clamber into the back before getting into the vehicle herself.

As the door slams behind her, I turn to Haedes.

"You stay safe, both of you. And if you—" I threaten, looking to Osiris now, "so much as think about trying to harm anyone, you'll end up looking like that disgusting green snot you served me at dinner!" I glare at him one final time, making sure my pissed-off expression is branded into his memory, before turning on my heel and hurrying over to the platform.

I climb up onto the stage, hoisting myself with only the strength of my upper body before getting into the driver's side seat and inhaling the welcome scent of fresh polish and leather.

The Furies say nothing, and I watch as Haedes walks across the garage, flicking a few switches. The door opens before us, and a whirring sound signals the lowering of the platform.

I put the keys into the ignition, anxious, as a sudden sound leaves my nerves in tatters.

It's unbelievable— it's—.

Ain't no mountain high enough, by Marvin Gaye.

Please, God, let the stereo be fixed.

I stab at the off button with my index finger, sighing audibly as the motivational spiel dies into nothingness.

Phew.

The roar of the engine is all that can be heard as the leather of my seat vibrates, only increasing my anxiety as I find the bite point with the clutch. I pull forward onto the flat and spotless white of the garage floor, proceeding forward to the door and rolling down my window as Haedes steps around the side of the car.

"Be careful. I don't need to be resurrecting you again. I've already got too many grey hairs as it is," Haedes jokes, and before I can reply, he does something I don't expect. He leans in through the window, kissing my cheek with his dry thin lips. I flush.

"I'll be careful," I promise, not sure what to say as I cough, clearing my throat. It's uncomfortable to say the least, having a parent who cares after all this time.

With a final gaze at him, I roll the window back up before pulling out of the space and into the Exilia entrance, speeding off into Mortaria. As I focus on driving, I can't help but be filled with a growing sense of dread.

Finally, after a lengthy period of silence, I find myself so on edge I can't bear it any longer.

"So— uh— how do you guys like working for Haedes?" I ask them, at a loss for a more interesting question.

Erlea stiffens beside me in her seat as Ericka pops her head between the two of us from the back of the vehicle.

"He is— how you say— an asshole?" she observes.

I snort.

"True, but I kind of get the impression you guys think that all men are assholes? Am I right?" I ask them, putting my foot down and overtaking a slew of carriages, horses startling ever so slightly at the roar of the engine.

"Yes," Erin replies simply.

"Why? If you don't mind me asking?" I query them, trying to keep the conversation going. Anything so I don't have to think about killing Lucifer and breaking Xion's and Haedes' hearts forever.

"Kidnapped, raped, murdered," says Erin.

"Sacrificed to the gods," announces Erlea.

"Executed for refusing to marry the chief," says Ericka. I look back over my shoulder, carelessly weaving in and out of traffic without keeping my eyes on the road, staring at them all as they fall yet again into silence.

"Uh— right," Is all I can think to say.

I mean, how the fuck am I supposed to respond to that?

"I uh, got stalked and then stabbed to death—" I add, shrugging slightly, trying to find common ground even if that ground is soaked in blood.

"Did you grind his bones to make your bread?" Ericka asks me, eyes glinting, and I scowl.

"No—wait—what—that's an actual thing?" I demand, taken aback as I debate turning on the stereo again, anything to drown out this necessary yet torturous and immensely disturbing small talk.

"Of course. Men bones make the best bread—" Erlea smiles wickedly, and I grimace at her, sheepish as I try not to show the horror climbing within me.

"I uh, I did kick him in the balls— does that count?" I look at Erin in the rear-view mirror, eyes glistening with slight pleasure as they flick between her impressed expression and the road.

"Very nice—" she purrs, and I continue to smile at her, growing more uneasy by the second.

Remind me never to leave these guys alone with Jules— or Xion— or any male I don't want dead. I note, taking deep breaths as we reach the city limits.

The drive passes too slowly as the three women fidget in their seats, obviously restless as the metal and wood of their weapons clangs against their bony legs. I'd start up more small talk, but in all honestly, I'm trying not to think about death, about killing, which seems to be their only subject of interest.

It's a shame they don't have an interest in say— designer shoes, or cars, or— well hell, even discussing men in a relationship sense would be better than talking man bread.

The scent of ichor drifts in through the vents, which I promptly close, tapping my nails nervously on the steering wheel.

"You think there will be demons?" Erin asks me, her broken English drifting over my shoulder.

"I think if Anubis and whoever the hell else is pulling this little stunt have left the entrance to those mines unguarded, they're very stupid—" I mutter. Erlea frowns.

"I have never thought of Anubis as lacking in brains," she determines, and my lips twist into a thin line.

"Then you have your answer," I reply, palms beginning to sweat as I push my foot down even harder. The Icon's unmistakable silhouette is cast by the lilac sun, which hangs behind it. It's as I look at it, I realise I actually don't know the exact location of The Sinstone Mines.

"Hey uh, do any of you girls know where these mines are exactly?" I demand, looking over to find Erlea's acute features deadpan.

"We live in jars."

This is literally all she says.

291

"Okay— well, I better ask for directions," I say, slowing up as we enter the Plains Of Ichor. Around us, sinners toil, sweat dripping from their bent and broken silhouettes.

"Is good job you are not man— yes?" Ericka giggles, and Erin smirks. I roll my eyes.

"Excuse me," I call out of the window. "I was wondering if you could tell me where The Sinstone Mines are?" I demand of a sinner who is nearby, combing over the ichor-soaked soil with some kind of rake. As he approaches, the scent of infection, of human juices, leaks into the car, making my stomach turn.

"Yes ma'am. Just head up to The Icon. It's about half a mile to the left," he replies, turning before I've even had a chance to thank him and going back to what he was doing. His eyes are dead as he strokes the comb across the earth, but I don't have time to stop or stare, and neither do I feel pity for the sinner.

Instead, I roll my window back up and put my foot down hard.

I let the engine open up to its full potential, tired of the waiting, of the anxiety. I want to get this over with.

Reaching The Icon, I screech around the corner, ash flying up under the back tyres as I let the car drift.

As soon as I do, I realise that Haedes is not going to get his car back in one piece.

There are demons — *everywhere*. Gorgonians and Succubi, sitting, waiting— not as I would have expected. I thought they'd be feeding, killing sinners, but instead they're merely standing in formation outside the entrance to the mines about half a mile ahead.

"That is a lot of demons—" Erin announces.

"You don't say—" I mutter, putting my foot down even harder and changing to a higher gear.

"What are you doing?" Erlea asks, the long nails of her pale fingers clinging to the seat as I pick up greater and greater speed.

"I am going to teach you all a lesson in driving—" I speak calmly and Erin frowns at me in the rear-view mirror.

"A lesson?" Erlea swallows hard, and I nod, a small smile induced by the thrill taking over my face.

"A crash course if you will—" I continue, and the three women inhale as we near the wall of demons, faster and faster, with no hint of stopping.

"But Haedes said—" Erlea gasps, and I cock an eyebrow.

"He said not to let you drive— are you driving?" I ask her, and she shakes her head.

"Well then, I'm not breaking any rules. Everyone got their seatbelts on?" I demand, watching as the three women frantically scurry to belt themselves in.

"Right then—" I sigh, each passing second bringing me closer to a collision with flesh, teeth and bone— "Lesson the first— Emergency stops."

As I pull on the handbrake, I let the back of the car slide while yanking on the steering wheel, forcing the back of the car to smash into the front line of the wall of demons. The Furies don't scream, merely pursing their lips and steeling their muscles as we come to a standstill with an ear-piercing screech, the scent of burning rubber filling the vehicle. A pile of decimated demon corpses catch under the tread of the tyres, making it impossible for me to reverse like I wanted to, using the car as my main weapon, but I suppose it was good for taking out at least a dozen, so I can't complain.

Winding down my window, I shoot a quick ball of red-hot flames at the mass grave, watching as they burn, souls eviscerated within seconds. Their ashes blow away, indistinguishable from the surrounding flurry.

Getting out of the car, I feel them surrounding us, the hairs on the back of my neck warning me of their increasing proximity.

"Time for lesson the second—" I call back to them, too afraid to break eye contact with the encroaching hoard as I unsheathe my sword. "Kill everything that moves—" I hear Erlea open her door, her words ringing out into the air as she draws her katana from inside the car.

"Ah," she says, "this lesson we know very well."

24

SALUTE

LUCE

"SO HOW LONG DOES something like this take?" Anubis enquires, as though we're not trying to resurrect an evil god into the body of her mummified ex-husband but rather trying to change a tyre on her SUV. I cock an eyebrow at her.

"I don't know. I've never been blackmailed to perform a resurrection on a God of Ancient who could potentially doom the entire universe before—" The words fall from my lips, drab and lacking in sentiment or emotion. I'm numb, the fear having receded deep inside as the dark power in my veins takes over. Instead of drowning in the endless and awful possibilities, I'm now trying to work out how I can use my new powers to get Thane and me out of this mess.

"Lucifer, what makes you think the universe will be in any worse order under the rule of Ra than your boneheaded, blue-haired friend?" she demands, crossing her arms across the black fabric of her dress. I watch as the dim hot light of the surrounding torches steals all hue from her irises, making her eyes appear as bottomless pools of onyx, much like my own.

"You were the one who first helped claim back The Higher Plains, so why don't you tell me?" I demand, trying to keep the conversation going as long as possible as I clutch the book tightly in my palms.

I have the powers of the Ancient dark children of Uranus running through my veins— fear, illusion, murderous bloodlust, untameable savagery, and malice. There must be some way for me to get at least a moment alone with Thane, to ask her what I should do.

I know I should stop this, know that the right thing to do is abstain, and yet I am too weak to willingly let her go, too weak to let them take her from me. I have never needed her advice, her support, or her acceptance, more than I do in this moment.

"Mortals have too much power here, Lucifer. He's sleeping with them, letting them prepare his food, allowing them to walk among us in jest and without fear. That is not what this place is about. It's about repenting, suffering— giving back the darkness within them," she's preaching, so I turn away to the table on which the sarcophagus is set before slamming The Book of The Dead down with a heavy, irritated thud.

"And yet, for hundreds of years, the balance has remained. The scales have not tipped. Haedes has done his job. He just knows you don't need to be cruel to achieve such ends. Except, of course, I hope, in your case. How will you answer for your sins?" I enquire, sticking my nose in the air, superior. She smirks.

"You're far deeper into the shadow than I have ever been, Lucifer. So, who really needs to repent? Who drank from The Well to save her own lover's skin?" she retorts, turning on her heel, the long sleeves of her gown flying out behind her in a flurry of luxurious fabric.

As she paces around the space, I look at Thane, the high curve of her cheekbones, the deep set of her eyes. She has not changed since she was a little girl.

It is with this recurrence of memory that the world around me shifts, dissolves, and I'm transported somewhere I never thought I'd set foot again. The place where it all started, the place where we began.

The warm breeze stirs through the trees, the scent of Othrysian apples lacing the air, sweet with a bitter edge. Warmth shines through each individual leaf, the epitome of luscious emerald tipped malachite in hue. The veins within their lavish flesh silhouette, and as I stare down at my skin, I realise we are not so different. Dark veins mar my pallidity too, not showing that I am bad but perhaps merely more alive than I have ever been.

"Lucifer—" Thane's voice reaches me, a familiar birdsong on the wind.

"Thane— what is this?" I demand, wondering why I'm here as I seek her form.

Did I do this? Or did she?

She emerges from behind the trunk of a tree, the bark veined through with gold, silver, and platinum; it shimmers. Her tread echoes out against the powdered quartz that lies underfoot as she parts several branches sporting low-hanging apples. They glisten, their skin so pristine and flawless in texture that they could be made from crimson enamel. I know better though. I know that beneath the sheen of the too-crisp flesh, sweet ambrosia juices await, primed and ready to be let run down some lucky fool's gullet.

"I don't know— I thought you brought us here." She gives me a heartbroken look as she comes close to me, still wrapped in the black silk from the cavern. Her wound is gone, and so are the demons that bind her to the sheer rock face.

"Did I? I guess— I guess I could have. I don't know what this magic is capable of yet," I admit, looking deeply into the grey of her eyes. It's not stormy, but still. Extinguished even.

"Luce what did you do?" she cocks her head, lips parting ever so slightly as she reaches out and runs her fingers through my black hair. Her fingertips caress me, tracing the veins that crawl up my neck and over my cheekbones, visibly pained by her journey across my skin. "This—" she says, "it isn't you."

"It is me. It is now. I have to save you," I implore her understanding, squaring my shoulders and looking at her with unwavering determination.

"Luce, no. I'd rather die than let that monster, Ra, free. Please, don't do this—" She's pleading with me, and I feel my eyes dilate to black as rage builds in my chest.

"So, what? You want me to let you die? To let you go back up to those people in The Higher plains?" I accuse her, and she looks sad.

"If it's what we have to do. We have a responsibility as goddesses not to let our personal feelings mess with the balance of the universe." She sounds like my mother, like her mother, not placating me but instead, stoking the fires of my rage further. It blazes beneath my skin, turning ferocious.

"We don't have a responsibility to anyone, Thane! They abandoned us! They exiled me and left me for dead. They tried to force you to stay in The Higher Plains and be miserable. We don't owe anything to anyone. *Nothing*. We owe it to us to fight for this. Even if it means—" I'm breathless, heartbeat rapid as she interrupts me.

"Sentencing others to suffer and burn?" Thane demands.

"Yes," I scowl, and her face remains impassive, eyes glazing over.

"I'd rather die than be with someone who could make that choice with a clean conscience, Luce," she warns me, arms still at her sides, hair wild around her face as it catches the light of the too-pure plati-sun overhead.

"So, you want me to let you go?" I feel a tear threatening to spill from the depths of my dark eyes, scrutinising her as my heart breaks.

"I don't want you to let me go. Not ever. But you must." Thane plants a gentle kiss on my forehead, looking deeply into my eyes. "I love you," she whispers, lips sagging with sadness. I should be sad too, but I'm not. Instead, I'm simply defiant.

She would be torn from me so easily?

I did not drink from The Well to lose her. I did not willingly absorb such power to be made meek and victimised by a mere pissed-off Titan and her demonic playthings.

I look at Thane once more as she stares at me, waiting for me to tell her I love her too. Waiting for me to cry, or weep, or dissolve into a puddle of emotion, of grief for what I know is coming.

But I refuse.

Instead, I simply reach up, plucking an apple from a nearby branch that glistens gold in the heavenly sunlight. She cocks her head as I do so, giving her a dangerous look as my eyes deaden in my skull.

She might not want to fight for us any longer, but I will. If there's breath left in my body, I will fight for her.

"Luce— don't— please," she whispers, voice broken.

I turn the Othrysian apple in my palm, letting the light fall over the perfection of its bloody skin.

"You will thank me. Maybe not tomorrow, but someday," I call, turning promptly on my heel and digging my teeth into the flesh of the apple as my lips cup its sumptuous curve.

Juice wets my lips before dribbling down over my chin and dripping into my cleavage. I let the taste take me over as the Othrysian Orchard dissolves into nothing and the apple in my palm turns to bitter ash falling through my fingers.

I blink, and I'm once more standing beside Anubis, who is looking at me. No time has passed here, and she's still waiting for me to retort to her last comment. Thane's face is twisted in irritation as she stares at me, she and I the only two people aware of what had passed, unplanned, between us.

I try to recall what she was saying, but I'm too stunned by the illusionary experience that just took over all five of my senses to remember.

"I need to look at the body—" I murmur, taking several steps forward to where the sarcophagus lies, pried open, upon the enormous slab of marble central to the cavern.

I stare down into the depths of the solid gold burial casket, finding Horus' shrivelled, bandaged, and inhuman looking remains staring back up at me.

I gaze with a casual, fleeting motion back over my shoulder to Anubis. How can she sleep at night, knowing her ex-husband is sitting down here in this state? It's enough to make me feel sick just by looking at him.

I lean in, holding my breath as the scent of stale air and dust fills my nostrils against my consent, trying to work out if this body is even intact enough for a resurrection. This isn't like with Sephy, who had been dead a mere six months— this will be a little trickier, to say the least.

"Did you uh— were his organs removed before he was mummified?" I demand, voice thick with evident disgust.

"Of course. I am nothing if not a stickler for the traditions of my people," she raises her eyebrows, surprised by this question as if it's stupid.

"Do you have them? The organs— I assume you put them in canopic jars?" I enquire.

"Yes, except for the heart— the heart is left within the body. It is the seat of the soul," she explains, and I nod, exhaling heavily. I stare into the eye sockets of the corpse, pondering about what lies behind.

"And the brain?" I ask, and Anubis gives me an odd look.

"Usually destroyed, but I had Horus' brain placed in with his stomach— which is where it spent most of its time when it wasn't lodged in his—" I cut her off.

"I need the jars—" I order her, and she frowns.

"But they will be but dust by now, Lucifer," she insists, and I shake my head.

"Excuse me? Are you performing this ritual? You said you wanted me to resurrect Ra, so I expect you to do as I say!" I spit, throwing the three figures watching me my most furious glare.

"All right, no need to be a bitch about it—" Anubis mumbles, shuffling over to the wall behind me. Her skirt trails along the floor behind her, gathering shimmering crystal shards as it goes. I watch her, narrowing my eyes as she rolls aside a slab of stone I wouldn't have known was there. Behind it, the four canopic jars stand.

"Imsety— the liver." She passes the first to me, taking long steps as she glides across the earth, delicate in her handling of the artefact. I stare at it as I snatch it from her, a human head gazes back, unfeeling in solid gold. I screw off the lid, tired of this spectacle already as I dump the contents of the jar onto the top of the mummified corpse's torso. "Qebehsenuf— the intestines," she announces as I toss the first jar to the ground without care or caution. Snatching the second jar from her, I gaze into the precious falcon's face before upending the contents once more into the abdominal cavity. "Hapy— the lungs," the baboon's eyes flash this time as I spin the lid, sprinkling the contents like marinade on a steak gone well past its sell-by date over the top of the ribcage.

"And finally, Duametef, the stomach and in this very special circumstance, the brain." Anubis unscrews the jackal-headed jar and reaches inside without pause. She pulls out a large floppy pouch made from indigo velvet, passing the jar off to me before she moves to the head of the sarcophagus. She tips the contents into one of the eye sockets, assuming in her arrogance that this is correct, which luckily for her it is.

I do the same with the remains of the stomach, letting the jar fall to the floor with a hollow clatter as soon as I'm done.

"Do you have a tether?" I demand, looking at her with tired eyes. My lids flutter slightly, heavy as she draws something from a hidden pocket on the underside of one of her skirt's pleated folds.

"I had this recreated based on the original—" she passes it to me, an ankh made from citrine. It glistens like canary yellow flames made solid in the flickering torchlight as I glare at her.

"You have been the busy little bee—" It comes out as a snarl as I hold the tether so firmly it may shatter. Anubis looks at me, reaching into her cleavage for Thane's tether and pulling it out, dangling it right in front of me.

"I would start showing me a little respect if I were you," she bites out, as I snatch for the necklace. She takes a step back; smirking and shoving the jewel back between her breasts.

"Gorgon, Katerina. Why don't you come a little closer? Assist Lucifer here with the ritual?" she demands, eyes gleaming wicked.

"What the hell happened to you?" I spit, looking at Thane who seems to be falling close to unconsciousness as the wound on her shoulder continues to weep blood.

"Hell happened to me, Lucifer. And you. And everyone else who didn't fit into the tiny boxes Zeus created and deemed correct. I would have thought you, more than anyone, would relish the chance to work under gods and goddesses who believe that power is earned, not birthright." She glowers at me.

As she does so, Gorgon and Katerina stride over to me, grabbing me by the upper arms. I struggle, wishing I had more than a few moments to work out how to use my new power— how to harness this darkness within me.

As it is, only rogue emotion seems to be getting any results, and instead of letting myself feel, I'm currently quashing my conscience and forcing myself to do what I know I must.

I take a step forward, opening The Book of The Dead.

"I need you to bring her closer, to have her hold this, and I need aether—" I demand, gesturing to Thane as I shove the tether at Anubis. Thane's eyes widen as they connect with mine, the book in my palm becoming a welcome distraction as the dark ink begins to whisper to me. It's as if the words had been written by a quill first dipped in The Well of Eternal Torment itself, and where before I could feel the power within the pages, now it invades my every sense.

Gorgon leaves my side, quickly replaced by Anubis whose shadow falls over me, obstructing the light by which I'm trying to read. I look back at her, glaring, and she moves an inch to the right as I turn back to the pages. Thane's body is bound tightly by the Gorgonian demons that slither too easily around her limbs, and Gorgon whispers to them in a harsh hissing tone until they lower her to the ground. He grabs her injured arm, yanking it hard as he forces her to walk with him, snake-like demons still wrapped around her throat, legs, and arms, ready to constrict at any moment. She cries out, but I ignore the sound, trying to focus on the task at hand. I need to remain impassive, need to concentrate if I'm going to do this right without killing her.

"Sprinkle the aether in a circle around the sarcophagus please—" I bark at Anubis, wondering how the sun will impact this ritual. In the mortal world, I had told Haedes to spread it counterclockwise, because the sun rises in the east and sets in the west— but in Mortaria, the sun never rises or sets.

"What now?" Anubis asks, pushy as ever. I turn to her, taking a deep breath and placing my palms, mapped black with dark veins, flat upon the cool marble table in front of me.

"Now," I say simply, "we begin."

XION

"We should hold up in the throne room. That way we can keep an eye on the hourglass," Haedes suggests, and I look at him with a surprised expression as he flicks the switch to close the garage door.

"You think that might be a target?" I demand, folding my arms and trying to ignore the sinking feeling that overtook me as I watched Sephy drive away.

"I think I'm not stupid enough to take the risk that it might be," Haedes mumbles, giving a sideways glance to Osiris who is waiting at the entryway to the garage even still, looking bored.

"And what about him? Do you think he's telling us the truth? Or is this some ruse like Sephy said?" I ask him, and he shrugs, face sullen.

"I'm not sure of that either, what I do know is that regardless of whether he's lying or not, Anubis has a lot to answer for. I mean, what the hell was she thinking?" Haedes asks me, frowning.

"I don't think even Anubis knows that. She's power-hungry, and if you ask me, she seems to think that the grass is always greener on the other side of the fence. She's switched sides a lot historically, even tried to play Ra under Cronus' rule. She's not an easy woman to pinpoint. Regardless, I'd say keeping her son close isn't a bad idea. We just need to be careful we don't trust him with anything important," I suggest. Haedes seems to wordlessly agree, expression growing increasingly morose by the second.

As the garage door closes behind him, I sigh.

"Do you think she'll kill Luce?" I ask him as we head for the exit, climbing the stairs without so much as gesturing for Osiris to follow. He does though, his melancholy and adolescent tread bordering on stroppy behind us.

"I think that she's capable of whatever she deems necessary," Haedes replies, blunt.

"Oh, I do not doubt that. I just hope she gives her a chance to prove she can handle the darkness, that her moral code hasn't gone out of the window, I suppose," I muse.

"Whatever she decides, I'll support, Xion. I love Luce like a sister, but I can't doom the entire world for her. I sacrificed Sephy to keep control over this place, and she's my daughter. If I must sacrifice Luce to maintain the same balance, there's no question in my mind." He's clearly given this a lot of thought, and I frown as we begin to make our way back down the corridor.

"I understand that." I sigh, rubbing the back of my neck with my calloused palm as we exit the narrow hold of the hall and enter the chasmic entryway.

"Now, onto a more important question," Haedes breathes, not making eye contact with me as his words hit the air.

"Which is?" I demand, anxiety pooling in my stomach.

"Are you fucking my daughter because you're in love with her, Xion?" he demands, and my mouth pops open slightly as we approach the hall doors, guarded by stoic-faced sinners. They step aside, opening the doors for us and letting us inside, before closing them after Osiris trails in behind us.

"I uh— I—" I stutter and Haedes moves to the throne at the head of the room, eyelids fluttering in relief as he finally sits.

"So that's a yes then. I thought so. Look, I'm going to cut the shit with you. I think she loves you too. But if she has to choose, at one time or another, between you and the universe, I expect you to make that choice for her. You will remove yourself from the equation. Even if she hates you for it, even if she cries and begs and screams, you remove yourself. I won't let her become her mother. Understand?" His eyes twinkle with serious devotion, and I think perhaps this is the first time since Demi Sinclair's death that I've seen him display such potent affection publicly.

"Yes, sir," I vow, watching as he gets to his feet, visibly wincing.

"Hey, you know you could just convect—" I suggest, as he holds out a hand to me and I place a hand on his shoulder, steadying his fragile posture.

"That's the thing though, I can't. Not anymore. My powers are all but gone, Xion. I sacrificed them for her. The only person I can claim to love as much as, if not more than, Demi. So, I expect you to honour her and her uniqueness, her power, her role in this universe, even if it means unimaginable pain. Even if it means death," Haedes implores me with his gaze as I grasp his hand in mine.

"I promise." At my words, he gives a sigh of relief.

"Thank you."

SEPHY

It's been too long since I felt this much control in any aspect of my life. Even with Xion, when he's touching me, I feel a loss of control to my desire for him. This though, this is pure thrill.

The Furies are a force to be reckoned with, and we whip through the mass of demons, caught in an artistic dance of clattering swords and the spattering of arterial blood coating hot flesh.

I use my free hand to throw fireball after fireball, taking out demons in every direction, but more just keep crawling out from the depths of the mines. It's been ten minutes, or so I guess because I've not really paid attention, and we've barely made it into the mouth of the tunnels leading deep underground.

"Sephy!" Erin calls from behind me.

Spinning on the spot, I'm just in time to see the long arm and outstretched gangly fingers of a Succubus heading right for my skull. I duck, bringing up my sword and resting it against my forearm in a makeshift brace as I put one leg out behind me for stability. I look up into the crimson eyes of the demon, its too-large mouth and excessively shard-like teeth glinting, moist with spittle in the unrelenting lilac sun.

I take my chance, dropping my guard and wasting no time in plunging the sword deep into the pale flesh of the demon's gut. I yank the blade back, blood spraying across the pale skin of my forearm. The demon falls forward and with the wave of a hand, the body is ablaze before it even hits the ground.

As I turn to make sure my back is covered, I see a Gorgonian slithering, wide jaws agape. However, before I have the chance to so much as aim at it with a fireball, the prang of a releasing bowstring reaches my ears, and in the time it takes me to blink, the demon is dead, killed by an arrow through the skull. My breath is rapid and deep in my lungs, and I wish now I knew where it was we're headed. If I could visualise the location, I'd be able to convect, but as it is, I'm stuck hacking my way through demon after demon.

Erlea can be heard, her harsh Chinese battle cries unmistakable whilst her Katana slices through corpses as if they're no more than rotting cucumbers.

I twist, realising that if we continue to plough our way through this mess one demon at a time, we may very well be here forever.

"Erin!" I call, gesturing for the African warrior to come closer. I watch as a Succubus makes a grab for her throat, taking it out with a flaming projectile before it can so much as scratch her flawless cocoa skin, returning the favour she had done me not moments ago.

"What?!" she calls, throwing one of the knives in her belt directly at me. I twist, shocked at the act, but find her aim flawless as a Succubi which had been silent at my spine crumples to the ground. I set it ablaze without mercy or second thought.

"We aren't getting anywhere! They just keep coming!" I gasp, breathless, and she nods. "Where are the souldiers?" she asks, bringing the heel of her leather boot down onto the skull of a Gorgonian trying to bite her ankle.

"I'd bet Anubis has them all occupied on the other side of the wall—" I muse, looking to the enormous slab of obsidian that separates Mortaria from The Ashen Waste, and beyond that, The Fallen Kingdom.

"We need to get inside! Bottleneck them," Erlea suggests, her cobalt war paint and blood-spattered skin making her appear as if she's been to a Day-Glo paint party. She approaches with haste, swinging her sword and cutting a Gorgonian on her left in two. Blood spurts out from the body, soaking into the grey ash of the ground, now tinged an unmistakable and dominant crimson.

"Bottleneck them?" I demand, flexing my fingers and feeling the flames ignite in my veins like someone's struck a match against pure gasoline. I throw a stream of fire to my right, clearing the way for Ericka who is reloading her bow faster than I'd imagined was possible.

She jogs over to us, her tan skin peppered red as her long dark braids sway from the left to the right, orange war paint moist with sweat across the bridge of her nose.

"I guess we don't have a choice but to force our way through—" I suggest, and they frown.

"Perhaps— perhaps we could create a blaze as a distraction— something to draw them out— just thin them so we can get inside?" Erlea suggests, looking back at the smoking Mean Machine.

Haedes is going to kill me.

I roll my eyes, sighing as my breath falls from me in a heavy exhale.

"Hold my sword," I shove the weapon at Ericka.

The Furies turn in synchronised time, facing outward toward the demons, covering me.

I let fire run rampant down the veins of my left and then right arm, shoving my palms out from my body, and projecting a scorching stream of flame through the air. I smile, having missed this use of my power, this projection of my anger, my rage.

Maybe all I've needed is to be reminded of who I am. Not just that I am under so much scrutiny, that the weight of so much bears down on me, but also that I am strong enough to bear it. I am a demi-goddess. I have power.

I am nobody's victim. Perhaps I never was.

The flames reach the newly painted body of the car, the polish so fresh that the entire vehicle acts as a mirror for merely moments before the flame reaches the gas tank.

"Run!" I yell out, turning on my heel and feeling the ash fly up around me as the four of us make our way through the demons, who stand stone still, watching the fire rise into the sky. Mere seconds pass before—

BOOM.

The entire thing explodes, causing pieces of car body, engine, glass, and metal to fly through the surrounding crowds of demonic flesh as flaming shrapnel. The air around us vibrates, heating too fast as we cover our heads with our arms and make a dive for the mines.

Once we get inside, I find myself staring, dumbstruck, at the walls encrusted with semi-precious stones as the smell of burning rubber and gasoline fills my nostrils.

"I thought there would be more demons," Erin notes, looking around.

It would seem that the demons within the mines have already been lured out by our earlier arrival and the onslaught that followed.

"Watch my back?" I ask them, looking down into the labyrinthian corridors of the mines and squinting, wondering exactly how long of a walk I've got ahead of me.

I don't look back at them, but I feel the sentiment between them as they draw swords, palm knives, and nock arrows. I don't take my sword back from Ericka, knowing I have the most important weapon already; my pyromancy skills. They crowd my spine, and I feel safer than I thought I would at this point. I never realised the perks of having a team with me, and I especially never thought that team would be three furious women with a mission to make the Spartans look civilised.

I guess it's true what they say.

Hell hath no fury like a woman scorned.

25

MY SONGS KNOW WHAT YOU DID IN THE DARK

<u>PANDORA</u>

WE ARRIVE.

Side by side, our shadows crisp as they grace the smoky quartz of the floor. Sinners are everywhere— or so it would appear, but I know differently. I know they live and breathe just like me. I also know that they've been waiting for us. Not a single body moves or calls out for aid. They've been patient for this moment, and instead of the expected clashing of weapons, there is a silent awe as they bow their heads in respect.

"Welcome, gentlemen," I purr, lips caressing the syllables of each word as my face turns joyous in expression.

As the last of the demons follow us in through the portal, I close it, stashing the box in the pocketed pleats of my well-worn leather ball gown.

"Please— make yourselves at home. This is our Exilia now," I command them, looking to Barbas. He extends a long arm, ending in a pointing, shuddering, and bony index finger.

"You heard the pretty lady," he speaks, voice cracking as it travels over his shoulder and the Phobias accompanying us scatter.

I watch as they climb around the bannisters, arachnid forms crawling the length of the walls, the ceilings, in seconds. After a few moments, the light in the place dims, torches extinguishing as lightning flashes across the room from seemingly nowhere. It's startling, as if someone is running an electric current through the very stone the place is carved from. It continues to flash in a staccato of fear-inducing sequences, brighter even still as each stark and momentary penetration of light gleams from the shining facets of the surrounding walls, floor, and ceiling.

They quickly drape the room with thick black cobwebs, victory banners of our presence, the sound of their crustacean-esque legs clicking sharply against the stone above and below them. I hear a scream come from nowhere and smirk as it echoes out, hollow but undeniably realistic.

"Very nice," I compliment Barbas, who cocks a single eyebrow, the left side of his mouth curving upward into a victorious smile.

"Oh, we're just getting started," he vows, his acute bony skull hosting a respectful glance as his eyes fall over my form, drenching me in a cold chill only too resonant of his affinity.

We take steps forward, gesturing for the surrounding mortal fodder to follow us with sweeping and grandiose motion.

Treading up the stairs, I hear each of my steps echo harsh like a victory bell. This is what I've been waiting for, what I've been craving ever since the day Zeus took me in under false pretences and then spat me back out for daring to question his rule. True, his brother might not be quite as arrogant, but he's hardly deserving of such power either.

"I think I'm going to like it here," Barbas mutters beside me, letting Mr Skinny Legs loose from beneath his sleeve and watching as the tarantula climbs, spindled legs working fast.

As I watch it, distracted, I fail to notice the change in my surroundings. After a few seconds though, I raise my head, blinking in awed confusion. The place has been taken over by fear and illusion, every shadow cast into the shape of a demonic smile, or the devil's most wicked glare— one which now she uses often. Bloody light moves over the space as if the sky is bleeding into the earth. The bannister beneath my cool palm goes from smooth to porous, and I look down, finding vertebrae curling up the side of each step where there used to be smoky quartz. It's attached to the floor by a gargantuan ribcage splayed wide open, each rib now replacing a stair and morphing seamlessly into the sick decor.

"If you can do all this— why leave The Fallen Kingdom in such disrepair?" I demand of them both, turning to face one and then the other with a confused stare.

"Do you know how dangerous it can be to glimmer somewhere in disrepair? We make the floor look flawlessly terrifying and you find yourself breaking your neck by tripping over a crack you didn't know was there. Safety first," Barbas smirks. I roll my eyes.

"Sure, whatever you say," I brush off this odd comment, finding excitement in both their eyes. Dark artists that have been painting bloody fantasies onto cave walls now have a blank and perfectly prepped canvas at their disposal. The smell of burning flesh fills my nostrils as I smile, pleased they are having fun.

"You two are masters of the craft, truly," I compliment them, feeling generous as I reach the top of the skeletal staircase. Here, two ceiling-high double doors await me, dark and formidable, just like my destiny.

All I have to do is step through.

"Ready?" I enquire, looking first to Barbas and then to Abraxis before glimpsing back at the masses of mortal guards who have formed an organised and single-file line behind us, formidable in formation.

Beautiful, I muse, glad I'd taken the time to train them. Like animals, I must teach them what to expect from me should they disobey. I must follow through with my punishments and stick to reasonably made and practical threats if I'm to keep control.

Taking a deep breath, I inhale, pulling the dark veil over my face, wishing to remain impassive in my expression, to hide my emotions from he who may try to read them for his own personal gain.

I gesture now for the two Demon Lords to open the doors before me, and they do so, taking one each and sending them flying as though they've been caught in the eye of a malicious yet theatrical hurricane.

I step forward, skirt sweeping over the floor in grandiose motion as I watch phobias and the fear fuelled illusion of the entryway sprawl like a disease through the doors and across the delicately embellished and warm ceiling of the throne room. The torches on the walls extinguish, plunging the room into temporary darkness as a single fork of fortuitously timed lightning illuminates the raw power and allure of my silhouette.

"Honey—" I call, catching Haedes in my sights, "I'm home."

XION

Shit.

That's my first thought. Then I see the sinners following in their wake.

Double shit.

What the hell is going on here?

Pandora's voice echoes out into silence as the walls begin to ripple around us and lightning strikes from seemingly nowhere, flashing within the crystal of the walls. The torches surrounding us extinguish, and the hairs on the back of my neck stand on end as the delicate clicking of Phobia legs reaches my ears. Osiris is at my spine, and I feel his too-quick breath hitting me in the back of the neck as he peeks around my shoulder, staring out into the depths of the room like a timid and terrified woodland creature.

"Osiris? Oh, how perfect. Anubis will be thrilled!" Pandora taunts him, spinning on the spot and letting her wide skirt billow out around her, revealing boots which climb, in no tasteful way, to her mid-thigh. She prances forward, face masked by the mess of dark hair and net veil falling over her pale skin and distinguished features.

I debate turning on Osiris where I stand, accusing him of orchestrating all this, but the look on Pandora's face, the wicked glint which is just visible behind the mask of her black shroud, tells me that he knew no more about this than I did.

I glance at the sides of the room where sinners stand, motionless. It is clear their alliance no longer resides with us. They are not malicious in expression though, merely awed as they watch the scene before them unfold.

I back up, pushing Osiris out of the way and moving to defend Haedes.

"What do you want?" I demand, heart picking up pace as I feel the familiar cooling of obsidian against the flesh of my chest.

"What do I want? Oh, nothing really, simply the death of the old man behind you." She tilts her body sideways, peering at Haedes around my broad gait as she stifles a laugh.

"Well, well, you really are looking old, Haedes. If I were you, I might not consider even bothering with a suit any longer— not much point. After all, a pig in a dress is still a pig, is it not?" she asks.

Haedes rises from his seat, stepping down beside me.

"Hey, shut up! I'll have you know I look fucking fabulous!" Haedes yells in reply, tossing his head back and pretending he has a supermodel's luscious locks. "And I'll also have you know, I *was* born with it, and it's definitely not fucking Maybelline!"

"Haedes—" I whisper, trying to warn him as he gets on a roll.

"And— who the hell are you to lecture me on fashion, little Miss Morticia, Queen of The Damned Ugly. That look is over!" He's puffed, out of breath as he snaps his fingers at her. He turns to me, cocking an eyebrow.

"Okay, I'm done now, but it had to be said!" He throws up his hands, and I groan. If we were any more credible as adversaries, we'd be at risk of hurting ourselves.

"Look, you'd better let me handle this," I whisper, pushing him behind me as he grumbles.

"What you mean my sass wasn't actually cutting anyone?" he asks me, sarcasm dripping from his tone like too-pungent cologne. I wrinkle my nose.

"Just— let me handle this!" I snap at him as I turn my attention back to Pandora who is staring down at her nails, bored.

"Done now?" she asks, crossing her arms across the plunge of her corset's square neckline.

"Yes, we're good," I reply, the atmosphere becoming awkward.

"Great. I would hate to have the momentousness of this moment diminished by your petulant attack on my sense of fashion—" Pandora rolls her eyes, and I hear Haedes clear his throat to speak up again. I let a low feral growl emit from my throat as I shove the two gods back another pace toward the throne.

"There's nothing momentous about this. You're about to get your ass kicked. There are only three of you. I can take three," I growl, not actually sure I can take three, especially when one is my own father and the other has access to all my deepest fears.

"Three? Why only three? I think you might have underestimated the loyalties of these mortals to me," Pandora quips, her lips trembling with the beginnings of a smile.

Mortals?

"Yes, mortals. You see, it's easy to find people to stand beside you in overtaking hell when they are the future of its people— many of them, understandably as you might imagine, don't quite relish the thought of penance," she explains, twizzling her fingers as she gestures for the guards lining the walls of this chamber to come closer.

"Come, defend me," she beckons them, and they oblige, silently moving to surround myself, Haedes, and Osiris on all sides. She smirks at me as I breathe in deep and Barbas cocks his head, taking a step forward.

"I find it interesting that as soon as you discovered they were mortal, your fears became crystalline to me. This means that you, yourself, are experiencing fear right now, Xion. But why fear mortals?" he ponders, stepping in front of Pandora as he nears me for closer inspection. Abraxis watches me too, his eyes dead in his face but posture visibly stiffening.

Does he care?

Why should he? He's never cared before.

I see myself in him so astutely in this moment I'm caught staring at him longer than I should be. His hair is thick and black, just like mine. The chameleonic metallic irises are a mirror image of mine, the strong jaw, the broad shoulders. I am no doubt my father's son in appearance, if nowhere else.

Barbas turns back to look at Abraxis.

"Ah, seeking daddy's approval in killing them?" he demands, and I grit my teeth, tearing my gaze away from my father's face and staring back into Barbas' dull eyes. He smiles, crooked teeth alive with tiny arachnids that crawl, spinning webs between his incisors. "You see Xion, this is where fate has aligned the stars of your destiny, and ours. You are afraid of blackening your soul, of feeding the demon within you by taking the lives of soulful mortals— and Pandora here just so happens to have procured them as our driving force in this little takeover. Isn't that clever? Makes you wonder if it is not the fate of the Ancient Gods to return after all, does it not?" he asks me.

I shake my head.

"It'll never happen. I don't have to kill them to stop you," I bite out, not showing the desperation beginning to fill my chest like icy water, drowning my confidence.

"Oh, of course not— but I can make it increasingly difficult for you—" Before I can reach out to stop him, his hand waves in front of my face and my vision changes.

I'm no longer surrounded by people but by naked vulnerable bodies filled with visibly beating hearts. I can see the glowing of each soul within their chests, the flashing network of their live-wired brains, their humanity becoming all too visible as I cry out. I look down at myself, seeing not my clothed body, but straight through the skin of my torso to where my soul and heart lie within my chest, visibly rotting. The stench creeps up into my nostrils, infecting me with the scent of death.

I watch on as my soul crackles, a cloud of abyssal black sparked through with bloody red lightning, rage afloat in a sea of dark and vicious intent.

It's the soul of a killer.

I blink, and the backs of my eyelids become a blank screen upon which my past is projected in a flickering and faulty sequence of cinematic pain.

No. Please.

Not this.

Anything but this.

Her eyes are cerulean, pools of paradisal waters with the power to heal any broken man. Her hair is a sweet strawberry blonde, tumbling over her naked shoulders.

"Lilly." Her name is a prayer as I whisper it against the soft rose petals of her lips. It's not me speaking, I'm only an observer here, but I can still feel everything. She's so fragile, small, and petite in stature, her shoulders smaller than the size of my palms. I feel her taut abdominals stretch beneath my groin as I hover above her, kissing her intensely. The creamy silk of her perfectly pure and untouched skin glistens in the early vanilla twilight pouring in, unrestrained, from outside the window. The pale white net of her curtains flutters in the early spring breeze, the white of her sheets casting each of her features in stark and stunning beauty as I caress her cheek with one finger.

"Alex—" My name is a precious sigh which she exhales in a fully invested breath as she leans up, kissing me back.

My erection grows, aroused for her purity and the wonder in new sensations, for her sureness about who I am, who we are together.

She trusts me.

I stare at her, dread filling my gut but not able to stop actions that have already been performed, the events which have already unfolded like a bloody flower in bloom.

"Ready?" I ask her, and she nods, smiling as she leans back against the fluffy down of the pillows. The scent of her skin— fresh linen and jasmine— fills my head as I bury myself first in the crook of her neck and then into the warm clutches of her body.

I inhale deeply as the first waves of pleasure take me, but suddenly my focus is drawn by the pulsation at my left ear. Her blood. Rushing into her brain, pushed by every pump of her heart, the heart she's giving to me.

Something within me snaps as I thrust, pleasure unlike anything I've ever known making my insides tumult like a dark and dangerous tide, washing away my consciousness with it and leaving only with the fractured debris of something instinctual.

This is where I usually black out.

Where everything fades to denial and fear as if my mind is cocooning itself from such harmful substance. Now though, I know these thoughts aren't my own. I know they're being externally forced upon me by Barbas. They're real, but I know that this time there is no escape.

I hear a mangled cry escape my chest as I rear up, skin scorching black as Lilly's eyes snap open from where before they'd been lost in a cloud of explorative ecstasy.

"Alex?!" Her voice echoes in my head, but I'm lost to her now as my fingers twitch, hearing the beating of her hungry heart, too fragile, too tender, in her porcelain chest.

The demon has been locked up for too long, and now she will suffer.

I put my fingers around her neck, feeling the life drain from her as it snaps, too easy to break within my grasp, stealing her life without even so much as a flex of my muscular biceps. She's a limp dead thing now, so it plays with her.

I play with her.

I rip her arms from their sockets, twisting them up and posing them so I can get a full view of her body. The demon in me approves; it purrs like a contented newborn kitten, deciding that death is not enough.

Only desecration can satiate such a sick fuck.

I come back to myself after it's over. After he's finished, empty, and drained of whatever it is he needed to unload. I know what happened after. I had woken, found her dead and decimated at my side. Blood everywhere. I had fled the scene, tried to kill myself, put a barrel, cold and unforgiving, between my lips. Unfortunately for me, the demon had presented before I could pull the trigger.

I'm on my knees in the hall, and all I can hear is Haedes yelling behind me.

"Xion! Xion— *get up!*" he pleads as Barbas and Pandora glide forward, effortless in their agenda.

Mortal guards pass me, boots clattering against the floor, but the sound of it falls only too late and too redundant on my deaf ears.

The world is slow, and all I can feel is the unstoppable beating of my rotting heart within my chest.

I need it to stop.

Please.

Is there no mercy for me?

I cannot live with this pain.

I must end it.

End it all.

I feel arms restraining me, pulling me to my feet. I feel my father's firm stare penetrating me as he orders mortals to take me to the dungeons. Shoving me to my feet, four of them push me forward, weapons poised against my rapidly throbbing carotid while Haedes and Osiris are lost in a cacophony of clatter as they try to fight off the men.

I could transform, become the demon, let it out— but what if that's all I am? A murderer of mortals who don't know any better. What if I turn on Haedes and Osiris? What if that's what the Demon Lords' plan has been all along? They want to use me as a weapon, use me for what I really am.

A demon in a human skin suit.

I hear it all even now. The frail beating of their hearts. The spindled veins that decide their fate— pleasure or pain. I hear the susurration of the blood, a tonic for my demon's never-ending rage, the frantic effort of every living breath, the emptiness of their souls— searching forever for love, for purpose, which I could deny them in but a moment. With one hand, their necks could be broken. In one of my breaths, I could steal the rest of theirs.

I should help Haedes, help Osiris, should fight— but I'm surrounded, surrounded and not sure what I'm even doing here.

I'm no hero.

26

POISON

LUCE

IT'S AS I BEGIN to chant, and Thane unwillingly takes the tether in hand while restrained even still by Gorgon, I realise something I had not been privy to before. The Book of The Dead, lying flat on the table before me, is much more than it appears. It is not merely a guardian of knowledge, but a key to the magic itself.

As I feel the familiar words begin to form on my tongue, I watch as the matte, jet writing begins to glow violet at the edge of each cursive stroke, imperceptible to anyone but me.

"Sanguina— hear me. Nocturna— hear me. Moloch— hear me." As the words fall from my lips, the world around me begins to tremble. Dust and minor debris fall from the ceiling of the cavern as I brace myself against the marble stone of the table. The crackle of dark magic sparks in my veins, summoning the Gods of Ancient with far more ease than before.

"Bone, blood, spirit, breath. I am yours in eternity," I cry out, my heart beginning to pound ferociously against my ribs. I ready myself for the pain, for la douleur exquise of my true nature.

I feel them, my pupils dilating to black as every muscle in my body tenses, steeling in synchronised time. I groan, not finding the pain that I expect but rather a craving that I fear may never be satiated. I hold up my hand, finding it blurred in motion as it glides through the air in front of my face. My saliva has become sweet blackberry juice, trickling with a tempting zing down my gullet, and my nostrils have filled with the scent of pine. My eyelids flutter, the pale wings of dark butterflies, as his voice becomes clear above the din of my ecstasy.

"You dare to incite me again, child?" The voice is low, deep, but with an edge of sibilance, summoning the voices of dragons I'd heard my

mother imitate as a child, delivering with it stories of Avalon in a nostalgic wave.

The world around me dissolves, fading to black.

I stand, a void above me, a void below me. Every motion I make is blurred, fragmented, and every breath I take in feels like the final inhale before climax. It's delicious, addictive, and as he walks from the shadows, I am not afraid.

Straightening my spine, I stare into his reptilian gaze.

"Father," I address him, black hair blowing around me in the non-existent breeze of this non-existent place.

"My darling daughter—" he sounds sentimental as his tongue caresses the words, and I examine him without restraint, eyes hungry. Mother would never allow me to learn of him, but that didn't stop me finding records, murals, and etchings of him in The Minerva Library of The Mercury Heavens. It didn't stop me from devouring every stroke that made up his face. Not for knowledge of him, but of myself so I might pinpoint exactly why I was shunned at every turn.

His forehead is broad, two enormous ram's horns protruding from the bony protuberance of his skull. His eyes are wide, dark, cruel perhaps, but as they gaze upon me, they shimmer, becoming soft like a puddle of oil in the rain, dilute yet opalescent. He lacks irises, and his eyes are entirely blackened like my own. I see his pale flesh beneath his robes, the way it fades in and out of scale, the way black veins weave in and out of the armoured patches of his skin. His fingernails are long, pointed, and his stature is broad. I have his face, the firm jawline, the large eyes, thick lips. I can also see my own silhouette in his broad-set shoulders narrowing into a slim waist, and in his daunting height.

I can see why my mother could not bear to look at me now.

She had not seen the face of a daughter but the face of her rapist.

"Why am I here?" I demand, wanting to get the ritual over with.

"I might ask you the same question—" Moloch whispers, his voice the meek rumble before a roll of thunder.

"I did this?" I demand, brows pinching together as I let my long fingernails caress the skin of my arms through my jacket sleeves, a solitary comfort.

"You do not know?" He cocks his head. I frown.

"No," I retort, impatient. He laughs.

"It interests me that you wish to resurrect another being, this time more powerful, and yet you know nothing of your abilities. Your

317

emotions are driving you unknowingly in and out of Delyria's dark kingdom, a world of illusion— a world of the mind, of the surreal— of simulacra." Moloch appears troubled after this sentence vanishes into the darkness of the void where we're standing, still as statues, refusing to drop one another's gaze.

"So, you're not real?" I surmise, and he shrugs.

"Is anything— *real*?" he asks me, and I frown. I don't have time for mind games.

"I don't want anything to do with this. Any of this. I just want to stop Thane being taken from me," I snap, still feeling like that tiny child who had been caught drying her own herbs, carving her own pestle and mortar, deep in the forest by her mother.

"Child, you need not lie to me. You drank from The Well; you cannot think to deny your lust for such power. You know that Uranus does not impart such potent dark energies to one not certain of their desire." He gets a look of wicked malice as his thick lips spread wide, snakelike in their fluidity, across the bony features of his skull.

"You don't know me. You raped my mother and gave me the life of an outcast. I hate you!" I yell, suddenly angry. I ball my fists at my sides, the muscles in my abdomen turning rigid in disgust.

"It is not me you lust for child; it is the dark half of *your* soul. The call to embrace who *you* truly are— that is the summons you cannot ignore." I don't reply to this, the truth of his words ringing out too pointedly into the nothingness. If I'd been able to resist, Thane never would have taken flight and been shot down. If I'd been able to resist, Sephy Sinclair never would have been resurrected, and Haedes never weakened. If I'd been able to say no, The Book of The Dead would never have been found. It would have remained lost.

All of this could have been prevented.

Pandora and Anubis wanted to commit acts of treachery, of evil, but I gave them the tools, the keys to the doors of Mortaria.

I did this.

It is with this realisation that it occurs to me that perhaps I deserve everything that is happening. I've been reckless, been stubborn, not listened when I had been warned.

But— now it is too late to turn back, and I can't lose Thane. She is perhaps the only person who can help me get this darkness under control. I need her, or others might be doomed at my hand as well.

So perhaps this resurrection is not entirely selfish? Perhaps it could prevent me from falling further down this rabbit hole if Thane survives. After all, together we can accomplish anything— why should that not include taking down Ra once he is made flesh?

"You are certainly my daughter—" Moloch announces into the silence, raising a hand to my cheek and trying to examine both the left and then right sides of my profile. I step back.

"I'm not your anything," I hiss. He smiles, and I wonder what it is he finds so endearing.

"That— is yet to be determined," he replies, lips twisting into an amused smirk.

"I determine it now. I'm good. Despite what you might think, despite the colour of my hair, my eyes— I'm good— I am!" I plead, and he turns from me, beginning his walk back into the void that surrounds us. Before he disappears, he looks back over his shoulder, staring at me with his endlessly deep, dark eyes.

"If only you believed that—" he whispers.

As his words echo out into nothing, putting a firm dent in my sense of self, I blink, and am back in the chamber once more. My knuckles are white, matching the marble they cling to as sweat beads, hot and defiant between my shoulder blades.

"Sanguina— hear me," I pant, my heart continuing to race in my chest, my mind a fog of pleasurable impulses and sensations I had not expected. "Nocturna—" I begin, but the words are stolen from me as I am swept up in an unexpected swell of dark ecstasy. My head hangs back momentarily as my eyes close, savouring every second, the waves of energy rippling throughout my nervous system. This peace lasts until I hear her cries.

My head snaps up, my body hovering a clear foot off the crystal dust scattered beneath my now dangling soles. I stare down at her, physically able to see the life energy being pulled from her as her jagged frame becomes eroded smooth and frail. Her eyes, windows into the devastation raging inside her head, colour every memory we've built through the years dark with the tainted debris of my unforgivable acts.

I want to stop it, but I can't. I know this needs to happen. I have to do this, for us.

Ecstasy starts rolling in across my flesh in waves, rendering me utterly helpless as I want to do nothing other than surrender to it. I feel the eyes of the Demon Lords, of Anubis, on me, pupils dilating as they take in the spectacle. Awed.

Thane cries out louder, harrowing and bone-deep in intensity, and I see the mummy beneath me in the sarcophagus begin to tremble.

It's happening— he's coming back.

I smile to myself, victorious as an overwhelming state of calm settles over me.

Everything will be fine now.

Everything will be fine.

Me and Thane— together forever. Just as it's supposed to be.

I look at her, at the pain and betrayal in her eyes.

It will pass, and if it doesn't— I can always make her forget.

A gift from me to you my darling Thanatos. The gift of ignorance.

It's as I'm thinking this, a sudden and abrupt flash of red light flies past one of my shoulders, startling me from my self-indulged monologue, my desperate vows.

The next thing I know, I'm falling unceremoniously to the floor and everything goes dark.

SEPHY

I skid around the corner, the scent of burning filling my nostrils as I throw a fireball toward Luce. She's floating, hair black as night, skin mapped over dark with black veins. I've never seen anything like it.

The flaming projectile goes where I will it, not hitting her but instead, following a simple arc through the air and landing inside the sarcophagus before her. It's a lucky shot, one I've decided to make in an instant, but luckily for me, it pays off.

"*No!*" Anubis cries out, spinning on the spot to find me with my next round of fire already sizzling in my palm. I glare at her, irises alive with the light of both my fury and the flame, which I raise, threatening to unleash it on her at any second. Luce has crumpled to the floor beside her, and I wonder how she'll react when she once again finds consciousness.

"Oh yes," I reply, taking a step forward as The Furies spread out at my spine, ground crystal crunching beneath my tread.

I grow the ball of flame in my palm with my free hand before thrusting both palms out from me and directing The Eternal Flame to the object that started all this trouble. The Book of The Dead.

It's an accurate shot, and I watch as the leather-bound book catches light, the pages curling at the edges, turning to nothing more than ash before my very eyes. I find Thane behind the rising flames, which crackle into the air above the sarcophagus. She's injured, a crude arrow made of bone jutting out of her shoulder, black circles unmistakable around her eyes. Her mouth is slack, skin drained of all colour. She looks like she could use a serious vacation.

"Go, help her," I order The Furies, who scatter, moving to disable Katerina, Gorgon, and the demons crawling around each of Thanatos' limbs. I turn to Anubis, tilting my chin as I observe her.

"How— how did you know, where to find us? This is Pandora's doing!" she exclaims, and I shake my head, smirking.

"Oh no, think closer to home," I suggest, cocking my head and letting my hip jut out to one side as I twiddle the end of my long ponytail around my index finger. Looking up at her, I flutter my eyelashes, trying to appear more innocent than I am. Knowing Anubis, she will underestimate me, as she does everyone she deems inferior.

"Osiris?!" The name comes to her, a hollow whisper. I nod, satisfied as I embrace the power simmering in my blood.

"Ding, ding, ding— we have a winner!" I purse my lips in a smirk as I cross my arms, taking a leisurely step toward her, my body shielding Luce's crumpled form.

"Never. My son would never betray me!" She shakes her head, the heavy gold of her earrings swaying, frenzied, with her denial.

"Sure. You believe that. Let's just say I magically guessed exactly where you'd be." I raise an eyebrow, satisfied further by the grunts of Katerina and Gorgon as The Furies corner them. I look over my shoulder a second, balling my fist at my side as Thanatos falls to the floor, the demons around her body taken out one by one by Erin's quick knifework.

"It's a trick," Anubis hisses, her too-white teeth bared in a feral grimace as her thick lips pull back.

"Look, whatever. You believe whatever little fantasy you want to. Either way. The party is over. So— the only question that remains is whether you're going to hand over Thane's tether, or if I'm going to have to take it from you and then burn you to a crisp for being a stubborn bitch. I'd say dear old dad won't be very pleased with you either way, but there might be some remorse if you hand it over willingly." I brush the handle of my sword with my palm as I let my hand fall to my side, holding the left one out to her, extinguishing the flames as though they had never been. Her eyes follow me, nervous suddenly. I get an enormous kick of pleasure from seeing her so uncomfortable.

I haven't felt this level of comfort in my own skin in a while, this level of control. It's the first time I've felt like me, the old me, since the night I'd been murdered. There's no way I'm giving this feeling up again, not for anyone or anything. Ever.

"Well, Anubis?" I ask, grinding her down with my gaze. After a few moments, she reaches down into her cleavage, relinquishing the tether as she drops it into my palm.

Clutching it, I shove it into the pocket of Xion's leather jacket before turning my back on her. As I spin, I come face to face with abyssal black eyes and pale skin. It was a face I had known once, and I'm taken aback by how starkly she has changed in appearance.

"Lucifer," I address her, voice betraying nothing. I watch her, fingers twitching at my sides, ready to do what I have to.

"Where's the tether?" she barks, eyes narrowing as she inches closer to me.

"I have it; don't worry. Anubis is—" I begin, but she interrupts me.

"Gone. You let her go—" Her voice is a snarl, and I roll my eyes.

"No, I didn't let her do anything. She has nowhere she can run where Haedes won't find her. She *will* pay for what she's done—" I insist, and Lucifer's eyes narrow.

"But I should be the one," she announces, and I shake my head.

"No. You've done enough," I say, noticing the dried blood peeking out from beneath the black sleeves of her military-style jacket. A cape hangs from one of her shoulders, her slim legs made hard and rigid inside velvet pants. Her hair is unkempt, lacking its natural glossy sheen as it hangs, matted with dry blood, past her shoulders.

"But she—" Luce begins to protest, but I snap. I'm not having this debate with her. I won't have her killing more people. The Luce I know would never forgive anyone for murder, so I don't see why I should let her commit the same crime.

"Enough." I wave a hand, dismissing her as I watch Gorgon and Katerina bowl past me in a flurry of velvet and too-pale skin. They're fleeing now, the demons they had at hand dead upon the floors of the chamber, blood and pieces of flesh the only evidence of their otherwise seamless dismemberment.

"Go. Follow them," I command The Furies, who nod, taking off into the labyrinthian mines in a clatter of hard boots and bloody steel.

I turn to Lucifer, who is staring at me, hands trembling as she takes several steps back towards the far wall, her shadow becoming smaller and more vivid as she nears the torches at her spine.

"Look who's all grown up now—" she snarls.

I shake my head.

"Stop this. Right now. Or I'll do it for you," I threaten her, fingertips sparking with the promise of a full and lethal blaze.

"I should've left you dead," she glowers, fingers twitching noticeably too.

"Yes. You should have. Hindsight's a bitch, ain't it?" I ask her, and she smirks.

"Quite."

"Still— I have the tether. We can go now. Everything is going to be fine." I reassure her, trying to be rational, and she blinks as the sounds of a sputter and then a cough hits the air. My head snaps sideways, finding Thane in a pile on the floor as I stride around the side of the Sarcophagus with hurried steps.

As I near her, Luce moves faster than I've ever seen her, fingers wrapping too tight around my wrist.

"Give me the tether," she demands again, and I shake my head with furious vigour.

"No." I retort.

"*Give it to me!*" she bellows in my face, breath laced through with the metallic weave of blood.

"No," I repeat myself, rage building inside of me. There's no need for this, for any of this. Surprising myself, I am not afraid either, not vulnerable. I am strong, having found my way again in this world of death and certain loss.

This is not hell to me, this is home.

I stare into the jet abyss of her eyes, weighing up whether I should just grab my sword and behead her right here, get it over with.

She's close enough; close enough for me to see the black veins that spider up her neck and the carotid pulsing just beneath, a frail thing despite it all.

I remember Xion's frantic voice as my free hand meanders in a subtle and fluid motion to caress the hilt of my sword yet.

She risked herself to save your life, Sephy. We all did.

Thane coughs again, and I watch as Luce's gaze flits from me to her lover's crumpled body. Her enormous pupils recede slightly as Thane groans, the grip around my wrist loosening before her hand slips away entirely. She takes three steps forward before dropping fast to her knees.

Shimmering dark crystal dust billows up around her. My hand slips from my weapon as I exhale heavily, watching the fine powder settle once more.

The danger isn't over, but for now, Luce is too busy worrying about Thane to be an immediate threat to me.

Thane whimpers as Luce pulls the arrow from her shoulder, blood spraying across her pale face. I watch as she looks at me, pupils dilating again so they're full of abyssal power, and stare, unmoved to show my abhorrence in any way, shape, or form.

"What are you looking at?" she snaps, waving a hand over the wound on Thane's arm and beginning to chant in a language I've never heard before, voice hypnotic like a seductive dark lullaby.

I exhale, leaning back against the marble slab as she does whatever it is she's doing with her dark magic, watching as the skin around Thane's wound begins to knit together. Relief doesn't flood my gut though. because while everything has found a temporary state of calm, for now, Pandora is nowhere to be found.

That, in itself, is never a good sign.

27

WALKING IN MEMPHIS

PANDORA

HIS LAUGH RIPPLES THROUGH the chambers of the vault, bouncing with the most irritating cadence from each of the golden walls and riding on my last nerve. I take step after careful step, concentrating on the clicking of my thigh-high boots on the cold floor as I run my fingers over the curves of each individual hourglass. The fine crystals tinkle as they fall successively through the narrow waist of each one, too bright flaming sconces catching upon the edges of each luscious glass silhouette. I continue to observe the gemstones inside crackling with firelight, patience wearing thin.

Picking up an hourglass covered in dust, I blow the cobwebs from its surface, looking up through the rows of shelves. Haedes is hung, suspended by thick black spiderwebbing at the end of the room. Here, another sound can be heard, the sound of a crowbar against precious metal as my mortal servants toil against the locking mechanism of the vault's innermost and longest-kept secret; the store of Haedes' tether.

Hearing his laugh echo out yet again, I let the hourglass fall from my grip, smashing audibly on the floor as jade crystals scatter. I stare after it, Haedes' hysterics becoming only more outraged with each inhale. My fury piques, causing me to take a flat palm, swiping four or five more hourglasses from the shelves and walking away as they smash against the floor, sending a rainbow of glistening sinstone shrapnel skittering to the farthest corners of the chamber.

"Barbas! What the hell are you doing?" I bark, sending several more hourglasses flying as I pass simply to hear them shatter. I take a random selection in my palm, gripping it until my knuckles turn white.

"I'm trying to torture him—" Barbas gives me an infuriated look, features becoming sharp, jagged even, in their fury.

"Yes, you're not doing a very good job, are you?" Haedes laughs, cocking an eyebrow at me as his head perks up from where it's hanging, slumped between his shoulders.

"I have no idea what you find so funny—" he mutters, lips pursing together.

"Just that you're showing me my fears. It all *pales*. Pales to what I've already had taken from me. It's kind of like being tickled, actually. I'd say tickled pink, but I'm not sure you've quite got the dextrous finesse for that." He bites his bottom lip, giving Barbas an ostentatious and aroused look, startling the Demon Lord of fear more than should be possible.

"Enough of this! If you can't elicit a scream, then I will." I crush the hourglass in my fist, feeling the glass splinter against the soft velvet of my skin. Letting most of the glass fall to the floor, I cling to a large, jagged shard, palm bloodied. It reminds me of a lightning bolt, representing a different brother altogether.

Taking a step forward, I stare up into the grey of Haedes' eyes, tilting my chin and dropping my gaze to fall on his oddly attractive torso. Age doesn't look bad on him.

I take the shard of glass to his pectorals where a smattering of silver chest hair curls up from the tan of his Grecian skin. The edge of the glass cuts into the flesh covering his chest muscle, smooth like butter.

"*Ooooh— Ahh—* just like that, *baby*," Haedes grunts in pain, but then his agony morphs into more hysteria as he looks up into my eyes, shooting me a cocky glare.

"What about if I mess up that pretty face you seem to be so damn attached to?" I growl, standing on my tiptoes as I hang only inches from his face.

He jerks forward, coming within touching distance of my cheek. I wonder if he'll kiss me as I inhale the scent of burning spices from the surface of his glistening skin.

"Come closer—" he whispers, and I oblige him, curious.

He places his lips on my cheek before promptly licking the side of my face from bottom to top.

What. The—

"Sure, chicks dig that whole rugged scar-faced look—" he winks, rolling his head as he pulls away. "Hey uh, by the way, I just wanted to ask, is this gonna take long?" he demands, and I sigh, exasperated as I turn from him. "It's just, I'm kind of bored. Thought I could put on some music— after all, it is my party—" He flicks a wrist, visible to me as I turn back to glare at him over my shoulder.

The voice of a woman explodes from nowhere as a cloud forms overhead, shimmering an opalescent cream as the sound deafens anyone close to it. She's talking about walking in Memphis, whatever that has to do with anything.

"I thought you didn't have any powers left?" I cock an eyebrow at him as he swings his head to the beat.

"Oh, I don't have enough power to bust out, but I do have enough to annoy the shit out of you. It's a speciality of mine. One I'm going to enjoy using immensely." Something stirs at my shoulder so I turn, finding Barbas tapping his foot to the beat.

"What are you doing!?" I snap, scowling at him and he shrugs.

"What, it's a good song. Even I love a good Cher number, Pandora." He glowers at me like I'm stupid.

"I think it's hideous," I spit at him, and he rolls his eyes.

"No soul," I hear him mutter, and I shove the shard of glass at him. He takes it in his palm reluctantly, lips pursing.

"I want to hear him scream," I growl, storming from the smirking scrutiny of Haedes' smarmy face and over to the door my mortals are still trying to wrench open.

"What the hell is taking so long?" I blurt.

"The mechanism is complicated, the electrical work was damaged in the Banshee attack, but it's still a heavy piece of metal to move forcibly," one of the mortal servants informs me with a know-it-all attitude. No prizes for guessing which sin landed him a future here.

"I don't care for excuses. Just open it!" I spit, spinning on my heel and finding myself face-to-face with a rack of urns. I pace over to them, uninterested but bored nonetheless.

I have waited for this moment for so long, and yet when it arrives, Haedes doesn't even have the decency to act scared, or pained, or even slightly annoyed. He's just as bad as his brother and owes me some serious respect.

"Assholes," I mumble to myself, eyes resting upon one urn sitting central to the shelving unit. It has a triangle carved into its surface, and as I turn away from it a flicker of recognition sparks between synapses I promptly ignore.

I don't have time for distractions.

"When I kill you, Haedes, and I will, I want you to deliver a message to your brother for me," I announce, picking up another piece of shattered glass from the floor before tossing it aside with a tinkle, deeming it not jagged enough for my purposes.

I select another, nearing him as I bring up a hand to grip the back of his head, fingers burying deep into his hair.

He growls, an irritating and irrational salacious joy spreading like wildfire across his features.

"If it's that you're coming for him, I think I'll just keep that little titbit to myself. After all, you're not much of an actual threat, are you?" He smirks, and my fury expands, blooming in my chest like a rabid mushroom cloud of noxious intent.

"I want you to tell him that he'll rue the day he ever crossed me," I bite out, immensely annoyed at how easily he's disarmed me.

"Oh, sure. I'm sure he'll start rueing any day now. He always was one for self-reflection." Haedes chuckles as I give a yank on his hair, silky in my palms. Relishing the glossy texture between my fingers, an idea strikes me.

Taking the piece of glass, I grab a fistful of locks, using the jagged edge in my palm to cut it at the root.

"Hey, what the fuck do you think you're doing?" he exclaims in an affronted baritone, struggling for the first time against the thick black webbing suspending him.

"Giving you a little haircut." I muse as he leans back, trying to evade my eager and malicious hands.

"Hey, no! Stop it!" he gasps, writhing like the worm he is, breath becoming frantic at last. I continue to grab chunks of his thick silver hair, cutting it uneven and patchy as I let the shimmering locks fall over his shoulders. Like the plucked feathers I had once lost, they float through the air, weightless and precious, before finding their place on the floor beneath the tread of my boot.

"There we are—" I bite my bottom lip, examining him as his eyes blaze furiously. Instead of saying something funny in retort though, he merely hangs his head as the last few pieces of hair flutter down around him.

Have I broken him at last?

As I'm wondering this, I hear a cracking sound before the grinding of metal upon metal hits my ears. I step back from my prisoner, eager for good news.

"It's open, Your Highness." One of the mortals bows his head as his words ring out through the air, pure in intent, and I hear Haedes snort. My head snaps sideways, glower vicious.

"Yes, Haedes?" I demand, and he shakes his head, eyes becoming dead in his skull as excess hair flutters to the floor, dislodged from where it had clung, hopeful, to withered crevices of skin.

"Oh, nothing—" he mumbles, and I roll my eyes.

I haven't been called Your Highness since brilliant white feathers tipped with violet graced my spine. It's odd but undeniably refreshing. I know now it was not what Hera made me that created a worthy Queen; it is who I have been all along.

"Let's take a look—" I feel Barbas tracing my path as I move to where the vault door has been pried open by the collective strength of my followers.

Within it, a colossally enormous onyx hourglass glints, surrounded by flickering torchlight. I smile, the beginnings of my checkmate begin to fall into place.

This should be easy enough to break. In fact, I don't know why I'm wasting time sitting here staring at it. The only thing remarkable about it is how it's not more remarkable, being that it holds part of a man so ridiculously ostentatious. It's just plain onyx, dull and massive, like a shadow of time itself, always looming just within sight but still invisible for all intents and purposes.

"Any last words?" I turn to Haedes, cocking my hip, and he bursts out into an enormous guttural laugh. My fury grows yet again.

"What is so funny? I'm about to kill you." I ask, wondering if he's too stupid to grasp what I'm trying to do.

"Oh, nothing—" He shakes his head like he's in utter and complete denial. My eyebrow cocks, as suspicion falls over me like a swarm of fire ants.

"Tell me. I'm going to kill you either way," I demand, crossing my arms.

"Oh, nothing. I just can't wait to watch my daughter kick every single square inch of your ugly ass all the way back to whatever hole you crawled out of, you stupid bitch. And you know, once I'm a full god once more, I'm going to help her in every single way I know how." He's breathless after this exclamation as laughs continue to wrack his body, bouncing from the walls.

My temper snaps as I storm to a nearby rack of antique spears. I select one. It's plain steel, the metal twisted into a spiral before ending in an unapologetic and cruel spike.

Gripping it in my palm, I watch him, wishing him all the pain and torment The Higher Plains have to offer. Then, making an artful pirouette on the spot, I use the momentum to simply launch the spear with a single and furious wrenching motion of my arm. It's not dramatic, not over the top, but rather practical and effective, just like me.

The weapon pierces the air, flying through the inner vault door and landing square in the middle of the narrowest part of the onyx hourglass. It shatters, an ear-piercing sound, as a wave of light is released from within. It explodes outward, rippling through the surrounding air as the hourglass itself promptly cracks into a million pieces.

I shield my eyes, hearing his laugh fall into nothing and the sound of Cher's horrific droning tones die into silence. The only sound now is the tinkling of onyx shards upon solid gold.

I exhale, a smile twisting my lips into an expression of extreme satisfaction. I stare over to where Haedes' body hangs, dead.

"Let him go," I call to Barbas, who gestures to the Phobias overhead. Their webs recede from his body, the bloody and bald carcass crumpling to the floor with a thud.

I take several steps over to him, giving the corpse a prompt kick in the gut with my boot.

"Who's laughing now?" I demand.

The world around me begins to alter as I tread back through the throne room of the Exilia, making my way in a relaxed air toward the entryway. A chill runs rampant through the hall, something unusual for the humid stickiness of Mortaria.

My mortal servants open the doors before me, and I find myself smiling at them, gracing them too with my joy, with my victory.

Haedes is dead.

I killed him.

The pleasure of success swells within my chest as the thought occurs to me that this place, Mortaria, will now answer to me.

Abraxis passes me in the hallway as my step begins to take on a jolly rhythm. I turn, expectant, to stare him directly in the eye.

"Xion is secured down in the dungeons, as is Osiris," he informs me, face blank. I nod, brushing my long hair back behind one ear.

"Haedes is dead," I announce. Abraxis nods, not surprised by this.

"I know," he replies. I cock my head.

"How?" I demand.

"How else? I suggest you take a look outside. You might get the best view from the Solarium in Haedes' room. It's that way." He points down the corridor on my left before placing his hands back into the pockets of his leather trench coat.

"How do you know that?" I demand, curious as ever.

"I used to be friends with him. When he first arrived here. We used to play poker. He's— I mean he was one of the only people who has ever beaten me at my own game," he informs me, shrugging, and my eyes widen.

"Right. This way?" I demand, pointing to the direction he's just indicated, and he nods. I'm ignoring the information he's just imparted. It doesn't matter now. The fool is gone back to where he belongs, to his doomed family.

"Yes, there's a secret panel on the far wall. Push on it, and you'll find the staircase to the Solarium," he instructs me.

"Thank you," I respond as he shrugs yet again, nonchalant as ever, before turning and moving into the throne room, no doubt to find Barbas.

I take off, making quick work of the corridors as I find several guards slumped against the walls.

Must have been sinners. I determine, passing them as if they're no more than decorative suits of armour, not dead Doppel bodies.

I reach a door at the end of a long corridor, pushing hard on it so the wood gives and swings open.

The inside of the room is decadent, no surprise, and I flit around the space like a ghost, taking in each of the individual details. I find a picture of Haedes and some dark beauty — I think I knew her once — on the bedside table and promptly throw it into the still-flaming hearth.

This will be my room now.

I stand by the edge of the four-poster bed, taking in my success as I let my fingers run through the flocked silk drapes. They're embellished with velvet fleur de lis and the entire piece of fabric slips, black as night, beneath my pale touch as I caress them, comforting myself in a quiet moment of self-reflection.

Shaking myself from the clutches of tranquillity blooming from my victory, I move to the far wall. Pushing in on the marble, it gives with unexpected ease, cool beneath my flat palms.

Behind the slab of dark stone, I find a narrow turret, the walls lined with a tight spiral staircase. I ascend, but the view when I get to the top is not what I expect.

Everything is dark; the only light now from falling purple flames, an eerie spark shower to say the least. The room around me was probably a deep blue in the sunlight but has now turned indigo, scattered with dim grey stars.

I squint upward, fascinated.

The sun is nothing more than a charred black spot, marring the otherwise deep wine hue of the unlit sky.

The street lamps have extinguished at his passing, and as I look over Mortaria from the clutches of this crystal cage, I find myself grinning from ear to ear. Carriages are at a halt in the streets below, the bodies of Doppels littering the streets, the apartment buildings, the floors of stores, and more importantly The Ashen Waste. I sigh, finally content after all this time.

Darkness has fallen, and a new era has begun.

28

WILDFIRE

LUCE

WE HURRY BACK THROUGH the labyrinthian passageways that make up the mines. I find myself treading over bodies, slumped, pickaxes still in hand. Did the demons do this? I can smell them rotting, their skin, bones, and organs starting to liquefy, to seep back into the Mortarian earth from which they came— and yet something odd strikes me.

There's no blood.

Surely, if this had been the result of a demon attack, the Doppel bodies would be drained dry—

"Did you do this?" I demand, head turning promptly towards Sephy, who is walking beside me. She's supporting Thane who, though is no longer injured, seems exhausted, bare feet dragging through the dirt.

"No. This wasn't me or The Furies. The sinners were just fine before," she replies, shaking her head so her vibrant red hair bounces around her shoulders.

I still harbour the quiet urge to tackle her and take Thane's tether for myself, but something tells me that wouldn't go down too well with either of them, so I refrain.

"Anubis and the Demon Lords?" Sephy suggests as we step over several more bodies splayed out in the dirt, eyes wide open and glassy as they stare up at the earth burying us beneath its moist and heavy blanket.

"There are no wounds—" I muse, pushing one of the sinner's cold skulls to one side with my boot as I pass and trying to discern any injuries that may have caused this loss of afterlife.

Something occurs to me, a click between two synapses that flood with electricity, my mind whirring fast.

"Shit," I exhale in a blunt exclamation, breath returning in only earthy wisps. Ignoring the shimmering of surrounding crystals, I increase my definite pace, panicked, pulling both Thane and Sephy through the remainder of the passageways. Weaving left and right, we kick up dirt, crystal dust, and stale air as we hurry forward, too distracted to keep count of how many corpses we tread over.

We reach the mouth of mines, a gaping hole in the earth with a gradual incline slowly peppered over with increasingly dense ash. My eyes are immediately drawn to the skies.

No.

"Luce, what's going on?" I hear Thane croak and look back over my shoulder to both her and Sephy as her grip tightens against the dark fabric covering my upper arm.

"Haedes—" I breathe, eyes dilating to black as my breath comes quicker and more desperate with each passing second.

The sky is the darkest I've ever known it, a deep bloody wine, the colour of rich merlot mixed in with hot arterial blood. The entire thing is only visibly red still from the dancing violet flames, which fall, much larger than any single spark I've ever known to tumble from the skies.

"The sun—" Sephy inhales, eyes widening as I turn to her.

"Haedes— Haedes is *gone*," I whisper, tone rife with a kind of underwhelmed disgust, as her mouth falls open. She's not shocked but displays more horror mixed in with grief as her eyes sparkle with sudden and unexpected tears.

It's a more sentimental response than I can give, and I watch her as she stands, awestruck beneath the darkness of the empty heavens. Thane stares up at the sky too, her grey eyes turning lilac in the face of the storm of a dying sun, a dying god and his era passing with him. It is with this, and the morose anxious expression that follows her gaze, that I know we cannot stand out here any longer.

My heart breaks at the thought of Haedes leaving me all alone, but still I stand, immune to my emotional turmoil as the darkness crashes through my mind like an angry wave, instead seeking a logical next act on my part.

Big Brother, I'll miss you. I make this final acknowledgement of his passing, digging my nails into my palms.

"Ow!" Thane exclaims, her bare flesh at my mercy as I've unwillingly clenched down with the fingers gripping her too.

"We need to get back to the Exilia," Sephy sounds panicked now, the dark leather of Xion's jacket painting her skin a stark porcelain and revealing that she's even more drained of colour than usual. She grips the long sleeves with her fingers, balling her fists beneath the leather, impatient.

I cock my head.

"If the sun is extinguished, Sephy, it means he's gone. There's nothing left for you there. We need to get out," I conclude, tone clipped. I gather the dark strands of hair that fall over one shoulder, brushing them behind me so my long locks fall down my spine in a matted tangle.

"No, Xion is there with him. I have to go." She looks furious as if she hadn't forgotten him for a moment.

"Oh—" I exhale, winded at the notion I'd not thought of him immediately. What if he's dead?

My gaze sweeps the area, finding more Doppel bodies strewn across the ground surrounded by piles of charred ash, as we step, haphazardly, out into the open space.

"If the Doppel bodies are dead, it means the souldiers in The Ashen Waste are dead too. That means the only thing standing between us and the demonic forces beyond are those gates," I explain, clinging to logic as I quickly locate one of the gates nearby.

I squint, the unmistakable white gazes of Banshees peering through the gaps as they rear up and cause the gate to rattle inside its frame. Paws smash, impatient, into the metal.

"I have to go," Sephy announces, shaking her head and letting Thane's arm slip from her shoulder.

"He could be dead, Sephy. Don't risk your life," I plead with her, not sure how I'm going to get back to The Hollow if she leaves me.

"Lucifer, I don't give a fuck what you say. I came out here and left them undefended because of your bullshit choices. I'm going." She turns from me, and I call out after her.

"And what about me? What about Thane and The Furies? What about Beelz? I need him! My Tether! How will we get back?" I call.

"You drank from The Well. Figure it out. I'll meet you there—with Beelz—" she snaps, relinquishing her attitude slightly before disappearing in an explosive plume of blue flames.

Shit.

I turn to look at Thane.

"Can you stand?" I ask her. She nods, face marred with disapproval. She's still wrapped in the black silk she'd been dressed in as Anubis' captive, and she stands, shivering slightly as a blanket of cold falls heavy over the world around us. Ash ceases to fall in place of the flaming purple embers, signalling the sun is well and truly gone.

"I think so. The solar presence would usually have me feeling fully healed by now," she complains, pulling away from me.

"One moment," I breathe, ignoring the rabid sounds of paws bashing in against the gate on the other side of the wall, only metres from where I stand.

Placing my hands on her shoulders, she grunts with the pain from what had been her wound. I've fixed the external gash, but the inside is still healing. After all, knitting muscle and sinew back together isn't a quick process, especially around a socket like you find in the shoulder. I'm not exactly practised in this kind of magic yet either.

As I close my eyes, power surges in ripples down my arms and into my fingertips, I clothe Thane in a skin-tight leather catsuit, opening my eyes and finding her edgier, more immovable, than ever.

"How did you do that?" she asks in an accusatory tone. I can only shrug.

"Magic," I mutter, sick of people asking me that question. I mean, what other response do they expect?

"Okay, so we have— no way to get back. How did Sephy and The Furies even get here?" I ask her, and she turns on the spot.

"Lucifer. Thanatos." Our names freefall through the air, broken and thick with a Nigerian accent.

I spin on the spot, cloak billowing out behind me.

"Erin," I extend the greeting as her eyes, and those of her fellow Furies, collectively narrow at my change in appearance.

"The Demon Lords and Anubis— they fled beyond the wall with the remainder of their Kindred. There were hundreds of Banshees waiting for them. We could not follow. We fear the only option now may be to flee," Ericka explains, her lower lip bloody. Her pink tongue flicks out over her cracked skin, wiping it clean.

"Haedes has fallen," Erlea announces, heartless in this assessment as her eyes flick up to the sky and a look of unwavering determination settles over her hard features. She sheaths the Katana, bloody, across her back with a fluid swing of one arm that is so well practised it takes only seconds.

"How did you get here?" I enquire, watching as Thane observes me, the chill breeze taking my dark hair up from the onyx-mapped skin of my cheeks.

"Haedes' car. Sephy used it to distract the demons. It's gone now," Erin explains, running her fingers back through the wild curly mass of her hair. I take a moment, pondering more traditional methods. Gondolas and carriages would be perfect, if they weren't manned by Doppels that now lie immobile and useless across Mortaria.

"So, we have no way to get back to The Exilia?" I exclaim, my rage toward a certain redhead building.

That's when something gold glints in the corner of my eye.

I turn, distracted, eyes settling on the solution to our problems. Well, almost.

Anubis' Chariot stands, unmanned, about a hundred feet from me. I take off toward it, my cloak floating out behind me, ominous in its seeming material apparition.

As I reach the chariot, I run my hand along the polished rim of it, but then exhale. The Jackals that had once pulled it are no more than four piles of neat bones among the ash.

"Crap," I cuss as Thane moves in at my side, reflection visibly golden upon the shimmering cart.

"The sun— it was keeping them alive too," she sighs, shrugging as she raises her uninjured arm and runs her fingers through her hair. "So much for that plan. Maybe I should just fly— try to find us some horses— I mean I doubt there's any still standing but perhaps Muerta—" she suggests, and I round on her before she can finish.

"Are you fucking crazy? You've already been shot out of the god-damn sky once today! You're not going anywhere, and if you try, I'll ground you myself," I condemn her. Her eyebrows rise fast on her forehead.

"*Excuse me*? Is that a threat?" she demands, voice a low rumble.

"Damn fucking straight. If you hadn't stormed off, we wouldn't be in this mess." I scorn her with my gaze as The Furies close the distance between us, kicking up ash in their wakes as they sense our unrest.

"And if you hadn't lied to me and broken your promises, I wouldn't have taken off!" Thane retorts, sucking in her cheeks so the bones beneath become defined and rigid like blades.

"We cannot just stand here. The gates will not hold forever," Erlea warns us, and so I turn to them, not giving Thane the courtesy of a response.

"So, what exactly do you suggest I do?" I bark, terror rising within me. I have all this power— so how am I still so helpless?

Think, Luce. I curse myself, mind racing to find a solution as the three Furies give a synchronised shrug. Escape isn't their forte, and if it was up to them, we'd remain here until not one of us was left standing.

As it is, the choice is not theirs. It's mine.

I wanted the power— so now I must rise, rise and make it do my bidding.

What do I know of myself?

I am the daughter of Moloch—

Moloch had lots of different powers but one I recall in particular is the power to influence.

As I hear paws thud onto the gate once more, I storm past the group, no idea whether I'm going crazy but lacking any other option than to wing it and see what happens.

I near the wall, its obsidian mass glinting a dualistic hue between plum and ebony and glazed over with a cobalt sheen like that of pure gasoline. I hurry, ash compacting harshly beneath my feet, and blink slowly, approaching the gate without fear as I keep my heartbeat steady within the cage of my ribs.

I see them, gnashing jaws, smashing both bone and flesh against one another as spit flies from the back of their throats, hungry as ever. I look through the metal lattice, trying to catch the eyes of one in particular.

Stop. I command, singling out a pair of rabid alabaster eyes framed by the steel rods of the portcullis.

I watch as the beast stills and reach out to make gentle contact. Its nose begins to twitch, curious, reminding me too easily of the kid.

Calm! I bark within my head, not breaking eye contact for a second as my fingertips contact the nose of the Banshee.

It recoils.

I fear it might snap, taking several of my fingers with it, but instead, it stills. Ears flattening against its skull, its packmates continue to push against the gate, but this one Banshee sits like a dog, too easily broken under my gaze.

My eyes narrow and my lips twist into a smile, a sense of invulnerability flooding my gut as I straighten within the square cut of my jacket.

I know what to do.

I turn, gesturing for Thane and The Furies to join me. They do so, sharing hesitant glances but forcing their feet to move, closing the distance between us despite their personal opinions of me.

"I need you to open this gate," I look to The Furies, and they each cock an eyebrow.

"Open it? Have you lost your mind?" Thane exclaims.

I shake my head.

"Go and get in the chariot," I order her, pointing toward the chariot with pursed lips. She falters in her reaction, pausing. I spin around, pupils dilating fast, chasmic with rage.

"Lucifer, who the hell do you think you are? This is not you!" she exclaims, frowning, expression a fusion of fear and fury.

"*Go!*" I yell, not having time for her attitude. I just want to get out of this mess alive.

She turns on her heel, stalking off toward the chariot, leaving me with the feeling that my soul is gradually freezing over, cracking but expanding too as it readies to take flight, finally harnessing the potential I've held inside all along.

"Now, I want you to lift it," I demand.

The three Furies look at one another, nervous.

"Just a little. Maybe a foot or so. Just enough to let one through, if any more get loose, you take them out," I instruct, not blinking or faltering in my speech. They exhale heavily as a collective, bare stomachs visibly tensing moments later beneath the leather of their crop tops as they hesitate several seconds too long.

"Well! Do it!" I bark. The gates continue to rattle, frame audibly weakening in resistance to the hoard beyond.

The Furies move forward with hesitation, all three bending in an identical squat. They grip the metal of the gate from underneath, somehow managing to ignore the snapping jaws on the other side that graze the calloused, rough skin of their fingers.

I hear them give a guttural grunt, several deep breaths, and then they all let out a horrific scream, each cry specific to their origins, as they hoist the metal spikes from the ground. It only moves a few inches at first, the tapered ends of each bar only just visible above the layer of thick ash. I keep my concentration, waiting until finally it's raised high enough for me to act.

Come. I command, keeping my connection as I seek out the calm alabaster gaze of The Banshee that I had lulled placid only moments before. The beast crouches, wiggling under the gap like a puppy trying to escape from a neighbour's backyard.

"Release the gate!" I call, keeping my eyes trained on the Banshee. It wags its tail, shaking ash from its furry underbelly before rising to the height of my shoulder as it straightens on all fours.

I hear a clang as the metal of the gate is released, re-piercing the earth with the harsh ringing of steel on hard ground. This is when I'm caught off guard by the weight of another person falling into the back of me. I am shoved forward, landing face-first in the ash of the floor.

Ugh! I cuss, shaking my face free of ash and spitting out the chalky texture and smoky taste that coats my tongue.

Turning onto my back, I find Erlea has bowled into me, not having managed to loosen her grip on the gate in time.

I shake my head, irritated as a saliva-thick growl hits my ears. I spin, launching myself to my feet as the Banshee I've let through bares its teeth, licking its muzzle with a hungry expression.

I've broken the connection.

Focus, Luce. I scold myself, squaring my shoulders and throwing my black hair back over one shoulder yet again, dislodging ash like sick snow.

I look down at the Banshee, which is creeping closer, widening my eyes and intensifying my gaze as I reach out with long, spindled fingers yet again.

This time, the connection takes hold faster. The pupils of the creature dilate and it stills, jaws going slack as its enormous tongue lolls out of one side.

Come. I demand, storming forward and leading it toward the chariot. I rest a hand on the nape of its neck, feeling the thick fur between my fingers as the scent of ichor, of death, billows up and into my nostrils.

"Luce— *what* are you doing?!" Thane exclaims as I near her, standing, ready to depart in the chariot.

"I'm getting us a ride out of here," I explain in a calm and even tone, making the connection with the creature beside me as steadfast as I can. I feel its compliance slipping now and again, the smallest motion such as a sudden rabid inhale or the protraction of a single claw hinting that I need to tighten my hold. It's exciting, a challenge, something I've been without for too long.

"But that's a demon!"

I sigh.

"Observant," I retort, not turning to her as I try to hold my concentration even still. Letting my pupils sweep over the equipment used to fasten the jackals to the vehicle, I realise quickly the shackles aren't large enough to harness the demon.

"Erin, come here." I gesture for her to step forward; aware that the three women have been trailing behind me, whispering to one another about my unorthodox methods.

"Yes?" She moves to my side, voice void of emotion as she stands, erect in posture, hands hanging open above her muscular thighs.

"I'm going to give you these to wrap around the Banshee's neck. You will be on the back of the demon, making sure we stay connected to it because I don't know how well this will hold. So, don't fall off," I explain. Her eyes widen, their chocolate depths doubtful. "Look, just do it. I don't have time for attitude."

I shove the solid gold chains of the chariot into her chest as she takes them in hand.

Kneel. I command the Banshee, which promptly lowers itself to the ground so that Erin may climb atop its wide shoulders. I watch with satisfaction as she loops the gold chains around the neck of the beast, holding the makeshift reins in her palms with a doubtful expression. With a loud clatter, I find my attention drawn behind us, where the gates within the wall suddenly begin to move, the sound of a chain being pulled through a winch hitting the air around us.

"Get in!" I shout, giving one last look behind me and hurrying Erlea and Ericka into the chariot. I get in too, finding adequate room for all of us because we are luckily petite, and push my way to the front of the semi-circular and archaic cart.

To the Exilia. I telepathically bark at the Banshee, not sure whether it'll understand something as complicated as a place name but feeling the rumble of paws against earth begin to vibrate beneath the chariot as the gates slowly withdraw from the Mortarian soil. This alone is enough to push me into action regardless of my uncertainty.

The chariot jerks forward, causing all of us to tilt backwards. Ericka and Erlea brace themselves against the wide-open back of the contraption, stopping Thane and myself from falling.

Squeezing my eyes shut, I try not to think about how insane this all is, to think about how many Banshees and other demons are about to run loose beyond the wall. I need to get to The Exilia, get Beelz, and get out of here.

The chariot picks up pace, the ungraceful and heavy tread of the Banshee echoing loudly in my ears as we leave The Icon's unmistakable silhouette behind us. The Banshee is fast, faster than I thought, but I can't help but wonder if we will be able to outrun the hoard once they're unleashed.

Mortaria is falling before my very eyes, and as we race through The Plains of Ichor, I feel my connection with the Banshee begin to wane.

No. No feed. I bark, hearing it whine and whimper. I watch as Erin adjusts her balance, the pace of the creature beneath her picking up yet again as we race alongside what had once been the slow-moving waters of The River Styx.

The sun may have been down for barely any time at all, but I can already tell that without the resurrection flame to call the waters to Golgotha, the river is filling to the brim, and fast. The cloudy current is tumultuous now, rabid and angry as it swarms within the banks of swan neck deformities and natural meanders.

The wind picks up as we gain speed, travelling in the opposite direction of the current on our left and finding dead bodies scattered with increasing abundance the closer we get to the city limits.

I look behind us a moment as we reach the outskirts, and when I do I breathe a subtle sigh of relief, finding the wall is not yet overrun. Turning once more, I watch Erin, looking less than comfortable on the back of the Banshee, as she is tossed from left to right with every single turn as though she weighs no more than a ragdoll.

Faster. I demand, the remark stinging as I lose patience. The demons aren't upon us yet, but it won't be long. We may only have minutes before they break through and make a run for the city, for their old hunting grounds. They aren't carting a chariot behind them either, so no doubt they'll be much faster than we are.

Once we are clear out of The Plains of Ichor, my control over the demon becomes more concrete. We skid around a corner as we reach the city, the chariot smashing into the front window of a local bar. Glass flies out, the sound of it shattering overwhelming me as I stand strong where everyone else ducks, trying not to lose my persuasion. The glass cuts into me, flying through the air and lodging in my skin, my hair, but I don't feel it, tightening my grip on the rim of the chariot and urging the monster driving us on instead. My breath is surprisingly even, my blood cool in my veins; despite the increasingly difficult path we're travelling, which requires all my concentration to navigate. Doppel bodies get caught under the wheels of the chariot, and carriages mounted by dead drivers and pulled by even deader steeds create unmovable and morbid obstacles. As we hit the leg of a dead horse and Erin almost slides from the back of the Banshee, only regaining her composure through sheer force of will, I know I must take evasive action if we are to reach anywhere in one piece.

Left.

Right.

Left.

Left again.

This is as much as I can focus on as the chariot weaves haphazardly in and out of fleshy debris; occasionally jolting as it unintentionally hits some stray limb or the corner of the sidewalk.

Eventually, as the lilac sparks seem to be all but lost from the sky and the world falls into darkness around us, we finally turn onto the road that leads directly to the Exilia.

As the streets become shrouded in shadow, I hear it, the collective howling of the Banshee pack. They must finally have broken through the gates, and now they're coming straight for us. I look up to the gothic streetlamps that line the paths as we rush past them in a blur. Not even one is lit, not an inkling of The Eternal Flame anywhere to be found, in the sky, on the streets, or otherwise.

The only hope we now have of outrunning the demons is Sephy Sinclair and the power which had once belonged to her father, and that in itself is a huge problem. She's far too busy running after a boy she supposedly doesn't love and probably getting herself killed in the process to worry about the fate of little old me.

I sigh out, feeling the chariot becoming far too crowded as the Banshee pulls us, step by ragged pounding step, closer to our destination, demons at our back, and the rising of a new dark ruler just up ahead.

29

HOT AS HAEDES

SEPHY

THE COBALT BLAZE DIES down, leaving me staring down the long corridor of the dungeons, lined on either side by cell after cell. I've been gone for what feels like hardly any time at all, and yet everything has changed. The torches on the walls are extinguished, the passages plagued by screams bouncing from each individual steel bar of every single cell, relentless.

I hear him before I see him, but it's not in a way I've ever known.

His sobs reach me as I rush forward, feet smashing hard into the cobblestones underfoot as my breath catches, a hostage to fear, in my throat. I find him in the farthest cell along the corridor, slumped in the corner and blanketed by shadow. I stare in between the bars, barely recognising the slumped form at all.

"Xion!" I exclaim, tapping on the bars with my knuckles. He doesn't move, simply continuing to cry quietly on the floor. His knees are drawn up to his chest, eye sockets deep dark caverns against the olive skin covering the rest of his face.

"Xion! Get up!" I hiss out once again, placing my hands around two of the bars and rattling them, trying to get his attention. He still doesn't budge.

For God's sake, I don't have time for this! I cuss internally, balling my fists at my sides and allowing the resurrection flame to engulf me. I pop up again, inside the cell, closer to him — but he still doesn't move.

"Xion—" I whisper, softening my tread as I take several steps across the hay-scattered floor before falling to my knees in front of him.

"Stay away, Sephy," he mutters, voice hoarse. He won't hold eye contact, simply staring down into his lap.

"No, look, we have to go. Haedes is dead. Mortaria is going to hell—well, more than it was before. We need to go now!" I try to impress the seriousness of the situation on him, placing a hand on the thick curve of his kneecap. His face rises from where he's been staring down, eyes finally meeting mine.

"No. You go," he breathes, like a pouty toddler.

Oh hell no. I curse, rolling my eyes.

"I came back for you. I'm not leaving without you, even if I have to beat your stupid thick skull in and carry you over my shoulder fire-fighter style," I reach out, placing a hand on his shoulder and shaking him slightly. His eyes are so empty, only making me more frustrated.

"Sephy— *enough.* I'm not worth it. You don't know what I've done," Xion implores me now, his tear-filled, molten gaze burning into me.

"Right. Well then, I have no choice." I let my fingers flex, The Eternal Flame to me.

It crackles as I hold it to his face, illuminating the shadows of his skull and lighting his irises a hot gold.

"Ready to die?" I demand, and he looks into the flame, eyes reflecting the fire back at me, desolate.

"Do it." He closes his eyes, and I narrow my gaze.

"Are you fucking kidding me?" I demand, and he frowns as I extinguish the flame in only a second before slapping him across the face.

"You're the one with the power to set the world free of me." Xion's head lolls to the side, his cheek pressing against the slick stone at the side of the cell, moving with my palm and not fighting me at all.

"*Are you fucking kidding me?!*" I yell at him. "You forced me back into this life, didn't give me a goddamn choice, and now *you* want to leave?!" I exclaim, slapping him across the face once more.

I don't stop there though. I continue to slap his arms, beating into his flesh with my fists, rage overtaking me like it had when I was a small child.

"*You. Are. Such. An. Assclown!*" I burst, letting my pointy knuckles pound into the hard muscle of his chest. "*Get the fuck up!*" I exclaim, grabbing him by the collar and hoisting him to his feet.

"Sephy, stop!" he exclaims, grabbing me by both shoulders.

I glare at him.

"No. You stop. Get a grip on yourself. We all kill people we love, boohoo! You won't be the last, and you certainly aren't the first. If I'm stuck in this suck-fest, then so are freaking you!" I demand, desperate

345

as I ram my lips to his. I inhale the scent of pomegranate and his husky perspiration, feeling his heartbeat turn turbo beneath my palm.

"Sephy stop," he murmurs as I push him back into the wall.

I open my eyes a fraction, finding the gaze staring back at me glowing orange.

"I'm not afraid of your demon, Xion. You bring him right out here. I'll kiss his stupid face too," I vow, watching as his skin ripples beneath my touch, fading from flesh to charcoal.

I do as I vow, continuing to kiss him, kiss the darkest part of him. He brought me back, gave me a beating heart and all the pain that came with it. I'll be damned if he puts that beating mass of fleshy pulp in my chest through anything more.

I let my palm heat, warning him as I the breathing of the beast before me becomes ragged, primitive, and volatile against my lips. I kiss him hard, eliciting a small moan from his lips as I keep him pinned against the wall. My arms and his are both mapped with popping veins, the tension between us never more physically evident as I snake my leg around his femur, pinning him to the spot.

I end the kiss, looking back at him, into the dark skin, the blazing orange eyes, and the demonic intent behind them.

He doesn't scare me.

And as much as I wish it weren't true, out there among the ash and fallen Doppels with Luce, I realised that it's his removal from my life, as a friend or otherwise, which truly terrifies me above all else.

"We done?" I growl, letting the glow of my white-hot skin sizzle into the surface of his, my hand branding its silhouette above his heart as his white t-shirt disintegrates beneath our scorching connection.

"Never," the demon vows, tightening his hold as his charred dark arms fall, winding fast around my waist.

"That's what I like to hear," I whisper, resting my forehead against his and letting my irises blaze with the orange glow of his. I'm bathed in the light of his swirling tattoos, stifling as I move to take off his jacket and pass it to him. As he pulls it over his shoulders, the sound of footsteps interrupts us, and I straighten, taking a step back from the wall. I pull the chainmail bolero from my shoulders, aware it's not a quiet garment as it hits the floor and the steel rings out into the air.

I look at Xion, watching as his demon form balls its fists, biceps bulging against his jacket sleeves. I prepare myself too, ready to convect and take out anyone who tries to stop our escape.

Stiffening in posture, we both stand, waiting for the footsteps to reach us. When they do, I instantly set my palm ablaze, raising my arm as I ready to throw the projectile.

"Wait!" the man exclaims, putting both hands up. Then I realise, it isn't a man at all.

"Father," Xion says, voice deeper now he's in demon form.

I stare at Abraxis through the bars, ready to convect and beat his ass if I must. His broad forehead, his sharp glowing orange eyes, and his well-oiled black hair make me frown. I can't help but wonder if this is his true face because it looks so remarkably like that of his son.

"You're here to rescue him?" he enquires, and I give a single jerk of my head to indicate this is my intent.

Abraxis reaches into the pocket of his leather trench coat, pulling out a key and walking toward the door of the cell. I tense, grabbing Xion's forearm in my palm and convecting us onto the other side of the bars, so we're stood behind the Demon Lord before he even has a chance to touch the lock.

"I was going to set you free—" he mutters, looking irritated.

"Yeah, nice try and all, but I don't have time for whatever you're trying to pull, dude," I explain, tucking my hair behind one ear. Xion frowns at him, cautious beside me as he remains physically tense and unwavering in posture.

Why would Abraxis want to help us? I wonder, scrutinising him.

"Go. Quickly. Before they find you," he whispers, voice hushed but desperate as it comes out in a snake-like hiss.

I want to ask him why he's doing this, why he would aid Pandora if he intended to undermine her all along, but I don't have time. I have to get Beelz and get out.

Xion and I rush down the corridor, looking into each of the cells and checking for any other prisoners I missed on my way in. The Fates don't seem to be in any of them, but as I reach the cells by the staircase which leads back up into the Exilia a flash of white catches the corner of my eye.

Osiris. I determine.

I could stop, could set him free, rescue him too. As it is, I don't have the time, and I have no idea how involved he is with the Demon Lords. Haedes is dead, which means this could have been a trap orchestrated by him all along regardless of whether he's in a cell or not. Swallowing hard, I make my decision, continuing up the stone steps and out into the corridor above, leaving him behind in the dank stench of the dungeons.

"Where to now?" Xion enquires as I turn to him, checking both directions of the hallway are clear. We stand in the open, side by side, aimlessly paused as I stare up at him. My heart is racing, adrenaline spiking through my system with the thrill of it all.

"Go and get Beelz. Then head out to where the docks run for the River Styx. You might find Luce and Thane there. I stopped the resurrection, so they are on their way back with The Furies. If not, I'll meet you, I have something I need to do first," I reveal. The skin of his demonic face creases right above his heavy brow.

"Sephy, what are you doing?" he asks, his tone a warning, and I cock an eyebrow.

"She killed my father, Xion. She can't just get away with that," I determine, and he looks surprised.

"Sephy, come on, this isn't the time for vengeance. We just need to get out of this alive," he exclaims. I roll my eyes, crossing my arms over my breasts.

"Says the demon boy with a death wish. Whatever. Just go get the panther. I'll be back soon." I turn on my heel, walking from him and hearing him calling my name, trying to get me to come back to him.

I don't turn back though; I just keep on walking.

I storm through the lobby, shooting flames from both palms at guards on either side of me as I twirl on the ball of one foot. Bodies and shadows come charging toward me simultaneously from directly ahead, and I grit my teeth, ready. Both demons and sinners close in on me, and as I ready myself to end each one in turn a realization hits me.

These guards can't be sinners. They're still walking around without the aid of the sun.

What the fuck is going on here? I wonder as the scent of burning flesh fills my nostrils, making my nose wrinkle. I'm distracted from this thought only when a Phobia drops from overhead and I let a stream of flame capture it mid-descent. It falls to my feet in a sizzling mess and I kick the corpse to the left, bowling over several of the encroaching guards in the process.

Strike. I muse, biting down on my bottom lip as my heart thrums a rhythmic beat within my chest. I watch as the disarmed guards tumble back down the stairs, no longer crystal in structure but bone.

Well, that's new— I frown, guessing Barbas is probably to blame. Several more Phobias try dropping down from the ceiling, but I soon catch onto their ploy, standing and covering the shadows above with a crackling blanket of flame, heating the space considerably and causing any remaining demons to perish. They fall to the floor like grim and heavy raindrops, landing with a bloody splat.

I turn, reaching the double doors with ease now, guards scattering behind me as I toss a line of flames over my shoulder. I light the torches on either side of the entrance to the throne room for good measure, chasing away the odd, bloody light that's fallen over the place.

Without hesitation I lean back, smashing through the doors with my boot as I kick them wide open, impatient for retribution.

A gust of cold air rushes me as the dank insides of the space are revealed, a drastic contrast from the now blazing entrance hall, blowing back my hair from my face.

I stand, feet wide, fists clenched, ferocious in expression.

"Pandora," I call, finding her draped over the throne at the end of the hall.

"Ah, Sephy. I was wondering when you'd be showing up. Better late than never," she tuts, looking at an imaginary watch on her wrist as she straightens. Getting to her feet and moving forward, Barbas and a fleet of guards assemble at her spine. Her boots click on the floor, leather skirt surrounding her in a heavy ring of shadow. The look is entirely over the top; then again, she doesn't have the face to pull off minimalist or classy.

"I'm kind of hurt you're not running in terror right now," I growl, fury hot in my veins. I take several steps forward out of the doorway, meeting her halfway across the slick and smoky dancefloor.

"And why should a queen run from her own castle?" Pandora asks me, tilting her head and pursing her lips.

"The only way you're even close to resembling a queen is if the one you're referring to works down the club on weekends and her name is Mistress Jazmeen," I quip, but I don't think she fully understands the insult. Doesn't make it less amusing for me though. A smile tugs at the corners of my lips, daring me to fully expose the expression.

"And you are— a queen I mean?" she demands, a laugh threatening to spill from behind her dark lips as well.

"Not even close. I'm a warrior," I state, sounding bolder than I'm feeling as I push out my chest. With this, I summon a flame, readying to fight her. It crackles intensely within my clutch, an outward symbol of my fury at Haedes' destruction.

I will not be made prisoner to this place. I will not become my father— either of them.

"Before you throw that, might I just remind you that as we stand here talking, Persephone, the entire demon population of The Ashen Waste, and a rather large mortal presence are charging right towards us? They have breached the wall," she informs me, smug.

I throw the fireball in my palm, watching it soar through the air, over her shoulder, narrowly missing her as intended. It lands upon the throne where Haedes had once sat, melting the heavy gold of the chair until all that remains is a pool of molten metal and the cinders of the padded seat cushion upon the raised platform. The metal drips down the incline, hardening too slowly as it spreads. Pandora startles as it approaches her in a slow-moving sludge, jumping sideways to stop her skirt being covered as I inhale deeply, steadying my nerves. She might have The Exilia, but she won't sit where he sat.

"And why should I care? You killed my father, you deserve to die like a dog," I snarl, taking another step forward, closing the space between us.

"You should care because if you don't go and aid the others in escaping this place, everyone close to Haedes will perish. Xion will die too. So, you have a choice to make. Revenge and certain death by demon hoards that you'd stand no chance of defeating alone— or flee with what little you have left."

As her words hit the air, a rumble begins to stir the stone beneath my feet. "They're coming. Tick tock, Persephone. Choices, choices—" she laughs, crossing one foot over the other and making a quarter turn as she saunters before me. I take a second, sensing the oncoming threat as the noise and trembling of the earth beneath my feet gets louder and louder. I can sense them too, their hunger, as it grows increasingly voracious the closer they get to what had once been theirs.

She's right. I have a choice to make.

I could burn her and everyone in this room to the ground; go out fighting, I could get my revenge.

But then, what about Xion, what about Jules? What about Lucifer and Thanatos? What about Haedes? He sacrificed his power so I could live. This entire disaster has unfolded because of the people who care so deeply for me, they ripped apart the universe to bring me back to them.

The price is too high. The sacrifices have already been made by others, made so I don't have to.

I observe Pandora, the way her violet eyes gleam at my misfortune, but I see something else too. Behind them, an emptiness lies. More barren than any Ashen Waste, she is void of a will to truly live.

Being alive isn't just a state; it's a choice. One of the most difficult I have ever had to make, but as I stand here, staring at Pandora, I can see myself in her.

Myself, if I choose wrong.

Revenge will ultimately lead to her downfall. She has no love in her life, not anymore. Nobody to live for. No cause greater than the destruction of those who wronged her.

What a shitty way to live.

I turn on my heel, her eyes burning into the back of my skull as I tilt my head upward, empowered by the realisation that life is not in fact a foregone conclusion. Because now I know, there is a difference between being alive and living.

As I take slow steps away from her, pushing my luck and testing to see whether she intends to fight me or let me leave, I smile. I have many things to live for. I just hadn't realised it before.

Living is me coming back to save Xion. Living is Lucifer rushing to save Thane. Living is Haedes visibly ageing so that I might regain my immortality. Living is not breathing in and out, it's how we strive to connect, the way in which we make sacrifices, take risks, and bear the pain of being alive for those people who make it worth our while to carry on. Living is loving, is fighting to love and for those we love no matter the hand we are dealt.

Revenge is for those who simply wish to exist, like zombies, walking through life to no avail other than to satiate their hunger for mindless pain. Revenge is an avoidance of moving on, it's a way to become the victim in a world where anyone can be one if they're meek enough, if they're helpless enough and desperate enough to deny responsibility and shift blame.

I am not a victim.

I am a warrior, as I've already assured myself. And one who, apparently, has realised she can pick her own damn battles.

This isn't one of them.

Haedes is dead, and if he thought I might die trying to end his killer after the fact, after the damage has already been done, he'd swear extremely loudly and then call me stupid for even contemplating it before going to pour himself a large whiskey.

I stride from the ballroom, throwing fireballs left and right as more guards attempt to take me out to no avail. Their mortal bodies are too slow, no match for my semi-divine instincts or speed.

Pandora doesn't come after me, neither does Barbas. They have what they came for, and my guess is they won't risk fighting me for the sake of it— because they know they'll lose, even if the demon hoard kills me afterwards.

As I reach the top of the now skeletal staircase, I find that the violet embers, which had been falling from the sky before, have ceased. Someone touches me on the shoulder and I spin, hand spitting flame as I rotate, ready to fight.

"It's only me!" Xion exclaims, Beelz growling at the flame as I promptly extinguish it, sighing with relief as my blood continues to pound in my ears.

He's in his human form now, skin flesh-coloured once more.

My eyes are drawn to the burn where my hand had scorched into the skin above his demonic heart, his human chest now also permanently branded with my palm impression.

The sound of howling fills the air, bringing me back to our current predicament.

"Okay, we have to go. The demons from beyond the wall are coming—" I express, feeling the rumbling underfoot even still as I race down the stairs.

"All of them?" Xion demands, and I nod.

"Yes, the sun is out. The souldiers fell. The wall has been compromised. We have to get out of here," I keep my sentences short and snappy, moving to descend the last step as he grabs my shoulder.

"I'm sorry— about Haedes. I should've—" he begins but loses the words halfway through the sentence as his metallic irises become dull and cold with shame.

"Xion, it's fine. There was nothing more you could have done. You were outnumbered, and besides, I have the feeling Haedes knew this might happen. We have to go!" I express, grabbing him by the hand and pulling him along behind me. I don't have time for his guilt.

What's done is done.

What we do next is all that matters.

My feet skid across the floor of the Exilia entranceway, and as we move close to the dock, I find myself gazing down the length of it, squinting for any sign of the others. The waters distract me a moment. They're higher now, rushing like rapids, frothing at the mouth and angry as they swirl too fast down the course of the river.

I'm taken back to the task at hand as I hear Xion speak, his voice barely audible above the rabid sounds of hungry beasts.

"What the—" He's lost in shock, or awe.

When I turn, I see why.

A Banshee is racing toward us, mounted by none other than Erin. The beast gallops, heavy flat paws pounding against the stone and claws scratching against the faceted floor with every single step.

As it nears, a chariot is revealed behind it, screeching to a halt right in front of us, sparks flying up from beneath the solid gold wheels.

Luce stares at me from atop it, hair blowing back from her face as her black eyes bore into mine, void of emotion.

"Get in," she says in a calm voice, looking back over her shoulder.

Xion and I clamber into the chariot, but there isn't enough room for Beelz. Luce stares next to the cat as I turn to see where her gaze had been focused. Behind us, a wall of teeth, fur, claws, and strangely coloured eyes are approaching, more formidable than I could have ever dreamed.

There are so many. Too many even for me to handle. Maybe even too many for me and Haedes to have managed together.

Fear climbs up inside of me, clawing at my stomach from the inside as it creeps upward, stilling my lungs, making my heart leaden, and finally robbing my breath as it creeps to the top of my throat.

I know now I did the right thing.

I've made the right choice.

There's no way I could take back Mortaria, even if I wanted to. The Demon Lords have well and truly conquered the city, and now the bodies of Doppels and the rest of the land they so seek will be relished as the spoils of a silent war nobody had known was coming, least of all me.

"Beelz, run! The Hollow!" Luce bellows at the panther, whose ears flatten as she pounces forwards and begins to sprint out of the Exilia courtyard, leading us onward.

The Banshee connected to the chariot pulls off once more after the slick black sheen on Beelz's coat, the added weight of two extra bodies noticeably slowing our speed.

353

I pull out my sword as Erlea unsheathes her Katana and Ericka readies her bow and arrow.

As we prepare for the oncoming storm, our Chariot passing under the high crystal arches of our now fallen kingdom, the demons approach, a growing mass of shadow edging closer with each passing moment under the now forever dark sky above.

30

STRANGE FRUIT

XION

THE WORLD AROUND US is a mess of sound, light, and sensation, blurring into one another as we race through the darkened streets away from the Exilia. My chest hurts, the burn Sephy made still stinging as the cold wind hits it through the hole in my t-shirt. I should mind, but I don't. I don't care about the pain. She's imprinted a part of herself onto me, perhaps not in the most conventional of ways, but for us, a pair of unconventional individuals, it means more to me than I'd ever tell her.

She came back for me.

She didn't have to.

She didn't need to.

But she did.

If I wondered where she stands regarding us, her actions have spoken louder than any words ever could.

My internal reverie is broken as the chariot hits something and tilts; I fall forward into Sephy who catches me, looking into my eyes for a moment before something distracts her.

They're catching up too fast.

"Here, take my sword," she hands me the weapon, eyes glinting at the challenge as we reel sideways around a corner, chariot wheels screeching. I look back as I right myself, at the demons, then at her.

"Won't you need this?" I demand, accidentally stepping on Erlea's foot.

"Ow," the Fury mutters, expression deadening. I give her an apologetic grimace.

"No. I've got these," Sephy waves her hands in the air, smiling as flames begin to flicker from the tops of her fingertips.

"Right then." I grit my teeth, watching as the demon masses close the final one hundred feet between us, and Sephy starts launching flaming projectiles.

She's continuous with her onslaught, missiles of fire flying into the air, but as Ericka begins to pull back her arm to draw the string of her bow, she almost elbows Thane in the nose. Thane moves, her face begrudging as she eyes Luce with concern. I can't deny I'm concerned too. When I'd first seen her, she'd been unrecognisable. Not even just in her appearance either, as her tone, her gestures, and the way she holds herself are now altogether more calculated, chill even.

The stampede of demons is impressive, but I don't have time to stare, the footfall of hundreds of paws, of claws, hitting the stone of the abandoned roads, ringing out into the otherwise silent dark, gaining on us with every passing second.

Ericka launches arrow after arrow, but her aim is consistently having to adjust due to the constant jolting of the cart beneath our feet. Even then, when an arrow does make its target, it rarely makes a kill shot, only slowing the demon down instead of taking it out.

I feel something nick the side of my neck and turn too late to see Erin throwing knives from the back of the Banshee, which she's now straddling in reverse. The blade hits its target, a Succubus trying to grab the chariot within its albino grasp that I'd been too distracted to notice.

"Duck!" Erin calls long after the projectile has hit its target, laughing to herself as she draws back another knife. Before she can launch it though, I take the sword in my hand, twisting on the spot and bringing it fast across the Succubus' throat with both hands, decapitating it. It wails for but a second, before its body falls in two separate pieces and is left beneath the tread of the demons following in its wake.

They begin to surround the chariot, so I grab Sephy, pulling her into me and shoving the sword beneath her arm, piercing the eye of a Banshee attempting to snap at her when she was otherwise occupied.

"Thanks—" she breathes, looking up at me.

We hang for a moment, words escaping us both, before her eyes dart beside me and she pushes hard on my shoulder. I bend at the knee, allowing her to jump up and dunk a ball of fire into the spine of a Gorgonian slithering in tandem with the cart.

"Uh, Sephy—" Luce calls out, voice barely audible over the din of rabid jaws snapping at our heels.

"Yeah, kinda busy here— what is it?" Sephy calls, turning and pushing me to her spine so I can cover her as I plunge my sword into the face of an Abraxian riding a Banshee.

That's novel, I muse, sighing.

Them working together is the last thing we need.

"The river!" I hear Luce call, and I twist, finding that her alarm is justified.

Before us, the River Styx separates the outskirts of the city from the beginnings of the Sanguine Forest, waters higher than I've ever seen them.

Shit.

"Luce, you're just gonna have to improvise!" Sephy exclaims, turning back to me and launching a palmful of fire over the top of my head. It lands atop the Banshee whose rider I've just slaughtered.

As the body falls away, it's replaced by another, who is shot through the leg by Ericka and falls, trampled beneath its Kindred brethren, lost in the chaos.

Hold on! I hear Luce's voice echo out inside my skull.

What the fuck was that?!

It's me you moron. Luce. Now hold on! The voice comes again, and so I brace myself, grabbing Sephy around the waist and pulling her close to me as The Furies and Thane flatten themselves against the edges of the chariot, holding themselves as steadfast as possible against the shuddering golden rim.

As the road turns to a ruddy riverbank beneath the wheels, my stomach lurches, and we take off into the air. We're at a narrow bend, and the Banshee before us is soaring through the air, following Beelz who had made the jump effortlessly before us. It lands with a thud, clearing the opposite bank of the river as the chariot crashes onto the edge, water sloshing up and in around our ankles. The beast rears, our weight dragging it back, but then catches sight of something far off in the distance and finds the strength to drag us up onto the blood-soaked soil of the forest on the other side.

"Xion! I need your phone!" Sephy exclaims.

I give her a quizzical look.

"But—" I go to question her, but she shakes her head, holding out a palm. I dig deep into the pocket of my jeans, finding the phone I had all but forgotten.

"Pray for a miracle," she instructs me before she jabs several buttons and puts the receiver to her ear as we continue to fly through the forest, blood spraying up from beneath the spin of the wheels.

I look back at the demons leaping across the river, keeping up the pursuit, and then to Beelz who continues to lead us through the forest.

Erlea takes out her katana, staring at me and nudging me with her elbow to do the same with my sword. We pass trees, and as we do, she shows me her intent, swinging her sword and cutting down branches that soar down as projectiles. The pounding of demonic encroachment is unceasing, but in the midst of it all, I hear Sephy.

"*Holy crap*! I got through! Who the *hell* is your long-distance provider?" she demands, grinning at me with one eyebrow cocked.

However, her face quickly returns to a more serious expression as we continue to hack down branches, only pausing now and then to lunge and take out a demon directly.

Ericka continues to pull back her bow time after time, and I cannot help but wonder how she's not yet run out of arrows.

"Yes, meet us by The Hollow— no not an axe, a *chainsaw*!" I watch her as she rolls her eyes at me, ducking one of the low-hanging branches right after it thwacks me around the back of the head. "Don't argue! I said a freaking chainsaw, Jules!" she exclaims, laughing at me, as I hear the tone of her prompt disconnect.

"Careful of low-hanging branches—" she comments, pursing her lips as I roll my eyes at her.

"Thanks for that—" I shake my head, reaching up to thwack at another branch, exhaling heavily.

"We're almost there!" Thane informs us.

Sephy looks around with desperate eyes.

"Does anybody have a—" she begins, but as she's staring at Erlea and me for use of our swords, I see Erin launch one of her daggers straight at us. I don't think, I just react, reaching out into the air and grabbing the blade before it goes flying off into the chaos of the pursuing demons. I pass it to her, smiling as she cocks an eyebrow at me.

"For someone with so little grace you can be a smooth bastard, you know that?" she asks.

I smile, blood rushing to my cheeks.

The chariot slows, and as it does Sephy is suddenly talking too loudly in my ear as she absentmindedly surrounds us with a layer of flame, which catches too slowly on the leaves scattering the ground.

358

This is not the only thing scattering the ground though. Here, bodies of guards have fallen from the trees to the ground, like a strange sick fruit, a greeting for the encroaching demons.

Beelz growls at them, slowing and pacing anxiously within the ring of flame separating us from the oncoming threat.

"When we get on the other side of The Hollow, we're going to cut it down. Well, you and Jules to be exact," Sephy tells me, and I stare at her, eyes wide.

"Sephy, what about The Fates, what about Yama and Muerta?" I demand.

"Are they worth unleashing this mess on the mortal world?" she asks me, her glance honestly curious. I sigh.

"No. They are not."

"Then the matter is settled," she decrees, taking the blade in her palm and slicing it across her pale flesh without wincing.

We dismount the chariot as a collective, and she passes the knife to me. I cut my own palm, letting out a hurried hiss before I pass it to Erlea. We approach The Hollow and I stay behind as Luce, who has Beelz in tow, Thane, and lastly Erin make their way into the portal, palms still bleeding as the Banshee who had brought us here rears up, no longer placated by Luce's dark influence.

With a final ounce of effort, I launch the sword in my palm forward, watching it spin through the air before landing firmly in the skull of the beast, which crumples to the floor, dead.

Turning, I let The Hollow take its last blood offering before stepping through and leaving a dark, burning Mortaria behind.

SEPHY

As Xion finally exits through the whirling portal of The Hollow, I release a breath that I've been holding captive until this very second. I shove the equipment in my palms to him, done with the dirty work for one day.

I'm freaking pooped.

The sun above is just falling from the grace of the sky, leaving behind a masterpiece of periwinkle blues, hot pinks, and creamy peaches.

As Luce, Thane, The Furies, and I take several steps back, Beelz takes off onto the grounds, and we watch as the two men in my life take down The Hollow in a glorious spray of splinters and cracking of wood. I take joy in watching Jules wield his chainsaw, thinking he's getting a little too enthusiastic as he and Xion attack one side of the broad tree base each. Their eyes glint behind protective goggles, destruction inherent in their testosterone-laced veins.

Finally, after around ten minutes of them exchanging masculine grins, I hear Jules call, "Timber!"

The Hollow falls to the ground, the sound horrific. Debris and dirt fly up as it impacts the earth closest to us, and I take a step back, giving Jules an irritated look.

Whoever asked if a tree still made a sound if nobody was around to hear it clearly never witnessed a tree falling.

"You can uh, dispose of this, right Jules, Xion?" I cock my head, giving the tree a swift kick. Jules nods, scratching his bald forehead with a gloved hand. I've blatantly caught him during cooking because he's still wearing an apron that says *Kiss the Cook* across the front. With this, I turn, gazing back at the group of women who look completely lost.

"Come on, you'll be staying here for a while. We should get cleaned up," I look at the state of them, Luce the best preserved out of the bunch with barely a hair out of place. The Furies sport multiple cuts and scratches over their arms and faces. Thane looks weary but otherwise unharmed, and I'm fine, except for a rather sore arm, which I'm pretty sure is a repetitive strain injury from consistently throwing fire. All in all, it could have been worse— but it also could have been better.

Mortaria has fallen, and now the continued survival of the universe hangs in the balance of its fate.

Still, it's not exactly my problem.

I'm sure The Higher Plains will be stepping in to help any day now, especially now Haedes is back up there and no doubt stirring up a storm.

"Come on—" I sigh, repeating myself and beginning to trudge back through the forest.

I don't look back again, but I can hear their footsteps, and so hurry forward as the sound of chainsaws revving up again drowns out all further sound.

We reach the edge of a line of trees and I stop, waiting for the group to catch up, taking in the house as Beelz creeps closer to me, belly sweeping the ground. I've seen it many times, but this is the first time I've ever appreciated it as home. Somewhere safe, somewhere away from the madness of The Underworld. Even before, it hadn't felt secure, but it's where I grew up, where I've found strength once again, where I had climbed from my own grave. It is undeniably home.

I wish I could still say the same for Mortaria.

Unfortunately, my connection to it has been destroyed, just as The Hollow has been reduced to nothing more than firewood.

I let the scent of clean air fill my nostrils, grateful for the lack of the metallic tang so resonant of the Sanguine Forest. I make my way across the lawns, swift as I approach the house, but as I move to make my way up the mocha stone steps leading to the front door, I hear the ear-shattering crash of metal on metal.

"Get behind me!" I exclaim, turning to face the source of the noise, fearing it may be Pandora, come to finish what she started, or worse, The Demon Lords.

As the women run to stand on the stone of the steps at my back, the panther leaping to stand in front of them, they collectively shield the door from whatever is approaching.

I glance around, finding not demons but vehicles.

Their tyres squeal on the gravel, a high-pitched crunch as the black SUVs rush directly at us. As the new rising moon is given a chance to shine down onto the scene through now intermittent cloud, I watch as five of the same black vehicles follow in the wake of the first, engines slowing as they brake only a few metres in front of me.

I stand, arms crossing over my corseted breasts, spreading my legs slightly wider and taking a deep breath as a chill moves the scarlet curls from my shoulders, ready for whoever might be inside.

The doors of the vehicles open, heavy-duty boots thumping down onto the ground, one after the other, as men identically dressed in black military camouflage exit.

I roll my eyes.

Fabulous. Just what I need. Jarheads. I sigh, stepping forward as the passenger side door of the vehicle that's leading the intrusion opens.

From within, a man with red, close-shaved hair disembarks, both feet hitting the gravel with a sharp pointed ring.

He's not an attractive brute either with a face that looks like a toe and some lovely scars which run in three parallel lines vertically from his eyebrow to his cheek on the left side.

"And who the hell are you? This is private property!" I exclaim, narrowing my eyes at him and pressing my lips into a straight hard line.

"Hello, Miss Sinclair. My name is Colonel," he introduces himself without a smile, his toe-face bulging in all the wrong places. Some people would think he looks intimidating, but I think he looks like he's compensating for something as I eye the gun strapped into a holster around his thigh.

"Colonel? Colonel—" I smirk, waiting for a name I can remember to put in my little black book of people I don't like. It's practically a novel by now.

"Just Colonel," he retorts without an ounce of humour in his tone.

"Ooh— *scary*. A man without a last name. Whatever will I do?" I snort, thinking about the escape I've just made. Compared to the demons, he looks like a plucked chicken with a superiority complex.

"We're here for it—" he gestures to Luce, who stands behind me.

I smirk.

"You mean Lucifer?" I demand, and he nods.

"We are under strict orders to detain her indefinitely," he explains.

"It's the whole anti-Christ thing, isn't it?" I cock my head, and he glares at me.

"That's none of your business," he sneers.

I bite my bottom lip.

Before I can think, I've acted. Convecting before his eyes and gripping him around the throat in a chokehold. With my free arm, I summon The Eternal Flame to me, letting the skin on the side of his face sizzle like wax ready to melt.

"Now seeing as how you already look like a human toe, I'm going to assume you won't care if I leave you burned to a crisp, but how would you feel about having your soul incinerated?" I whisper in his ear as I hear the audible click of semi-automatics being loaded behind me.

"Tell them to stand down, Colonel Toe. Or I will make sure your own personal hell makes Mortaria look like a nice little ocean-view bungalow for two—" I threaten him, and he chokes beneath my grip, trying to inch away from the flames.

"Tell them to stand down!" I exclaim, and he nods, signalling the men to drop their weapons. I relinquish my hold on him slowly, keeping the ball of flame alight in my palm just in case as the surrounding militants relax.

"Now, as I was saying, why exactly do you want Lucifer?"

"She's a threat to this world. We don't allow creatures with such dark potent power to just immigrate," he explains, rubbing his throat.

"And what about me? I'm powerful too—" I express, tossing the fireball up in the air and willing it to return to me, making it look like I'm about to start shooting hoops.

"So, it would seem. But you are not my concern. She is." He gestures to Luce once again, face unfeeling.

"Ah, well, you see, that's where we have a problem, you and I. She's my family. And I don't see you walking out of here with her. We take care of our own. If she needs putting down, I'll be the one to do it," I growl, and he blinks once, then twice, as I hear The Furies drawing weapons behind me.

"They're family too— and I wouldn't mess with them if I were you. They hate men— and you look sort of like a man to me— I think," I examine him with a grin, a mischievous glint born too fast in my eye.

As we're standing, tense, staring one another down— I see movement out of the corner of my eye. Jules and Xion must have finished dismantling The Hollow.

As they get nearer, I hear Jules' voice, addressing the man standing before me.

"Sandy?" he calls, coming into full view as his shiny shoes hit the gravel of the driveway. His apron has been removed and it is now draped over his arm, pristinely folded.

"That's right," the man responds, narrowing his eyes.

"Wait— wait! Your name is Sandy?" I chortle, and he nods, looking aggravated as I try unsuccessfully to stifle a laugh.

"What are you doing here?" Jules demands.

I cut in, further irritating Colonel Sandy Toe as is evident by his fast-furrowing brow.

"They want to take Luce. I'm in the middle of telling them over my dead body— well— you know what I mean." I wave away the technicalities of the situation and Jules frowns up at the red-headed Colonel.

"Tell the acting General I have this under control," Jules orders him, and he cocks his head.

"And who the hell are you?" the Colonel asks.

"I think you mean 'Who the hell are you, General—" he adds, and the Colonel's eyes widen.

"Call them if you don't believe me. I'll wait—" He brushes off the man as the surrounding grunts dressed in black remain silent, stone still, like ghosts. I stare at each one, finding the same haircut and the same broken spirit behind their eyes.

The Colonel does as Jules requests and pulls out his cell phone.

While he puts in the call, Xion and Jules both walk over to me.

"Who the hell are these guys?" I exclaim, tired.

"This is A.D.A.M. The unit I told you about," Jules explains.

"I kind of figured. They're not taking Luce out of here. Or anybody else. We need to stick together. If they try and separate Luce from Thane, we'll have a bloodbath on our hands."

"Agreed. They're not going anywhere." Jules nods, smiling up at Luce and giving her a small wave. I turn to face her, finding her waving back, though her posture shows how visibly tense she is as she clings to Thane, their fingers interlocked, Beelz pacing at their feet.

A breeze stirs around us and a shadow falls across my face as the Colonel approaches, hanging up the phone and stashing on a clip dangling from his belt.

"She says I'm to give you whatever you ask for," he grumbles, back poker straight as Jules looks at me with a grin.

"Awesome. Luce isn't going anywhere. None of us are," I decree, and the man shrugs.

"Whatever, it's your funeral," he mutters.

As he turns to call off the hounds, which still stand motionless behind him, Jules speaks up.

"Do you have any of those specialist medical doctors on hand?" he asks.

The Colonel stills mid-step.

"Yes, why?" he demands, not turning back to make eye contact.

"I think we could use some medical checks on everyone," he looks back at me and I nod.

I don't like doctors, but I do have some questions about how changed I've come back from The Nether.

Am I as I was?

Perhaps these doctors can give me the answers I've been searching for.

I turn to head up the stairs and into my home, when from behind me I hear Jules cuss, "Shit! The Soufflé!" before bolting forward, pushing me aside.

A Colonel called Sandy, a General fretting over a soufflé while sporting a Kiss the Cook Apron.

If I didn't know better, I'd think this was insane.

Turns out it's just my life.

31

SWAY

PANDORA

WE SPIN, GLIDING ACROSS the smoky crystal floors in a wicked ballet of dark intent. Barbas' dull gaze caresses me without so much as a hint of arousal as he twirls me from him in calculated time and my feet float across the crystal in an effortless pirouette. The violins played in the farthest corner of the room by several only too-willing guards whine out into the space, creating the perfect melodic majesty for such a dark waltz.

Barbas grins, clenching my waist in his palm as I return to him, our bodies flush. I wonder what he's so happy about, but before I can ask, the throne room around us is transformed into something different.

Where before the Exilia had surrounded us with shadowy facets on all sides, now I am within the clutches of another ballroom. This time though, my gut floods with resentment.

Solis Castra has the most stunning vertical ballroom you can imagine. With stained glass windows on all sides rising as high as five hundred feet, giving the Sephilim and Nephilim room to stretch their wings, holding their partners close and wrapping one another beneath thick blankets of glistening feathers.

Lilac, periwinkle blue, violet, and cyan panes catch the cobalt sun from outside the window, turning the space magical as the light is filtered and transformed even more beautiful before falling upon the faces of the blessed. I feel them at my back, a welcome weight I have missed. My wings beat against the cool fragrant air, laced with the scent of white roses as I hang, suspended amongst the grandeur. It is when I look back up, seeking the face of the Demon Lord, that I am reminded I am in the presence of Barbas. Now, the face of the man I had once thought of as my beloved is revealed instead. I can scarcely bring myself to stare upon him, let alone think or utter his name. So, I tighten my grasp on his arms, cocking my head.

"Barbas, enough—" I demand, the illusion of my fears, of being only one half of a whole once more, dissolving as quickly as they came.

I cannot wipe the smile from my face as I realise the reality of who I am now, of where we are now.

We continue to sway across the ballroom, floating on a cloud of effortless joy made possible by our utter and complete victory over the throne, which sits, now a cold puddle of warped and misshapen metal.

His long grey overcoat makes him appear rigid, spine perfectly straight beneath my hand that gently rests atop his shoulder. Mr Skinny Legs crawls over my fingers, making my stomach roll with unwarranted disgust, just as the doors can be heard opening at the farthest end of the hall.

"Xion is gone," Abraxis announces. I shake my head, his incompetence startling for someone supposedly so powerful.

"I assumed. Seeing as how I was paid a visit by Haedes' daughter—" I call, voice echoing above the rhythmic gut-made strings of the violins that continue to chirp against the stroke of their constituent bows.

"I don't know what happened— I went down to check on the prisoners, and he was just gone." He sounds put out, so I shrug.

"Forget about it. She can convect. It's no surprise she came for the boy," I'm feeling genteel in my condemnation, placated by success, and continue to dance with Barbas as I hear more footsteps approaching up the bony steps outside.

"Pandora," Anubis greets me, face lined with concern. Katerina, Gorgon, and Lilliana follow in her wake, entering the ballroom and staring at the décor with interest.

"Evening," I call, spinning even still within the confines of Barbas' spindled frame.

"The resurrection failed. Sephy Sinclair— she destroyed The Book of The Dead. And I see the sun is out as well. What did you do?" she demands, eyes blazing with fury. I smile at her.

"I did what you could not. I took the Exilia for myself. As for the resurrection, I am sorry to hear it failed, but you cannot be surprised, especially when your son is to blame," I remind her, watching Anubis' gaze dart frantically across the room.

"Where is he?" she demands.

"In the dungeons, I believe," I reply, curt as Barbas takes a bow and the melody that has been spurring us on fades into silence.

Gorgon takes a few steps across the floor, holding out a hand.

"May I have this dance?" he enquires, one of his eyebrows curving as it rises upon his slick forehead. Watching him hold out a hand I curtsey as the music begins to drum up again. He takes me in his arms as I look over his shoulder, watching Anubis turn promptly on her heel and make her exit, no doubt looking to recover her traitor of a son. Still, I suppose none of us should be surprised at his betrayal; the apple never falls far from the tree.

My fingers caress the velvet of Gorgon's bottle-green suit jacket and I observe as Barbas takes Katerina in his arms too. Abraxis offers a hand to Lilliana, which she accepts with half interest, and the six of us waltz in and out of the shadows cast down from the ceilings upon the floor. Phobias crawl among the chandelier, which hangs central to the room, and I watch as we revel in my victory.

I find myself looking into Gorgon's eyes, into his slits for pupils and finding admiration there, finding respect.

"You know, Lilliana is concerned," he announces, and I tilt my head, letting my dark curls fall over one side of my face in a torrent of inky sheen.

"I didn't realise she had the capacity for such a complex emotion," I muse. Gorgon smirks.

"When it comes to the hunger of her Kindred, she does—" he retorts.

"Hunger? I just took back their hunting grounds! They should be happier than Zeus in a whorehouse right about now!" I exclaim.

"Agreed, but I hear she has found her Kindred no longer satiated by Doppel Ichor. Apparently, you may have spurred their appetites toward fresher kills. Katerina is seeing the same thing amongst her Kindred too, an increased specificity to fresh blood," he explains.

"I'll take care of it. We don't need anyone but ourselves now. No Gods, no Goddesses. I will use our control of this place to tilt the Kindred Scales, to pull down the walls between dimensions. Then, I will bring Zeus to his knees," I vow, and he smiles.

"Vengeance looks good on you." He twists me out from his body as the compliment reaches me, and I smile. Glancing at the other two dancing couples, an idea strikes me, something unusual stirring in my gut.

"Would you like to come and take a look at the skies with me? It's quite the spectacle now the sun is dead." I extend the invitation to him, and he narrows his gaze, forked tongue flicking out to caress his bottom lip.

"Haedes' Solarium?" he enquires, and I nod.

"Yes, I've taken his room as my own," I explain. His brows rise on his forehead, surprised.

"I've always wanted to look at Mortaria from such a superior perspective. Lead the way." He finishes the dance, stepping back and bowing to me as I curtsey in return. I grasp his chill fingers in mine, pulling him behind me as I head out of the hall. We depart in hurried steps laced with unexpected anticipation, leaving the other Demon Lords behind to continue our dark waltz in melancholy time upon the grandiose floors of our new dominion.

"What a view—" Gorgon places his forearm against the window pane, staring out over the city below.

"It is," I agree, nodding as I let silence fall between us.

"I want to ask—" Gorgon looks at me, eyes glowing in the dark as we stand upon the midnight blue stone of the floor flecked through with gold.

"Ask— ask what?" I enquire, and he smiles, lips twisting and making him appear temporarily attractive as he places a hand on the back of his neck.

"I want to know about your story—" He looks embarrassed, a small chuckle escaping from between his lips. It surprises me.

"You know my story. I was a Kindred of Hera, then I ascended to become a Titan and was tricked into opening the box by Zeus. I fell here, only afterwards discovering I could not use the box to return," I recall, shuffling from one foot to the other as he shakes his head, slick hair unmoving.

"No, I mean you, your mortal story—" he elaborates. I cock an eyebrow.

"Not much to tell. I was a poor man's daughter who sold her body for survival— though my Aetherial union wasn't much better in that respect—" I sigh, remembering those nights, the nights he had climbed atop me and smothered me beneath his fast-beating wings as he took what he wanted. He would take to the skies after, disappearing beneath the glow of the golden moon and leaving me wanton, sore, as broken as an angel could be upon our wedding bed.

369

"Still— you must have found pleasure, at least once?" He eyes me, slit pupils caressing my silhouette in the dim light.

"Pleasure for women isn't important to men. At least not any man I've ever known," I retort, keeping my eyes fixed on the horizon.

"That's the saddest story I've ever heard—" Gorgon reaches out, taking my palm in his and bringing my knuckles to his lips. I feel an involuntary shudder run down my arm.

"Yeah well, heaven isn't all it's made out to be." I shrug, trying to resist the urge to weaken at the knees beneath the leather veil of my skirt.

"Good men might go to heaven Pandora, but bad men like myself we bring heaven to you. Come— my Queen." He blinks with both vertical and horizontal sets of eyelids, lashes fluttering closed as he delivers his free hand to my shoulder, turning me and caressing the side my neck as he leads me back down the spiral staircase and into the bedroom. I oblige him, swallowing hard, as moths flutter helplessly, decaying slowly within my gut as they struggle for freedom.

"What are you going to do?" I'm suddenly nervous as he takes off his jacket and slings it over an armchair near the now-extinguished hearth.

"I'm going to thank you for everything you've done for me and my Kindred. I'm going to show you how a man should pleasure a woman if he has any self-respect," he hisses the last two words, forked tongue flicking out to wet his bottom lip.

I can't speak, blood heating beneath my porcelain skin, fast breath caught hostage within my tightly buckled corset.

Gorgon looks down at me as he gets closer, unbuttoning his shirt and revealing his naked torso beneath. Snake tattoos climb up both of his arms, peeking out at me as I examine him, his thin waist, edgy pectorals made from scarce, thin muscle, and his protruding ribs. He's compact but well taken care of, groomed to within an inch of perfection, as all his body hair has been cleanly removed. I place my hand on the back of his neck, feeling the slick grease of his hair coat my fingertips as he tugs at the buckles of my corset.

Reaching up to my face as he does so, he buries his face in the nape of my neck, running his tongue down the curve of it as I inhale sharply, closing my eyes against my better judgement. The corset noticeably loosens, and I gasp as his lips travel down over my collarbone, tongue flicking in and out until he reaches and unleashes my remarkably swollen breasts. I've never had this feeling before, the way my stomach tenses and waves of electric sparks between synapses ripple down my limbs, causing my skin to heat but goosebumps to rise in regardless rebellion.

His lips tickle around the outside of each nipple as he drops to his knees, staring at me, eyes intense as they take in my vulnerable expression.

"Turn," he orders me.

I do without question, returning to a state of obedience easier than I've ever anticipated. I feel him unlacing my skirt before he lets it fall to the floor, leaving me standing in a garter belt, stockings, and thigh-high stiletto boots. He grins, holding out a hand to me as gets to his feet. He looks to the bed, leading me there.

"Lie on your back. I'll take care of everything else," he instructs me, and I frown.

What exactly is he intending to do?

My heart is thrumming in my chest, stomach tight with anticipation as desire unlike anything I've ever experienced drips slowly and evenly like sweet honey before pooling between my thighs. I crawl forward onto the sheets, my shoes still on, turning as soon as I reach the pillows close to the headboard. I lay, hair splayed out in loose curls around me as I remove the dark tiara from my hair, placing it onto the bedside table.

"What— what are you going to do?" I ask him, voice softening from its usual bark and spilling from me in merely a whisper.

"I'm going to make you come," he says, taking one of my feet and pulling the thigh-high boot from it so the velvet drags down my leg oh so slowly.

"But no man has ever made me— do *that* —" I express, weakening as his fingers begin to massage the ball of my foot. He only smiles wider.

"I know," he whispers, taking the other boot from my leg, this time by ripping it from my limb.

I expect him to climb on top of me, but he doesn't.

"Lie back. Relax," he commands me, and as I lay down against the plump pillows behind me, I hear him hissing into the air. I glance down at my almost naked body to where the air is beginning to ripple. Then I feel them, slick, slithering up over me and causing my skin to tingle, too sensitive from their master's touch.

"Relax, they're only to restrain you." He swallows hard, watching as the Gorgonians wrap around my wrists, pulling them to the bedposts, and then my ankles. They pull my legs apart, leaving me bare, exposed, and nervous. I swallow hard, heart hammering far harder than it should be.

"Ready?" he asks, kneeling on the wooden chest at the end of the bed.

"What— what are you going to do?" I repeat my prior question, completely out of my element as he lies between my legs flat on his stomach.

"Pandora, just relax. I promise you, you *will* enjoy this," he vows, and I exhale, not sure I have much choice. As I wriggle, the Gorgonians tighten around my wrists, stopping me from budging.

Well— I guess I don't really have a choice but to succumb— I reason, letting my eyes flutter closed as a small smile of foreboding spreads across my lips.

I don't watch, I surrender to sensation instead, afraid of what I might see. I feel him rip away my dark lace thong, position himself between my thighs, and begin to creep up my stomach with his fingers, teasing me. I let a tiny sigh escape my lips as forks of sensation strike across my skin. He reaches my breasts, and as his fingers of one hand close around my nipple, he does something that takes me utterly by surprise.

His hot mouth clamps over the apex of my thighs, hot and wet, causing my back to arch and a groan to fall from me. I'm unable to stop it, even if I wanted to, as I squeeze my eyes shut and a sensation more intense than anything I've ever known floods the epicentre of my pleasure, causing it to tremble.

He flicks his forked tongue over my trembling flesh, lapping at me, causing me to curse. I hear him laughing as he squeezes my breast in his palm, harder with each passing second. I writhe, the demons holding fast at restraining me, pulling my legs further apart as Gorgon pulls me closer to him and splays my labia wide with his fingers.

I don't open my eyes, not even for a second, letting myself become lost to his mouth, kissing me, caressing me in figure eights and endless circles. I groan over and over, and in my mind I'm in flight. Soaring above the clouds, banking left and right, climbing higher and higher with every motion of his tongue. I ball my fists in the sheets, the velvet soft beneath my clammy palms as the muscles in my torso, in my thighs, begin to tense.

"That's it— *Just like that—*" Gorgon encourages me, voice urging me only closer to the sun as I find myself unable now to even fathom the bed beneath me. I'm floating, gliding, bathed in a sensational light so intense that I could be drowning. My breath comes in quick desperate wisps, his name falling from me in too many moments of utter surrender.

Finally, I reach the sun, the intensity of the heat between my thighs building as my entire body tenses, clenching as he increases pace, refusing to relent until I'm unsure where there is left for my body to go.

I discover it, an explorer of these new skies as a final, intense, and gut-wrenching wave of ecstasy radiates out from where he laps at me, adoring my flesh, shuddering out through every single muscle within me. My eyes fly open as a cry bursts from my lips, and I begin to fall, so slowly, skin on fire, back toward the earth.

My descent from the skies is more pleasurable than anything I've ever known, and as the sweet ache within me works itself into no more than a gentle tide lapping at the shore, I bite down on my lip, the Gorgonians relinquishing their hold on me.

I look down at Gorgon, who is on his feet, an erection noticeably visible beneath his velvet suit pants.

I wonder if he'll climb on top of me— if he'll take me. I'm happy to oblige, happy in this moment to do whatever he asks of me, but instead he simply walks over to his shirt, which is discarded on the floor, giving a hiss as his demon Kindred return to him.

He stares at me, buttoning his shirt, as I run my long fingernails down between my bare breasts and then over my bare stomach, sore from such delicious clenching. I want to tempt him, but can only watch as he slips on his suit jacket and turns to me.

"Goodnight, Pandora—" he gives a curt nod, licking his bottom lip with a glint in one eye, as if tasting me is his reward.

He leaves me, spent and bare, splayed amongst the velvet sheets, without saying another word.

32

SOMETHING STUPID

<u>SEPHY</u>

THE NEWS HADN'T BEEN all that surprising. Most women would be devastated, but as the doctors had taken blood and run tests faster than should be possible by the current wait times at most general hospitals, it had been determined as true.

I'm barren.

I shouldn't be surprised. After all, I had come back from the dead, and even though I might physically seem perfectly normal, it's obvious from the way that the doctors had squinted at my biometrics that I'm anything but.

I sit, sipping whisky, processing the information, which I think I'd secretly known long before now.

I've never wanted a child. No part of me has ever desired such a thing. I think perhaps my childhood had been so lonely, and now with the discovery that I'm half Goddess, it seems unlikely I would ever be able to provide a child with the security and love I missed out on.

It's not the end of my world because it's never been a desire I've felt. I know I don't need a child to complete my life.

Beelz eyes me from the couch opposite, purring heartily.

"Jules, another—" I demand, sloshing my drink in the depths of the crystal tumbler, physically exhausted from everything that's happened.

We have taken it in turns to be escorted by the blonde female doctor to the makeshift clinic that's been set up on the opposite side of the staircase. So, I wait, patiently, pondering my results as the others take their turns.

As I down the dregs of my glass, I hear the metal rings of the flimsy blue curtain pull back over the steel railing. Luce and Thane step out from behind it together. Thane's arm is in a sling, and she looks pissed. Luce's expression is unfeeling.

I look to Xion who is sitting beside me, a glass of orange juice in his palm, the order of which had me rolling my eyes.

"Everything alright?" he enquires, eyes rising from the rim of his glass to Thane's arm.

"No. Luce screwed up," she spits, brow creasing in pain as she sits down beside Beelz with a sigh. She gives the Panther a scratch between the ears, as Luce folds her arms over her chest, continuing to stand over her lover.

"Well, I'm sorry. I didn't know that stopping you from bleeding to death was such a goddamn crime. Joints aren't exactly easy things to mend you know!" she growls, turning to me.

"Where can I sleep?" She's insistent as the request comes out more of a bark, and I think on this a moment.

"You can have my parent's old room, at the end of the hall down the left-hand corridor. It's pretty big so should suit you and Thane fine," I offer, and she nods, storming off up the staircase.

The truth is I don't care about the size of the room. I just want her close to mine so I can keep an eye on her.

As her hurried steps pound on the ebony velvet of the runner, her speed and force of motion cause the crystal chandelier overhead to tinkle.

"Sorry about her—" Thane sighs, rubbing her temple with her free hand.

"It's not your fault," I remind her, and she shrugs.

"So why do I feel like the world would be better off if I'd never fallen in love with her?" she asks, eyes serious.

"I don't know. Because you know that isn't true," Xion answers so I don't have to, as Jules returns to me with a whisky upon a tray. Being the astute individual he is, he's also brought the bottle.

"Thanks," I say in a soft voice, tired of the noise, of the yelling as I take the cold crystal to my lips, the fire of the whisky coating my throat as two sharp cubes of ice clink together. Thane leans forward, swiping the bottle from the tray before Jules can set it down.

"Do you mind?" she asks, and I shake my head.

"Be my guest." I nod as she removes the stopper from the fine vintage bottle, tilting it back and taking several huge gulps and slumping back into the sofa. As she lets the bottle drop back so it rests against the black fabric of her sling, I notice her eyes are visibly watering, though from the alcohol or emotional pain I can't tell.

"Jules, can you go and make sure that my parent's old room is stocked with towels and the like? Thane and Luce will be staying there for the duration of their time here," I ask, watching as he gives a curt nod and turns on the spot before beginning his ascent up the staircase.

He's been, as usual, amazing. Not asking any questions though I'm sure he's dying to. He's also made sure that the A.D.A.M assholes have kept their distance by stationing The Furies to watch over them, which I personally find a special kind of genius.

"Do you want any medical checks?" I look to Xion, who shakes his head.

"Nah, I'm fine," he replies, face void of expression. I can't help but wonder what they, Pandora and Barbas, did to him in the Exilia. I've never met anyone so withheld, restrained, and stoic, and yet when I'd found him on the floor of that cell he'd been bursting at the seams with emotional turmoil and practically unrecognisable.

I slapped it out of him, made the quick fix to get us out of Mortaria, but I know that no internal trauma can be fixed that easily.

"So— what now?" Thane stares at me, eyes intense, and I allow my expression to turn confused, like I haven't heard what she's just said.

"Excuse me?"

"Well, you're the one with the firepower now, right? What do you propose we do to take back the Exilia?" she hounds me, relentless as she takes another mouthful of alcohol. My heart deflates in my chest.

"I'm not the person who should be making any of those kinds of decisions," I protest, and she narrows her gaze.

"Are you kidding me?" she asks, and I shake my head.

"Nope. I'm not Haedes. I'm a demi-god with twenty-five years of reckless abandon under her belt and a thing for fast cars, leather pants, and well— apparently half-demons. Not ruler or decision-maker material I'm afraid," I sigh, bringing my glass to my lips and drinking deep.

"We can't just leave Mortaria in the hands of The Demon Lords and Pandora, Sephy—" Thane condemns me, and I glare at her, blinking a few times and trying hard not to lose my temper.

"What do you propose I do then? Go on— I'm interested to know what you think I could do that would be of any use," I challenge her, and she leans up, straightening her spine.

"You could convect back there and—" she begins, and I cock my head, interrupting her.

"Do what? Become demon food? The sun is extinguished, there are no souldier forces, the city is crawling with demons, and the Exilia is guarded by not only those demons, but apparently mortals— which I don't understand. What the fuck is up with that by the way?" I turn to Xion, assuming he knows as he exhales heavily.

"Pandora, she's been recruiting mortals and taking them to The Underworld using that stupid box—"

I feel my eyes widen.

"The disappearances downtown—" I whisper, fidgeting atop the couch, uncomfortable that I hadn't identified it as something mystical before.

It all makes sense now. Of course, Brad hadn't been responsible. I should have seen this a lot sooner. No mortal could just make humans disappear without a trace while leaving a trail of half-eaten demon snacks in their wake.

"Christ—" I exhale, leaning back into the chair and eyeing Thane.

"I'm sorry Thane, but this isn't in our hands anymore. I'm just a demi-goddess. I have no clue how to fix this. The best bet we have now is hoping that Haedes can fix things from The Higher Plains," she frowns, taking yet more alcohol into her mouth before wiping her liquor-soaked lips on the sleeve of the leather monstrosity she's wearing. I mean, hell, she's got the figure for a leather catsuit, but compared to her usual aesthetic, she looks like a teenage comic book nerd's wet dream. She gets up from the couch opposite, patting the side of her leg and indicating that Beelz should follow her.

"Can I take this?" she gestures to the bottle in her hand, and I shrug.

"If you like—" I reply, and she smiles, grateful and on the verge of drunk as she moves to leave.

"Oh— hold on—" I reach into the pocket of Xion's jacket he's still wearing, pulling out a string of black velvet attached to a glistening violet gemstone.

"I don't think I need to tell you to put this somewhere safe—" I say, offering her the necklace. She takes it from me, looking down at it with sad eyes.

"No. You don't. Thanks," she sighs, gripping the tether within the fingers of her injured palm and letting the whisky bottle fall to her side with the other. Xion and I watch as she climbs the stairs, slow but steady in pace, head dropped and staring at the floor as she ascends.

"Well, that was about as much fun as a lava enema—" I mumble, letting a sigh fall past my lips.

"Poor Thane, I've known her and Luce so long. I've never seen either of them this way, especially not her," Xion expresses, and I chew on my bottom lip thoughtfully.

As I'm pondering their predicament, I hear the front door open. Erin and Erlea escort Colonel Sandy Toe in, one of them on each side, weapons drawn and expressions serious. I almost laugh, mainly because the Colonel is giving them both the side eye and walking like he might pee himself.

"Colonel Sandy Toe," I address him with a smirk, and he glares at me. Erin unsheathes one of her daggers to examine it in the light with hilariously convenient timing, causing him to adjust his facial expression and cough, clearing his throat as anxiety possesses him.

"Are you all done with the doctor?" he demands, and I watch his gaze dart to the top of the staircase. Here, Jules appears from the left-hand corridor before promptly descending the stairs with the gentle pitter-patter of his beautifully polished loafers.

"Yes," I reply, setting my empty glass down on the coffee table.

"Very well. I have my orders. We will be going now," he dismisses himself as Jules finally reaches the bottom of the staircase.

"I'll escort them off the property," he informs me without breaking stride.

The doctor behind the opposite side of the staircase, a blonde woman whose name escapes me now, collapses the final privacy curtain and slams several metal cases full of medical equipment shut. I watch as the front door opens and several armed men in identical black camouflage come to help her with the equipment.

Within seconds, the entire troupe, equipment, Colonel, guards and all, have gone, leaving no trace that they were ever here except for the faint smell of too-potent boot polish.

"Thank god for that. I thought they'd never leave," I relinquish as the final echo of Jules slamming the front door shut behind him falls into silence.

I rise to my feet, manoeuvring around the coffee table and taking to the staircase, stretching my back, which gives an audible click.

I look back to Xion as I reach the halfway mark of my ascent to the landing, peeking back over my shoulder and the finely polished dark wood of the balustrade to where he remains, clueless, sipping his orange juice on the couch.

"Are you coming?" I demand, flicking my eyes upward in the direction of my bedroom. He startles, downing the rest of his orange juice and stumbling to his feet. He trips over the edge of the coffee table, and I push my lips together, trying not to laugh as he clambers after me.

XION

The last time I was in this room for any considerable length of time, I'd been sitting at her bedside, watching the shell of who she had become after returning from the dead. As I step in through the doors now, though, she's remarkably Sephy, perhaps more so than she's ever been.

Moonlight drips in through the window and down onto the pale carpet, creating a relaxed atmosphere. Silence falls momentarily between us as I shut the door behind me.

"What did the doctor say about you? Everything okay?" I demand as she walks through to the bathroom, turning on a tap and wetting her face. I watch as she unfastens the corset from her torso, letting it fall carelessly to the floor. She walks back down the steps of the bathroom, a strapless bra and thong her only attire once she strips off her pants.

"Yeah. Everything's fine. I'm barren, but you know, other than that little revelation, I'm perfectly— well— better than mortal fine, but not quite full god fine. If that makes sense?" She's rambling as she walks across the carpet to me, placing her hands around my waist and looking up into my eyes, expectant.

"Wait— what?" I double take, blinking slowly as I stare down into her porcelain face, into the heated depths of her cognac irises.

"I'm barren— you know, *infertile*?" she cocks her head.

"Yes, Sephy, I know what barren means," I retort, staring at her hard, trying to work out if she's about to break down in tears. "Don't you care?" I ask. She lets a hysterical giggle escape her lips in a sudden unexpected burst.

"Are you kidding? Can you see me at 'Mommy and Me'? Do I strike you as the bedtime stories and midnight feeds type of girl? Because

379

if so, I'd say I need to reintroduce myself." She smirks, and I feel my heart sink a little. She's so cavalier about it.

"But— what if— what if you *want* a baby in the future?" I ask, face serious, and she shrugs.

"Look, we've been all worried about that stupid prophecy ever since The Fates told us a child made by you and I could potentially end the world or whatever, now we don't have to worry anymore. I thought you'd be happy," she admits. I sigh.

"You and I won't always be together, Sephy. As you've already said, there's nowhere for this to go. You can't love me. I can't make you. It's fun, right? It'll run its course, and then you'll move on. What about if you want someone else, want his child?" I ask her. She pauses a moment, looking down at the floor, and then shakes her head, her fiery hair becoming voluminous as she bites her bottom lip.

"And what about if when I look into the future all I see is you?" she asks me, face earnest.

I inhale sharply, breath caught in my chest as my heart flutters unwillingly like a stupid fragile butterfly or something equally as pointless.

She inches closer to me, moving in to kiss me as her breath becomes husky and wanton in my arms. I inhale the scent of cinnamon, head swimming in her, close to being pulled under by the weight of my feelings. The hot red of her hair, the cool white of her skin, the fiery sizzle of those cognac irises— she's like a drug made specifically to torment me. The kiss deepens as she pushes my jacket from my shoulders and it falls to the floor. I feel myself becoming erect fast as she pulls my t-shirt over my head next but stop her, grabbing her by the shoulders.

"Stop," I snap, fear running riot as every one of my muscles tenses beneath her scorching fingertips.

"Why?" she asks me, and I shake my head.

"I can't. I *can't*—" I repeat, unsure of how to explain what I'd been shown, how to expose the sickness inside of me.

"What did Barbas show you?" she demands, reaching up and touching the side of my face with the soft pad of her thumb.

"Nothing I don't already know. I'm a demon. A killer," I murmur, and she looks up at me, eyes wide.

"I don't care," she retorts.

"I do. I don't want to hurt you," I challenge her, balling my fists and trying to restrain myself as I stand before her, throbbing and bare.

"Oh, don't make me laugh! I'm the one who can't commit to you. Can't find the courage to feel for you. The only one of us at risk here, Xion, is you. And that's not stopped you before. I won't let it stop you now. You need this, after today. So do I. We deserve it. Don't you think?" she pleads, looking guilty as I take a deep breath.

"Besides—" she adds, eyes glinting, "You could try and hurt me all you like, but I can't promise you won't end up burned to a pile of not-so-handsome ashes in the process." It's a valid threat; she has the power to end me, to decimate my soul— and I'm not only talking about her ability to conjure The Eternal Flame either.

She'd kissed my darkest face, looked me in the eye when I'd presented the worst part of myself.

And yet, she's still standing here, after everything, so why am I waiting?

I'm no saint, no pure thing.

She's everything I want.

So, I take her.

My kisses run rampant across her hot flesh as I stare up at her from where my lips are caressing her navel. She's lying back on the bed and I'm hovering above her. The room is dark, the lights dim, and outside the window, stars twinkle. She's not pure, at least not in the virginal sense. She's pure fire instead; untameable, heat quite irresistible after the merciless chill of the real world outside these four walls. I feel her eyes tracing me as she lies back against the pillows at the head of the bed, tracing the palm print she'd left above my heart.

"Kiss me," she demands, reaching down to my face and guiding me up the length of her naked body. Her lips find mine, desperate as her tongue flicks in and out of my mouth, hungry for me and me alone. Her scent blankets me, the warmth of her skin leaving me drowning in her presence as my erection lies flat, throbbing and hot against the taut muscles of her stomach.

I bring a hand to the side of her face, caressing her cheek before burying my fingers in her hair and pulling to expose her neck. I bury myself in the nape of her and let my tongue caress her until I reach her earlobe. Sucking, I hear her emit a groan, which only spurs me on with greater ferocity.

As I crawl back down her body, lining myself up, I feel her, wet, hot, ready— *mine*. As she envelops me, I cry out in a hollow exclamation, filling her to the hilt.

I thrust, feeling her clench around me, her legs cradling me as her heels dig into my muscular, bobbing ass. I crawl back up her body, kissing slowly as I make shallow thrusts, enjoying the anticipation of her trembling folds.

"Sephy—" I breathe, before kissing her and stroking her jaw with my free hand. I let it trail down her body, stroking around the outside of her breast as I enter her fully again, placing both arms on either side of her body and rearing up so I can go as deep as possible.

I need this.

Need her.

She's mine like this.

I groan as I inch in and out of her slowly, teasing her as her eyes glisten with malice, building my own release slowly, too slowly almost. I'm playing a game of control with myself, and I'm winning. She makes me a winner, makes me the dominant, as I know that with her, demon or not, human or not, she can take whatever I'm willing to give.

I plunge deep, twisting my hips and experimenting as her eyes widen.

"You like that?" I whisper in her ear, lowering myself so I can feel her erect nipples pushing into my body, scorching points like small stars in the galaxy of our sexual pleasure.

Our hips grind together, inching, thrust by thrust, stroke by dripping stroke, towards a supernova.

She looks up into my eyes, pupils dilating as I continue the slow torturous rhythm, making her squirm and writhe beneath me, helpless to my whim.

She orgasms, tightening in an explosive gush of hot and sticky nectar, coating me, and pushing me over the edge in a torturously slow wave.

It overcomes me inch by inch, causing my fists to ball in her hair as I breathe in the scent of cinnamon, feel her pulse against my lips, hear her cries turning to small whimpers of ecstasy.

The words slip from me in a desperate cry, right beside her ear.

"Sephy— oh god, *Sephy— I love you so much.*"

33

BEWITCHED, BOTHERED, AND BEWILDERED

LUCE

THE HOT WATER RUNS, bloody, down the drain. I reverse its polarity, causing the scarlet to spin the wrong way as the tiny tornado rages beneath my feet. I look up into the onslaught of the water, raining down from overhead, letting it bathe me, clean me, purify my sins, and wipe away what I have done.

It's over now.

I look down at my naked body, at the way black veins mar what had once been flawless porcelain, alabaster silk pulling taut over my skeleton, making me beautiful. My black hair is made only darker by the water too, and I watch as the streams from the locks falling over my breasts run gradually clear. Jules had brought towels, white towels, reminding me of the bloody mess beneath my clothes. I want to be clean before Thane gets back because I don't have the energy for another argument.

Pushing my hair flat against my skull with both hands, I think about the way she'd condemned me for not healing her shoulder completely. I had done my best, gone to save her, sacrificed so much to keep her here with me.

So why isn't she grateful?

I try not to let her expression, the way she continues to glimpse at me with disgust, disarm me, but it's difficult. Her eyes have always held such adoration, and now that seems to have all but diminished.

I turn off the hot water, stepping out of the shower and into the pastel green of the ensuite bathroom that had once belonged to Sephy's mother and father. The tiles beneath my feet are cool, the colour of sand, and cut into perfectly angled hexagons, a pattern far more precise and simple than anything else in life can claim to be.

I drip onto the floor as I reach for a towel on the heated rail beside the sink, wrapping myself in it and finding a stark dark contrast against the white linen where my skin is clean but unmistakably marked by The Well, water droplets beading over every inch and magnifying the intermittent inky paths beneath.

The mirror doesn't lie to me, the light fluorescent and unforgiving, relinquishing a truth about what will be my existence from now on. A truth that cannot be ignored.

I succumbed to it, the dark.

For her.

And now there is no going back.

I made my choice, and I know now I would choose the same again in a heartbeat.

There is no question in my mind; she is and always has been the answer to every query that means anything to me.

I step out of the bathroom, tightening the towel around the top of my breasts and inhaling the scent of fresh red roses as I enter the bedroom. I remember this scent, the pungency of it unforgettable. It surprises me, but after all this time, traces of Demi still linger, no matter how small.

I tread over to a vanity on the far side of the room that stands, delicately carved in pale wood, beside the extinguished fireplace.

Darkness prevails outside the arched window, which looks out over the grounds opposing the bed, the moonlight drizzling in, unhindered, before it falls too pure upon the cream of the carpet.

Sitting down in front of yet another mirror, I look down at the objects before me. A wooden hairbrush, a box of tissues, and a pump bottle of old perfume, the glass of which is twisted into an odd statuesque shape. I look at the items, cocking my head. Before I realise what I'm doing, they're rising from the surface of the desk, protesting gravity. I let them ascend, rotating slowly in a threesome before me.

Staring at them, I find myself absorbed, so much so that the sudden slamming of the bedroom door behind me causes me to startle, the objects falling unceremoniously back to the desk with a clatter.

"What are you doing?!" Thane demands.

I shrug, watching as Beelz crosses the room, curling up by an armchair near the window in a puddle of moonlight.

"Nothing," I reply, fear flooding my gut as the feeling that I've been caught like a child with my hand in the cookie jar clutches me, causing my heart to struggle within the confines of my ribcage, frantic.

"Don't lie to me. I've had enough," she sighs, taking a swig from a dark bottle clutched in her palm. I watch her in the mirror as she swallows, not turning to face her.

"I'm not lying. I'm just sitting here," I exclaim, allowing my eyes to widen in frustration. I cross my bare legs beneath my towel and watch as she shakes her head.

"Whatever," she snaps, slumping onto the side of the bed and placing the bottle of whisky on the pine of the bedside table. A glisten of indigo catches my eye and I breathe out, relieved as I figure she's at least got her tether back in her possession. "I'd super appreciate it if you'd whip up some clothes for me that don't make me look like a prostitute if you're using magic like a party trick now, by the way," she blurts, and I wonder how much she's had to drink. I don't remember her ever speaking to me this way before.

"What the hell is your problem?" I burst, spinning on the padded blue stool of the vanity, glaring at her.

"Me? Well, how about the love of my life drank from the most potent source of dark magic in the universe and didn't give a damn about the consequences?" she exclaims.

"I didn't have a choice, Thane!"

"No! You did have a choice! You chose wrong, Lucifer!" She's on her feet now, muscles visibly tensing beneath the leather of her catsuit.

"Choosing you was wrong, was it? Choosing to keep you here with me instead of sending you back up to those— *those hypocrites*— that was *wrong*, was it?" I demand. I've known this argument has been brewing, but it doesn't make the words spilling from either of us any less shocking.

"Yes! Putting our personal lives over the balance of everything in this universe is wrong! It's selfish. I thought you were better than that, purer than that!" she crosses her arms, and I scowl.

"Well, maybe, maybe I'm not! Maybe I'm not some blonde-haired, doe-eyed angel who is just misunderstood. Maybe I am really what they've always said I am. Maybe I'm selfish. Maybe I'm just like him, my father! But you said you loved me, all of me. Was that a lie?" I question her, heart pounding and blood roaring, tainted, in my ears.

"I didn't fall in love with this—" She gestures to me, standing in a towel, vulnerable and exposed in my darkest shades.

"And I didn't fall in love with a stuck-up bitch! But here you are!" I spit, blinking several times after the words fall from me.

This isn't how I intended this to go. I don't even know if I just meant what I said. All I know now is that my temper has just unleashed something I don't know if I can take back.

"Nice." Thane glowers at me, grey eyes darker than I've ever seen them. Tumult lies, unmistakable, beneath the glassy surface, indicating a lack of willingness to back down.

"Look, I'm sorry. I know this is not how either of us thought this would go. But you can't deny, Thane, that I saved you," I implore her, and she smirks, shaking her head.

"No. Sephy Sinclair saved me. You tried to put my life force into a malevolent God of Ancient just to keep me here. And what's worse, you compromised and cheapened whom I've always thought you were to do it. How is that *saving* me exactly?" she asks, and my fists ball at my sides.

"Please, Thane. Don't say that. Nothing about me has really changed. I'm the same Luce I've always been. Except now I'm not as helpless as I was before." I rise from the vanity stool, closing the distance between us as I tread around the width of the bed, gliding to her with wistful slow strides.

As I get within touching distance, I wave a palm, and before she gets a chance to move, which I think she contemplates, the leather catsuit is gone, replaced by a thin cotton white shirt and black slim-cut slacks. She looks like her again, like my Thanatos.

"There. I'm sorry about the clothes. I was— I wasn't thinking," I make the excuse and she visibly slumps, the sling holding her arm more noticeable now against the white of her shirt. "And I'm sorry about this. I didn't mean to screw it up. I just couldn't bear to see you hurting—" I whisper, softening my gaze and allowing my pupils to return to their usual baby blue. I reach out to touch her shoulder, but she leans back, flinching so she's flush to the bedside table behind her.

I want her so badly. Want to touch her, to tell her I love her and make her remember who I am, who we are together, but the way she looks at me is no longer the same.

Maybe if I—

I let dark intent seep down my arm, as I move my palm to her cheek, caressing it. I watch as she wavers a moment, swaying left and then right, before her brow furrows and the connection forming between

387

us frays too fast to be repairable. It snaps, and she shakes her head, a sudden ferocity lighting beneath the surface of her gaze.

"What the fuck was that?!" she spits, shoving me back with her uninjured arm.

I stumble slightly as I move with the force of her action, sighing out.

"I just thought— I thought it would be easier if I could make you relax—" I stumble over my words, and she lets out a guttural grunt of disgust, like she might be sick.

"So, you thought if you could placate me, you could *fuck* me into loving you again? You thought you could just use your fucking magics to make this go away? To turn me into your what— dog? Who the fuck are you!?" she yells, more furious than perhaps I have ever seen her.

"Thane wait, no, I didn't—" I stutter but she puts up a hand.

"Shut up. No really. Just stop talking. I've had enough. You aren't who I thought you were Lucifer. You're not who I fell in love with. Not anymore."

She turns on her heel, grabs the whisky bottle and her tether in her long willowy fingers and storms out of the room.

I'm left, standing as the sound of the door slamming within its frame echoes out into nothing.

I didn't mean any harm— I just wanted to fix things.

I didn't want to drink from The Well— but Pandora hadn't given me any choice.

I didn't even want Thane to be happy about my choices, but I at least expected her to respect my reasons for making them.

Why is it that I can't seem to catch a break?

I no longer have a home, Haedes is gone, my relationship is in tatters and none of this is even my fault.

It's not fair.

Still, maybe I can salvage my relationship.

I ponder this as I let the towel fall to the floor in a mess, taking a moment to stare at Beelz who lies, motionless in the dappled moonlight. I envy her, envy her contentment, her stillness. Nobody questions her power or whether the innate savagery running through her veins is right or wrong. It's just who she is.

Moving to the closet on the opposite wall, I find a towelling robe with the Sinclair monogram embroidered on the breast and wrap myself in it, frozen inside and out.

The chill doesn't relinquish when I rub my arms or when I get into bed with no inclination to do anything but find unconsciousness.

When I wake, I'll find Thane. I'll make things right. When I wake, I'll mend what needs to be mended.

After all, I've never been so powerful, and there's nothing I won't do to fix whatever I've broken between me and her.

She's my life, my world.

But first, I'll find solitude and comfort in the darkest recesses of my mind.

First, I'll rest, and when I wake to a new day, everything stained by my darkness will be wiped clean once more.

SEPHY

I lie awake, bewildered. My bare skin is chill as I stare up at the ceiling, going over the last few hours in my head.

When I look into my future all I see is you—

I cringe.

Why had I said that?

I know deep down it's true. I know that despite the fact I'd been slightly tipsy on whisky, and that I'd been relieved after the terror I'd felt at the thought of losing him, it's not even close to being a lie or an over-exaggeration. But why had I let those words loose on the world? Why was I being such a sentimental idiot?

But then— then he'd gone and done it. I mean, *really* gone and done it.

Putting the final nail in the coffin of my uncertainty about him.

I love you so much.

Fuck.

I am so not equipped for this.

I could justify it when I thought he had feelings, but *love*?

My stomach rolls, fear clutching at me as if by this admittance, Xion has doomed us both to hell.

Haedes' voice echoes out in my restless mind too.

Your mother would have been the undoing of this universe. A part of me thinks that's why fate took her so soon. If I'd had to choose between her—and my duties as a god, it wouldn't have even been a question in my mind.

Maybe I do love him, despite myself. Maybe that's what this constant concern, constant terror for another is.

Is this love?

Even if it is— I'd never admit that. I mean come on. It's asking for trouble. Everyone around me is doomed to suffer and die, or so it would seem. After all, Haedes had been just fine until making my acquaintance. He didn't even make it a year once I'd walked into his life, and he's a god. So, what the hell kind of chance does Xion have?

I don't have the energy to fight fate, or the powers that be. I just want to stay out of it all, but it would seem, as much as my desire to cleave myself from The Underworld grows with each passing disaster, that the universe has other ideas.

I sit up, feeling him stir beside me. I hadn't replied to his confession, hadn't even acknowledged there was one. Instead, I'd simply written him off as being mind-numbingly close to orgasm and completely out of his mind.

I should be so lucky.

Deep down though, I know. I know he means it. I feel it every time he looks at me. The way his fears show their true face in my presence and then seem to disintegrate beneath my gaze.

What is it about him that I find so hard to step back from, so difficult to break free of? I never had this problem with any of the other men in my life, but for some reason, he and I are like a moth and a flame, doomed to continuously enthral until one of us is burned to a freaking cinder or worse.

Seeing as I'm the flame in that analogy, I doubt the cinder will be me.

I'm more likely to just kill everything and everyone around me than succumb to death myself, especially after everything I've been through.

That's what makes me who I am. The fact that I don't care what anyone takes from me, because I've already lost it all— now though, that doesn't seem to be true.

When I thought Xion might be in trouble, I'd become passionate and driven in a way I had thought long lost to me. It was the way I'd felt desperate before I'd been murdered that night, the way I'd been willing to change everything about who I am to claw my way to a better life for us.

Once I'd crawled out of the grave, though, that had been gone, I'd thought forever.

I'd been wrong.

I get out of bed, pondering this as I stretch up to the ceiling, before making my way around the bed and over to my closet. The night is still fairly young, and though before I'd felt exhausted, my tumble with Xion and his little confession has left me wide awake despite everything that has already happened today.

"Sephy—" I hear his voice call into the dark before the bedside light flicks on, illuminating me. I don't stop walking, restless even more so now I'm under the scrutiny of his gaze.

I walk into the closet with speed, grabbing some jeans, fresh under-wear, and a tank top before yanking on the clothes as quickly as I can. Once I'm dressed, I grab a pair of boots and exhale, wishing I could mentally block his words out or erase the memory entirely.

"Wait— you're leaving again?" he demands as I walk back into the bedroom, fully dressed, with the pair of boots in one hand.

"I want to go out," I shrug, and he sighs.

"This is about what I said, isn't it? About the fact that I said I love you."

"Oh, yes, *that*," is the only reply I can come up with as I push the tangled, red curls of my hair behind one ear and lean down to pull on a boot, not meeting his gaze.

"I meant it you know—" he whispers, voice hoarse, like he's afraid.

Pulling on my other boot, I press my swollen lips into a hard line. I can feel where he's been, every inch of my skin humming or sore.

"I don't doubt that," I reply, and his eyes become hollow.

"I see—" he whispers, and I feel my heart break.

If I say it back, even if it were true, it wouldn't mean anything. Not really. They're just words, right?

"I'll be back later," I inform him, bending to the floor to grab his leather jacket before placing it around my shoulders and inhaling the scent of pomegranates, forbidden as the day we'd met.

He doesn't try to stop me, just shuffles down under the sheets as I turn and walk from the room, closing the door behind me and leaving him in the dark.

I make my way through the silence engulfing the estate, exiting through the front doors and leaping down the two front marble steps, feet hitting the gravel with an audible crunch as I try to stay distract-ed. I enter the garage, select a pair of keys, and unlock the Vanquish, which I haven't driven in far too long.

Shoving the keys into the engine and putting on my seatbelt, I close the door and sit back a moment, trying to relax. I press the button on the steering wheel to heat the underneath of my leather seat, relishing the warmth seeping into the sorest part of me as I lean back against the headrest, breathing hard.

I need to get out on the open road, feel the tarmac swallowed beneath my tyres, I need to get away from this house, away from everyone even slightly linked to Mortaria and the mess I've left behind.

I turn the keys and rev the engine as I find the bite point, easing up ever so slightly as I push down on the accelerator once more. The garage door opens automatically and moonlight floods the silver hood as I draw the car out into the night.

I edge down the gravel driveway, looking out into the copses of trees on either side, somewhat paranoid that I may be being hunted without my knowledge.

Then again, why would Pandora hunt me now? She has what she wants.

As I reach what had once been the electric gates at the end of the estate, I sigh, rubbing my forehead with long warm fingers. The gate has been damaged and needs repairing, no thanks to the jackasses who had busted in here like I was harbouring a goddamn criminal less than several hours ago.

I mean where were they when Pandora was hunting me before or when these demon attacks and abductions were taking place?

They don't seem to be of shit use to me— but maybe I'm just an overachiever.

I pull through the damaged gates, taking a moment to glare, irritated, at the scrapes and dents in the metal before I accelerate onto the open road and set to driving the normal route I take into central Chicago.

It doesn't take long for the trees of Forest Glen to become sparse, replaced by the concrete arteries that make up the interstate as I join it, the traffic barely existent at this time of night.

I rev my engine, putting my frustration into the car as I speed up, watching the world flash past me in a blur. I wonder as I speed toward the city if it will look like this in just a few days— a few hours.

How long will it take before the universe begins to unravel at Pandora's hand? Will the skies bleed red? Will demons start to encroach on every continent— or will it be gradual— an under-acknowledged slew of unexplained murders, which escalates over years into total unrestrained chaos, death, and bloodshed?

I'm such a ray of fucking sunshine. I muse to myself, wondering when everything became so complicated.

Was that before I was unceremoniously murdered, or after I was resurrected from beyond the grave?

I guess I'll never know, because everything on a personal level in my life is beginning to bleed slowly into the mythical. I can feel it, and I know I am being dragged, kicking and screaming, to hell.

That doesn't mean I have to accept it.

So, I race toward the city, toward Retropolis, toward a time in my life that had been simpler and, by no small understatement, far more fun.

I don't know what's coming, but I know how to comfort myself and placate the growing sense of fear that everything in this world is about to disintegrate.

All I need is a fine whisky, a good beat, and some disco lighting to boot.

34

I'M NOT IN LOVE

LUCE

THE SUNLIGHT FALLS THROUGH the window, a chill breeze stirring me from the depths of sleep. I roll over, hands splaying through the sheets, searching for her, but she's not there. I can't hear Beelz's usual purring either so sit up, blinking and disoriented.

Her silhouette is cast from the bright sunrise outside the window, and I exhale with lead-like relief settling over me, finding her sat with her back to me in an armchair across the room.

"You came back—" I whisper, but she doesn't reply. She doesn't even move.

I know I need to make this right, fix things, so I promptly swing my legs over the side of the bed, letting the cold from the window she's opened clutch at me, causing goosebumps to rise in protest across my skin.

I pad over to the armchair, its tall back facing the room, shielding her from view.

"Thane, baby—" I whisper, placing my hand upon the silk of the armchair's decadent upholstery. As I round the wings of it, I find her, still, looking out at the sunrise, unblinking.

My heart stops in my chest, spluttering and failing in its rhythm.
No.

I scramble forward, dropping to my knees as a begrudged Beelz moves out of my way without so much as a sound.

I look into her eyes. They're glazed, empty, the endless calm after the storm. Her pale skin is bathed in sunlight, but she's cold as ice. One of her hands is stiff upon the arm of the chair, but the other, the other is wrapped tightly around something.

I take the chill skin of her body into my palm, which is now scorching as adrenaline hits my system.

Prying her fingers open, I find it.

The shattered pieces of a single indigo stone, broken and jagged upon the soft pallor of her lifeless palm.

I fall back onto my naked heels, staring at her, shocked as I begin to hyperventilate.

I can't cry; this is so beyond what tears can solve.

All I can do is panic.

Thane— is *gone*.

She left me.

SEPHY

Sitting at the bar in Retropolis, I notice how Simon stares at me, making his final checks on the stock behind the counter.

"Hey, it's closing time," he hints that I should leave, so I shrug, hopping down off the lime green stool I used to frequent far more often than I have of late. He'll add the drinks I had tonight to my running tab, which I clear at the end of every month, so I don't need to pay for them now. I'm left feeling empty, not wanting to return home and deal with any of the emotional unrest that I know is coming from my sudden departure. Not to mention, I now have a house full of fiery women, including but not limited to one extremely unstable Lucifer and three archaically feminist Furies.

Sighing, I move towards the exit, the club empty except for me, which I didn't even notice until I glanced over my shoulder.

This place doesn't hold the appeal it once had; that's for sure.

Before, when I'd come here after crawling my way back from oblivion, I'd thought it was the trauma of the world, the realisation of vulnerability that had diminished the joy I feel. But it isn't.

It's not even the club.

It's me. I know it is.

I'm numb, unable to find the joy to dance, unable to want to drink myself stupid for fear I might say something I regret to Xion on returning home. I'm buzzed, having consumed a fair amount of whisky, but over the many hours I've been sitting, going over and over the events which have passed in my head, I've failed to reach the point of drunk.

I'm not the Sephy Sinclair who had danced with many different men upon the flickering square disco lights of this dance floor, I'm the Sephy Sinclair who is fighting the fact that she only ever wants to dance with one man. One man who wants the exact same thing.

And yet—

If I hope— if I try— failing— losing him, will utterly destroy me.

Even death wasn't as irreversible as breaking the pull I have to Xion, that level of understanding without having to utter a single word. I've never had anything like it, never met anyone like him. If I admit it's real, admit the truth— it's one more thing to be used against me and then taken away.

So instead, I'll hang in limbo, as painful as that is— and try to forget in between the brief glimpses of what could be when I'm consumed by his touch and cradled in his arms.

I descend the stairs, turning my back on the nightclub, on what had once been, and heading out into the bright early morning sun of the Chicago city streets.

The sky is a burnt orange, a new day breaking over the horizon as I hear the hollow ring of my boots upon concrete. I place my hands in the pockets of his leather jacket. Unwillingly inhaling him, missing him so deeply it makes me feel sick.

I can't go back to the Estate yet. I can't. The whisky has made me weak, and who knows what I might say— what I might do.

I mustn't ever tell him the truth because if I do, then it'll be almost impossible for either of us to walk away when the time is right.

I turn a corner, heading back towards my car, debating on sleeping in the front seat just so I don't have to go back home. I can't drive— I'm over the limit, and convecting is too fast, too simple.

It's as I'm pondering how comfortable the driver's seat of my Aston Martin will be that I hear it.

A scream.

My ears prick at the sound, almost as if I've been waiting for something like this to happen.

Before I know what I'm doing, my feet are pounding against the pavement, my heart rate skyrocketing, blood rushing in my ears. A sudden downpour of light rain causes the sidewalk to turn slick beneath my frantic pace as I skid around the corner, finding the source of the scream to be a side alley which is still encased in the shadow of the night, not yet chased away in this early hour of dawn.

"Help! Help me!" The voice belongs to a young man dressed in black trousers and a black shirt. He's probably a bartender from one of the clubs that's only just closing its doors, but that's not what makes me smile. What makes me smile is the Banshee and two Succubi that have him backed against a wall.

"Hey!" I yell out, letting my instincts take over.

I step into the cover of the alley, Eternal Flame striking a scorching blaze in both palms.

The demons turn, allowing the man the time he needs to run in the opposite direction and out onto the well-lit main road opposite.

"You don't belong here," I growl, widening my stance and preparing as the three demons launch forward without pause, eyes narrowing on me as their single focus and new target.

As they get closer, with each paw pounding upon the slick concrete, every snarl that hits the fresh spring air of the morning, my lips curve into a wicked smile, revelling in their challenge.

Love— *never*.

But this, *this* I can handle.

EPILOGUE

HAEDES

I LIE BACK, FEET propped on the opposing armrest of what had once been my couch. Now, though, it isn't. Now, it's some hideous, blue, silken monstrosity with seaweed embellishments, belonging to a couple of burly sea gods living in my, again, once stylish and relatively peaceful apartment on the Elysian coast.

Panpipes.

All I hear now is freaking panpipes.

Lir and Sedna aren't exactly what I'd call terrible people, but their taste as a couple is downright criminal.

What the hell had Zeus been thinking, giving my apartment away to the two most flamboyant male bodybuilders in The Higher Plains?

Oh right, he had been thinking he's an asshole and it would irritate me greatly, resulting in his endless entertainment.

Asshole.

Ugh.

I sit up, restless and on edge as the music filling the apartment from no discernible source changes track, this time not punishing my ears with panpipes, but something worse.

A fate worse than death.

Fucking bagpipes.

Considering I had just had my mortal form murdered quite brutally, I hadn't thought I'd be in a position of torture quite so soon.

And yet, here I freaking am—

I peer into the flawless looking glass on the opposing wall. I had adorned this space with a life-size nude portrait of Aphrodite myself, but now it's a mirror because apparently Lir and Sedna would rather look at their own rugged beardy-ness than a nice pair of tits.

To each his own.

My reflection graces me as I stare into it. Flawless smooth skin now covers my skull, my hair has returned to vibrant cobalt, shimmering with the odd silver hue from my recent rebirth in the Divine Pastures. My chin is as ever, flawlessly smooth, not a trace of stubble in sight, just the way I like it, and as I begin to hum one of my favourite Cher numbers under my breath, and the bagpipes reach an unceasing and entirely unnecessary high note, my fists ball at my sides.

I don't know how much longer I can take this.

As if listening to the kind of thunder they're making on my bedcloud at night isn't goddamn bad enough.

It's enough to make me want to drown myself by mixing the copious floral perfumes they keep in the bathroom, an insult to any bachelor pad, let alone mine.

A knock at the door breaks my aromatic and suicidal fantasy. Lir and Sedna aren't even here, not that they'd turn off the incessantly grating music while they're at yet another Circle of Eight meeting, so I walk slowly over to the frosted glass of the door, pulling it open.

I expect it to be a messenger, yet another from Zeus who hadn't felt it necessary to greet the brother he banished on re-entry to The Higher Plains, but it isn't.

"Thane?" I know I sound incredulous, but I am. I'm utterly shocked.

"Hey—" she mutters, looking at me with a shy smile, cocking her head. Her eyes are stormy, black hair spikey around her face. She looks— *good*.

"What the hell happened?" I demand, letting her across the threshold with a wave of one hand and raising my voice so I can be heard over the droning and torturous music— or what the two owners of this apartment *claim* to be music.

"I uh, I left Luce," she admits as I slam the door behind her harder than I intend to as I feel it slip from my grasp with surprise.

"What? But— you can't. You two are like— you're like—" I'm lost for words and Thane sighs, rolling her eyes.

"We're like over, Haedes. It's done. She's not the same person I fell in love with," she informs me, looking around the apartment with a curious expression.

"God— I didn't feel this lost when my parents got divorced," I admit, and she smirks.

"Divorce— hmm. Would you call Titanomachy followed by banishment to another dimension divorce?" She quirks an eyebrow, amused at my oversimplification of world-altering events.

399

"Whatever." I wave away the technicalities of my family history, bored by it entirely.

"We've been together a long time— it was a tough decision to make. But there are more factors at play than just she and I," she reveals, examining the décor with a half-smile. "I didn't peg you for the dolphin lover type—" she adds, picking up a vile, crystal statue of two dolphins diving out of the water, their bodies forming a wretched frothy heart.

I stare at it and, naturally, bile rises in my throat so fast I have to stop myself from gagging.

"Uh, Zeus— he uh, gave Lir and Sedna my place. Ease of access to the Olympian Council chambers and all that." I cough, sighing. "So, what's going on with you leaving?" I press her for a more comprehensive answer.

"Mortaria fell after you left— as I'm sure you gathered. But Sephy isn't intending on trying to get it back, and I can't just sit there and do nothing. This whole thing is my fault." She sighs, and I put my hands into my pockets.

"And how, dear Thanatos, do you figure that?" I demand, cocking my pristinely arched eyebrow and giving her a little razzle-dazzle with my irises.

"If I hadn't been captured, Luce never would have drunk from The Well. I knew she was struggling with the magics, but instead of—" she begins, but I raise a hand cutting her off.

"Short of chaining her up in the dungeon, what else could you have done? The Fates saw this coming; you know they did. Nothing you did or didn't do would have prevented this. You're not to blame. Pandora— she is the one to blame for this," I spit her name, a small smile possessing me as I think about how in my last moments I had succeeded in thoroughly infuriating her. Thane looks to the floor, jagged frame enviable. I bet I would be seductive as all hell with a body like that.

"I came here because I want you to come before The Aetherial Court with me. I want to convince them to intervene, but without you, I don't think they'll take me seriously. Especially because two of the members blame Luce for this in its entirety—" she explains, face grim. I narrow my gaze.

"Nemesis and Hecate— and how are those two hypocritical man-haters by the way?" I demand, remembering how much I'd disliked both of them when I lived here before.

"Well, you can imagine that my mother is full of *I told you so*— and well, Hecate is feeling all justified in abandoning her daughter. It's a mess— Not to mention my visions are back, so that's causing me a bunch of headaches," she admits, exhaling as she stares into the mirror above the fireplace. I recall, before she had fallen, her ability to see death, all death across the universe. It had almost driven her mad as a child, but with Lucifer, she'd harnessed it, somehow found peace among the desperation and pain. Then, when Lucifer had been banished, she'd gone after her and given up the visions to live in a mortal body. Where someone like myself found only disdain and hatred for my loss of total godly power, loss of eternal youth, Thanatos flourished without hers.

"I just think going to Zeus about this is a waste of time— I don't really want to stand before a council and be hung out to dry for what I did and didn't do in my godly duties either." I pout, nervous now.

I haven't been to see either of my brothers since I've been back, and I haven't intended to either. It's the only reason good enough to keep me trapped in this hellhole of an apartment.

"I'll do you a deal then?" she proposes, and my eyes widen, curious.

"I'm listening."

"If you come and do this with me, I'll let you have the spare room in my place," she offers, and my mind begins to whir. She knows what I want, and she isn't afraid to barter with me, something I've always respected about her.

"A spare room you say? Does it have its own bathroom?" I ask, thinking about the nightmare that has become my morning grooming routine. A communal bathroom is a big Haedes no-no.

"It does. With a tranquillity pool—" she coaxes me, and I relinquish. Dread fills my gut, but my heart simultaneously rises at the thought of forever escaping the panpipes, bagpipes, and any other kind of pipes Lir or Sedna might decide to inflict upon me.

"Sold," I retort, and she smiles, jumping slightly as she heads for the door, clearly as tired of the music as I am.

"You need to pack anything?" she demands, and I cock my head, giving her a death stare.

"Have you seen this place? It's got less flare than a pair of skinny jeans. I have no idea what happened to everything I own— though I would be interested in finding out what became of my portrait of Aphrodite—" I mumble as we walk from the apartment, closing the door on the wailing with a determined slam of finality.

401

"Oh," I add, thoughtfully, "And you should also know that Cher will be a regular feature in the mornings. I love a good sing-along while I'm in the shower—"

"Are you serious?" Thane groans and I smile, feeling a rhythmic joy returning to my stride as I swing my hip, knocking her off course slightly.

"Oh yes, Thanatos. You see, every man has his price, and Cher is the one thing in life I simply won't negotiate."

ACKNOWLEDGEMENTS

This book is over— phew! That marks fifty percent down on The Queens of Fantasy Saga! A huge thank you to everyone who helped me get to the end of this one- it wasn't easy! This is the hardest time I've ever had finishing a novel, with health crises and self-doubt more crippling than ever, I am so relieved to finally write the end! A huge thanks to two very special people in particular- Mark my wonderful partner and Leeah Rochelle Minick who both spent hours upon hours reassuring me that I shouldn't just delete the entire book and start over! Also, a huge thanks to my Nanny, Mum, Dad, my amazing Editor Jaimie Cordall who never fails to make me smile, my incredible betas Dawn Yacovetta and Amy Lynn Lockhart, and of course the person to whom this book is dedicated- Angie Pfeiffer-Senft. Angie, you in particular have fuelled the journey for this book, with your struggle so resonant with that which Sephy goes through in this novel in so many ways. Thank you for all your encouragement, and your unceasing bravery in spite of everything, you are truly an inspiration. I also want to thank Kirsty Adams, Tilly Broad and of course, the absolutely whimsical Winter's Rage, who as my PA never stops working to get my books noticed. My new street team is amazing, so thanks to all three of you wonderful ladies for helping me keep it going! You're the best!

Well, I guess that's it— until next time!

ALSO BY

QUEENS OF FANTASY SHORTS AND NOVELLAS

TIDAL KISS SHORTS AND NOVELLAS
Beyond The Shallows
Waiting For Gideon
Vexed

ASHEN TOUCH SHORTS AND NOVELLAS
Death Blooms
A Touch Of Smoke And Snow

AETHERIAL EMBRACE SHORTS AND NOVELLAS
Ambrosia Nights

EXTRAS
Infiniflash Fiction Volume One

OTHER GENRES FROM KRISTY NICOLLE

DYSTOPIAN ROMANCE:
Something Blue- A Dystopian Romance Standalone

POETRY:
I Am Arcana- A Tarot Inspired Poetry Collection
Starsong- A Zodiac Inspired Poetry Collection

To keep up to date with the latest release dates, spin offs, and exclusive content, head on over to kristynicolle.com

ABOUT THE AUTHOR

30-Year-Old British Author of Award-Winning Indie Fantasy Romance, Kristy Nicolle is escaping the pain of Ehlers Danlos Syndrome by crafting intricate and immersive worlds for her readers. She lives in Norwich, Norfolk, with her long-time life partner Mark, and can often be found writing in her local coffee shop - *Botany and Beans,* with a peppermint mocha, surrounded by beloved witchy paraphernalia and plants she knows only too well she'd kill at home.

FOLLOW KRISTY NICOLLE ON SOCIAL MEDIA OR FIND HER AT KRISTYNICOLLE.COM